LO
Lucy

Also by Tracy Culleton

Looking Good

Loving Lucy

TRACY CULLETON

POOLBEG

Published 2004
by Poolbeg Press Ltd
123 Grange Hill, Baldoyle
Dublin 13, Ireland
E-mail: poolbeg@poolbeg.com

© Tracy Culleton 2004

The moral right of the author has been asserted.

Typesetting, layout, design © Poolbeg Press Ltd.

1 3 5 7 9 10 8 6 4 2

A catalogue record for this book is available from the British Library.

ISBN 1-84223-156-1

Typeset by Patricia Hope in Palatino 10/14
Printed by
Litografia Rosés S.A., Spain

www.poolbeg.com

About the Author

Tracy Culleton lives in a little granite cottage in County Carlow, along with her husband Peter and son Tadhg. When they bought the cottage they could see its potential. Five years on, they can still see its potential . . . Strangely, on the TV, makeovers take only half an hour, so it was a bit of a shock to realise it takes longer in real life. Still, Tracy feels she has a good excuse since she's writing all these novels. Yes! Result!

For more information, writing tips etc, Tracy invites you to visit her website: **www.tracyculleton.com.**

Acknowledgements

First of all I'd like to thank everybody who bought *Looking Good* and who said such nice things about it – I hope you enjoy *Loving Lucy* just as much.

It has been such an adventure since *Looking Good* was published this time last year, and I've had many wonderful experiences leading out of that. And one of the most amazing was the opportunity to meet and mix with the self-proclaimed Irish Girls – Irish women writers whose names I have known and admired for years. Sarah Webb was kind enough to contact me and invite me to join them, and I would like to thank you so much, Sarah, for that, and to thank the rest of you for your warm welcome and for making me feel that maybe, possibly, I was a real writer and wasn't being a *total* fraud for being there!

I would like to thank my beloved sister, Frances, for her never-ending support and encouragement and for reading this book in manuscript form and giving it the thumbs up. Also for being great fun and a wonderful sister all round!

Big huge hugs and thanks to Michael and Heather who should have been thanked last time, but in the panic I forgot (thanks for forgiving me!), who have also encouraged and supported me and read manuscripts.

Thanks also to Sinead Tynan who, in addition to saying nice things about *Looking Good* has really proven herself a true friend – much appreciated.

And to my mother and father who are like my own private PR company, telling everyone to buy my books and making sure bookshops the length and breadth of the country stock them!

Thanks as ever to Gaye Shortland for her comprehensive and sensitive editing.

Thanks again to Peter and Tadhg for supporting me as I do this, and for keeping my feet on the ground whilst giving me the space to reach for the clouds. Love you both.

Finally, thanks to another Peter for help about Garda procedure. You'll see I've taken liberties for the sake of the story.

For Tadhg,
whose every breath fills me with joy.

Chapter 1

"You got a *what?*" I hissed, staring disbelievingly at him.

"You heard me," he muttered sulkily to his feet.

"Oh, yes, I certainly heard you," I agreed bitterly. "I just couldn't believe my ears, is all."

"Look, it's not so bad," he began.

But he didn't get very far with that line of argument before I jumped in to disabuse him entirely of it.

"It's not so *bad*?" I shouted. "You're after getting a *drugs* conviction, and you have the *nerve*, the sheer *gall*, to stand there and tell me it's not so *bad*?" My voice had risen so much on the final words that it was squeaking slightly.

"Now hang on, Tory," he blustered, holding his hand up. "Yes, yes, I got a drug conviction. I admit that –"

"You admit it," I spat the words out, nausea sharp in my gut, "because your solicitor rang here assuming I'd

1

know all about it. All you confirmed were the details, Ray. You've kept it from me all this time, and probably would never have said anything about it if I hadn't found out."

His shamefaced expression was its own admission.

I went on, speaking more slowly now, more calmly, but still totally incredulous. "You managed to cover it all up. Being arrested, the court case. Oh God – no wonder you kept disappearing all those days, in what passes for smart clothes with you! I thought you might be having an affair," I laughed bitterly. "I never thought of this."

His sharp thin face was anguished, and his slim body almost cowered as he tried to evade my tirade, the first I had ever dared launch at him. He'd probably thought I didn't have it in me, and his expression was shocked, but there was a kind of respect there too, I noted, and realised that this was one of the rare times I had seen respect for me in his eyes. And, I acknowledged ruefully, one of the rare times I had acted in any way which would command respect.

As I'd been thinking this, Ray had been talking away, putting his case for the defence, and I tuned in to listen to him just as he was saying, "It was a *suspended* sentence, for Christ's sake! It was only a first offence. And even that was only for three months. It was only a bit of hash. Tory, for God's sake. Cannabis barely counts as a drug! It wouldn't even be classified as illegal except for crooked knee-jerk politicians wanting to keep on the right side of the middle-aged, middle-class voter. It's safer than cigarettes and alcohol, and *you're* going on as if I'd murdered somebody," he finished indignantly.

"The solicitor said the conviction was for dealing."

"I was only sharing it with a friend!" he protested.

I took a deep breath at that, filling up on air so I wouldn't have to restock halfway through sharing with him my opinion of *that* statement, and he held up a hand in surrender. "Okay, okay," he admitted begrudgingly, "I know the law sees it as dealing, seeing as I took money off him." He sounded most aggrieved at this, most hard-done-by, and then he went on, "But I only charged him the cost of it – that was only fair, wasn't it?" He smiled at me then, his supposedly cute smile whose subtext was, 'I know I'm a rogue but at least I acknowledge it and it's quite appealing really, isn't it?'.

I don't suppose Ray ever met a situation he couldn't charm his way out of, or through, or around. He certainly had always been able to get his way around me. Until now.

I released the breath that I'd been holding, in a long sigh. He noted the sigh, and I saw a little half-smile cross his thin mouth. I knew him well. I knew what was going through his brain as clearly as if it were written in neon over his head. She's calmed down now, he'd be thinking. She's got it off her chest. Okay, he'd be telling himself, I knew she wouldn't like it, not a drugs conviction, but she'll get over it. She'll get used to it. We can carry on. He thought that that was what my sigh was: an acceptance, a capitulation.

But Ray was about to get the second shock of the

evening. Because I *was* about to give in, but not in the way that he thought, and sometimes giving in can be far more devastating than even the worst anger. In anger, there is still somewhere – no matter how little, no matter how deeply buried – a kind of caring. Giving in is all about indifference, about no longer caring.

"You know, Ray, I don't think this is working," I told him wearily.

"Me getting done for drugs? I totally agree with you, and I promise you, Tory, on my mother's grave, that it'll never happen again."

I gave a mirthless laugh. "Your mother's grave? Ray, my dear, do the maths. She was only sixteen when you were born, so that would make her – what? – forty-one now! She hardly has a grave at forty-one, for you to swear by. And even if she did, you wouldn't know, and you wouldn't care, so it's not much to swear on. No," I said, studying him intently, "if you want to convince me, swear on something important to you. Like your guitar."

His face paled, and he reflexively reached for it where it sat beside him – *of course*, beside him – and caressed it.

I smiled ruefully to myself – there was never any doubt where Ray's priorities lay – before continuing, "Well, admit it, it's hardly every girl's dream, is it: living with a convicted drug-dealer? Okay, okay," this as he opened his mouth to protest, "living with somebody who's kind enough to share his stash with his friend and the State are so unreasonable about it that they call it dealing. But, Ray, admit it, we weren't exactly getting on anyway, were we? Not since I got pregnant last year, really."

"No," he agreed sulkily. "But that's not *my* fault. It wasn't *me* who changed."

"True," I agreed. "Getting pregnant changed my priorities. I moved on. But the end result is the same: we're focussed on different things now."

"Yes. Yes, we are."

I looked at him as he sat there on the tweedy-brown sofa of our rented flat. Ray, oh Ray. Ray of the clever thin face, the wiry muscular body, the long brown hair, the capsule denim wardrobe, the guitar always with him like an extra appendage. Ray of the infectious laughter, the entrancing smile, the careless infrequent generosity which was all the more precious for its rarity. Ray who was congenitally laid-back about everything except his music.

And as we sat there in silence, I was thinking, and perhaps he was too, of how it had been between us.

We had met when I was twenty-six and he twenty-two. We joked about him being my toy-boy, never knowing that that four-year age gap would later become an issue. We joked about his inability to do housework, his tunnel vision when it came to his music. In fact we joked about most things – it was a very light-hearted, fun-above-all relationship.

He was a guitarist and singer, trying to break into the big time, and I loved his music, knew how talented he was, was as determined as he that he would make it. I happily followed him around from gig to gig. They were great times – even now I have to say this – sitting in the crowd with the current girlfriends of the current fellow-band-members as the men played, and all going on somewhere else afterwards. It was mad and manic, a bit frenetic.

Before long Ray and I were living together in this upstairs one-bedroomed flat. Actually, it was a maisonette rather than a flat, because it had the distinction of its own entrance: the front-door led to a tiny hallway from which stairs gave access to the living space – a literal and metaphorical step above a mere flat.

Although, when I say we were living together, I have to admit that we had never discussed what exactly that would mean – what commitment, if any, it implied. In practice it turned out that it meant we carried on exactly as we always had done, except that our clothes now shared a wardrobe, and we didn't have to ask, *'Your place or mine?'*.

We lived a post-student lifestyle – Ray signed on the dole and picked up bits and pieces of off-the-books work in between equally off-the-books gigs, and I worked at the check-out of the local supermarket. I know, I know, and me with a degree in business studies and marketing. But to succumb to the lure of a professional job would have been selling out, joining the establishment, bringing down onto my bowed head the left-wing scorn of Ray and his friends (they didn't *join* the establishment; they just lived off it). And I, feeling for the first time ever as if I belonged somewhere, as if I were part of a group, wasn't going to risk that wonderful, secure, safe feeling for any job.

And then, two years down the road, I fell pregnant. It was, needless to say, a huge shock for me. How could I possibly be pregnant when we'd always been so careful? But nothing's a hundred per cent guaranteed, I reminded my anxious, stricken reflection in the bathroom mirror, as I tremulously clutched the pregnancy test with its unequivocal blue line.

For a couple of days I kept the news to myself, trying to figure out how I felt about it. Shock, as I've said. Trepidation. Fear. But, with those pregnancy hormones relentlessly flooding my system, I adapted very quickly, grew excited about the idea in no time at all. A baby, I thought, a baby!

But how was Ray going to react?

It won't be a problem, I firmly told myself. It's a surprise – sure. And he'll probably be shocked just as I was, need a little while to get used to it. But it'll be okay – we're together all this time; it'll be fine.

And so one autumn evening I plucked up the courage to tell him.

"Ray," I said, "Ray, do you mind putting that down and listening to me. I've something important to tell you."

"What?" he said, his voice a mixture of mild irritation and indifference, as he reluctantly closed his *Hot Press* magazine and placed it onto the sofa beside him.

"Ray," I was annoyed to find that my own voice was squeaking slightly, "Ray, I've just found that that I'm . . . well, thing is, I'm pregnant."

"Pregnant?" he asked, puzzled. Almost as if he had never before heard of the concept.

"Yes. Pregnant. You know, as in: there's a baby growing inside me."

He didn't seem to notice my admittedly feeble attempt at humour. His confused expression grew stronger as he asked, shaking his head in bewilderment, "How the fuck did that happen?"

"How did it happen?" I said lightly, desperately trying to steer this conversation into a relaxed direction. "Well, you see, men produce sperm, and women produce –"

"I know *how* it happens," he interrupted, irritated at my levity. "What I want to know is, how did it happen to you? I thought you were on the Pill?"

"I was. But nothing's a hundred per cent guaranteed," I said, repeating to him what I had told myself. But it turned out that *I* had been a lot easier to convince of this than was Ray.

"Were you not being careful to take it every day?" He was still looking shocked, disbelieving, but I could see a measure of realisation and its attendant panic seeping in too.

"Of course, I was!" I said indignantly. "I didn't do this on purpose. Is that what you're suggesting?"

"No, no," he said hastily, urgently backtracking, "but I just don't understand how it could have happened, that's all."

8

"Well, it *has* happened," I pointed out to him, and at that we both fell silent. Give him time, I told myself. He has to take it in, get used to it. After all, I reminded myself, I had had a few days to come to terms with it – I couldn't expect him to get his head around it instantaneously.

Despite this, after a few painfully long minutes of silence I cracked. "I know it's a shock," I babbled, "and I certainly hadn't planned it. But now that it's happened, well, we'll manage, won't we? After all, we're a stable couple. We can offer the baby a good home. A happy home."

He spoke then, as though my speech had freed him to talk. But what *he* said was in no way related to what *I* had said. I don't think he had really even heard me.

"I'm only twenty-four," he said wonderingly. "I'm too young to be a father. And, Tory, I still haven't made it as a musician. I can barely look after myself financially; how can I possibly support a baby? I have to concentrate on getting my career sorted. I just . . ." he shook his head sadly. "Tory, it's just not the right time for a baby. I'm sorry," he added softly. "I really am. Look, we can talk about it again in a few years. Four or five years. When I'm older, and more established."

I listened in mounting horror. "What exactly are you saying?" I asked then.

"Tory. You know what I'm saying."

And I did, no matter how I had hoped I was wrong.

He added compassionately, "I'll come with you, help you through it."

9

I stared at him, shocked and dismayed. "I suppose that's your version of being a New Man, is it?" I asked him. "Coming with me while I abort our baby?"

He shrugged, standing up, visibly uneasy with the whole conversation, with the heavy emotion and importance of the subject matter. "Well, if you'd rather do it on your own, I don't mind. I'd understand." He picked up his *Hot Press* and went and locked himself into the bathroom.

I had sat there stunned. I can take a hint as well as the next woman and I could accept his not-so-subtle clue that the conversation was over. But what now? I had been *sure* he'd come around to the idea once he got over the shock.

And I went away and thought about it, and I was shaking. I didn't want an abortion. True, I hadn't planned to be pregnant, but now that I was, I wanted the baby . . . but I had never stood up to Ray about anything before . . . the enormity of doing that overwhelmed me.

Maybe it would be better to have an abortion after all? We could always have another baby in a few years as he had said. Not this baby, granted, but another baby, a planned baby. An abortion would guarantee peace in the house, and God knows I was well-accustomed to compromising (well, I called it compromising; it was probably nearer capitulating) to ensure peace.

I'd think about it for the rest of the day, I promised myself, and I'd decide then. But the end of the day came and I was no nearer making a decision. Another day, then. But that day passed too. In some ways it was very simple: I wanted this baby, Ray didn't. I couldn't please both of us. Of the baby itself and what he or she might want, I refused to think. Of the rights and wrongs of it all, I refused to think. Perhaps it might have been easier if I had. It might have swayed the balance sooner.

So . . . I wanted the baby, but since when had what I wanted been a compelling factor? Ray didn't want the baby. How would he react if I said I was going to keep it? Would he leave me? My heart clenched in fear at that prospect. How would I manage without him? Particularly with a baby to look after. I debated asking him what he would do if I decided to keep the baby, but knew that that would tactically be a *very* bad move. I might as well go up to him and say: 'Threaten me with all sorts of dreadful things if I keep the baby.'

And the days passed, each one with its decision-deadline going unmet. And after about a week or so I realised that I was going to keep the baby. I don't think I ever made a proactive decision, as such. I just let the indecisiveness seep away through attrition until all that was left was this knowledge, this certainty: no matter what the repercussions, I was going to keep the baby I was carrying.

And so I found some courage from somewhere and I went to him, as he sat on the sofa playing his guitar one afternoon, and I told him that I wasn't going to have an abortion. I waited for the eruption, but he surprised me.

"Okay, suit yourself," he shrugged, and didn't even lift his eyes, his attention, from his guitar, as he went on to ask, "Where do you fancy going tonight? I wouldn't mind going to Darcy's. There's a new band playing there that are supposed to be shit-hot, and I heard a rumour they're not getting on with their guitarist."

He looked up at me then and I read so much in his expression, saying what he couldn't articulate out loud. There was fear there . . . terror, in fact, not to put too fine a point on it. How could he provide for a baby? it asked. How could he be a father when he'd never learned what fathers do? it asked.

There was anger and annoyance at his wishes being thwarted. There was a kind of love for me which wanted to give me my heart's desire and was glad of this decision. There was compassion for us both, and for the baby, at the untenable situation in which we three found ourselves, which could never ever have ended totally happily for everyone. There was a tiny, glimmering, nascent respect for me too, for my having had the courage of my convictions.

As he spoke on about the new band in Darcy's, his eyes told me all this, and I tried to make my own eyes answer him, and thank him and promise him it would all work out.

I still think I was reading his expression accurately that day, but maybe I was wrong. Maybe it was just my own wishful thinking and projection, because he never referred to the pregnancy again after that. He, who always dealt with life's issues by avoiding them, dealt with the pregnancy by totally ignoring it. And I, accustomed all my life to avoiding confrontation, to doing my best to make sure all stayed peaceful, dealt with *that* by letting him, by hiding as much of its limitations from him as I could. I struggled through morning sickness, doing my best to retch quietly, and making my own dry toast. I quietly went for the ante-natal checks, never told him about them, never showed him the ultrasound scan picture of our baby *in utero*. I was engrossed in the adventure of my burgeoning body, in the journey towards motherhood. But I adventured alone, journeyed alone.

And eventually I went into labour.

"I'm in labour," I told him late on a summer's evening two years ago. "I need to get to the hospital."

"I'll ring a taxi," he said, and he did so. When the taxi arrived he placed my suitcase in the boot, helped me into the back seat and said: "Good luck."

"Aren't you coming with me?" I asked, shocked, *horrified!* And even the taxi-driver swivelled his head around to look at him in surprise and, it seemed to me, not a little derision.

"Oh, babe, I'd be no good to you," he said swiftly, urgently. "I'd need more attention than you would! Ring me when it's over and I'll come and see you."

"Oh . . . okay," I said in bewilderment as he gave me a thumbs-up and closed the car door.

As we drove to the hospital I reasoned desperately to myself – he had never said he *would* come, after all. It was a bit unfair of me to blame him for not doing something that he hadn't even said he would do. He hadn't wanted anything to do with the pregnancy. It made sense – if only I had let myself realise it – that he wouldn't want to attend the birth. He'd be fine after the baby was born, I told myself. Men often have trouble with the concept of a baby – I knew this from reading carefully hidden pregnancy magazines – but were thrilled once the baby arrived and they actually got to see it, got to meet their son or daughter.

It didn't take long to get to the hospital – only about four contractions long. Each time the taxi-driver turned his head. "You okay, love?" he said compassionately, and what's more, didn't even expect an answer, which was just as well because I couldn't have responded anyway.

He pulled up outside the entrance to the hospital, and got out, opened the back door and helped me out of the back seat. He looked down at me and I dimly registered, now that I could see him, what he looked like. In his fifties, running to fat, pleasant face.

My timing was a bit off – I was no sooner on the pavement than another contraction hit. And he held my elbows and braced me as I breathed through the contraction. Afterwards I breathed, "Thanks," and he nodded. He looked at me then, appraisingly, and then seemed to come to some conclusion. He reached into the car and switched on the hazard-lights, in that quintessentially Irish code of, 'I know I'm parked illegally but I'll only be a minute, honest,' lifted my bag out from the boot, and took my elbow.

"Come on," he said, and walked me into the hospital

building, carrying my bag in one hand and holding my elbow with the other. As we neared the reception desk he muttered to himself, "Oh, what the heck, why not?" and then he turned and whispered to me, "Say I'm your da, and that I've just gone to park the car," and he winked at me, and grinned a little – possibly at my astonished expression – and he turned and left.

In the event he arrived back just as I – ensconced now in a wheelchair – was about to be pushed into a lift and brought to the labour ward.

"Hi, darling," he said, and laid a proprietary hand on my shoulder. I was growing more and more bewildered – who was this guy? Maybe he was some weirdo who got his kicks from attending women's labours. But somehow, I didn't think so, somehow it seemed that – while I didn't understand what was going on – my best bet was to go along with it. At least for the moment.

So we carried on like that – me in the wheelchair which the orderly was pushing, he walking alongside with his hand on my shoulder – until we reached the door of the labour ward and the orderly asked him, "Are you attending the birth, Mr – ?"

"Yes, yes, I am. I'm her father," he said proudly. "Isn't that right, darling?"

"Yes – Dad," I said faintly.

"Yes, indeed," he said to the orderly as we made our way through the door and along a corridor, "I'm going to be with my precious daughter seeing as her partner's abroad at the moment and can't get back in time, and her poor mother's no longer with us," and he raised his eyes sorrowfully and piously to the corridor's fluorescent-lighted ceiling. And as he said this he reminded me of the opening scene in really bad plays, where the whole background is clumsily given, something like, 'Yes, here I am, Mary Murphy aged forty-two, schoolteacher, all alone in this big house with neither chick nor child and the bills unpaid and the wind howling through the hole in the roof and the evil property developer trying to leave me homeless,' and I had to stifle a giggle.

But the orderly didn't seem to see anything contrived in it. Probably he was used to all sorts of bizarre monologues spurting out of people at this emotionally intensive stage of their lives.

We arrived in the labour ward and the orderly helped me up onto the bed before saying, "The midwife will be here in a minute," giving me a reassuring smile and leaving the room.

I took the opportunity. "What on earth are you doing?" I hissed at the taxi-driver, at the same time as he was turning to me and saying urgently, "Sorry, love, just say the word and I'll go. I just felt so badly for you, going through all this on your own. I was with my Margaret through all four of our children's births and she always said me being there was the only thing that kept her going. So I thought I'd stay with you if you like. Be your birth partner. You know, you can hold my hand and dig your nails into it and shout at me if you like."

I looked into his broad face, with its fleshy red-

16

veined nose and kindly, wrinkle-set eyes, and thought about the kindness of strangers, and said, "I'd like that. 'Dad'."

He smiled at me, and took my hand, and then, as we both heard the door opening, whispered urgently to me, "What's your name, anyway?"

The procedure turned out to be that there was a senior midwife who came and checked periodically on me during this dilation stage of labour, and a junior trainee-midwife who was with me all the time. She, the trainee, appeared to be about fourteen, and looked even more scared than I was, hard though that was to believe. I got the distinct impression that this was her first time doing this, but refrained from asking her because a 'yes' answer would probably have ended up panicking us both, and certainly I for one was hanging onto my calm by the proverbial thread. In fact, if it hadn't been for 'Dad', I probably would have lost all semblance of composure.

After one particularly strong contraction I growled, "Oh God, why does it have to hurt so bloody much?"

It was probably meant rhetorically – to be honest at that stage I wasn't sure what exactly I meant by anything – but the trainee midwife took it literally and answered, "It's the price we pay for walking upright and all the evolution that that's made possible."

"You mean," I said after the contraction had passed, "that evolving from monkeys meant that men could have palm-pilots and Saturday-afternoon televised football, and we have painful labours? Doesn't seem fair to me."

It was supposed to lighten the mood – probably – but she took this literally too. "Oh," she said, "we women have benefited from technology too, you know. What about washing machines and dishwashers?"

My eyes met 'Dad's', and we grinned at each other. But just then there was the beginnings of another contraction, and I took his hand again, considerately trying to find a part of it without the red welts which marked the previous contractions, and clung on – grateful beyond describing for his presence – while I rode the pain. Dimly in the distance, beyond the agony, I could hear her high clear voice going on, ". . . and hair-straighteners, and eyelash curlers, and . . ."

To my eternal gratitude the contraction took over then, and I didn't hear what else she felt was fair recompense for the pain of labour. I did manage to think viciously, though: wait until you go through it; we'll see how philosophical you are about it then.

And eventually, as daylight began streaming through the windows, Lucy was born, and I took one look at her and fell in love, totally and irrevocably. There was an actual physical pain in my heart with my love for her.

"She's beautiful, love," said 'Dad'. "Well done, good luck." And he bent and kissed my cheek, and Lucy's too, and went off, his good hand kneading and massaging the hand I'd been hanging on to.

And that was it. I never learned his name. I never saw him again. If I were fanciful I would say he was an angel come to earth to help me when I needed it. I know he wasn't. It was better than that: he was just an ordinary Dublin taxi-driver who was kind beyond the call of duty to a stranger who needed support.

As soon as I could I rang Ray. "Ray, we have a daughter! She's beautiful!"

"Great, well done! I'll be in to see you later."

And he did come, and brought flowers (garage-flowers, but still . . .) and a little teddy for the baby (blue, and in a bag marked with the logo of the hospital shop, but still . . .). And as he put the little blue teddy down into the cot, his eyes were caught by the enormous pink one sitting there. He looked at the gift tag attached to it. "From your father," he said, "how strange. I wouldn't have thought, from what you told me that he would be sending you presents . . . and why has he put 'Dad' in inverted commas?'

"Never mind," I said, "have a look at your daughter."

And he looked at the baby in my arms and pronounced her beautiful, but he declined my offer to hold her.

"No, no, I won't," he said, shifting awkwardly. "I wouldn't know how. I'd be scared I'd drop her or something."

He wouldn't be persuaded otherwise. And he didn't stay long that first day.

On the second day he came again, scarcely glanced at Lucy, but was full of news about a new gig he might be getting. As he left he said, "You'll be coming home tomorrow, won't you? So I won't bother coming in. Just get a taxi home, and I'll see you there."

Once home, things were strained. I resented his lack of interest in her, and I was exhausted from doing everything myself. He, in his turn, resented her being there. Not so much herself, I thought, but the disruption she caused. He sighed when I got up at night to feed her, his face tightened when he came home to find chaos in the house and me still in my dressing-gown. He was *furious* when I came into the sitting-room once to ask him and his friends to keep the noise down in case they woke her. And he went nearly apoplectic when he realised that I had given up my job and was going to be staying home with Lucy for the foreseeable future.

But worst of all, far worse than all of that from his point of view, he couldn't believe it when I told him I wouldn't be able to go to gigs with him for a while, that she was too little to go that long without a feed.

"Can't you put her on a bottle," he asked, "and get a babysitter and come anyway?"

"No," I said stubbornly, standing up to him for the second time, "I can't. It'll only be for a few short months, Ray. It's not forever."

But Ray was, I realised, very like a child in many ways. And one of those ways was in instant gratification. If he wanted something, he wanted it *now*. To children and Ray, the concept of *a couple of months* is totally ungraspable, totally meaningless.

And as for Lucy herself, Ray just didn't get her. I don't mean that he was cruel or nasty – of course not. Ray was many things, but being proactively cruel and nasty was definitely not one of his faults. (A cynic might suggest, someone far more sceptical than I might say, that being proactive about *anything* wasn't in Ray's make-up, as a fault *or* a virtue.)

But, as I said, he just didn't get her. I could see him looking at her sometimes with a puzzled look upon his face. As though he was trying to figure out what she was, where she had come from and, above all, what on earth was she doing here? Even when she got bigger and began doing more, reacting more and generally being more fun, he just never seemed to get the *point* of her. You couldn't eat her, drink her, or smoke her – his baffled expression seemed to say – nor play any music on her, so what was she *for*? What was her purpose?

Occasionally he would make an effort. Mostly whenever he felt he was in my bad books for some reason (an increasingly regular occurrence), and was looking for a quick way back into my favour. He would look at me as if to say, 'Is this right? Is this what you're expecting from me?' and he would reach out a tentative hand and ruffle her meagre hair. I never had the heart to tell him that hair-ruffling was more appropriate for older children, that babies wouldn't understand. But it didn't hurt Lucy, and, although I knew well why Ray was doing it, at least it was *some* contact between father and daughter, so I just nodded my endorsement and let him on with it.

And whenever those incidents happened I would feel a solid hollowness in the pit of my stomach, and I would wonder to myself: had Ray always been this manipulative? And if so, how come I had never noticed before this? Or was this a new trait?

This was the pattern of the first six months of Lucy's life. For his part ninety-nine per cent annoyance and one per cent charm, and for my part an ever-growing awareness of the vast space between us, an ever-growing weariness with having to either facilitate him or put up with sulks if I didn't. No surprise, things became very strained between us. As I had just told him, we were now focussed on different things. The drug conviction was simply the last straw, the final nail in the coffin and other assorted clichés. The end, anyway.

"So you'll go," I urged gently on that evening I found out about the drug conviction, sad now that this was truly happening, no matter its inevitability. And scared too.

"I'll stop smoking anything illegal," he pleaded. "I promise I'll go straight, honest I will. I was going to anyway. It's a fool's game anyway, drugs."

"Good," I said evenly, "good. You're right, it *is* a fool's game. But that's not really the point, Ray. The drug conviction is only the catalyst, really. It's all over between us anyway, has been for ages. You know that."

He nodded miserably, but although his head was bowed, his eyes downcast, I felt sure I could sense something in the way he was holding himself. Some sort of relief, perhaps, some sense of excitement of new beginnings. In fact, he stood up then, and – Freudian or what? – took a half-step towards the door.

"But Ray –" I said.

He stopped in his progress.

"Ray, you're going to have to help provide for us. You know that. Lucy *is* your daughter, after all, and I don't want to go out to work and leave her. It'll be tight enough – I'll have to go on Social Welfare, but you're going to have to pay your bit too. Do you hear me?"

He shuffled from foot to foot, looking embarrassed. "Well, you know, I really don't think I can. I just don't have that much ready cash. And, you know, I wanted you to have an abortion. It was your choice to have the baby. Doesn't seem fair to make me pay for the rest of my life for your choice."

"But she's your daughter!"

He shrugged again. "Okay, I'll try and send you what I can," but we both knew he wouldn't.

I waited for him to say something about visitation rights, about organising a schedule to see Lucy, but he didn't. And I didn't suggest it, disappointed in him, disappointed too that it looked as if Lucy wouldn't be growing up knowing her father. But glad also, and relieved: I certainly didn't want her growing up with a convicted drug dealer in her life. And maybe as I stood there, on the windswept high moral ground, I was able to half-admit to myself, that my relief had more to do with a selfish wish to have that darling girl all for myself, and with not having to share her.

Ray silently packed his bags, and came into the hallway.

"Well," he said awkwardly, "goodbye. Look after yourself. I'll be in touch."

"Where will you be?" I asked. "You know, in case I need to contact you, if something was going on with Lucy, or something."

He shrugged, "I don't know. I'll kip for a few nights with one of the lads, and I'll see from there. You have the mobile number anyway."

And then he wished me luck the way you wish luck at journey's end to the stranger who happened to sit beside you on the aircraft, and walked out the door and out of our lives.

I stared at my sleeping baby, my Lucy, in all her six-month pudginess and innocence, and I asked her, "Now what, love?"

But she didn't seem to have any answers – or wasn't offering any solutions, at least. It was all up to me. Despite what I had said to Ray, I did contemplate getting a job, but the thoughts of leaving her, of letting someone else have the joy of rearing her, repelled me.

So in the end I did go on Social Welfare. It was a humiliating experience, filling out the forms and explaining my situation to the young oh-so-together-looking woman behind the counter, no matter how the Department now refers to us (officially, anyway) as 'clients' and not 'wasters-who-are-living-off-the-rest-of-us', and no matter how kind and efficient she was. But – maybe it was my imagination, my paranoia – there seemed a sort of weariness about her, a weary, half-sympathetic, half-irritated 'Here we go again: another stupid woman who believed a man and who has ended up holding the baby while her boyfriend gets off scot-free and leaves us, the taxpayer, to clean up the mess'.

Actually, it turned out that even if that weariness did say anything, it didn't mind too much about the burden to the taxpayer. Because, I learned, those sensible folk in the Department of Social Welfare now expect the errant father to contribute, via themselves, to the upkeep of the child of his loins, to pay *them* a portion of what they pay out.

I found this out when she asked me about contact details for Ray, and I have to admit I took a sly pleasure in being able to inform her that while I didn't have those, *they* should, given that he was also a recipient of their largesse. I gave her his name and date of birth and she seemed happy with that, confident they would be able to identify him. It cheered me up no end, thinking of Ray having to fork out money for Lucy's keep despite himself. I wondered if he would try his, 'It's not my fault the child's there, I wanted her to have an abortion' argument on the implacable face of officialdom, and laughed to think how little that would get him anywhere.

Mind you, I had little else to laugh about. The Social Welfare money kept body and soul together, but barely. No matter how often I told myself how lucky I was, that many other countries didn't have this resource at all, I was still struggling to make the money stretch far enough.

And so began a year which turned out the be both the most special and also the most horrendous I had ever experienced.

The year was special because it was just Lucy and me, and I relished every little thing about her, and watched entranced as she flourished and grew and thrived. I celebrated each of her milestones, no matter how little, no matter how unimportant they might be to anybody else, hugely grateful that I could share them with her, witness them. I laughed at her laughter, at her expressions of intrigue and wonder and fascination as she explored and experienced the world.

Yes, it was all fantastic, but there was a very high price demanded for it. And that price was two-fold, with the second half of it arising from the first. The first was poverty. As much as I told myself I was lucky to be getting this payment at all, that people all over Ireland were working hard and paying taxes so I could get this money, as much as I reminded myself of this and tried to be grateful, the fact remained that it wasn't a huge sum of money. It was a struggle to make the proverbial ends meet. I'd never had much money, had never been rolling in it, but there had always seemed to be a little bit more than enough before now. Now there was only Enough, and sometimes not even that.

And that poverty led to something else. Something debilitating, and wearying. And that something was loneliness.

There certainly wasn't money enough for the cost of a baby-sitter and a night out, so my social life was non-existent. It wasn't that I missed meeting men, I never really thought about them, about the possibility of meeting one, of maybe having a relationship that led to the proverbial living happily ever after. There was no point. I might as well yearn to go to Mars.

So the lack of a boyfriend wasn't really an issue. I didn't let it be.

But to have no women friends . . . that ground me down. I was truly alone.

Okay, I knew that when Ray and I split up I was also saying goodbye to that particular social life. Having Ray's ever-changing band-friends and *their* ever-changing girlfriends as pals had been easy, handy. There was always somewhere to go, and somebody to go there with. And if I had noticed a certain superficiality, a certain lack of true friendship, a lack of intimacy – well, I hadn't really minded it. Or perhaps, if I'm to be really, painfully, honest here, maybe I had preferred it. It was easy to mix with these people at whatever level, without having to invest too much of myself.

I hadn't really had any friends in school because of – well, for various reasons – but I had made good friends in college. As luck would have it, most of those friends had emigrated, and I kept in text and e-mail contact with those, which was great. I had to reluctantly admit that it was likely that very distance which kept us being friends. Because I had slowly drifted apart from those friends who had remained in Dublin. It wasn't that I was jealous, as such. It was just that it was . . . difficult . . . to see them, to see what successes they were making of their lives while I . . . well, wasn't, not to put too fine a point on it, making a success at all of mine.

And whatever contact we had managed to retain when I had had at least some disposable income withered totally once I could no longer even manage to meet them for a coffee.

When Lucy was very young I had joined a couple of local mother-and-baby groups, and I had really enjoyed them. But because Ray needed to sleep during the day and couldn't be disturbed, I couldn't invite anybody back to my place. Which meant I couldn't accept invitations to their houses. I know I got a reputation for being pleasant yet distant, and although everyone was perfectly friendly to me when we were there, there was no possibility for outside friendships to flourish. It was difficult overhearing others making plans to meet over weekends, promising to call up for coffee and so on.

Once Ray had left I could have made some overtures, could have invited mothers back, sprung for some cakes or biscuits. Except that I had left it too late, it seemed. The friendships were formed, the cliques were set. Perhaps if I had made an effort it might have been different, but lack of confidence held me back.

And so, although nobody there would have guessed it – well, maybe they would – but I ended up living for those brief hours in the week that the Mother-and-Baby groups ran. Because . . . for the rest of the time I was so incredibly isolated. Nobody called or phoned. I called or phoned nobody. I made a point of going out every day, whether it was to the shops or the library or the park, just to have some human contact beyond my darling Lucy. But no matter how I dawdled, there were still hours and hours of each day when it was just Lucy and me. And the weekend! I don't even want to think about the weekends. Family time, inflicted upon somebody with no family.

My mother rang at least once a week, sounding furtive each time. Every so often I would manage to get her to promise to come up to Dublin to see me, to spend the weekend with me and her granddaughter. "After all," I reminded her, "you've still never seen her." And she'd agree, "I know, I know. I must. I will."

But each time, a day or two before her expected arrival she would phone with some reason, some excuse, as to why she would have to cancel. For a while I amused myself – albeit bitterly – trying to guess each time what the excuse might be this time. I have to give her credit, she never used the same one twice. "Your father's hurt his foot," might be one, and, of course, there was no point saying that he could possibly still fend for himself – he didn't even fend for himself when he was in the whole of his health, or what passed, with my father, for the whole of his health.

"Mrs Quinn's after up and dying," might be another, "and of course I have to go to the funeral."

"Of course, you do," I'd agree. "Maybe next weekend, so?"

"Maybe, maybe," she'd agree, worriedly.

But after some time, I gave up on inviting her. I could tell that it was stressing her, this constant pull between her genuine love for me and wish to please me and desire to see Lucy on the one hand, and fear of confronting half a lifetime's indoctrination on the other.

From then on I contented myself with that regular call, always furtive, sometimes abruptly cut-off.

Chápter 2

And so that year passed in mixed joy and struggle. But, as time passed, I had to begin facing an unpalatable fact: I was falling further and further behind financially. Lucy was getting bigger and more expensive. Not her fault, God knows, but a fact nonetheless. Each month seemed to widen the gap – very slightly – between my income and my outgoings. But slight widenings, over time, was what put us in Europe and Africa three thousand miles away from the Americas. In my case it didn't take millennia – it took just over that year before I had to admit defeat. Before I knew I had to get a job.

When I finally accepted the reality that I had no choice but to go back to work I was – like thousands of women before me – faced with the issue of finding good childminding. Making that decision was, for me, like asking a condemned man if he'd like to pick a good

31

executioner – it was a decision I didn't want to have to make at all, but yet it was crucial to get it right.

There were a couple of really reputable crèches locally and so I went and had a look at them. The friendly staff showed me around and I admired the immaculate surroundings, the cute murals, the child-friendly gardens, the abundance of play equipment and toys. And I was impressed by the way they spoke to the babies and children already there: with affection and respect. But somehow it was all a little too sterile, a little institutional. No question, the standard was very high. But . . . somehow . . . if I could no longer be home with Lucy myself, I wanted to replicate for her, as much as I could, what home would be like.

And so I continued to look around, asked neighbours and acquaintances, read the cards on the notice-board in the local shop, and I went and interviewed a number of unofficial childminders. The majority were mothers themselves, minding other women's children to subsidise keeping themselves at home, and for the most part were very pleasant. I was spoiled for choice, I felt. But something made me go to see just one more person, someone who had placed a card in the local newsagent's window, and many's the time I congratulated myself on that decision, for that last person turned out to be Carol.

I phoned her and we had chatted pleasantly on the phone, sussing each other out. I liked what I heard – she sounded warm and friendly. And so, when it seemed as though we might be able to help each other out, she invited me to come over and meet her, see her house.

She lived, it transpired, about ten minutes' drive away from me, and about three or four minutes' walk from the DART station, so that would be handy for work – I could drive to her, drop Lucy off, and get the train into town. Her house was an ugly terraced square, one of thousands built in Dublin's expansion of the 60's. However, I noted with approval its immaculate upkeep as I walked up the short driveway, Lucy on my hip, and rang the bell. She answered almost immediately.

At first glance I judged her to be in her late sixties, plumpish and motherly, dressed in a floral polyester two-piece, her mostly grey hair short and carefully curled, and soft grey eyes crinkling with her kindly smile. But then I looked more closely and realised that she was actually only about fifty-five, certainly not more than sixty, no matter that she was dressed and coiffed like a much older woman, or a woman of her age in a previous generation. I was reassured at her relative youth – she should have enough energy to look after my little girl.

Even as I was thinking all this she was speaking to me. "Hello, you must be Tory," she smiled, and then she beamed at Lucy, "and you must be the beautiful Lucy! Come in. Come in!" She stood back to allow us admittance. She brought us into an orderly – albeit dull and dated – sitting-room.

My eyes were caught by two ornate silver frames on her television, each containing a photograph of a young man in a classic graduation outfit: black cloak, that funny hat, a scroll of paper, and an huge beam of delight and pride.

"My two sons," she said when she saw me looking at them. "Larry and Sean," she told me, pointing to each in turn. "I'm so proud of them: they've both got great degrees, and they're working in London. But I miss them now that they're gone. It's – well, it's very lonely. The house is very empty. My husband's dead these past few years, so it's just me. Which is why I decided to do childminding. It's wonderful for me to have children around the house again. I really enjoy their company. And it's great to be able to provide a home-from-home for the little ones."

And when I saw her pride in her sons, and the love in her voice as she spoke of them, I knew that this could be – would be – the right place for Lucy.

"I don't really have any special equipment," she continued, worriedly, "just the sort of toys any household would have. Come and I'll show you."

She led the way out of the sitting-room, into what would have been, in another life, the dining-room. But she had turned it into a bright and cheerful playroom. The walls were sunshine yellow, the floor was covered in mid-blue lino, and one whole wall was taken up with shelves upon which rested a cornucopia of children's toys and books.

"That's lots!" I exclaimed. "Any household would be delighted to have that many toys for their children." And her face brightened, and she lost her slightly worried expression, even as Lucy was registering the treasure trove and had wriggled out of my arms to begin a delighted investigation. Carol, I noted, was smiling indulgently at her.

"How many children do you mind?"

"I limit it to three. It's few enough to allow me to give each one individual attention, but three means that they can be company for each other. At the moment I only have two: Shay, who's three, and Laura, who's two-and-a-half. I did also have George, but his mother's a teacher, so she's home all summer, and since he's going to school himself in September, he won't be back. It's difficult to let them go like that, especially since I often mind them from babies, and you grow to love them, you know. I had George from when he was about four months old, and I do miss him." She sighed philosophically. "But that's the way it goes. It does mean, however," she said, her face brightening, "that I now have room for one other, which is why I put the card up. And," she gave a big grin at Lucy, "I certainly think this little one would fit in well . . . wouldn't you, pet?" she raised her voice to include Lucy.

And Lucy paused in her ransacking of the riches-laden shelves long enough to turn and grin at her, obviously taking to her immediately. And as for me, I was smitten. If I couldn't look after Lucy myself, Carol would clearly be the next best thing. In fact, I wondered, would she look after *me* too? It would be wonderful to spend my own days in this clean, shabby house with its tranquil atmosphere, with motherly, bosomy Carol to take care of me.

And the decision was clinched when Carol mentioned casually that she was a retired nurse. A nurse! Great! If, God forbid, Lucy got sick or anything, Carol would know how to deal with it. Probably better than I would.

"So would you take us on?" I asked. "Take Lucy on?"

"I'd be delighted! I do love all children, but I have to admit that I've really taken to little Lucy here."

It seemed, also, that Lucy had taken to her. She was chatting away in her own unique babble to Carol, showing her all the different toys she had discovered.

"The only thing is," I said, embarrassed, "I don't know how long – I mean, I need to find a job, but I didn't want to look for one until I had Lucy sorted out. So I'm not sure –"

"I understand totally," said Carol maternally. "I wouldn't have wanted to commit to a job either, not until I knew my little girl was going to be in good hands. Don't you worry, Tory. You go off and look for your job. I'll keep the place open for you. And if you need to leave Lucy here while you go for interviews, I'd be delighted to mind her then."

"Would you?" I asked, my eyes glistening and pricking a little. After so much stress and worry these past few years – being pregnant, trying to keep both Lucy and Ray happy, then him being gone and me struggling on, and finally the despair over having to get a job – it was beyond wonderful to have someone offer to do even this for me.

"Sure I would. I'd love to."

I was so happy with Carol, felt so good about her, that I felt almost guilty, almost underhand, ringing Shay and Laura's parents to get references – no matter that it was Carol herself who had pressed their phone-numbers into my hand as I was leaving, encouraging me to ring. But ring I did, and wasn't in the least bit surprised to get glowing recommendations from both families.

So I began looking for a job. Not a supermarket job, oh no. This time I was going to use my qualifications, my degree. And perhaps meeting Carol had signalled a change in my fortunes, perhaps she was my good-luck charm, because within three weeks I had landed myself a brilliant job with one of Ireland's top recruitment consultancies.

It was such a wrench leaving Lucy in Carol's arms – no matter how loving those arms were, they weren't mine. But I think I minded more than Lucy did, because she settled in quickly and well. And so I settled back into work, and life began to look up for me. Over the next six months or so I got a promotion at work, had managed to get out of debt, and was even building up some small savings!

Best of all, Lucy and Carol continued to adore each other, and Lucy never minded being left there, going happily into Carol's welcoming arms each day. And she got on well with Laura and Shay, Carol's other charges, and played happily with them – as much as any toddlers will play with any others, at least.

But, I was also glad to see, Lucy was also overjoyed

to see me again when I collected her each evening, abandoning Carol's arms without a backward glance in order to reach for mine. I knew I was lucky there – I'd often heard colleagues share ruefully the news that their babies had clung to the childminder rather than go back to them, their mothers. So I was thrilled with how well it had all worked out.

There had been another bonus as well – Carol and I had become good friends.

Because one thing still hadn't really changed – my social life. Yes, I had more money now, could have tried to catch up with those college friends. But after being apart from Lucy for most of her waking hours all week, I found that a potent mixture of guilt and desire for her company conspired to keep me home with her when I had the chance.

And while I got on great with my colleagues, was starting to get to know people, to be work-pals with them, a lot of them were single, ready for the pubs and clubs while I was into nappies and purple dinosaurs.

And as for those who were parents like me . . . well, for a start they were all couples, and that made it awkward. And they all seemed so *grown-up* compared to me, organising their lives much better – I didn't really want them to see my one-step-up-from-student accommodation, and if I couldn't return their hospitality I couldn't take it. A recurring theme in my life, I acknowledged ruefully.

It was ironic, it really was. All my life I had had the gift of being popular. People were attracted to me, wanted to spend time with me. But my circumstances at each stage of my life had made it impossible, and eventually they had moved on.

So, yes, I was still lonely, although less so. And therefore it was great to know Carol, to become friends with her. I'd often stay for a cup of tea when I got to the house to collect Lucy, and we had started doing the Sunday-dinner thing at each other's houses every so often. And we shared the details of our lives in order to get to know each other; trading pasts and secrets and joys and disappointments the way women do.

I heard all about her dead husband, Phil, and her two sons; stories of when they were all young and a family still together – scraped knees, broken windows, trips to the zoo. I heard of the scare when Phil found a lump in his testicles, and the bigger scare when it turned out to be malevolent. And the operations and the hospital stays and the slow painful decline into widowhood. And the two boys, spending their teens under this shadow; it was understandable, said Carol, that they wanted to move away as soon as they could. But they rang often, she said proudly, and sent flowers for her birthday and Mother's Day, and came home at least once a year, regular as clockwork.

And in my turn I spoke of the Ray-days, the mad, almost manic fun we had had, the bands and the music and the dingy, magical venues, and the long nights and the hopes raised and dashed. And Lucy – I spoke often of Lucy, and two pairs of eyes would turn to her as she played, and I thought how lucky she was to have Carol for her childminder, Carol as kind, as loving, as committed, as any blood-grandmother could ever be.

As our friendship flourished Carol grew more and more determined that I should get a new boyfriend. Preferably one of her sons, either of which, she seemed to be indicating, would be perfect for me. Actually, I wouldn't mind . . . not that I was for one minute falling in with her wild matchmaking schemes. But I wouldn't object to meeting somebody nice at some stage, and as the photographic images of her sons smiled benevolently at me I acknowledged that they were both very presentable-looking. And even allowing for justifiable maternal exaggeration, they sounded like intelligent, kind, decent men. I wouldn't mind *meeting* either or both of them some time. And if romance did blossom . . . it *might*, I argued to myself, that's all I'm saying, it *might* . . . then Lucy and I would truly be related to Carol and it would all just be so perfect.

But I hadn't had the opportunity to meet them yet, so we were limited thus far to the charms of other men. Such as the postman. One day he and I happened to arrive at Carol's front door simultaneously and we exchanged polite pleasantries . . . and she remarked to me afterwards how good-looking he was, wasn't he? And very nice, she assured me, always cheerful and kind. And a few days later she reported that he had expressed an interest in me too. Oh God, I thought I would *die* with the embarrassment – she had obviously corralled him and demanded his opinion of me and he, politely, had probably agreed with whatever flattering assessment of me she had suggested. Which agreement she had turned around and brought back and proffered to me as if it were an unsolicited compliment little short of a marriage proposal.

I felt a surge of irritation at her transparency, her lack of subtlety, which irritation I immediately transmuted into amusement. Carol was so good to me, so good *for* me and Lucy that I wasn't about to let a little foible get to me.

And, I reminded myself firmly, remember how well she had reacted to my name.

Mostly when I finally had to admit to people that my name was Tory, they asked, "And why did your parents call you after a British political party?" and laughed themselves silly at their wit, never realising that a) their so-called wit wasn't remotely funny, and b) I'd heard it a million times already.

But Carol just said, "Tory. That's a lovely name. Very unusual. How did you come by it?'

And gratefully I answered, "My parents spent their honeymoon on Tory Island – you know, off the coast of Donegal – and I was born nine months later. So, long before David and Victoria Beckham thought of it, I was called after the place of my conception!"

"What a lovely idea! Just as well they didn't honeymoon in Termonfeckin!"

"Isn't it!" I said laughing. "What would be your name, if you were called after where your parents honeymooned?"

"Cilltubber," she grimaced. "Doesn't exactly roll off

the tongue, does it? I was born four years after they married, though, so it wouldn't have applied. Having said that," she mused, "we spent all our summer holidays there all my life – my father was a teacher, and they owned a cottage there, still do, I go there often – and I was born in April, so you can work it out yourself! Oh, what about," and she started laughing as another example struck her, "if your parents had had their honeymoon on the Blasket Islands!"

"Too right! Blasket O'Neill! I don't think so!"

And as we came up with more and more outrageous suggestions for holiday destinations which would make silly names (Benidorm, for example, Beni for short, one of us suggested), we laughed and laughed, and Lucy laughed too, not getting the joke, but enjoying the atmosphere, and our friendship was born and sealed.

Chapter 3

But God forbid you start relaxing, or thinking things are going your way. I can now understand the belief ancient peoples had about not speaking out loud about any good luck they were receiving, in case the gods heard and grew jealous and conspired to mess up that person's life.

I think the gods who were assigned the job of checking me out must have been especially petty, particularly jobsworth, because I wasn't exactly announcing to all and sundry about winning the Lotto, for example. Nor about having patented some brilliant invention which was going to make me a millionaire in a year's time. Nor shouting about having been signed to a prestigious record-label (I can't even sing, so that last was especially unlikely).

No, I was just thinking quietly and contentedly to myself that I was beginning to make sense of my life, that things were beginning to fall into place. I was just congratulating myself (maybe that was the mistake) on enjoying my life, and on having found a childminder for Lucy who was so good to her, and to me, that I could go to work without remorse, and on doing such a good job in that aforementioned work that I had been promoted and was being appreciated.

Was that too much, was that the hubris against which we are warned? Evidently it was, no matter that it wasn't my ideal life. My ideal life would definitely have involved being able to stay home with Lucy. My arms itched as I went to collect her each evening, itched to hold her again. I yearned to breathe in the sweet scent of her, to hear about her day. And I felt, each and every day, an overwhelming sense of envy of Carol, being able as she was to share the bulk of the waking hours of the day with my gorgeous daughter, to hear her laughter, calm her fears, enjoy her hugs. I could have hoped that this was enough to balance out my good fortune, to satisfy those gods. But evidently not.

Because one Sunday evening as I was sitting watching the telly, glass of juice to hand, the doorbell rang. Who on earth could that be? I wondered. Nobody ever called, as I've said. Immediately my heart clenched with fear. A fear much worse because it was a formless fear, a fear in my heart without knowing from which direction, or in what form, the danger would come.

I leaned out of the first-floor window but I couldn't see anybody. I called out a questioning, "Hello?"

All that happened after was, although I didn't know

44

it then, set in train at that moment. Could I have averted it, by not responding to the doorbell? Perhaps not. Perhaps what happened was inevitable, and all that I could have achieved, no matter what I did or didn't do, would have been to change some of the details. In many ways I hope that that's the case – it would be too painful to consider that I could so simply have averted what happened later.

And yet, and yet, considering *all* that happened after . . . would I have averted it even if I could? That's a thought I try not to dwell upon – for that way madness lies.

But call out the window I did, and my caller stepped back a little and came into view: it was Ray. Ray who I hadn't seen since the day he left.

"Oh, it's you," I said. "Hang on until I open the door." I wasn't overly thrilled to see him, but I certainly wasn't upset either. Indifference was my strongest emotion. (Is indifference even an emotion? And can you feel indifference strongly? It's a lack of emotion, perhaps. Whatever, that's what I was feeling. Or not feeling.) Oh yes, and a mild curiosity too. But that was it.

I closed the living-room window, went down the stairs, and opened the door to him. "Come in," I said, and he did so, stepping into the small hallway. I began to walk up the stairs, saying over my shoulder, "Do you want a coffee?"

"Sure, sure," he said, and followed me up into the flat's main hallway, and then into the tiny kitchen.

I filled the kettle and flicked the switch, and then

turned my attention to spooning instant coffee into mugs. As I was doing so I asked him, still not really looking at him, trying to sound casual, "Ray, what brings you here? It's hardly a social visit."

He shrugged nonchalantly. "I was just in the area, and I thought I'd pop in and see how you're getting on."

"I see." Although I didn't. Not yet.

He cleared this throat, and I realised that he was now getting to his real motive for calling, "And Lucy? How's she?"

My voice softened, "She's great, Ray, wonderful! Here, come on and I'll show you."

I led the way into the bedroom, where Lucy lay sleeping. She was lying flat on her back in her cot, arms and legs flung wide in innocent abandon, her covers – obviously having been kicked off along the way – crumpled at her feet. A beam of light from the streetlight outside fell onto her face, somehow not disturbing her, but showing her little plump face in all its beauty. But yet, the yellow colour of the light gave her beauty a somewhat macabre tint, made her look ill and jaundiced. Her abundant black curls were surrounding her head like a dark halo, and her button nose and full lips were so dainty and tiny and kissable that I felt a familiar ache of love in my chest.

I leaned into the cot and tucked her covers around her again.

"She's beautiful," breathed Ray.

"She is," I agreed fervently.

And for some little time, some time that is still precious to me, no matter all that came after, we stood there in silence, in mutual admiration of our mutual offspring, as parents have done since time began probably. In a way that Ray and I had not been able to do before.

After some moments I said softly, "The kettle's probably boiled. I'll go and make the coffee," and I went back into the kitchen and left him alone with his daughter, gave him privacy with her, delighted that he seemed, at last, to be showing an interest in her.

He came back a few moments later and accepted the steaming mug which I offered him. We both stood, leaning against cupboards – there was no space in this tiny room for a table and chairs. I did think of suggesting we move into the sitting-room, but that seemed a bit *too* hospitable, a bit too cosy.

"Cheers," he said, raising the mug to me in a slight toast before lifting it to his lips and taking an appreciative drink. As he was doing so his eyes were darting restlessly around the room.

He then studied his mug intently, cleared his throat a couple of times, took a few breaths and released them again, before saying hesitantly, "Thing is, Tory, I was wondering . . ." his voice trailed off.

"Yes?" I prompted when he didn't seem inclined to elaborate.

"I'd like to see more of Lucy," he burst out, his eyes still focussed on his cup. "I was wondering if we could arrange for me to have regular access to her. Say a day a weekend, or something. Or a day every second weekend," he went on hurriedly, "if every week is too much."

I felt a rush of something for him. Not love, certainly – that emotion had withered and died a long time ago. But affection, maybe, or fondness. And I felt a gladness on behalf of Lucy that she might, after all, be able to enjoy a relationship with her father. She might . . . if one issue were sorted.

"Sure," I said, taking a sip of my own coffee, "of course, we could agree something. You two *are* father and daughter, after all – it's much better that you know each other than that you don't."

"Thanks," he said awkwardly, and took another sip of his coffee.

"That is assuming," I said evenly, "that you're drug-free."

"I *am*!" he protested. "I told you I would stop, and I have."

"That's good," I said, relieved.

As we drank our coffee, still standing, like guests at a canapé-ridden function, I asked – more to make conversation than anything else – "And why now, Ray? Why have you decided to be in Lucy's life now, after all that time ignoring her?"

He shrugged, his gaze absently on the far wall. "I had a bit of a fright a little while ago. Thought I was done for, to be honest. And I was just sitting there tonight, and it occurred to me that when I'm gone, I'm gone forever. I don't believe in life after death, you know I don't. So my only immortality is my child. And it got me thinking about her, and I was wondering what she was like now . . . got to thinking about how strange it is, that she's a whole new person, who wouldn't even exist if it wasn't for me, and how she's somewhere in the world growing up without me and –" he shrugged then, unable to explain further what had brought him in pursuit of a relationship with his daughter.

But I wasn't really pursuing that line of thought. I was thinking of what he had started off saying.

"A bit of a fright?" I questioned. "You mean you thought you might die?"

He nodded sombrely.

"Dear God, how? Were you in an accident?"

"No," he shook his head. "No, it was more along the lines of a . . . of a health scare."

A health scare? What kind of health scare does a twenty-six-year-old man suffer? Even as I was pondering the question, the answer came to me. As did the realisation that all the time he had been in the flat, he hadn't looked me in the eyes once.

"Ray," I demanded, "Ray, look at me."

Slowly he lifted his head and faced me square on. I looked at him, and sure enough – his pupils were pale blue orbs, almost unblemished by any sign of a pupil. Pinpricks were huge discs compared to the size of Ray's pupils now.

"You're still on drugs," I said flatly. "You're still using."

He shrugged, unconcerned, it seemed, at being found out.

49

"Yes, yes, I am. But I promise I won't use when Lucy's with me."

I gave a hollow laugh. "Ray, your promises are worth nothing. Less than nothing, if that's possible. But it's all academic. There's no way I'm going to let Lucy next, near, or nigh you when you're using. Come back to me when you're clean and we'll reconsider it. I *do* want you to have a relationship with Lucy, Ray, honest I do. But only when it's in her best interests."

"In her best interests," he mimicked cruelly, his whole manner changing abruptly. "You're so square, so pious, so bloody superior. Who do you think you are, appointing yourself the monitor of who will and who won't see Lucy?" He was waving his arm around for emphasis, possibly forgetting that he still had the mug in his hand. Drops of coffee were flying around. I looked at them staining the wall, the floor and decided that that was the least of my worries.

"Ray, you can go now," I said, trying to make my voice strong. "You're not having access to Lucy, and that's it."

"I'll apply for custody," he said then. "I'm her father. You can't keep her away from me."

I laughed scornfully, which perhaps wasn't the wisest thing I ever did, and then said something very unwise indeed, because I took away his last hope of getting access to her. "You'd never get custody," I sneered. "Don't forget the drug conviction, no matter how brief or suspended the sentence. No judge in the land is going to give custody, or even access, to a convicted drug dealer!"

I had no idea if this was true or not. But I hoped it was true – it bloody well should be if it wasn't. But, even more to the point, Ray had no idea if this were true or not, and by his reaction it was clear that he believed that I did know, he believed that this was true.

He stared at me then, his whole demeanour changed, drooped, the fight went out of him and I thought I could see sadness in his eyes.

"They wouldn't?" he asked, somewhat plaintively.

I buried the thought of what a loser he was and pressed home my advantage. "No, Ray, they wouldn't. But listen, you get clean, and you stay clean, and we won't have to take it to court. We'll work it out ourselves. Okay?"

"Okay," he said, and he still sounded defeated.

He put down his coffee mug then and took a deep resigned sigh.

"Okay," he said, "okay. If that's the way it is. I *will* get clean. I *will* be a fit father to her, you'll see." He looked around, almost as if wondering where all that brave fightin' talk had come from. "I'll be off now. Goodbye."

So I merely said, "Goodbye," and watched him as he walked out the kitchen door and towards the stairs. At the top of the stairs he turned to me, where I stood now in the kitchen doorway. "I *will* get clean," he said again. "You'll see." He turned and a few steps down the stairs brought him out of my sight, and then a second or so after that I heard the front door open and then close again.

He *would* get clean, he told me. And I am one

51

hundred per cent sure that he actually even meant it at that moment.

I sighed and began to wash the mugs and clean the coffee-drop stains off the walls and floor. It would be interesting to see if he did indeed manage to stay drug-free in order to see Lucy. Whether he could or not was one question, but even before that was the question of whether he would try. After having lived for many years with Ray's passing fads (around everything except music, to which he was eternally and perennially faithful), I had plenty of experience of how quickly what passed for enthusiasm with him quickly arose and equally quickly fell. And hadn't he said himself that it was only tonight that he had been thinking about it?

So, it was very possible I would hear no more about it. And if I did . . . well, I'd worry about it then.

Once I had cleaned up I got ready for sleep, and en route to my bed I stopped again beside Lucy's cot. She was still sleeping, the visit from her father having passed unnoticed. She had, however, thrown the covers off again. I smiled fondly, replaced the covers, laid the back of my hand against her soft cheek, relishing the so-faint-you-nearly-couldn't-feel-it sensation of her breath on the back of my wrist as I did so, before climbing wearily into my own bed.

Chapter 4

The next day. Monday, ugh. I flung back the covers, got myself and a sleepily protesting Lucy up, fed, washed and dressed, and then out the door to Carol's. The day passed uneventfully, but as I sat on the DART on the way home that evening I began to think again about Ray's visit. Maybe I should go to a solicitor, I debated, see what the story really was about shared custody, or even access visits. Forewarned is forearmed, as they say. But then I pondered the fragile condition of my bank account and thought that maybe I wouldn't, that it could turn out to be an expense I didn't need, Yet, the argument turned again, information is power.

I was still debating this quandary when I arrived back at Carol's house.

"Hi," she grinned, "come in!"

Lucy was busy pulverising some playdough at the kitchen table when I arrived into the kitchen. She raised her head at the familiar sound of my footsteps, my voice.

"Mamma!" she shouted exuberantly, and she quickly slid off the chair on which she had been standing and came to me. I picked her up, heedless of her doughy hands, and held her to me, absorbing the sound and feel of her heartbeat against me.

"Cuppa?" asked Carol.

"I'd love one," I said and sat down with Lucy on my knee.

"Any news?" asked Carol as she poured the tea.

"You'll never guess what happened last night," I told her, and caught her up to date with Ray's visit.

"That's a turn up for the books," she said when I finished. "I thought he had no interest in her. Which I have to admit I always found a bit bizarre – how could anyone not have interest in the little dote?"

"He didn't," I agreed, "but it looks as if he found some. Hit by the realisation of his mortality, or something!"

We laughed at Ray's expense as we sat there, two women drinking tea, and Lucy laughed too, not understanding the joke but enjoying the fact that it was happening.

And then I thought I could ask Carol's advice about whether or not to contact a solicitor. She would surely have something wise to say. Sensible Carol, kind Carol, Carol who had become nearly as much my surrogate mother as she was Lucy's surrogate grandmother. And so I did.

"Gosh," she said, taking a delaying sip of her tea. She thought about it for a few moments. "To be fair," she said, "I'm probably not the right person to ask. I don't know Ray, after all. I don't have any idea what he would do. How can I advise you?"

"Please, Carol," I pleaded, "I'm just looking for another opinion."

"Okay," she conceded. She thought some more and then said, "I think – now Tory, this is only my opinion, it mightn't be right, you understand that?" I nodded as she continued, "I think you shouldn't do anything for the moment. See what – if anything – Ray does next. There's no point going to the trouble and expense of seeing a solicitor when you don't have to. And if Ray does initiate any proceedings, you'll still have plenty of time to organise stuff from your side. So I wouldn't worry about it."

"That's just what I was thinking!" I said in relief. Well, it was . . . it was along with the fact I was thinking exactly the opposite. "Okay, that's exactly what I'm going to do – nothing!"

"Nothing except get this young lady home! We've had a busy day, haven't we, Lucy?"

"What did you do today?" I asked, agog as ever to hear the details, the minutiae of how Lucy spent her time. So Carol regaled me with the particulars of their day shared together. I felt my familiar mixture of guilt and regret and sadness that it wasn't I who was sharing this with Lucy, along with delight that at least Lucy was with someone who cared for her so much and so well.

"And how are you, Carol?" I asked when she was finished. "Have you heard from Larry or Sean recently?" And we sat together with the evening sunshine spilling into her kitchen as she caught me up on the latest endeavours and successes of her two beloved sons.

For a week or so, it seemed as if Carol was right. There was no word from Ray, either in person or in the form of dry precise legal correspondence. I decided that clearly his interest in Lucy *had* just been that passing fad I had predicted, which suited me just fine.

A cheerful May turned into a bright June, and life went on in its even, contented way. I didn't know then that the gods were only biding their time.

On that day, that June day on which everything changed, I had no premonition. None whatsoever. Everything progressed as normally as you could wish for. Until about three o'clock that afternoon. Until I answered my phone at work.

"Tory O'Neill," I introduced myself crisply into the receiver.

There was silence for a moment or two, but the sort of silence in which you can somehow hear that the line is open, that there is somebody there.

"Hello?" I asked. "Hello? Can you hear me? Can I help you?"

And then I heard an unrecognisable whisper. "Tory," it said.

I felt the first trickle of fear. What on earth was going on? I took a reflexive glance around the open-plan workplace, trying to gain reassurance from the bright normality of office-life going on around me.

"Tory," the voice rasped again, so quiet I had to strain to hear it. "Tory, it's me. Carol."

"Carol?" I asked, the fear growing, overpowering suddenly. "Carol, what's wrong? Is Lucy okay? Carol, please, tell me? You've got to tell me."

I heard a muffled sob and my heart clenched. "What's happened?" I asked urgently. "Carol, is Lucy all right?" My voice was rising now, trying to get through to Carol, and out of the corner of my eye I could see my colleagues focus their attention on me, concern and worry sharp on their expressions. Mary, the woman with whom I was perhaps closest, began to move towards me.

"Come home," said Carol's weak voice. "Come home now. I'll explain when you get here. She's . . . all right, but . . ." she gave a sharp sob again, "I can't explain, Tory. I would if I could. Just get here as quickly as you can."

"Carol!"

But she had hung up.

I was on my feet and grabbing my bag even before I had hung up.

"An emergency," I explained wildly to my colleagues, "I have to go – I can't explain – but – Lucy – I have to go."

"Sure, sure," they soothed, the various voices melding into one concerned tone. "Don't worry, Tory. Take all the time you need. We'll cover your clients.

We'll explain to Sinead – let us know how she is – is she in the hospital?"

But I wasn't listening, was barely taking it in, certainly wasn't answering, was rushing already towards the door. I flung myself down the stairs and out onto the street. I began running towards the nearest taxi-rank, but as luck would have it, an empty taxi passed me. I flagged it down and got in, pulling the door behind me. Striving to slow my words, struggling for coherence, I gasped the address at the taxi-driver. "Please, as quickly as you can," I said. "It's an emergency."

"Be as quick as I can, love, without breaking the law," he said, and off we sped.

And for that awful half an hour I had nothing to do but to sit and worry. What could possibly be wrong? She had said Lucy was all right, at least there was that. And she obviously wasn't badly injured or she'd be in hospital, not still at the house. So what was it? I could think of no other possibilities, none at all. But yet . . . yet it had to be something serious enough to upset Carol this badly, to have her call me out of work like this.

My mind turned uselessly over and over, and my stomach churned in nauseating symphony for the whole of that agonisingly slow journey.

I tried to ring Carol again on my mobile, but she wasn't answering, which worried me even more.

In the end I spent the remainder of the journey praying uselessly, kneading my hands over and over. "Please let her be okay," I begged. "Anything, just let her be okay."

It seemed to take an eternity, but eventually the taxi was pulling up outside Carol's house. I flung some money at the driver and threw myself out of the car, and up Carol's drive.

She was obviously looking out for me, because the door opened as soon as I reached it and I rushed into the house.

"Carol, what's going on?" I was asking even as she was telling me.

"Oh Tory, Tory, Ray's got her!"

That stopped me in my tracks. "Ray's got her?"

"Yes," she whispered. "I answered the door, not thinking anything of it – it was him. He pushed his way in. I couldn't stop him, Tory," her face creased at the memory. "I tried. I tried to close the door again but I wasn't strong enough. I was so frightened," she finished on a sob, and buried her head against me, the muffled sounds of her sobs and her fear and her upset making their way through our joined bodies. I patted her awkwardly on the back but right now I didn't care what she had been through.

"Carol," I said urgently, insistently, "Carol, listen to me. Get a hold of yourself. Calm down. We need to sort this out. There's no time for hysterics. Do you hear me?"

Eventually my words penetrated and she nodded against me – I could feel her rather than see her – to indicate that she had understood. She straightened then, wiping her eyes, and spoke in a much calmer voice – but under the calm I could hear the tension, the fear, the uncertainty.

"First things first," I said, trying to keep on top of my own tension and fear, knowing that the panic which was threatening to overcome me would do me no good at all. "Let's call the gardai, if you haven't already."

But Carol was shaking her head. "No gardai," she whispered, "he said not to. He said –" she broke off for a sob, which she hastily swallowed, "that it wouldn't be in Lucy's best interests if I involved the police. He said to ring you, and he left a note for you. He said it would explain. But I didn't dare call the police, just in case –"

"What note? Where is it?"

She looked around vaguely, as if the note would walk up to her and say hello. I tsk-ed with impatience then. Yes, I know, I know, she was an older woman who had just had an awful shock, but I needed information from her for God's sake.

"Where is it?" I asked again, forcing my voice to be gentle.

Her puzzled expression cleared, her face brightened. "It's on the kitchen table," she told me and then her expression darkened again as the reality of it must have hit her.

I turned and walked into the kitchen. On the table was lying an unaddressed envelope. I picked it up and noted that it was sealed. I impatiently ripped it open, too late remembering that this was probably evidence. But still. I tugged out the paper inside and unfolded it. As I read the typed text I could feel all heat drain from my body:

"Tory, I've got Lucy, and I'm going to look after her from

*now on. You had your choice, you could have shared her with
me, we could have worked it out. But you wouldn't so this is
on your own head. Don't worry, she'll be safe with me. But
do not contact the gardai. Look what happened to Charlotte
Riordan – she was safe with her father until the police got
involved. Ray."*

I looked up at Carol, who had followed me into the
kitchen, and silently handed her the note. She took it
and read it. When she finished she lifted a face to me
which was – and I wouldn't have even thought this was
possible – even chalkier than before.

"Charlotte Riordan," I whispered, anguished.

"Charlotte Riordan," echoed Carol brokenly.

Was there anybody in Ireland who didn't know the
tragic story of Charlotte Riordan? The way her father
disappeared with her during a custody visit, and
managed to evade all capture until one day the gardai got
a tip-off. And how they got to the house just too late to
prevent the father killing Charlotte with a shot-gun. He
was in prison now, unrepentant. "If I couldn't have her,
damned if her mother was going to," he was quoted as
saying. And her mother was reported as having sobbed
to journalists, "Oh why didn't I leave her with him?
She'd still be alive if I hadn't got the gardai involved.
Better her alive without me than dead."

"Dear God, what am I going to do?" I said, feeling
alternating waves of cold and heat washing over my
body.

"Sit down," said Carol. "I'll make us a cup of tea."

She seemed to be regaining her own strength a little in the need to look after me.

She laid a gentle hand on my elbow and I allowed her to steer me to a kitchen chair. I sat on it, rested my elbows on the white formica table and rested my head in my hands as I tried to make sense of it all, to come to terms with the new reality.

Ray has Lucy, I told myself, trying to make the words sound real. He's told me not to contact the gardai. He has not-very-subtly threatened her life if I *do* involve them. I have no idea where he is. I have no idea what to do now. And every minute is bringing her further away from me, and I'm just sitting here, paralysed with fear and indecision.

And all the time I heard the comforting sounds of Carol boiling the kettle, her footsteps soft on the lino as she walked to the fridge, the gentle sound of it opening and closing again. Eventually I heard her say, "Here you go," and I raised my head to see the mug she was holding out to me. I took it and curled my fingers around it, the warmth feeling good, but I couldn't bring myself to take a sip.

"He's a good man," I told her defiantly, as if she had been arguing to the contrary. "Well," I corrected myself, "he's not a bad man. There isn't a malicious bone in his body. I know he's not dependable, and totally selfish. But he's totally without nastiness. She'll be safe with him. Until I find them. I don't have to worry about her," I insisted. But then I had to go on, had to say, "Or, at least I don't have to worry about him *actively* hurting her. But he doesn't know how to look after children. He might neglect her, leave her on her own while he goes to gigs. And he does drugs, that was why I wouldn't let him have access to her – I told you that. He seemed to accept it, you know, when I told him he couldn't see her unless he was clean, I thought he'd accepted it. But it looks as if all he had accepted was that he couldn't get her that way, so he had to think of something else. Oh God," and I rubbed a weary hand over my forehead, with a massive effort of will fighting down the nausea and the tears which threatened to prevail over me. I could hear the tremor, the squeakiness in my voice. I forced myself to speak slowly, as strongly as I could. "But it's all okay. I'll find him soon. She won't be with him for long."

"But can you? Can you even look for him? His note . . . what he said about Charlotte Riordan . . ." She broke off, stricken.

"I won't involve the gardai. That was the mistake Charlotte's mother made," I said, a sudden expert, "but I won't rest until I have her back. But he won't hurt her. I know he won't. The note was just to frighten me. He's not like that. I know him. He's very gentle." I knew I was protesting too much. But then the realisation hit me. "I don't know him at all!" I burst out, and the tears came, and through the tears I sobbed, "I would have sworn he would have been the last person to do this. First of all that he has any real interest in her, it's just so out of character! But to abduct her . . ." I shook my head in disbelief. "I just don't understand." I felt cold now, so cold. Shock hitting me, I realised. "Tell me how it happened," I asked. "Tell me from the beginning."

"I was here with the three children, just like any day," she began.

I interrupted then as it occurred to me to ask, "Where are Shay and Laura?"

"When it happened I rang their parents to come and get them. I was so upset I couldn't possibly cope. I told them I was ill. And they both work locally, you know that, so they were here soon. They were both a little annoyed at first, I think," she laughed bitterly, "but I think they felt remorseful when they saw me. I surely looked ill.

"Anyway," she continued her tale. "the three children were having their Quiet Time on their mats when the doorbell rang. I thought nothing of it, I just went and answered it. And Ray – although I didn't know it was Ray then, of course – pushed in the door. And he told me who he was. Lucy's dad he told me. He said, 'Where is she?' And I asked him who he was looking for, even though I knew really. And he said, 'Lucy, of course, where is she?' And I said, 'In the playroom, having Quiet Time.' And he said, 'Go and get her. I'm taking her with me,' and I said I wouldn't, but honestly, Tory, I was so scared then."

Sure enough, she was physically shaking as she recounted the tale.

She took a deep breath and continued, "And when I said I wouldn't get her, he said that if I didn't get her for him, he would go and get her himself. But wouldn't it be better, he said, if I were to get her calmly and just hand her to him without distressing her? Because

64

otherwise he would go and get her, and if I was trying to resist and it all got upsetting then she would get upset and that wouldn't be good, would it? He was going to take her one way or another, he told me – surely it would be better for Lucy if it was all relaxed and low-key?

"And Tory," she wailed, "I saw the sense of what he was saying. There was no way I could physically stop him, he was so much stronger than me, I found that out when I was trying to close the front door against him. So I did what he said. I can't believe it now, but it did seem the best for Lucy. So I went in to her and I told her brightly, 'Look Lucy, a surprise. Your daddy's here to see you.' And she said brightly, 'Dada!' She knows the word, you see, from hearing Laura and Shay say it. So I picked her up and brought her and her nappy-bag out to the hallway, and I handed her over to him. And I was trying to tell him things about her, about the care of her, but he was just saying she would be fine, that I wasn't to worry. And I *was* worrying. Of course, I was.

"And then he gave me that note for you, and he told me to ring you and to get you home, but I wasn't to tell you what had happened on the phone. He said I was to get you here first, and make sure you read the letter. He said you would decide what to do then, the responsibility would be yours then, he said. But if I told you over the phone you might call the gardai, he said, so I was to get you here first."

"Okay, okay," I intervened, reaching out and putting an arresting hand on her arm, to stop the flood of information mixed with remorse and distress. "Just tell me – how was Lucy when you handed her to him? Was she upset? After all, he's a total stranger to her."

"No, she wasn't upset. At least there was that. But you know Lucy, Tory. She thinks the world is her friend. She'd go with anybody."

I was reminded again of how much more time Carol spent with Lucy than I was able to do. I knew that Lucy thought the world was her friend, she never made strange, loved strangers making a fuss of her. But I had thought that that was only when I was with her to give her that confidence. I hadn't realised she was trusting enough to go happily with a stranger. Guilt pierced me, at how little I knew my daughter, compared to the kindly woman sitting across from me, who, let's face it, spent far more of Lucy's waking hours with her than I did.

"I am so, so sorry," Carol said then, her face drawn, her eyes red. "You trusted me to look after her, and . . . and I didn't!" she ended on a sob.

I reached out a hand and placed it over hers as they kneaded together on the table. "It's not your fault," I soothed. "It's me who should be sorry to have brought this on your shoulders. You shouldn't have had to deal with that. Oh God, Carol," I burst out then, "what am I going to do?"

"Stay calm," she urged, turning her hand around so that it grasped mine. "You must stay calm – you won't be able to do anything if you're panicking."

"I can ring him!" I cried in relief, suddenly realising I still had his mobile number programmed into my phone. "I have his number! I'll ring him and talk sense to him! Yes, that's what I'll do. I'll promise him that I *will* share custody with him. God," I said fervently, "I'll promise him *anything* if it'll get Lucy back."

And as Carol watched me, anxiety and fear etched sharply on her face, I quickly tabbed through the phone address book until I came to Ray's number. I pressed the key to dial it, and as it rang I felt my chest ease, felt the tight band which had been encircling it loosen, and I could breathe again. Any second now I'd be talking to him, could explain things to him. It would all be over in no time.

But I didn't get to talk to Ray. I got to talk to – or rather, listen to – an unfeeling electronic voice informing me, *"This number is out of service"*. I kept holding the phone, kept listening, maybe hoping that it was all a joke, that any second now Ray was going to answer the phone himself. But after a while there was a beep and then some static. And that was it.

After some time I shook my head, pressed the 'end-call' button and shook my head. "He's not using that phone number any more," I said. "Makes sense – if you're in the business of abducting your daughter you probably don't want to be contacted."

"No . . ." said Carol softly. And then: "So, now what?"

I shook my head in despair. Good question, not one to which I had the answer, unfortunately.

She thought for a moment and then asked, "Do you know where he lives?"

I shook my head in despair. "No. I never thought to

ask him where he was living – I wasn't that interested, after all."

"What about his friends?"

"I don't know them," I wailed. "They were always changing as the bands changed. I never knew surnames, or usually even first names, only nicknames. They all blurred into this amorphous beer-drinking, guitar-playing, denim lump! And I never had their phone numbers. I never needed – or wanted – to phone them. Hang on, though," I said, as a thought occurred to me. "His grandmother! I can contact her!"

As Carol gazed at me, her expression anxious – God knows what my own face looked like – I lifted my mobile phone again and dialled Directory Enquiries.

"Directory Enquiries, Joanne speaking, can I help you?"

"Yes, please, would you have a phone number for a Maisie Rafter, in Dunfarney, Co Kildare?"

"Do you have an address?"

"No, I'm afraid I don't."

There was silence except for the sound of a distant keyboard being tapped. And then she said, "I'm sorry. We have no listing under that name."

"Oh. Maybe the phone would have been in her husband's name, which I don't know. Could you try for *any* Rafters in Dunfarney?"

More typing.

"We have three listed, and there are two others which are ex-directory."

"Could you give me the listed ones, please?" I

asked, quickly lifting my bag to fetch a pen and the ubiquitous back-of-an-envelope, and then I wrote down the names and numbers given.

"And can you give me the two others?" I asked then, even though I knew what the answer would be. And I wasn't wrong.

"No, I'm afraid we can't. As I told you, they are ex-directory."

"Look – Joanne, was it – I'm really sorry to put you in this position, but it's *so* important that I get those numbers." I took a deep breath, determined to slow my speech so that she could understand me, reaching for whatever it would take for her to give me the information I needed. "My ex-partner has just abducted my little girl from her child-minder, and I need to find his grandmother, to find out where he is. Please, please," I begged, aware that she was trying to interrupt, but desperation making me assertive enough to talk over her, "please help me! I need to get my little girl back. He has no idea of looking after children. I need to know she's safe."

Her voice was rising now and eventually she spoke over me and I had to listen, but there was compassion in her voice too, "We don't *have* ex-directory numbers. It just comes up that there are two other people of that name with a phone in that area. But we have no access, no matter how important it is, to the numbers. Do you understand?"

My silence must have answered for me, as she went on, softer now that she didn't have to shout to be heard, a world of sympathy in her voice, "But look, it's not as bleak as that. It really isn't. The police can get the numbers, if they request them officially. So as soon as you report the crime, they'll be able to start organising getting the number."

"Okay," I said morosely, "thanks for that." And I disconsolately hung up. And after some moments looked up, looked across the table at Carol. She was looking at me with compassion and concern on her face.

"Well?" she asked.

"Maybe, there are three Rafters listed. I'll ring them. But there are also two unlisted, and it might be one of those, but I couldn't get the number."

"Try the listed ones," urged Carol.

I did, and got through to each one. But no, they weren't Maisie's house. They didn't know Maisie or Ray Rafter.

I thanked the last one and replaced the receiver, shoulders slumping. I felt so exhausted. I wanted to go to bed and sleep for ages, and wake to have all this behind me. To realise, with heart-thudding relief, that it had only been a dream, a nightmare.

But it wasn't. It was reality. My daughter was out there somewhere and I was going to find her, and there would be no rest for me until I did so.

"I'll drive to Maisie's house," I told Carol. "I was there a couple of times with Ray. I think I can find it again."

"Good luck," she said. "Let me know how you get

on. And if there's anything I can do – anything! – to help, let me know. I feel so bad about my part in this – I'm so sorry."

"It's not your fault," I told her softly and we stood and made our way to the front door. Once there I hugged her, and she hugged be back, holding tight, and I drew strength from her solid capable warmth, and I said, "I'll let you know how I get on."

Chapter 5

And so I drove to Dunfarney. Which makes it all sound very easy. But in fact it took hours and hours as I became part of the Great Dublin Commuter's Traffic Crawl. It took me an hour alone to get across the giant carpark officially known as the Red Cow Roundabout, but which was aptly renamed by Dublin's wits as the Mad Cow Roundabout. It was stop-and-start the whole way along the N7. And I sat and fumed and a scream was building up inside me. But I knew that if I started screaming I wouldn't stop, that I would end up in total hysterics. Which wouldn't do me, nor Lucy, any good whatsoever. So I pushed down the scream-sensation, smothered it. It still lurked there, waiting, ready to pour out of me. But I pressed it down, held it down. My hands were slippery on the steering wheel and my heart was pounding hard in my chest. 'Ray's-got-Lucy! Ray's-got-Lucy!' the beat of my heart chanted.

And I was experiencing another form of frustration, an exquisite torture. Even as I was going through this horrendous journey I knew, somewhere deep in the heart of me, that this journey was actually bringing me further *away* from Lucy.

I didn't for one moment think that Ray would have brought her to his grandmother's house – they were most likely still somewhere in Dublin. But even as I was crawling in first gear, inch by tortured inch, lengthening the distance between Lucy and me, I knew I had no choice. Ray's grandmother Maisie was the only link, the only lead I had. But still, in every moment I felt a screaming urge to turn around, a tension like an elastic band being pulled harder and harder, the further away I got from Dublin, from what I was sure was Lucy's location.

And there was another problem. I didn't know exactly where Maisie lived. Her house was out in the countryside somewhere in Dunfarney's hinterland, I remembered, but I didn't know its location. As I had told Carol, I had been there twice, sure. But the first time Ray had driven on his motor-bike with me as pillion passenger and all I had really seen was his black-leathered back, the passing lanes a peripheral 70mph blur.

And the second time I had gone, it had been in a car, sure. My newly bought elderly car, purchased to provide a safe method of transport for the newborn Lucy, who was the reason for the visit – to introduce her to her great-grandmother. And since that had been another issue for Ray, having to stop riding his beloved motorbike simply because I refused to take a baby on it, he had insisted on driving, the threat to his virility from being a passenger way too serious to be contemplated. And because he was driving I hadn't really been watching the route, too nervous at wondering what the redoubtable Maisie would make of my Lucy.

The only thing I had in my favour was the fact that I'd recognise the house when I saw it, with its stone eagles on the gateposts, and its location right on a bend in the road, on the right-hand side.

There was another problem with the stop'n'start traffic – it didn't require enough concentration. It left way too much energy for me to think about Lucy. And so as I crawled along the infamous N7 I was nauseous with nerves and fear, wondering what Lucy was doing now. Wondering if she was okay. Was she anxious, missing me, crying for me? Was she wondering why I wasn't coming for her, why I wasn't there when she needed me? But under the nausea there was the steel of determination running through me too. *I am coming, Lucy*, I projected my thoughts towards her. *I am coming to get you.*

Once in Dunfarney I took the exit out of town which seemed the most familiar. I drove down the country road slowly, looking anxiously for any sign of Maisie's house. It had been a few minutes outside the town, I remembered, at the rate Ray drove, so much longer for anybody else. At my snail's pace, I'd better drive for ten minutes to be sure.

A few minutes outside the town I came to a right turn. Had we turned there? I couldn't remember. Okay, I'd keep going on the current road for another five minutes, and if I didn't find Maisie's house I'd come back and try that right turn. And failing that I'd then try any other turns I encountered. I'd do it logically. And if none of those worked, I'd go back to town and take another of the roads leaving it.

I carried along that road for the designated time, passing two more right turns, and two left turns. And God knows, I thought despairingly, how many turns *those* roads had. It didn't matter, I told myself fiercely. This is the only game in town, and you're going to do it, no matter how long it takes.

Ten minutes down that first road I admitted defeat. I turned back until I came to the original right turn, now on my left. I took it and began driving down it. Luckily within ten minutes of driving I only passed one turn off that. I returned to it and took it.

Whenever I passed walkers I stopped and rolled down the window. "Do you know where Maisie Rafter lives?" I asked, but nobody did.

Eventually, defeated, I returned to the main road and drove along it until I came to the next turning, and repeated the process.

That side-road, and its tributaries, were a blank also.

Okay, the third turning. Another blank.

Near midsummer it might be, but night was falling as I drove down country lane after country lane, despairingly looking for Maisie's house. It was after ten o'clock now, almost full dark. Maisie would be in bed, I thought despairingly, if not now, then soon. She was an old woman. Did I have the right to wake her up, impel her from her bed? Yes, I told myself fiercely, I did have that right! I was in pursuit of my daughter, and all other considerations were nothing compared to that.

Of course, my brave words were all very well, but she mightn't answer a knock coming late at night. She mightn't even hear it.

It became almost surreal: driving endlessly through the deepening dusk, the twists and turns and bends seemed to blend into an eternal, dizzying, circle. Full-leaved summer trees swayed above me, silhouetted against the last vestiges of light, seeming to dance and mock. Time and again I had to force my mind back to consciousness as it began to drift in the ever-changing but always-the-same scenery.

I was tiring, I realised. The day had been long and bizarre enough, and it was not surprising that I should be finding it difficult now.

But something kept me going. Not so much determination, more an awareness of a lack of other options. More a fatalistic sense of this being what I was destined to do, on this particular June evening, to drive and twist, and try and remember which roads I had searched, and which I hadn't.

I sighed as I turned into the fourth turning off that original 'main' road. If I remembered correctly, this turning was nearly ten minutes outside Dunfarney. Maisie's house was certainly no further than this. So, I told myself, it was this turning. It had to be. Or else, I had taken the wrong original exit from town.

So I began down that smaller road, feeling a little as if I would never find the house. Perhaps it had never really existed, perhaps I had only ever imagined it. Perhaps it was like Brigadoon, arriving and disappearing. Perhaps I was destined, like a vehicular Flying Dutchman, to forever drive the country roads of County Kildare, over and over, even after I died, always looking for my daughter. Get a grip, I told myself acerbically, aware that my thoughts were really getting strange. Fear and weariness and shock were conspiring against me.

I decided, trying to force myself back to sense, to reality, that I would keep going down that road for at least ten minutes. If I didn't find Maisie's house by then I would have to stay the night locally, and then try all other roads around the town once morning came. And, yes, of course, I suddenly realised with a slight lifting of my heart, the post office would know Maisie's address – her local postman would. But the post office wouldn't open until nine the next morning and I couldn't wait that long. Even assuming they would give out her address at a stranger's request. At the moment, my memory of Maisie's house was my only link, my only lead. I had to keep following it.

I was so numbed, so sure I wouldn't find it, that I nearly drove past it. I slammed on the brakes and reversed. There it was, the little bungalow, and illuminated in my headlights were the gate-pillars and their oversized stone eagles at which Ray and I had laughed long and loud. Now I thought them the most beautiful sight I had ever seen.

I pulled the car into the lee of the driveway, switched off the ignition and got out. With my headlights turned off there was nothing but blackness. The house itself, a barely darker shade of black against the night sky, was also dark, no light on anywhere. It seemed to glower at me as it crouched there. Nobody home, it seemed to mock, no answers for you here, no daughter for you here.

I stood irresolute, shivering a little in the cold night air. Now what? I didn't care, I decided. If she had reared a grandson who could steal my baby, then she could cope with the consequence of being woken up.

I carefully manoeuvred my way up the driveway in the pitch dark, with hesitant stumbling steps, until I reached the front door. I found and lifted the heavy iron knocker. The metal was cold in my hand. When I released it and it banged against its companion metal the reverberation of the sound crashed through the otherwise silent night. Never mind waking Maisie, this sound would waken the dead. I stood there on the doorstep, and waited.

Once the last resonance of the door-knocker had faded away the night returned to its former silence. It was oppressive, such a level, such a depth, of countryside quiet. I realised how accustomed I was to the ever-present sounds of night in the city: cars, sirens, even footsteps and laughter and arguments and fights.

As I waited I studied the black-satin inlaid-with-diamonds sky. I had never seen so many stars! I looked at them, and told myself that I, and hence my problems, were insignificant in the grand scheme of things, tiny amongst such enormity, such infinity.

But I didn't feel that, couldn't feel it. My problems *were* real, my hurt when I thought of Lucy was chest-piercingly real. Was she sleeping now? Her thumb having fallen out of her mouth, her dark curls scattered across some strange pillow. Were there tear-stains on that pillow? Had she cried herself to sleep, looking for me, calling for me, despairing as I didn't come? Had Ray fed her? Of course, he had, I swore, trying to convince myself. You don't have to be a parenting-skills expert to know that children need food, I reasoned. And what about her nappy? Surely he knew that two-year-olds still had nappies, which needed regular changing. Or was she lying somewhere in her own filth, the ammonia slowly corroding her silken skin as I stood there, waiting for my one link to her to answer the bloody door.

I turned and banged the door again, hard. There was still no response. Was Maisie sleeping through this noise? Or maybe it had woken her, and she was lying terrified in her bed, wondering who was demanding entry at this late hour, too scared to answer the door. All those stories of elderly people attacked, even killed, in their isolated houses for whatever pittance of money was left over from the weekly pension – she would surely have heard those.

Oh Tory, I demanded of myself, what kind of monster

are you, terrorising an innocent old lady? Lucy's with her father, I reminded myself. He is not a bad man, I reminded myself. She would come to no harm between now and tomorrow morning, I told myself. And even if Maisie's terror were worth getting the information a few hours sooner, and hence reclaiming Lucy that few hours sooner – even if I could defend that – that situation didn't apply. She wasn't going to answer the door.

I leaned down, pushed open the letterbox and yelled in: "Maisie, it's me! Tory! Ray's girlfriend! Are you there? Please open the door. I'm not going to hurt you. And if you don't want to answer the door, at least know that it's me, nobody who's going to hurt you!"

There was only a resounding silence. I suddenly thought – is she even here? Maybe she was in hospital, or some old-folks' home. Or dead, even, the house abandoned and deserted. Oh God, how would I find Lucy then, if any of those scenarios applied?

Suddenly I shivered, the night was getting colder. I turned and made my way back to the car.

I sat in the driver's seat, indecisive. I had three choices, I realised. I could go back to Dunfarney and try to get a B&B. Assuming anyone would let me in at this hour, with no luggage. Or I could go home and come back in the morning. But I'd hardly be home before it was time to leave again. And I didn't think – despite my earlier exhaustion – that I could sleep anyway. Or I could stay here all night – it would be uncomfortable, but the night wasn't freezing, I wouldn't die.

And maybe there was part of me which felt that it would be right to spend an uncomfortable night in the car. If Lucy was suffering in any way, at some level I'd be helping her by making sure I was suffering too. Bizarre thinking I know, but I was tired, traumatised, hungry and not thinking straight.

So, for right or wrong I spent the night in the car, sleeping fitfully, always aware of the cold. I clutched my coat to me, tried to get my legs and feet tucked in under it, and rested my head against the window. At times I would waken with my head jerking up, realising that I had fallen asleep, my head sinking downwards as I did so, until the discomfort of that dragged me awake again. The window was cold against my head, and I adjusted my position so I was resting it against the car seat. But that meant that my body was twisted uncomfortably. My back began hurting, so I moved again. Now my feet were sticking out from under the coat, and getting cold.

It was a protracted, cold, lonely, uncomfortable, exhausting night.

Chapter 6

Slowly, imperceptibly, the total darkness began to lift to a dark grey, and then a lighter grey, and then the sky was pink-grey, and then the grey was replaced by blue. The new day had come. A chorus of birds began to sing – they, I thought bitterly, hadn't a care in the world. Ha! They should try being in my shoes, see how much singing they would do then!

It was dawn on the first full day of being without my daughter.

I was aware that I was starving. I hadn't eaten since lunch-time yesterday. And I urgently had to go to the toilet. I looked at my watch – it was only seven o'clock. But surely somewhere would be open. I started up the car and drove back into Dunfarney.

I found a greasy-spoon café, and I negotiated my way around the various trucks and articulated lorries parked outside until I reached the front door. I went in and ordered a full Irish breakfast. Cholesterol 'R Us. While I sat waiting for it I couldn't help but be aware of the atmosphere: hot moist air redolent with piquant smells of fatty meat and over-used cooking oil, the loudness of the shouted meal-orders and the booming conversation of hefty tattooed men. I was aware, too – even through my downcast eyes – of the alert, interested, gazes of many of these men. I sighed to myself.

Whoever said that beauty was a curse didn't know the half of it. Far, far worse was to be in my position: the object of men's interest without even the consolation of being beautiful. Okay, I granted, my waist-long hair, brown-with-a-tantalising-tease-of-dark-red, was fairly arresting, thick and bountiful. Okay, I often acknowledged, if I wanted less attention I could have cut it all off. But every time I contemplated that act I remembered my father's voice, clear for once, saying, "Tory, you have beautiful hair," and how he reached out a tentative hand and caressed its length. There was no way I could cut it. I compromised, however, by keeping it resolutely plaited at all times.

But apart from my hair I had no beauty, no reason for these men to be staring greedily. My eyes – not that those men could see them, focussed as they were on the plastic grubby tablecloth – were an indistinguishable mix of green and brown, without even the distinction of a hue to call their own. *And*, to add insult to injury, they were too far apart in my head, with thick red-brown eyebrows lording it over them. And my mouth, too, too big and full. And my nose – I reserved the deepest, strongest loathing for my nose. Why couldn't I have a sweet little retroussé nose, instead of this strong imperious one? And then there was my figure. I was tall-ish for a woman, about five foot six. But thin. Skinny. All angles and sharp corners. I clung despairingly, half-amused, to the description of *gamine*. But I was the only one to use that word. I remember Ray, in a rare affectionate moment, telling me I was a fine thing, all right, all I needed was breasts and hips and I'd be beautiful. I had stifled my hurt and thanked him for what he had obviously meant as a compliment.

The meal came then, and I began devouring it hungrily, relishing each bite and the taste and heat of its accompanying mug of strong milky tea.

But then I suddenly paused, fork midway to my mouth. Was Lucy hungry? Had he thought to feed her? Was she crying even now for some food? What right had I to be eating when she might be hungry?

Ray isn't a monster, I reminded myself. Of course he'll feed her. Also, I acknowledged, regardless of the conditions in which Lucy was being kept, I was going to need all my strength to get her back. I needed to look after myself to be any use to her. It's like on aeroplanes – they always tell you to put your own oxygen mask on first before tending to a child, because if you can't breathe, you surely can't help them.

So I finished the breakfast, but the pleasure was gone out of it.

I got back to Maisie's house at about half past eight. I went and knocked on the door again, my heart pounding. If she wasn't there, what on earth would I do? She was my only link to Ray, and hence to my daughter. And if she wasn't here I had no way to find her.

But after some eternity the door opened slowly and a wrinkled suspicious face peered around the doorway, ready to slam it shut again, it seemed.

"Maisie," I said gently, "Maisie, it's me. Do you remember me? Tory. Ray's girlfriend."

She appraised me for a few moments, and there was no telling whether or not she recognised me.

"What do you want?"

"Can I come in for a moment?" I spoke slowly, measuredly, for fear of panicking her.

"Okay," she said, "for a moment only. I was just having my breakfast."

The front door opened straight into the threadbare grubby kitchen, and on the oil-clothed table I saw thick-cut bread on a plate, with bread-crumby butter and a jar of marmalade out of which stuck a knife-handle.

I heard a hissing and I turned towards the big black range which sat under the large chimney. On the chimney-breast the archaic pictures of John F Kennedy and the Pope still reigned. Not the current Pope, no, Pope John XXIII. The hissing came from the blackened cast-iron kettle which was just coming to the boil.

She followed my gaze, and said begrudgingly, "Would you like a cup of tea, so?"

"I'd love one," I said, forcing enthusiasm into my voice, agreeing to the offer more out of the need to get on her right side than any desire for a cup of her tea. Maisie was *famous* for the strength of her tea. Ray told me once that a few years ago there were some council-men working on the road outside her house, and they ran out of tarmac, so they begged a pot full of tea from Maisie and used that to complete the road-works. I *think* he was joking, but Maisie's tea was so strong that you could actually, almost against your will, easily imagine it being moulded into place to fill potholes.

I sat at the big kitchen table without being invited, and there was silence while she made the tea, and put on some bread for toast for herself. She didn't offer me any toast, which made me wonder how much she was accepting me, how kindly she would look with favour on my request. But then, to be fair, money was probably tight. Each loaf of bread probably had to last a precise number of days.

She brought the tea to the table, and when it was drawn (and hanged and quartered, it looked like) she tilted the teapot and the tea oozed out gently until both mugs were full.

"Do you remember me?" I asked her again as she did so.

"I do. You used to be Ray's girlfriend. But you're not any more. He told me."

"That's right. But the reason I'm here is that I need to contact him urgently, and I don't know where to find him. Do you know where he's living?"

"Why do you want him?"

Ah, that was the rub, all right. What to say? She

mightn't have that much sympathy if I told her the truth. Obviously her first loyalty was to him. She might well feel that she would rather he had his child than I did.

"I just need to contact him." I tried the tactic of evasiveness. Without success.

"Why?" she repeated tenaciously.

As I tried to think of a good story she must have picked up on it because she said sternly, "The truth, mind, and I might help you. Anything else and I'll say nothing." And I realised she was sharper than she was letting on.

"He's taken Lucy."

"What!" She couldn't have been more surprised if I had said I'd been abducted by Martians. "But he has no interest in her. He told me that's why you split up."

Hm, I noted, didn't mention the little matter of the criminal record, I see.

"Yes, that was true. But obviously he's conjured up some interest in her, because he took her yesterday from her childminder's." I decided that I was bringing enough grief with me, telling her this, without her knowing that Ray was violent enough to overpower and threaten the child-minder, so I improvised, "He conned his way into her house, told her I had sent him to collect Lucy."

She nodded at that. "He could always charm the birds off the trees," she agreed. "I've often thought to myself that life might have been better for him if he had had to work harder to get people's trust. He might then have thought that trust was a precious thing, something to be valued and kept."

She studied me for a moment then, thinking, and I held my breath, forcing myself to let her think it through, forcing myself not to burst out with a plea, to ruin it.

"I love Ray. Always have done since Concepta – you know, Ray's mam – left him here as an infant. I reared him as well as any old woman can rear a lively boy. I love him," she said again, "no matter what he does or doesn't do. In my book, that's what love is." She took a deep breath, "But, love is also *not* lots of things. Love is not covering up people's mistakes. Love is not loyalty beyond reason. And taking a woman's child is *wrong*."

She sighed deeply, an old woman who deserved peace at this time of her life, who deserved not to have to deal with this information about her beloved grandson's misdeeds, no matter how diluted that information was.

"The thing is, I don't know how much help I can be," she said. "I haven't heard from Ray for some time. He sent me a card for my birthday in February, but that's the last I heard. I kept it because it did have his address on it –" my heart sang at that news! "– but I don't know exactly where it is. Hang on until I try to find it."

She slowly and unsteadily got to her feet and went over to the battered wooden dresser. She began rooting through the chaotic piles of papers which were heaped upon it, and I released my breath in a rush. She was going to help me. It was all going to be okay. As long, of course, as she did actually manage to find the card.

She filtered through the papers slowly, methodically, and it was all I could do not to jump to my feet, elbow her out of the way, and sift through them more quickly, more efficiently. I sat there, cradling the hot, undrunk-from mug of tea, and concentrated on breathing slowly, deeply, calmly.

The not-Ray's-birthday-card pile grew slowly larger and larger, and the pile which could possibly contain the card grew disconcertingly smaller. As each piece of paper was rejected my heart sank a little more. *Please let her have it*, I begged. *Please let her be able to find it!*

At last, after about twenty agonising minutes, and when there were only three or four pieces of paper left in the possibly-Ray's-card pile she said, "Here it is," and I let out a breath of relief in an audible whoosh.

She made her way back to the table and handed me the card. And inside it was what I'd been looking for: an address!

"Thank you, thank you so much," I said, as I carefully copied it into my diary. "Look, you'll understand if I rush off now. I have to get to Lucy as soon as possible."

"Of course," she said.

But as I was at the doorway she called after me, "Tory!"

I turned to look at her.

"It really hurt me the fact that you haven't brought Lucy to see me since she was a baby. She's my great-grandaughter. I've missed her. It's lonely here all on my own. I haven't heard from Concepta since she left Ray with me all those years ago, and as for Ray . . . a card for my birthday, and one for Christmas is the height of it."

Remorse hit me. I came back and stood over her where she sat in the chair. "I'm sorry, Maisie. I never thought of it. As soon as I get Lucy back I'll bring her down to you." And I bent and kissed her on her wizened forehead, grateful beyond measure for her help to me.

I ran down the driveway, and into the car. One more job to do before I went to get Lucy. I rang the office and asked to speak to Sinead, my boss and one of the partners of the company.

"Sinead," I said nervously when I got through to her, "I hate to do this to you, but I have to take the next day or two off. A personal emergency. Lucy's not well. You may have heard that I had to leave early yesterday? No, she's not in hospital; she's not that serious, thank God. No, we're at home. I should be back by Thursday, okay?" That would give me a couple of days with Lucy once I found her – time for us both to recover from our ordeal. That, it appeared, was fine by Sinead.

Thanking God for nice bosses I then turned the car and headed back to Dunfarney, and from there to Dublin. I needn't have bothered writing down the address I reflected as I drove, it was all there in my head: 19 Cardiff Way, Marino.

My heart was thumping as I drove, impatiently willing the miles away. I knew where my daughter was! I was going to get her! We would be back together by lunch-time!

Chapter 7

It took too long but eventually I was parking on a Marino sidestreet. I went into a nearby shop, and asked for directions to Cardiff Way which they willingly supplied.

I followed the directions and made my way there, and it wasn't long before I reached the road. I glanced at the numbers of the houses near me, and counted my way up the road. There, that one, the one with the blue door. That must be number 19! My daughter was in that house right now, only a few minutes away from me.

And suddenly nerves hit me, and I turned and walked away, into the first café I found. I ordered a cup of tea, and sat and thought. How would I approach it? Ray probably wouldn't be too thrilled to see me. After all, his whole plan was to take her away from me entirely. And he was physically much stronger than I. Maybe I should ring the guards, get them to take Lucy.

But no, that was not an option, I realised, remembering what he had written. No gardai, he had said, and the not-too-veiled threat of harming her if I did. I was just going to have to knock on the door and play it by ear. Maybe once I reassured him that we could share custody? Maybe then he wouldn't mind giving her back to me. Or maybe the stress of looking after a toddler was already getting to him, and he would be delighted to hand her back to me. I won't borrow trouble, I promised myself. I'll just go and check it out.

So I paid for the tea and headed up the road until I reached that blue door. I looked at it, and its surrounding windows, and the tablecloth-sized patch of front lawn either side of the red-tiled path. They were all immaculately kept. Way more so than I would ever have expected of Ray. Maybe he had a conscientious flatmate.

Recognising all this surveying the house-front for the delaying tactic it was, I took a deep breath, and marched up the driveway and knocked on the door, more excited than I could remember ever being. Lucy was the other side of that door, and in a few short minutes – seconds, even – I was going to have her in my arms again. I hoped. If he agreed to give her back to me.

After a moment or two I heard footsteps the far side of the door, and then it swung open. I was already beginning to say Ray's name when I realised that it wasn't him. It was a stranger. Mid-thirties maybe. With dark-brown sharply cut hair, blue eyes, a navy-blue sweatshirt and pants covering a tall, lean body, rolled-up sleeves displaying firmly muscled biceps. All this I registered dimly even as I was saying breathlessly, "Excuse me, could I speak to Ray please?"

"He's not here."

My disappointment that he wasn't there was overlaid by a feeling of relief that at least I had the right house. I wouldn't have put Ray past it to put the wrong address on his card, either through carelessness or disinformation.

"Do you know where he is? Or when he'll be back."

The man gave a short unamused laugh, "No, I don't know where he is. I wish I did. And I think I can safely say he won't be back."

I felt as if I had been kicked in the stomach. Or more, I felt as if I were a marionette whose strings had just been cut. I swayed slightly, and the world went out of focus, seemed a long way away. Something must have registered on my face because the man stepped forward a pace and grabbed me by both my elbows, balancing me and even supporting some of my weight. I surely would have fallen otherwise.

"Come here," he said, a mixture of concern and irritation sharp in his voice. He guided me into the house, and into a sitting-room off the hall. He positioned me in front of a sofa, onto which I collapsed.

I indistinctly thought, I'm in this house with a total stranger. I'll be no use to Lucy if I'm raped and murdered. But I couldn't have moved if indeed my life depended on it, if that statement were more literal than the cliché it usually is. I was numb with disappointment and, to be honest, in that moment would nearly have welcomed being murdered – it would have taken me out of this nightmare.

And at the thought of the nightmare – Ray isn't here! Which means Lucy isn't here! – everything looked blurry again, and I felt dizzy.

The man quickly placed his hand on the back of my neck and gently but firmly pushed my head down. "Put your head between your knees," he commanded, and I did so. "Breathe deeply," he said, and even as I was complying part of me wanted to demand how I could breathe deeply when my lungs were scrunched up like this. "Hang on a sec," I heard him say. "I'll be right back."

I heard him move away and there was silence. I sat there, keeping my head well down, trying to take it all in. Ray wasn't there and it didn't look like he would be returning. The man didn't know where he was. Where could I go now to find him?

Fear, exhaustion, hopelessness caught up with me, and when he returned I was crying, tears coursing silently down my cheeks. He sat on the sofa beside me. "Here," I heard him say, "drink this."

I raised my head and he was proffering a glass of water to me. Gently he held it as I drank. Eventually I moved my head back to indicate I had had enough. "Thank you," I gulped.

"What's wrong?" he asked then. "Looks like you wanted to see Ray really badly."

"I do," I said. "In fact, I *need* to see him."

He gave a cynical laugh. "What's his secret, eh?" he asked bitterly. "How does *he*, of all people, manage to inspire such loyalty, have such a gorgeous woman turning up *needing* to see him. Please, please do tell me – I'd like to know. In fact, you could say I *need* to know."

"He's got my baby," I sat flatly.

His long face blanched and he said, "Oh God, I am so, *so* sorry. Please, please, excuse my flippancy. You just caught me at a time – " he took a deep breath and said, "anyway, that doesn't matter. Look, tell me from the beginning."

I did so, sparing no detail, from arriving at Carol's house to get the news that Ray had taken her, to reading his note which explained – I told him – why I had to find her myself without involving the police, to spending the night in the car outside Maisie's before getting this address, and finishing, "So here I am".

When I had finished he looked at me for a moment, appraisingly. "He did live here for about six months," he said then, "but he left a couple of months ago. Owing me, I might add, two months' back rent. I came home one day and his room was cleared, all his stuff gone. Well, I can take a hint as much as the next man, so I just cut my losses and changed the locks. Don't get me wrong, I was *furious*. Not so much about the money, although, of course, that too. But at having been ripped off. But been ripped off for two months' rent is a bit different to losing your daughter, isn't it?"

I nodded.

"Look," he said. "Here's an idea. It's a long shot but . . .

I haven't really used his room since he was gone. I'll go and search it now, see if he left anything behind, anything that could let us know where he is. I mean, the room *looked* cleared, the wardrobe and drawers were empty and so on. But I didn't really check it out, why would I? But I will now, if you like?" I nodded as he continued, "And in the meantime, you look all done in, which isn't surprising since you spent the night dozing in a car. I'll bring you down a pillow and a duvet, and I'd suggest you have a sleep here on the sofa while I'm looking."

A sleep sounded wonderful. Resting while somebody else took up the hunt, no matter how briefly, sounded wonderful. I nodded.

"Good," he said, and quickly got up and padded across the room. I heard him go upstairs and he returned a few minutes later with the promised pillow, which he placed at the end of the sofa, and a duvet. I shrugged off my shoes and laid my head gratefully down on the pillow, and he placed the duvet over me, tucking it in gently as if I were a child.

He smiled at me, and through my already-half-closed eyes I registered what a nice smile he had, kind and compassionate. As he left the room I thought how weird it was – here I was sleeping on the sofa of a total stranger, breathing in the healthy-man scent of him on his clean-but-obviously-slept-in duvet and pillow, while he looked for clues as to my ex-boyfriend's, and hence my daughter's, whereabouts. And I didn't even know his name.

Am I mad, I wondered, to sleep in a stranger's house?

But somehow I knew I was safe, that it was okay to sleep.

I think I heard him begin to climb the stairs, but I might have dreamed it.

Some unknown time later I felt a touch on my shoulder, and a whispered, "Hello? Are you awake?"

I struggled to wakefulness, opened my eyes to see him hovering over me.

I sat up. "Hi, thanks for the sleep. Did I sleep long?"

"About four hours."

"Four hours!" I gasped. "I'm so sorry. I didn't mean to –"

"Hush," he said, "it's okay. You needed the sleep."

"But all the time wasted!" I said anguished. "But listen, did you find anything?"

"I'm not sure. At least, I did find something, but I'm not sure how much use it is. Here," and he handed me what turned out to be an empty envelope, addressed to Ray at this house. Puzzled I looked up at him. What use was this?

"There's something written on the back."

I turned it over and looked. Scrawled there was: *Murtagh Levi, The Derby Rig, 9.30, 17th.*

"That's Ray's writing," I said, excited at this tangible evidence, no matter how little. "I wonder what it means, though."

"I thought it seemed like a pub name, so I looked it up in the phone book. And it is. It's down near the Quays."

"Oh! That's great, thank you – er, I don't even know your name."

"Connor, Connor Brophy."

"And I'm Tory O'Neill."

I waited, but he didn't crack any stupid joke, just said, "Very pleased to meet you, Tory," and incongruously, given that I had already cried in front of him and slept on his sofa, he held out a large hand. I took it though, and we shook hands. His touch was warm, dry.

"This is great," I said again, referring to the piece of paper in my hand. "It looks like the details of a meeting between Ray and this Murtagh guy at that pub. So maybe Ray goes there, or is known there. Or failing that, this Murtagh guy does, and he should know Ray. I'll go there tonight!" I looked at my watch – it was just gone four o'clock.

"No point in going earlier," he agreed, "so maybe you don't have to feel guilty about sleeping for those four hours."

"No," I agreed gratefully, "good point."

"Do you know this Murtagh Levi?"

"Never heard of him."

Connor said, musing, "I wonder if he's Jewish, with a name like that. Mind you, the Jewish surname is usually spelt with a 'y' as far as I know."

I knew little about Jewish genealogies and usually, no disrespect, cared less.

"Even if he is Jewish, how does that help us?"

"The Jewish community in Ireland's very small. My ex-boss is Jewish, and I get the impression that they all know each other. It's a long shot, but wouldn't it be great if he did know him?"

"It's more likely a nickname – you know, something to do with Levi Jeans. Especially with a first name like Murtagh which doesn't exactly sound Jewish."

"True," he said, rubbing his chin, "but it's surely worth a phone call."

He stood and went to a little table at the other end of the sofa on which sat the phone. He picked up a little red-covered book from the table, flicked through it until he found what he was looking for, and then dialled a number. As he was doing this I looked around the room, registering my surroundings for the first time. The walls were painted a light, bright yellow, and the blue full-length curtains matched the sofa on which I sat, and the armchair in the alcove beside the fireplace. The wooden floor was stained a dark oak and was partially covered with a red, yellow and blue abstract rug. It was bright, cheerful, welcoming.

And as Connor stood listening to the phone ring, I studied him too: tall, lean – as I had already noticed. But, I saw when I looked more closely that his leanness was deceptive, that he was well-muscled even so. And he held himself with the grace of a big cat, a panther maybe.

The phone must have been answered then. "Hi David, it's me, Connor. Yeah, doing great thanks. It's going well. No," he laughed a little, "I'm not ringing to ask for my job back – don't worry, you'll be the first to know if I'm back in the market. No, I was actually wondering if you could help me." He explained what he was looking for. "Right, that's what I thought. Oh, will you? Thanks very much. You still have the number here? Great, I'll hear from you soon then."

He hung up and turned to me. "David's never heard of him. He doesn't think he's a member of the Jewish community. But just in case, he's going to make a few calls for us. He'll ring me back."

"That's great," I said, feeling overwhelmed at the kindness of strangers. "You're so good to do all this for me."

He shrugged. "What kind of man would I be to have turned you away from my door? Not to do whatever I can to help in such an awful situation?" He changed the subject then, seeming uncomfortable with my gratitude. "Listen, are you hungry?"

"Oh, I am," I said fervently. "I've only realised it now you've said it. I haven't eaten since early this morning."

"I'm hungry too, I skipped lunch as I was on a roll with work. So, will you join me while we're waiting for David to ring back?"

"Yes, please!"

"Scrambled eggs okay?"

"Sure," I said. At this stage I was so hungry cardboard would have sounded good.

"Come on into the kitchen," he invited, and I followed him into a cream and yellow room, complete with gleaming stainless-steel appliances.

As he skilfully prepared the scrambled eggs, and grilled toast and tomatoes, and I stood leaning against the work-surface, neither use nor ornament as they say, we spoke, got to know each other a little.

"How old is your daughter?" he asked

"Lucy, her name is Lucy," I said, "and she's just gone two."

"Is she pretty?"

"Of course! Actually, I know I'm biased, but even people who have no connection to her find her beautiful – I've even had people stop me in the street to comment on her looks. Look," I said, reaching into my bag and pulling out my purse, "look here – a photo of her."

I handed it to him and he took it and studied it gravely. I didn't have to see it myself to be able to visualise it. It showed Lucy sitting on my sofa at home, her plump pretty face grinning and laughing at the camera. She had on red dungarees with a blue T-shirt underneath and her abundant black curls were framing her face and shoulders, and her blue eyes – the one legacy she was ever going to get from Ray, probably – were shining with joy and the love of life. And although the photo didn't, couldn't show it, I remembered that moment well and could hear again in my head the infectious sound of her laughter as she sat there and we celebrated the joy of life.

"She's pretty," said Connor, handing the photo back to me.

"S-s-she is, isn't she?" I agreed on a sob.

He stopped what he was doing and came towards me. He took me in his arms, and held me tight against his hard body as I cried. "I miss her so much. I want her back. I want to know she's safe." And even as I cried I was aware of the warmth of his strong solid body, and thought how wonderful it was to be comforted, to be embraced like this in my fear and grief. No matter how fleeting, this gift he was giving me was powerful, a gift from his humanity to a stranger.

I lay against his flat chest – a rare pleasure in itself, at my height I was more accustomed to lowering my head to rest it on a male shoulder – and for that one brief moment I allowed him to carry my grief and fear for Lucy's safety. For that brief moment I rested from that pain and stood there in the embrace of his strong arms, listening to the steady beat of his heart, breathing in the clean and wonderfully male scent of him.

"You'll get her back," he promised, rubbing my back.

I pulled back in his arms to look up at him. "Do you think so?" I asked anxiously, grateful for the reassurance, desperate to hear it again even though I knew, I knew, that he had no right to be promising such a thing.

"Sure," he said confidently.

And I breathed in that certainty, absorbed it, relished it, and refused to listen to the little niggling voice which wanted to remind me that Connor didn't know, couldn't know, whether or not I would find Lucy again.

As I stood there in his arms, absorbing his certainty, I became aware that the beat of his heart had changed, it was no longer so steady now. Even as I was realising this he pulled gently away from me.

"I'd better –" he indicated the saucepan, "– get on with this."

He turned back to the meal, continued the preparations. I asked him then, changing the subject, "What do you do? It sounds like you work from home."

"I do. I'm a software engineer," he said, "and I've just set up my own business. I'm working on a software project at the moment, which I'm going to sell when it's finished and make my fortune!" He grinned at me before continuing, "It's a big step, giving up my job – although David has said he'll take me back whenever I want. But I have been saving hard for years until I had enough to do this, and I'm using these savings to follow my dream. The money should last me a year or so, if I'm careful, and the project should be well out in the market-place by then. I hope."

"Well done, you!" I said. "I think you're great, going for what you want to do. And especially in software! I always admire people who have anything to do with that. I'm so computer illiterate it's not funny. Even though I use a computer at work, I just do the bare minimum."

"Oh, software's not so hard," he said modestly, "and as for setting up on my own, well, now is the time to do it while I've no responsibilities. It would be different if I had a family, but I don't."

I snorted. "Ray didn't think like that. He didn't let having a family make him do silly things like actually take responsibility for them."

"Sounds like Ray, okay," he agreed, nodding. "Pleasant guy, don't get me wrong. But, let me put it this way, I wasn't exactly surprised when I discovered he had skipped on me. He's not one of life's responsible people, is he?"

"No," I agreed dully, "and while I know – I think I know – that he wouldn't hurt Lucy deliberately, I'm terrified he might neglect her."

"I know what you – " abruptly he stopped, and turned away from me. He began to serve the food with studied concentration.

"What were you going to say?" I asked him. "What?" I insisted when he didn't answer.

He sighed, turned towards me. "Just leave it, okay."

"No, I won't leave it. Tell me."

He sighed and capitulated. "I was just agreeing with you that he's not responsible. I went away for ten days while he was here and asked him to water my plants, and he didn't, and some of them died. But," he added hastily, "he wouldn't forget about Lucy. And don't forget, plants can't ask for food, they just fade a little every day. I'm sure Lucy would asked for food if she was hungry."

"Yes," I said, "yes, she would." But although this information about Ray forgetting the plants wasn't telling me anything about him that I didn't already know . . . it was still troubling to be reminded of it.

He served up the food just as the phone rang, and went to answer it while I started tucking in anyway, too hungry for manners.

He came back a moment later. "That was David. No luck on Murtagh Levi in the Jewish community."

"I guess we knew that."

"Yes, but we had to check it out." He sat and began eating his own meal. "Have you given any thought to contacting a private investigator, since you can't contact the gardai? I don't know much about them, but I presume they could check bank transactions, and so on."

"Ray doesn't use banks. He operates strictly on cash. He says it's because banks are part of a capitalist plot, part of a Big-Brother-ish way of keeping tracks on people. I personally think it's far more to do with not declaring his music income to the taxman, nor having that income come to the attention of the Department of Social Welfare." Connor gave a quick snort of recognition as I continued, "But yes, a private investigator might be a good idea. I hadn't thought about it. I suppose I have been just operating reactively so far, haven't really had time to think. How do you even go about contacting such a person?"

"They might advertise in the *Golden Pages*. Hang on till I check."

He got up and strode out of the room, and again I was struck at how confident in his skin he seemed, his long rangy steps seeming to announce, 'Here I am, as I am, totally happy to be me and your opinion is your problem'. I shook myself. That was being a bit fanciful.

He came back a few moments later with the telephone book. "Here we go," he said, handing me the open book. "You'll see there's quite a few." He glanced at his watch. "Just gone five. Too late to ring them now, though."

"First thing in the morning," I promised. God knows how I'd afford to pay a private investigator. But I would. Somehow I would. Amazing how something like this puts everything else in perspective. Before I would have said I didn't have much money, but now I knew how important it was I'd do anything. Sell the car – sell the clothes off my back even. Nothing – *nothing* – was more important than getting Lucy back.

"What I'd suggest for tonight," he suggested, "is that we go to that pub, and try and track down this Murtagh Levi."

"We?" I asked.

"Sure thing," he said easily.

"You've done enough. More than enough. I'll go on my own." I felt I had to offer this, even as I was seriously hoping that he wouldn't take me up on that offer.

He didn't. He laughed, his generous mouth open, showing his white teeth. "I do not think so. Judging by that address it's not the most salubrious area, and I doubt the pub is any different. I wouldn't let you or any woman go in there on her own. No, we'll go together."

"Thank you," I whispered. "What time should we go?"

"Late, I'd suggest. Certainly not before ten o'clock."

"Okay, well what I might do is go home, have a shower and get changed." I grimaced at my attire. "I've been wearing this since yesterday morning, and I've slept in it twice. I feel very grubby."

"Okay," he agreed easily.

"Thanks," I said then, "thanks for all you've done so far."

"No problem. So will I see you back here about half past nine?"

"Sure." I stood up and hovered a little uncertainly. I hardly knew this man, we had only met some hours earlier. So a handshake would be the most appropriate gesture. But yet, we seemed to have shared so much in this time, and he was helping me so much. He stood up too, and held out his two hands. I took them, one in each of mine. This was good, I decided, and silently blessed him for his thoughtfulness. More intimate than a formal handshake, not as much so as a kiss.

We stood like that for a moment, I looking up at him, he looking down at me. He smiled and I smiled back.

"I'm looking forward to meeting Lucy," he said, and it was exactly the right thing to say. It held again that promise – more, an inherent assumption – that I would get her back safely, but it held also a suggestion that he wouldn't be disappearing from our life then which was somehow reassuring.

"I'll see you back here later," I said, and I turned to go.

I got home and wearily let myself into the flat, and took off my clothes, throwing them into the laundry basket. I stepped into the shower and let the warm water bless me and caress me as I scrubbed myself clean.

Lucy, I thought as the water cascaded down on me, has he thought to give you a bath yet? Does he know how to make sure the water is the right temperature? Does he know to make sure you're properly dry afterwards, even between your toes?

As I was drying myself the phone rang. I wrapped the towel around myself and dived for it. Oh, let it be him, I begged. Let it be Ray saying he's changed his mind, that I can come and get her.

It wasn't Ray. It was Carol.

"Have you any news?" she asked urgently. "Did you get his address from his grandmother?"

"Yes and no," I answered. "His grandmother did have an address for him, and I went there. But he hasn't lived there for two months, and his ex-landlord doesn't know where he is."

I could hear her breath shoot out of her body. "That's awful," she said. "So what do you do now?"

I quickly explained to her the plans for the evening. "It's a long shot, I know," I told her, "but I can't think of anything else. I'm going to ring a private investigator in the morning."

Concern was sharp in her voice as she said, "Oh Tory, I'm not at all sure that's the right thing to do. Maybe he'll include private investigators under the same heading as the gardai. The last thing you want to do is to endanger poor Lucy."

"He didn't say no private investigators," I said, "and anyway, aren't they working for the client, not the State, so unlike the gardai they have to do what you say. So if I tell him just to give the information to me, for me to act on, that's what he'll do."

"Good point," she conceded. "Well, I'm very sorry you haven't managed to track him down, but I'm delighted for you that you have another lead. I'll be thinking of you tonight. Let me know how you get on."

"I will," I promised, grateful beyond telling for her support. I did try and tell her, though. "Thanks, Carol, so much for your interest, your concern – it means an awful lot to me."

"Oh no," she brushed off my thanks, "what else are friends for?"

After I was dressed I sat with a notebook on my lap and a pen in my hand, and willed my brain to remember the names of any of Ray's friends. But nothing came, nothing I could use anyway. There was an Anto, I seemed to remember, and a Derek. But I couldn't match a face to the names, nor did I know any more details about them, anything which could help me identify them.

What bands had he been in? They had all been small-time bands, all waiting for – and in some cases, even working towards – the big time, in the meantime gigging at various pubs around the city. But there had been a *lot* of different bands. The proverb, 'Far away hills are green' could have been invented for Ray. He had tended to get impatient with slow progress, and instead of working within a band to speed things up, improve their sound, put the effort in to get bigger gigs, the interest of record companies – he had abandoned ship quickly to move to another band. And yet another one. "This is it, Tory," he'd say to me excitedly. "I've heard their sound, and they're *great*. And they need a new guitarist/vocalist, so I'm in! I'm telling you, Tory, they're going to be the next U2, and *I'm* in there with them!" At first his excitement was contagious, and I believed him, and was so excited for him. But after a few goes of witnessing the excitement wear off, the disillusionment creep in, the complaining begin, the looking around for another band – in short, witnessing the whole cycle – I had become jaded with it, and had given it only perfunctory attention.

I would have been a *lot* more interested, I reflected as I chewed the top of my pen, had I known it was going to be this important.

Sunset, was one, I recalled. I wrote it down and gazed at it. *Reality Check.* Slowly some of the names began returning. *Archery. The Fundamentals. Whispers and Shouts.* And that was it. Chew my pen as much as I wanted, my brain still wasn't giving up any more band names. Had there even been any more? Maybe that was all there had been. Still, it was something to go on. Now all I had to do was to find the bands. Assuming any of them were still existing. And see if any of the band-members had kept in touch with Ray, a man who had usually managed to leave on bad terms. No problem.

I needed to buy a copy of *Hot Press* and see if any of those bands were playing anywhere. I glanced at my watch, it was just before eight o'clock. I grabbed my keys and left the house, and drove the sinfully short distance to the local newsagent's. As expected, they didn't have a copy of the magazine, so, blessing my foresight in bringing the car, I headed into the city centre. The big bookshops like Eason's were closed at this hour of the evening, but there were other newsagents, not so big, but not so small either, which were still open. I parked outside one and ran in. I was doubly lucky: I got *Hot Press, and* I didn't get a parking ticket.

Clutching it to me I drove home. As soon as I got there I opened it anxiously and looked for any of the band names I recognised. I turned page after page and with each page my hand moved more slowly, dreading to run out of pages to search. But nowhere did any of the band names appear.

So I abandoned that useless exercise and commenced another useless exercise: worrying about Lucy. She had now been missing for over twenty-four hours. What am I doing just sitting here, I asked myself despairingly, when she's out there somewhere? But short of knocking on every door in Dublin (and that's assuming he was still in Dublin – he could be anywhere else in Ireland, after all, or even in the UK) I was doing all I could do, I knew that.

"I'm coming for you," I said out loud into the empty room. "I'm coming to find you, I promise."

Chapter 8

And so I left the flat again just after half past nine and drove back to Connor's house. It felt good to be moving again after the enforced inactivity of the past few hours, to be resuming the search. The door opened as I parked outside, and he came out, and opened the passenger door.

"Hi," he said, "how are you doing?"

"Not great," I confessed. "I feel better for the wash and the fresh clothes, though."

"I'm sure you do," he answered, getting into the car, seeming to fill it entirely. "Do you mind driving? I think my car might be a bit conspicuous where we're going." He indicated through the windscreen to the long, low silver car parked in front of me.

"Sure," I said, and started the ignition again. "Nice motor," I said about his car, as I moved off past it, being *very* careful not to hit it.

"It is," he said fondly, "although I think I'm going to sell it. It represents a good few months' living expenses. And it's a bit of a pretentious car for someone who is, let's face it, unemployed!"

"You're not unemployed," I said. "You're self-employed. Very different."

"True. But to paraphrase some famous quote, he who works for himself has a fool for a boss!"

I glanced at him, at his sharp uncompromising profile flickering in and out of shadow as we passed streetlights. "You don't really feel that, do you?"

"No," he said ruefully. "It's just hard to keep the faith sometimes. You know, working on your own all day every day, with no feedback. It's easy to lose perspective."

"At least you're doing it," I insisted. "I admire that so much."

"Ray did it too," he said, looking sideways at me, "pursuing his dream of making it in the music business."

"Hmm," I said, not really wanting to get into the fascinating topic of Ray's flirtation with musical success. "It's down near the Quays, isn't it?"

He gracefully accepted my change of subject. "It is. And I looked up the address in the street directory, found out where the pub is. I'll direct you."

"Thanks. Again, I have to say how much I appreciate this."

"Oh well," he said lightly, "it's not every day that a man gets to be a heroic knight! Oh, turn left here."

I did as instructed, and as we continued our journey he said, "I was thinking after you were gone. You should write down all the bands Ray has been in and do a search on them."

Excitedly I said, "Great minds think alike! I did just that this afternoon." My excitement dimmed as I remembered. "But I didn't find any of them."

"Oh," he said, disappointed. "Oh well, worth a try, though."

He continued directing me and eventually we pulled up outside The Derby Rig pub. It certainly looked rough enough, surrounded as it was by deserted factories and workshops, barbed-wire topped walls, steel-shuttered doors. Rubbish was swirling like tumbleweed around its door. The door itself may once have been red, but there was hardly any paint on it now, not from any designer's distressed effect but rather through honest-to-God neglect. The windows were smeared and dirty, but we could see lamps on inside, the feeble light doing its best to penetrate the murk and spill outside.

We looked at each other, braced ourselves.

"Well, shall we?"

"Yes, let's go."

We walked into the pub and immediately it became obvious that this was not a pub which was accustomed to strangers, nor to passing trade. Nor, indeed, one which encouraged either. At our entrance all conversation abruptly stopped, all heads swivelled to look at us, each head wearing an expression which ranged from inscrutable to hostile without ever swivelling anywhere near friendliness or welcome. Out of the corner of my eye I saw Connor give a confident nod to some of our viewers, while I managed a tremulous smile: neither of these had any noticeable effect. I felt him reach for my hand, and I clasped his hard hand gratefully.

He guided me to a stained and cigarette-burned table at the far edge of the room and I sat down on the edge of the red plastic leatherette banquette, carefully avoiding the places where it was ripped and torn.

"What'll it be, love," he said loudly. "The usual?"

"Yes, please," I answered, wondering what on earth he would judge as being my usual. "Thanks . . . darling."

I wasn't a great actor, I realised. I didn't think we had fooled anybody into thinking that we were just a couple trying a little walk on the wild side.

He went up to the bar and ordered a pint of Guinness, and a vodka and diet Coke. That, it appeared, was my usual. Actually, he wasn't so far off. It's vodka and orange juice, usually.

At the bar Connor was getting his change. "Thanks, mate," he said to the barman, loudly enough for everyone to hear. "Hey, I was wondering, I'm looking for a friend of a friend of mine. Fella named Murtagh Levi. Is he here?"

"No, no," said the barman, but his eyes flickered.

"Pity, I've a proposition to put to him. Our mutual friend said he drinks here. He said Murtagh was into music, and I'm getting into band management. I've a few connections to some pretty good venues, which is why I was looking for Murtagh. Do you know him?"

From my vantage point I could almost see the cogs whirring in the barman's head. On the one hand, I gathered, it was an automatic reaction to deny all knowledge of any of their patrons, but on the other hand, if Connor actually *were* able to involve him in the big time, it probably wouldn't go down too well if he, the barman, let that opportunity pass.

Eventually he decided, and he said, "No, I don't know him. But if you have a business card you could let me have it and I could ask around, you know. See if anybody who comes in here knows him."

"Sure thing," said Connor easily, and opened his wallet again. He took out a card and handed it to the barman, who studied it.

"Hey, it says here you're a software designer," he said suspiciously.

"I am," said Connor easily, and I marvelled at his calm. I'd have been a puddle on the floor at this stage. "As I said, I've only just started getting into band management. I did software design for a few places, you know, the Point, the RDS, places like that, and that's how I know the people there. It was when talking to the managers there that I learned they're always looking for new talent. So I decided to see if I could do something about that. Thing is," he said ruefully, "there's not too much money in software these days. Not since the dot-com bubble burst. You know how it is yourself."

The barman nodded shortly, obviously not knowing how it was himself, and not appearing to be overburdened with sympathy for these whingeing software types. There wasn't much money in bar-work at the best of times, after all. They didn't even get the chance to *have* a bubble to burst.

He placed the card on a shelf at the back of the bar. "I'll ask around," he said dismissively. "Yes, Jack, same again?" turning his attention to another customer.

Connor brought our drinks back to our table and placed them down. He sat disconcertingly close to me, took my hand, and bent and kissed me hard, swiftly, on the mouth. His kiss was like his hand: hard, soft, warm, dry. I tried not to show my puzzlement.

"Just marking my supposed territory," he whispered into my ear, his breath warm against me. "All the time I was talking to the barman I could see the rest of his clientele eyeing you up through the mirror behind the bar. That long red hair of yours is just too damn attractive, even tied up in a plait like that, and the rest of you doesn't exactly let the side down. I don't want any of them getting any ideas."

I smiled at him, "Yes, I saw them looking. But anyway, that was thoughtful of you."

"One of the more onerous parts of this project, I concede," he said, his eyes creasing with his smile, "but hey, superheroes like me do what they must."

"Oh you," I laughed, and immediately felt guilty for the laughter. How could I laugh when Lucy was missing? But neither did I want to be always dragging Connor down into my sadness. "If we weren't supposed to be a loving couple I'd clock you one for that."

He laughed in his turn and then lifted his glass. "Slainte!" he said. "Here's to successful searches."

I clinked my glass against his, and echoed, "Successful searches!"

I asked him then, "What do you think we should do now?"

"Now, we wait. It's like we've thrown a stone into the water and there's all these ripples, and we're going to see what turns up. I know that sounds like a well-thought out plan, but the truth is," he said glumly, "that I'm totally out of ideas about what else to do. I know genuine superheroes would probably have lots of plans ready to go, but I'm not really a superhero," he confessed, "just an ordinary guy. Worse, a computer nerd."

"Well," I said, taking a sip of my drink, "superheroes usually have a whole team of scriptwriters coming up with their plans – we're on our own, so don't be too hard on yourself."

And so we sat and waited, getting another drink some time later. I could feel my heart thumping with the need to be moving, to be doing something towards finding Lucy. Even though I knew rationally that this was it, it was hard to accept that sitting drinking in this grotty pub *was* the way, the only way we had at the moment, to find her.

The conversation in the pub had eventually resumed, but you'd swear there was some invisible force-field around us. Even as the pub filled there was a no-man's land surrounding us, where nobody sat or stood.

I muttered, "Well, I showered before I came out, so it must be you."

He gave a quick grin in acknowledgement. He drained his second pint and said, "I'm going to the toilet now. Just in case anybody does know anything but doesn't want to approach me in front of everyone else. Will you come and wait in the Ladies' for me? I don't want you sitting out here on your own. We'll leave then, if nobody approaches me. Review our options."

He glanced at me as he said that last, and neither of us spoke it out loud but we both knew that there weren't many – okay, any – options to review.

So we picked up our coats, and I my bag, and made our way into the concrete-lined hall which led to the toilets. We went through the respective doors, and I thought I might use the facilities since I was there. But then I looked at them, shuddered, and decided I wouldn't. I didn't need to go *that* badly. So I just hovered inside the door and waited.

After a few minutes there was a knock on the door, it opened a crack and I heard Connor whisper, "Tory."

I opened the door and rejoined him. There was some sort of suppressed excitement about him, and I said, "What is it?"

"Shush, I'll tell you in a minute. Come on out of here."

He walked me quickly to the car, his hand on my back urging me on.

Once in the car I turned to him. "What is it?"

"Someone followed me into the toilet. It's what I had been hoping for. Tall guy, balding, brown leather jacket, standing at the edge of the bar, do you remember him?"

I shook my head.

"Doesn't matter. Anyway, he came up to me. Asked me how much it was worth for information about Murtagh Levi."

"How much was it worth?"

"Doesn't matter," he said again. "Fact is, I got the information."

Excitement coursed through me. "You got it!"

"Yep!" He turned and grinned at me, his teeth white in the darkness of the car. "An address, and directions. Come on, let's go."

I turned on the ignition and moved down the road.

Connor said, "Turn left here."

I did, and followed his further instructions until he said, "Pull in here." I did, and he said, "It's along here somewhere. Number 27."

We got out of the car. I certainly didn't have the same excitement as I had had that morning when I was knocking on the door of what I now knew was Connor's house. I knew that Ray, and hence Lucy, wasn't going to be behind that door. But Murtagh Levi, whoever he might be, was, it appeared, behind that door, and he was a link – a direct link – to Ray, and hence to Lucy. So, sure, there was a bubble of excitement in there.

We got out and peered at house numbers until we found the right one.

"There's a light on," said Connor. "I didn't think there'd be anybody home, this early. I thought we would have to wait for him. Oh well, don't look a gift horse in the mouth."

We walked up the path to the front door and I rang the doorbell. After some moments the door was opened – to show us an elderly man.

"Excuse me," said Connor, "we're looking for Murtagh Levi. Does he live here?"

"No," said the man, looking bewildered, "no, he doesn't. I don't think he lives anywhere on this road, I've never heard of him. But – hang on a sec." He turned his head and yelled into the house, "Gloria, did you ever hear of a – what was his name again?"

"Murtagh Levi," I said, holding onto my patience with an effort.

A door opened, spilling more light onto us, and an equally elderly woman joined her husband in the doorway. "What is it, Charlie?"

"This couple here," and he indicated us, "want to know if there's a Murtagh Levi living anywhere on this road."

"No, dear, there isn't."

Disappointment stabbed me, a feeling of let-down. "Are you sure?"

"Dear, we've lived on this road for more than thirty years, you know, and I can tell you straight that there's nobody called Murtagh Levi living on it."

"What about any Murtagh?" I asked desperately. "Levi might just be a nickname."

She thought about it for a moment, but then, "No, dear, no Murtagh of any surname."

I turned in despair to Connor, but he was already speaking to the couple. "Thank you very much," he was saying. "We're sorry to have disturbed you."

"That's okay," they said. "We hope you find him," and they closed the door, leaving us standing on the doorstep.

"What now?" I asked, and as I turned to look at him I noticed that he was clenching his fists in fury.

"Your man set me up," he hissed. "Just chose any old address. What we do now, my dear Tory, is we go back and insist on our money's worth."

Your money, I thought, but didn't say. Time enough to organise refunding him when this evening was over.

This time he got into the driver's seat – I didn't comment, just handed him the keys. As we drove back to the pub he remarked conversationally, "As our acquaintance is so short I never got the chance to tell you this: I'm a black belt in both karate and judo."

"Really?" I asked, impressed.

"Seriously. Something about being small and thin growing up – well, I'm still thin –" (hardly, I thought, lean and muscular), "– but at least I took a stretch in my late teens, so I'm reasonably tall now. But for most of my boyhood I was the shortest boy in the class, and the thinnest. Add to the mix," he said dryly, "the fact that I was a computer-geek, even then . . . Well, you can imagine the rest. It didn't take too many times of being beaten up before I decided to take matters into my own hands.

Funnily enough, after a while they stopped picking on me!"

"I'd say they did."

"Having said that, to this day people sometimes underestimate me. Like that guy tonight."

Just then we reached the pub again and he pulled up outside and switched off the ignition. There were still lights on – through the grimy windows we could indistinctly see figures still at the bar.

"Now what?"

"Now we wait." He peered as best he could, given our limited vantage point, through the dirty windows of the pub. "I can't see him. But I'd say there's a fair bet he's still in there. A hundred euro buys a good few pints, even in this day and age."

"A hundred euro . . ." I echoed faintly. "Connor, listen, I'll pay you back as soon as I get to a cashpoint."

"Don't worry about it," he said absent-mindedly, his attention focussed on the pub door. "We'll sort it all out when we get Lucy back."

There was silence for a few moments then, which was broken as it began to rain, and the water bounced loudly off the car's metal roof, and poured down the windscreen, impeding our view still further. Connor switched on the wipers, and so there was now silence except for the rain and the soft swish-swish of the wipers as they transversed the windscreen, back and forth, back and forth. It was almost hypnotic, I found, as my eyes followed them. But when I pulled my attention back to the inside of the car I saw that Connor was not in the least bit sidetracked by the wipers, he was still watching the door of the pub intently.

"Connor," I said softly, reluctant to break the silence. But it had to be said.

"Mm?"

"Connor, what if that man doesn't even know Murtagh Levi? What if he made it all up, not just where he lived?"

"Good point. The answer is, I don't know. But it's the only link we've got, so we have to follow it. The thing is: you saw yourself, this isn't exactly a pub which gets much passing trade. And the barman certainly knew the name, no matter how he denied it. So I'm hoping that Mr Would-be-conman also knows him. He'd better hope so too, or I'll be looking for my money back!" He laughed, a little bitterly.

In truth nothing seemed very funny, sitting there in a rapidly cooling car, with the rain beating down on us, in darkness broken only by the orange street-lighting, waiting for some thug to come out of the pub so we could follow the one tenuous link we had to my daughter.

"I wonder what she's doing now?" I whispered.

"Sleeping, I hope," said Connor. His eyes didn't leave the pub door, but he reached out his hand and covered mine, where it kneaded my other hand in my lap.

"I'd never gone away for a night without her, ever," I went on, "and now this is the second night she's had to go to sleep without me. I hope he isn't leaving her to cry herself to sleep. Some parents do, you know. They think it trains the baby to sleep easier."

He didn't say anything – what could he possibly say to make me feel better? There were certainly no reassurances he could give, no promises he could make. But his hand tightened on mine, and gripped me hard.

"I miss her so much," I whispered, everything suddenly harder to see as the rain beat down more heavily on the windscreen. And then I realised it wasn't the rain beating more heavily – it was tears blurring my vision. "I'm so scared for her. What if she's calling for me, and I'm not coming? Will she hate me forever? I swore to protect her, and now . . . I have no idea where she is, or how she is. I've totally let her down."

Connor still didn't speak, but he kept a tight hold on my hand.

"She's scared of the colour yellow, you know." I gave a hiccup of a laugh which was more of a sob. "I've no idea why. But she screams if you try to dress her in yellow, or give her a yellow toy. I know that, and Carol knows that, so it's not a problem. But Ray doesn't know that. He might dress her in yellow, and she would become hysterical, and he wouldn't know why. He just wouldn't know. And he might get impatient with her, and hit her, and that would probably make her worse –"

"Hush!" said Connor roughly, so roughly that it shocked me into a silence, stopped my tears. He went on, "Tory, you've got to stop torturing yourself like this. You can think up awful scenarios like that forever. But it's doing you no good, and it's certainly doing Lucy no good.

You have to keep yourself strong for her, and that means good sleep, good food, keeping focussed and staying optimistic. No matter how Lucy is now, the stronger you are the quicker you'll find her, the sooner you'll be able to take her away from whatever situation she's in. Don't put yourself through this. There's no point."

I stopped, I knew he was right. But I couldn't stop my mind conjuring up awful images, images taken from a hundred kidnap-plot films: a bare camping-style bed with a thin mattress, and chains attached from the bed to the prisoner, and a room with boarded-up windows . . . Stop it, I told myself firmly. It's not like that, why would he do that? He just wanted to be a father, to get to know Lucy, to spend time with her.

And I deliberately tried to picture a roaring fire, and Ray sitting in an armchair before it, with Lucy on his lap snuggled into him, sucking her thumb – as she does – as he read a children's tale to her. It was a struggle – Ray was not a cosy fireside type of man, he wasn't a children-snuggling-into-him man, and he certainly wasn't a let-me-read-you-a-story sort of man. But I worked on that image, insisted on it, to replace the shadow of an image of the lonely bed in the dark room, and the little girl sitting on it with tear-track stains on her face.

"Here he is," said Connor then, and I snatched myself back to the present. A man was reeling his way out of the pub, swaying almost poetically to music only he could hear. He turned and staggered off down the road. Connor left it a moment or two, and then switched on the engine and began to follow him at a distance of about a hundred metres.

He said, "If I need to, I'm just going to abandon the car and run after him, say if he notices us and makes a break for it, so be prepared to jump into the driver's seat at any moment."

But oblivious of us following – he probably would have been oblivious of a passing tornado – the man zig-zagged along his way.

Eventually, he turned into a gateway and wandered up the short path to the door. Connor drove slowly past, saying to me, "Check out the house, the number, so we recognise it again."

I did so, and he pulled in at the next available space, a little further on.

"Come on, then," he said, and he undid his seat-belt and got out of the car. I did likewise. We walked side-by-side down the road, our arms touching ever so slightly, back towards the house, and I suddenly felt I had to stifle a fit of the giggles. Connor looked down at me, obviously having felt my arm vibrating with the effort not to laugh, "What is it?"

"If it wasn't so serious, it would be funny. All we're missing are the raincoats. It's like something out of a 1940's film, us following the baddies."

"It is a bit," he agreed. "except that it *is* so serious. But for now, it's important to keep focussed."

Yes, he was right. I swallowed my erstwhile giggles, which in truth probably had more to do with hysteria than humour.

We reached the house, and in our turn walked up the short path. Connor pressed the door-bell, hard and long. There was no answer. "I hope he hasn't passed out," he whispered with a curse. "That's all we'd need."

He pressed the bell again, leaning on it this time. I could hear its persistent buzz through the black wooden door. No matter how drunk the house's occupants were they had to, surely had to, be able to hear it too.

Eventually we heard muttered curses, and a slurred, "I'm coming, I'm coming," and the door was opened to us by a tall, balding, middle-aged man. He blanched when he saw Connor, but it was all he had time to do. Connor said, "Hi, Baldy, remember me?" stepped forward, grabbed his hand and in a movement too quick to be anything but a blur for me, was soon standing inside the hallway behind 'Baldy', twisting his arm behind his back.

"Come in, Tory," Connor instructed, "and close the door behind you."

I did so, grimacing despite myself at the threadbare carpet and the dirty wallpaper hanging in strips off the walls. There was a musty smell too. But I didn't have time to criticise their interior design further before Connor was speaking to me.

"Open that door there," he said, jerking his head to indicate the one he meant. "I presume that's the sitting-room."

And so it turned out to be. And the interior designer hadn't yet reached this room either – the wallpaper

128

was equally peeling, and the bare floorboards were unvarnished and stained. Connor and 'Baldy' shuffled into the room and Connor put him sitting in the furthest chair from the door.

"You sit down there," he instructed me, indicating the chair nearest the door.

Gingerly I did so, mentally consigning my jeans to the bin. Connor himself stood in front of the fireplace, in between me and the other guy, and I'm sure that that was no accident.

"Now," Connor said conversationally, but his expression was hooded and bleak, and after taking one look at it *I* certainly wouldn't have been fooled by his relaxed tone, "I gave you a hundred euro earlier in return for good information. But the information wasn't good, was it?"

'Baldy' looked at him, clearly trying to focus. It was clear that he had already managed to convert a large proportion of the hundred euro into, shall we say, liquid assets.

"I asked you a question," said Connor, and he took a step towards him. "Look, I don't want to hurt you. But you took my money, and I want the information I paid for. I'll hurt you if I have to," he said, and he took another step, and if he was bluffing it certainly wasn't clear to me.

Nor, it seemed, to 'Baldy'. "Don't hurt me," he pleaded ingratiatingly.

"I won't," said Connor again, "*if* I get the information I paid for. Where is Murtagh Levi?"

"I'm sorry, I'm sorry," 'Baldy' blubbed, "Murtagh made me do it. Murtagh don't like people asking questions about him. Not strangers. He told me to do it, what to say." He continued in tones of amazement and gratitude: "He even let me keep half the money!"

"I'm kind that way," said a voice from the doorway. I jumped about a foot in the air and turned around to see three men standing there. Two stood back a little, leaving one man very obviously to the forefront. A big man, dressed in denim jeans, denim shirt straining over his round stomach – the buttons definitely earning their keep – and a faded denim jacket.

This was obviously Murtagh Levi, and it seemed that I had been correct in my guess as to how he got his nickname.

I took all this in instantly, even as he was sauntering into the room towards me. He perched on the arm of the chair in which I was sitting, and placed a relaxed arm across its back. I twisted a little, to look up at him, and he smiled down at me. Benevolently. The way the cat smiles benevolently at the mouse.

"You must be Connor," he said to Connor, and he reached into his jeans pocket and pulled out a bit of paper. A business card. "*Connor Brophy,*" he read, "of *Cardiff Way, Marino.* Would that be right?".

"It would," said Connor shortly, "and," he gave a theatrical bow, "Mr Levi, I presume?"

"Indeed," grinned Murtagh. And to me: "And you might be?"

"Tory O'Neill."

"'Tory'" he said, grinning, "what an interesting name! Why on earth did your parents call you after a British political party?" He laughed uproariously at his wit, as did his two henchmen from the doorway, and even 'Baldy' managed a hesitant 'I'm not exactly sure what's going on but just to be on the safe side' giggle.

Murtagh didn't wait for an answer, though, as to the genesis of my name, as he went on, "Now, Connor," he added courteously, "I understand you were looking for me. And here I am. You can step away from poor Willie now."

Connor did, probably less because of the request, and more because of the subtle menace inherent in the soft voice and relaxed pose of the man sitting right beside me, and the equally understated statement made by the silent presence of the two other men, still standing in the doorway.

"Here, Willie," said that soft voice from behind my head, and something shiny flew through the air towards the hapless bald-headed man. He reached for it, missed, and it landed on the floor. As he bent to pick it up, I could see what it was: a front-door key. "Thanks for the lend of that, Willie," said Murtagh, "and for agreeing to be the decoy. You can head off to bed now."

And Willie did so, stumbling out of the room and up the stairs. Once he was gone Murtagh said kindly, "So Connor, why don't you sit down, over there. We might as well be comfortable as we're chatting."

Connor complied, sitting in the chair recently

vacated by Willie. It seemed to be no accident, and certainly Connor seemed to be as aware of it as I was, that Murtagh and his cronies were much nearer me than was Connor.

Murtagh said pleasantly then, "So you two were looking for me? You know, I really don't like strangers looking for me. I prefer to keep a low profile."

"It wasn't you we were looking for, specifically," I said, "more someone else, but we don't know where that person is, and your name was the only link we had. We found a piece of paper with the name of the pub and your name on it in a room he had vacated."

"I see." He inclined his head a little, thinking about it. "And who might this person be?"

"Ray Rafter," I said, holding my breath. In two more seconds I could have the whereabouts of my daughter.

But no, Murtagh was shaking his leonine head slowly. "Can't say the name rings a bell. But you know, one meets so many people in my line of work, I couldn't possibly keep track of them all."

"We need to find him, Murtagh," I said. "We just have to. He was due to meet you in the Derby Rig on the seventeenth, but we don't know which month."

"It might have been February or March," put in Connor. "Does that remind you of anything?"

Murtagh shook his head and I went on urgently, "Try and think. Please. He's a slim guy, medium height, with long brown hair. He always wears denims, and he's got a tattoo of a guitar on his right wrist. He might have met with you about getting a gig," I added. "He's a brilliant guitarist, but he hasn't really made the big time yet. So he's always trying to hustle gigs."

Murtagh put his head back and laughed. "Not me, love," he said. "People don't come to me looking for music gigs. No, shall we say I'm an entrepreneur of a totally different kind. If Ray did come to me, and I have to say your description is sounding a little familiar, ringing a few bells, he was buying from me, not selling!" He laughed again, and his two cohorts obediently laughed too.

"Right," I said flatly. Well, it had to be something to do with music, or something to do with drugs, and since it wasn't music . . .

"Drugs," said Connor flatly.

"Drugs," I echoed, equally flatly. "Is he dealing?" I asked then. If he was it would – or could – give us another lead, somewhere else to look.

But Murtagh was shaking his head. "No, or at least, if he is, he's not buying wholesale from me. I'd know all the people down-line from me, and your Ray isn't one of them."

He got to his feet then. "Well," he said politely, "nice to have met you both. Sorry I couldn't help you. I think I'd prefer if you forgot about meeting me, and then *I'll* forget about having met you two. I'll keep this, though," and he held up Connor's business card, "so that if it turns out that you remembered me to, shall we say, people I wouldn't like to be remembered to, then I'll be able to return the compliment." He smiled at us benignly, but his eyes were sharp narrow slits.

"We take your point," said Connor tiredly.

"Don't go," I said in despair. I even stood up, reached out and put my hand on his arm. At least I did until he looked pointedly at it and I hastily removed it. "You don't understand," I begged. "I really, really need to find Ray. And you're our only link."

"But I've just told you I don't remember him."

"But you had dealings with him. And somebody must know you both. Someone must have sent him in your direction. Businesses like yours don't exactly advertise in the *Golden Pages*!" I laughed lightly, trying to win him over any way I could, even forced humour.

"Why do you want him so badly?" he asked, seeming to be mildly curious at my persistence.

"He's got my baby," I said, "my little girl. She's only just two. I need to get her back, and I have to do it myself – he's threatened her safety if I go to the police."

He paused then, studied me for a moment. "Your little girl?"

"Yes, my Lucy."

"Why would he do that?" he asked.

I could only tell him the truth. "She's his daughter. But he never had any interest in her – he left us about a year ago, refused to support her. I don't understand why he should have taken her now."

There was silence while he thought for a moment and I waited in anguish for his verdict.

"Okay," he said at last, "I'll see what I can do. I genuinely don't know him, but as you said, there must be some link. I'll ask around. No promises, mind."

"Oh, thank you, thank you," I said, almost incoherent.

"Don't thank me till I've got somewhere. I'll give you a ring, Connor," he said, indicating the card again. "I know your number after all."

And he turned on his heel and walked out, followed by his cohort.

And Connor and I were left alone in this strange sitting-room, in this stranger's house, in this unfamiliar part of Dublin, looking at each other from opposite ends of the room.

"Come on," he said. "We'll go home."

Wearily we left the house, closing the door behind us. We walked back up the road, got into the car, and I turned on the ignition, turned the car around in the empty, silent street, and we headed for Connor's house.

"What do you think?" I asked him as we drove.

"I don't know," he said. "I don't know what to think"

"Will he help us, do you think?"

"He certainly sounded as if he meant it. But, Tory, don't get your hopes up too high. Even if he did mean it, he might forget, or change his mind in the morning. And even if neither of those things happen, he might just draw a blank. We've no idea how Ray got to hear about him."

"Mmm," I said, dejectedly.

"But it might work out," he said, "and in the meantime, there must be other leads to be followed."

"That's right," I said, even more depressed as I realised just how few, and how tenuous, any other leads might be. "I'll contact all the venues where he has played before, and see if they're still in touch with him. And there must be loads of other things I can try." But right then, in the middle of the night, driving through dark streets after an encounter with a daunting criminal, and no nearer finding my daughter, I found it hard to think of any.

"You're tired," said Connor gently. "Things always look worse when you're tired. You'll feel better in the morning, I promise."

"Hmm," I agreed, "I'm sure I will."

We drove in silence then until we pulled up outside his house.

"Thanks for everything you've done," I said. "You didn't have to get involved at all, and I really appreciate it."

"No problem," he said, stifling a yawn. "Listen, you must give me your phone number, so I can contact you if – when – Murtagh phones me."

So we programmed each other's land-line and mobile numbers into our respective mobile phones.

"Good night," said Connor then, lifting a hand and briefly touching my cheek. "Sleep as well as you can. I'll talk to you." And he undid his seat-belt and got out of the car, and closed the door. With a goodbye tap on the window he turned and made his way to his house.

I started the ignition and drove home.

I was so tired I was leaning on the front door as I was opening it, and I nearly fell into the small hallway, and the stairs leading from it to the flat seemed like the North Face of the Eiger, and took nearly as long to climb.

My head was spinning as I washed my face and brushed my teeth, and threw on a sleep T-shirt. Spinning with thoughts of Lucy, memories of her. The first time I saw her after she was born. The way she used to cling to my little finger using her whole hand. Her laughter and giggles. Her head tucked into my shoulder.

I sighed as I got into bed, imagining a sleepless night. But to my surprise I fell asleep the minute I got into bed, due, I suppose, to a mixture of the late hour and nervous exhaustion.

But in my dreams I heard Lucy cry. Not a distraught cry, more her usual cry, confident that she would be responded to, her 'I'm awake and I need something so please come and sort it out for me,' cry. In my dream I struggled to get out of bed to go and tend to her, but a dark amorphous mass was pressing down on me so that I couldn't move. After some time Lucy's cry progressed, grew stronger, louder, with annoyance and a sense of urgency in there too. She wasn't accustomed to being ignored and she didn't like it one little bit. And the louder and more urgent her cries, the more I – still dreaming – flailed and struggled to get to her, but I was still pinned to the bed and unable to move, and couldn't go to her aid. And her cries grew stronger and stronger as I grew more and more frustrated, unable to help her. Until at the end her cries were frantic screams, and I was screaming too, "Let me go. Let me go. I need to go to her," and I realised that I was awake, that it had only been a dream. But there was no 'only' about this dream, it had seemed so real. And my heart was pounding and my skin was clammy with sweat as I lay there, trying to come to terms with the fact that I hadn't really experienced this, that I hadn't really been pinned to the bed while my daughter cried in vain for me.

Except, of course, it wasn't a dream, it was real. Oh, sure, the details weren't real. I couldn't actually hear Lucy's crying for me, I hadn't actually been pinned to the bed. But her crying was real – no matter that I couldn't hear it, her tears were happening somewhere on this planet – and I was as helpless to answer them as if I was, indeed, pinned to the bed by some daemonic malevolent force.

I waited for my heart to calm a little, slow a little, and then I got out of bed and went into the kitchen for a drink. As I sat there in my pyjamas in the middle of the night, sipping from a glass of water, a wave of the purest grief overwhelmed me. And a wave of pure fear, and pure exhaustion. She could be anywhere, I thought despairingly. How can I possibly hope to ever find her? And I ached for her, my arms were so empty. I thought of her little laugh, the raspberries I would blow on her tummy and the giggly hysterics we would share. And how she would climb onto my knee, sucking her thumb when she was tired or cranky, and how just being with me would give her back her equilibrium.

And just then, just there, for one long dark moment, I felt like giving up. I thought, I can't go on. It's too great a task and I am too weak a woman.

But then, like an aftershock, a wave of anger overwhelmed me. Good anger, resourceful anger. Anger that had me pounding the table and shouting abuses at Ray, for putting me through this, and putting Lucy through this. Anger that had me swearing that I was not going to give up, that I was never going to give up, that if it took me the rest of my life I was going to find her. Anger that had me swearing that I was not weak, I was a strong powerful woman and by God no jumped-up pup of a wannabe rock star was going to take my daughter away from me and get away with it. And a wave of determination rose then, to support and embrace the anger, a wave of surety and confidence and tenacity that, as I sat there in the cool of the night-time kitchen, had me sure, and certain, and confident that I was going to find her.

And after my cup of water, and war of emotions, I went back to bed., telling myself that it wasn't selfish to sleep, that I had to be strong for Lucy, in order to find her.

And I tossed and turned for some unknown time, but eventually I must have slept, because the next thing I knew it was daylight.

Chapter 9

When I awoke the room was bright. I looked over at my little radio-alarm clock, and sat up urgently – dear God, it was nearly 11 o'clock! What on earth was I doing sleeping when my Lucy was out there somewhere, waiting for me to come and get her?

I washed and dressed quickly, then threw a cup of coffee into me in lieu of breakfast.

But then I hovered, uncertain. After all that rush, all that efficiency, I didn't know what to do next. Until we got that call from Murtagh Levi, there didn't seem to be much I *could* do.

But no! I was going to be way more proactive than that. If I could just think of a way in which to be more proactive.

Of course! I was going to call a detective agency. I pulled the *Golden Pages* out of the telephone-table drawer, and quickly began looking up the listing which

Connor had showed me yesterday. I was surprised that there was any call for private detectives in Ireland. It seemed such an American thing, such a California thing. But maybe I was just watching too much television. I flicked the directory pages until I reached the right one. I read through the choices, wondering which one to ring. How did you decide which was a good detective agency anyway? In the end I decided to ring one that had various branches throughout the country. I lifted the phone and dialled the number.

The phone was answered by a man with a kind-sounding voice, a voice which reassured by its very tone: even though you've got problems, which is why you're ringing us, we can sort them out; we can look after it all for you.

"Hello," I said to that kind-sounding voice, "I'd like to talk to someone about finding a missing person, please."

"Sure thing, hold on a second," and I was put on hold, and a few seconds later I heard another kind, we'll-sort-it-all-out voice (did they hold training days to get the right tone, I wondered), say, "Hello, Damien Moriarty here. Can I help you? I understand you're enquiring about a missing person."

"Hello . . . Damien," I said, timid now, finding it difficult to believe that this was real, that this was me, plain ordinary Tory O'Neill, actually talking to a real-life private detective. "I'm wondering how you go about finding one – a missing person, I mean."

"There are lots of ways, depending on the situation. Do you have a specific circumstance in mind?"

"I certainly do." And I explained, my voice catching: my musician ex-boyfriend, my daughter, this was the third day now.

"Hmm," he said, "You know, we kind of step in where the police can't or won't. You know, getting evidence of infidelity or fraud, stuff like that. But a situation like yours, that's the sort of stuff the police are there for. And they have better resources than we do, after all, so my immediate advice would be to go to them," he said kindly. "I'm not trying to do us out of business here," he explained, "but it's my job to give the best advice, and in this case I honestly think that would be best solution."

"I can't," I said miserably, and explained that too.

"Hmm," he said again, "I can certainly see your problem. But you know, maybe it would be worth going to the gardai anyway – you'd be amazed how discreetly they can work."

"No," I said, feeling panicky. "No, I'd be terrified to do anything that would put Lucy in danger. I don't think he would hurt her. I think he's just bluffing. At least, I *hope* that he's just bluffing. But just on the off-chance . . . You see, Damien, Ray was always a pacifist, very gentle. It would be totally out of character for him to hurt a child, it really would. But . . . it's also totally out of character for him to want to have a child, so I'm totally confused. Sorry, I'm not explaining it very well. I mean that if he would do something out of character like take Lucy, he's quite likely to do something out of character like hurt her."

"Hmm, I can see that you would be. Confused, I mean. Well, we wouldn't concern ourselves overmuch with his character or motivation or anything like that, but with his actions. And I think we could certainly try to help you. And it would be in the strictest confidence, needless to say, so you needn't fear the gardai would get to hear about it. Okay, let me take a few details."

"But first," I said, hating to ask, "how much do you charge?"

"It usually works out to about   500 per day," he said.

I physically rocked. "What?" I whispered. "Did I hear you right?"

There was compassion in his voice as he explained, "It's   50 per hour, and our operatives usually put in a ten-hour day. Er –" he hesitated before going on, "that doesn't include travel or other expenses. And," he almost-whispered, "it doesn't include VAT."

"And how long would it take you to find her," I asked desperately. Maybe if it were only a day or two . . .

"I've no idea," he said. "Every case is different. We could be lucky but . . . I've known cases where operatives have been working for three or four months before they found someone. I tell you what, Ms – ?"

"Tory. Tory O'Neill. Call me Tory."

"Tory. Look, I really feel for your situation. And I have an hour free this afternoon. Would you like to come in and talk it through with me? No charge. Maybe, even if you can't hire us, I can help by giving you some ideas as to where to look."

"Would you?" I clutched the phone hard in gratitude.

"Sure. I don't know how much help I'll be, but I'll try. Would four o'clock suit you?"

"Yes, yes. Of course."

"Grand so, we'll see you then. You have the address? Good, see you later."

After I hung up, I sat and thought hard. What was Lucy worth? That was an easy one: every penny in the world. But the harder question with its equally harder answer was: how much money did I have to spend on getting her back? And the answer to that was: a lot less than every penny in the world, an awful lot less than that. I stood up and went to the kitchen drawer, pulled out a pen and paper, and sat down at the breakfast bar.

And then I wrote, and crossed out, and calculated and recalculated until my fingers were numb and my head was spinning. But no matter what way I did my sums, the answers came up the same: I had just under a thousand in the bank, which was there for emergencies, and maybe, possibly, I had hoped, a bit of a holiday later in the year, when it was off-season. Obviously I'd spend that in a heartbeat. Indeed, didn't I owe Connor a cool hundred out of that already? But apart from that . . . I had no assets at all, except my car. And my car could only be called an asset in the very loosest sense of the word. I had to face it square on: truly, what would a ten-year-old car be worth? A couple of thousand maybe? If I was lucky. And even that was only use to me if I got a quick sale. And, realistically, there was no way I could afford the time to be selling a car when I had to be pounding the streets and pounding on doors looking for Lucy.

So, say – optimistically – a couple of thousand for the car, assuming somebody came magically knocking on the door looking to buy it, and what I had saved. Which would add up to six or so days' hire of the detective. Oh God. I put my head in my hands and let a wave of abject misery and frustrated helplessness overwhelm me.

And as I sat there I realised that this, truly, was the difference between being wealthy and being poor. They say money is power, and I always thought that that was the case for those who are interested in power. I, I had always said, was not interested in power, so didn't need much money. But I realised, that sunny Wednesday in June as I sat despairing in my small dated kitchen in an upstairs, badly furnished flat, that I had misunderstood what is meant by power. Sure, power can mean – as I had always thought – the power to influence politicians, to finance lobby groups, to pay for advertising to bring public opinion around to your opinion.

But power means, I realised that day, much, much more. It means power over the demon of worry. There's very little that can go wrong that can't be fixed by enough money, so if you're rich you simply don't have to worry. It is the power to decide for yourself how you are going to spend your life rather than selling those precious days and hours and minutes simply to live.

But above all, money is the power to protect your children. If I had had money I would have stayed at home with Lucy, and Ray would never have got his hands on her.

And . . . if I had money, and assuming that somehow this situation had arisen, I would have had the power to pay for expert help in rescuing her. As it was, it didn't matter that my love was deep and my determination to find her endless: love and determination are not saleable commodities.

Eventually it came down to this: I didn't have money, so I didn't have the power that money could have bought. So, my love and determination were just going to have to be enough.

I raised my head from my elbows, stood and went to the sink. I ran the tap and splashed the water over my face and my weary eyes.

I was just going to have to find her myself. Murtagh Levi hadn't phoned yet, and possibly never would.

It seemed clear to me that the next step was to contact various venues where he had played, and see if they knew where he was now. A long-shot, I knew, especially since I knew how high the staff turnover in the bar trade was, and how many bands came and played and went over the years.

But it was, so far, the only game in town, and I had to be doing *something*.

So I turned to the relevant section of the *Golden Pages*, and marked those pubs and other venues in which I remembered Ray as having played. I then tried, without huge success, to remember when he had played at each venue, and with which band, and wrote those down.

I lifted the phone and dialled the first one. "Hi," I said, deliberately upbeat, speaking quickly so as not to be interrupted, "I'm wondering if you could help me. I'm trying to trace a friend of mine who gigged at your venue once, I think it was about two years ago. His name is Ray Rafter and I think he was playing with a band called *Archery*. Or it might have been *Whispers and Shouts*."

"Yeah?" enquired the voice, and I *swear* I could hear gum being chewed.

"Well, would you, or anybody there, still be in touch with him? Or know where he is now? Or be in touch with any of the band members of either of those bands?"

"No, sorry," and he hung up the phone. He hadn't sounded very sorry.

I tried another place.

"Look, lady, it's lunch-time, we're up to our eyes, and you're asking us if we remember one poxy musician, and you can't even remember when he played here or who he played with? Get real!" Dial tone.

And another.

"Gee, I wasn't here then." Giggle. "Let me ask the other girls. Hang on." I could hear distant shouts, "Marcie, Suzanne, d'ya ever hear of a musician called Ray Rafter? Played here about three years ago. Band might have been called *The Fundamentals*. What? Oh, okay." She came back to me. "Sorry, nobody here has heard of him."

"Thanks for trying," I said. "I appreciate that."

I did too. I knew it was a useless exercise, wasting everybody's time, and it wasn't surprising that most of the people were getting irritated with me. But doggedly I kept going, until I had phoned, and had been shouted at, or sneered at, or sympathised at, by someone at every venue I remember him playing.

And Connor hadn't phoned yet. Which meant that Murtagh hadn't phoned him yet. What else could I do? I couldn't bear just sitting there not doing anything. In the end I rang Carol.

"Hi, Carol," I said when she answered.

"Have you any news?" she immediately asked anxiously. "Have you found him?"

"No," I said listlessly, "unfortunately I haven't."

I could hear her letting her breath out with a rush as I continued, "In fact, that's why I'm ringing you."

"What do you mean?"

"I'm really down about it all, and I could just do with some company now, and I was thinking I might drop over for a little bit."

"That's a *great* idea. I'd love to see you. We can be miserable together. But hang on, I've a better idea – I've a few messages to do in town – will I pop in to see you? It's on my way."

"Fair enough," I said, not really minding where we met, not once I got to spend some time in her calm presence, be with someone who knew Lucy and loved her, and who would be missing her as I was.

"Grand. I'll be there in about half an hour."

"Oh!" a thought struck me. "How are you going to manage with Shay and Laura? Maybe I'd better come to you after all."

"Ah yes," said Carol embarrassedly, "I was going to tell you, but the time didn't seem right. I've stopped minding them. I told their parents I couldn't mind them any more. I know it was short notice, and not very professional. But after what happened to Lucy, I just felt I couldn't be responsible for anybody else's child. It was too scary, too frightening. So I'm as free as a bird now," she finished with rich irony.

"Right, you come to me then," I said, thinking how many lives this situation had changed. Carol now without any of the three children she had minded so well and loved so much. Shay and Laura suddenly not seeing their beloved minder, and their parents stuck for new child-care arrangements.

But I couldn't really blame Carol. I was so overwhelmed and twisted with my own emotions I hadn't really the wherewithal to imagine hers, but on a rational level I could see how upset she must also be. She loved Lucy too. She was obviously missing Lucy too, worrying about Lucy just as I was.

"I'll be there in about half an hour," she promised, and she was.

We hugged tight in my hallway.

"Oh Carol," I said, my voice breaking, "it's been *dreadful*. Not knowing where she is, how she's doing. It's been three days now – I can't bear it."

"I know, I know," she soothed me as I cried in her

arms, patting my back, holding me to her. "It'll be okay, I promise. You'll find her. I know you will."

Eventually I calmed enough to bring her into the kitchen and make her a cup of tea.

"So, how are you doing with finding Ray?" she asked.

"Not very well," I told her. "We went to that pub last night like I told you, and we met the guy we were hoping to meet, but he doesn't know Ray."

"'We'?" she enquired.

"Me and Ray's ex-landlord. He helped me out yesterday."

"Oh yes?" she said with a wealth of meaning.

"Oh, Carol, will you stop?" I said brusquely. "Now is not the time to be doing your matchmaking. I'm sure I don't need to remind you that I'm hardly in the market for romance under the circumstances."

"But if the situation were different?" she persisted.

"I haven't thought about it," I said dismissively.

"Is he good-looking?" She wasn't giving up.

"I haven't thought about it," I said again, and then, as she opened her mouth to pursue the point I realised, with an internal sigh, that the only way to stop this line of questioning was to satisfy it. "No, he's not good-looking, not really. His face is too sharp and angular. But it's . . . fascinating, I would have to say. It makes you want to keep looking at it. He's quite dark-skinned for an Irish man. And fabulous blue eyes. And he has a lovely smile and his eyes crease up when he does smile. And he frowns when he's thinking about something, and he gets two little creases, just here," and I indicated the top of my nose, just between my eyes, even as I was feeling surprise at how much I had noticed about him.

"Sounds nice," she said.

"I suppose he is, I haven't considered him that way. He's just a friend, someone who's been helping me."

"And he's obviously a decent oul' skin, to be helping you out like this."

"Yes, he is. A very decent man indeed."

She nodded at that. "Anyway," she drained her mug, "thanks for the tea. I'd better be off now."

"Already?" I said, aghast. "You've only just got here!"

"I know, I know," she said, "but I have to do those messages I told you about. But listen," she put a hand on my arm, and her expression grew serious, "I'm really, really rooting for you on this. I'm," her face reddened in embarrassment, "well, I don't know how you feel about religion, but I have great faith myself. And, I just want you to know that I'm praying for you and Lucy every night, and I've lit candles in St. Ronan's." She laughed a little. "I don't know if it does any good, but it's all I can do –"

"Well, all you can do apart from listening to me, and being there for me, like you are," I interjected.

"Well, yes, thank you," she ducked her head in embarrassed acknowledgement, "but I hope you don't mind that I'm praying for you both as well."

"No, not at all," I said flatly, feeling that usual surge of discomfort whenever people started talking about religion, despite knowing that most people weren't like . . . well, anyway. I then realised how flat I had sounded, so I tried to inject some enthusiasm into my tone. "No, I really appreciate it, Carol. I certainly could use all the help I can get!"

"What's the next step?" she asked.

"I don't know," I said despairingly. "We're waiting for that drug-dealer guy to ring. If he does. He said he'd ask around about Ray. And I have an appointment this afternoon with a private detective."

"Have you now?" she said interestedly. "Are you going to hire him?"

"I don't know," I laughed bitterly. "Have you any *idea* what private detectives cost?"

"Well, no, I haven't actually."

Beginning to laugh a little hysterically I told her. " 500 a day. *Before* VAT. *Plus* expenses."

"Ah." Her soft grey eyes looked at me sympathetically. "That's a lot of money."

I nodded, not trusting myself to speak.

"And," she said softly, gently, "I wouldn't imagine you have that kind of money?"

I shook my head.

"Well, you know, I wouldn't like to see you stuck. I don't have much . . . but, I would love to help. After all I feel partially responsible for the situation. I could certainly contribute, I don't know, two or three hundred."

"Oh, Carol, thanks so much." I looked at her in sheer gratitude. "Hopefully it won't come to that, but if it does . . . well, yes, I might take you up on it."

"Do," she said. "I really mean it. And," she paused delicately, "could your parents . . .?"

"No. No way," I said. "No. That's just not an option." Funny, but with all else we had shared, I had never told her about the situation at home. "No," I said again. "That wouldn't be possible."

She nodded in the understanding she couldn't possibly feel, and flashed me another look of sympathy.

She reached down to her feet and picked up her handbag, then stood up. I stood too.

I walked her out the door, and we kissed and hugged goodbye. "Keep the faith," she whispered into my ear. "It'll be fine. You'll have her back before you know it."

"Thanks," I said. I appreciated her saying it even though I knew that such a promise wasn't in her gift to give.

After she had gone I sat and stared at the phone for a while. But no matter how much I stared, it didn't ring. Eventually I cracked and I rang Connor.

"No," he said softly, "he hasn't phoned me. You know he hasn't, that I would have phoned you immediately if he had."

"I know," I said miserably.

"How are you bearing up?"

"Oh, you know," I said listlessly.

"I don't know what good it'll do," he said kindly, "but if you like you'd be welcome to come over here for a while."

"No, thanks, Connor, but I won't. I have an appointment with a private detective later." Quickly I brought him up to date with that, then finished: "And I know you need to get on with your work."

"It would be good," he agreed gravely, "but Tory, honestly, I'll ring you the minute I hear from Murtagh." He didn't say, and I didn't point it out either, '*If* I hear from Murtagh,': the big '*if*' of Murtagh actually caring enough to remember his promise and do something about it *and* come up with some good information – that was a very tenuous hope on which to hang my only connection to Ray.

"Thank you," I said gratefully. Bad and all as this situation was, if it wasn't for Connor it would be an awful lot worse. His help so far had been invaluable – both his practical help in finding the link to Murtagh, and his interest and support that so far had meant I wasn't going through it alone. Which I would otherwise have been, Carol notwithstanding. She was wonderful, and her interest and her support were proving essential, but at the end of the day she was a middle-aged, fairly unworldly woman.

"It's no problem," he said, gracefully dismissing my thanks. "I'm glad to do anything I can to help you get Lucy back. But for now I'd better get back to the keyboard this end. Will you let me know how you get on with your man, the private eye?"

"I will. And ring me the minute Murtagh rings. I'll be going out about half past three, but you can get me on the mobile then." He promised he would and I finished with, "Goodbye, Connor, and thanks again. Talk to you soon."

I got some food then, couldn't have said what it was, but it was fuel to keep me going for a while longer, and not too long after that it was time to get ready to go into Dublin to meet the detective, which was great. Minutes and hours hung heavy without doing anything to at least *feel* that I was getting nearer to finding Lucy. Just sitting and waiting wasn't nearly proactive enough. So doing *anything* made me feel marginally better. Or at least, marginally less-bad.

So, I quickly showered and dressed in something a little bit smart, and got the bus into town. While I sat on the bus as it meandered its way towards the city centre, I reflected on my life to date. I hadn't, needless to say, done too well on the family front. And I had done little better on the friends front, which was understandable given the circumstances. But, I thought, I had always been very lucky in the way that strangers went out of their way to help me. From my birth-partner 'Dad', to Connor helping me so much when I didn't know him, to this Damien guy giving me his time for free . . . I had certainly hit the jackpot there.

I got off the bus, and walked through the busy streets, until I reached the offices of the detective agency. Which is where I got my first surprise. I realised I had, subconsciously, been expecting something out of a 1940's film – all dark wood and seedy ambience. But it was bright and modern, and could have been any business at all.

"Hello," I said to the receptionist, "I have an appointment with Damien Moriarty."

"Sure, hang on a second." She lifted a phone and spoke into it, and within a couple of minutes I was issued into a smart contemporary office.

The forty-ish man standing behind the desk stood up and walked around it, holding out his hand. "Tory O'Neill? Hi, I'm Damien."

I held out my hand on autopilot, but I was gawking at him in a most unsophisticated way. *Gauche*, I think is the word I'm looking for. Despite having already seen the environment, so different from my preconceived ideas, I must have had, lurking down there, more preconceived ideas.

He laughed. "What is it?"

"You don't look like a private detective," I burst out. He didn't either. He was of just-above-medium height, a slim build, and sharply cut blond hair which went well with his sharply cut dark-blue suit. In short, he looked like a bank-manager. No, not a bank-manager: his expression was *way* too benign for that. Maybe an insurance salesman. No, he looked too honest for that. A civil servant maybe.

He was still grinning at me. "And in what way do I not look like a private detective?"

"You're not nearly seedy enough. Too smartly dressed. Too cleanly shaven. Too . . . *normal*-looking."

He laughed again. "You've been watching too many American films! We don't go around looking like Philip Marlowe, you know. It'd defeat the purpose, after all – it's hard to be discreet and inconspicuous if you're lurking looking like everybody's idea of a PI. We don't even get many busty blonde dames coming into our office! Anyway," his expression grew serious, "I do only have an hour, and you have a serious situation. Coffee, before we start?"

I shook my head, and he nodded in acceptance, and indicated a chair for me.

"Okay," he said, once we were both seated, "your boyfriend has taken your baby."

"Yes," I agreed, but then, anxious to be accurate, "well, I call her my baby. She's actually just gone two years old."

"Okay. And is he named as the father on the birth cert?"

"He is."

"But you have custody." He looked up at my silence. "Have you?"

"No, Damien, I don't. The thing is that he didn't want anything to do with the baby. He just left. So I never legally got custody. It just wasn't relevant."

"Hmm. You're looking for him unofficially, so it doesn't actually matter who has custody now. But given that he is, as we now know, interested in her, I would make it my business to get custody, if I were you."

"Okay. I will. But that's a bit academic right now, isn't it?"

"Right now, yes. But it could be relevant later, if it all gets into the courts. But yes, the thing to talk about is what we would do now. Okay, the first thing we would do, if we were looking for him, is to ask you for details of all his friends and relatives."

"I don't know his friends. They were always changing with shifting band allegiances anyway. And they were only ever known by first names, or even nicknames. And he doesn't have any family, except his grandmother. He was born to his mother when she was only sixteen. He never knew who his father was. And his mother left him with *her* mother, and said she was going to London to, I don't know, make her fortune or something. Anyway, off she headed and was never heard from again. As far as I know, they don't even know if she's alive or not. So Ray's grandmother, Maisie, reared him."

"Right – well, what we would do with that information is to get her address, and then go and root in her dustbin." He must have caught sight of my expression because he sighed theatrically. "I know, it's the glamour of the job that gets us all. But seriously, you'd be amazed at the information bins contain. Particularly, in this case, old letters with addresses on them, or phone bills with frequently called numbers on them. What is it?" He had caught sight of my glum expression.

"I've already been to see her. She's helped me all she could. She gave me the last address she had for him, but when I went there he had already moved out."

He looked at me sharply, concerned. "And do you believe her? Could it be a bluff?"

I thought about it. "I did take her totally at face value at first. I didn't really think about it. But to be honest, Damien, I think she was telling the truth. She seemed totally shocked when she heard he had taken Lucy. I honestly don't think she was faking. And, you know, I know she loves Ray, but she's under no illusions about him. She made that very clear."

"Okay," he said at last. "I think I'd agree with you, from what you're saying. Right, another thing we always suggest, is to tap your phones."

"Tap my phones?"

"I know it sounds strange, straight out of a spy novel. But often the abductor will contact the remaining parent, to let them know the child's okay. And there are often great clues in that conversation which you mightn't pick up on in the emotion of the call. Clues in what the abductor himself says, or clues in the background noise."

"The thing is, he hasn't contacted me at all."

"Oh." And I think he tried to hide it, but I definitely saw a worried expression fleetingly cross his face. "That's unusual. If he does, Tory, try to remember as much as you can of what he says, and get a commitment from him to ring regularly with news of Lucy. And we'll put a tap on the phone then." He sighed a little, and tapped his pen on his desk. "Okay, let's try another tack. Tell me about Ray."

"What do you want to know?"

He shrugged. "Anything. You say he is a musician. Does he have a day-job? What are his hobbies? In other words, what does he spend his time doing?"

"His work is the same as his hobby," I said. "It's his music. He's a guitarist. A brilliant guitarist, to be honest. And a not-bad singer. And he's always looking for the best band, the best gig, the big break."

"Oh right!" he said, very interested, and he leaned forward. "You know, that's exactly the tack we'd take, then. We might pretend to be journalists from *NME* or *Hot Press* and try to track him that way. It's amazing how many doors the possibility of an interview in a trade magazine will open for you."

"That's a brilliant idea!" I sat back in my chair and looked, stunned, at him. "We kind of did something like that – we pretended to be able to set up a band with a great venue, but we never thought it through this much."

"'We'?" he said neutrally.

"Oh," I shrugged, "remember I told you Ray's grandmother gave me his address. Which turned out to be his old address. His ex-landlord has been helping me."

"Right," he said, still neutrally. "Tell me, if he's as good a guitarist as you say, and a not-bad singer, why hasn't he made it before now?"

I shrugged. "Who's to say? I think a lot of it is probably down to luck – after all, there's a million talented people out there for every one who makes it. And also . . . I rather think . . . in fact I'm quite convinced . . . that persistence might, possibly, have something to do with it. He joins these new bands, and they spend some time doing the small gigs, sending the demo tapes off to the record companies. But when it doesn't work quickly, instead of keeping going at it, he thinks it'll be better with the next band, the next line-up. So he moves on. A bit like he does with families," I said bitterly, and pretended not to see Damien's professionally neutral expression, his expression which said, 'I'm not commenting on this, I'm used to hearing lots of vitriolic comments but I'm a professional and I'm equally used to ignoring them and keeping to the point'.

"Hmm," he said, "that makes it more difficult. Well, look, Tory, if you and your, er, friend, can take advantage of that idea about posing as music journalists, take that idea and welcome. Also, look up the *Golden Pages* for listings of management agencies – Ray might have registered with one of those."

"Oh yes!" Great! What a brilliant idea! "He might, you know. I know he often said he was going to . . . but either he didn't get around to it, or if he did approach one they turned him down, and he had plenty to say, I can tell you, about philistines who wouldn't know good music if it bit them. But that was a few years ago. He might have tried again. I'll ring them when I get home."

"Do that. And, feel free to ring me again. I can't spend too much time on this, not when I'm not charging it, but if you need any specific advice or information I'll try to help."

Taking the hint that the meeting was over, I stood up to go.

"Good luck," he said, standing and shaking my hand. "I really mean that."

I came out of that meeting feeling vaguely more

cheerful. It looked as if we were on the right track, and we had two new ideas we could pursue.

'We,' I thought to myself. I was using that word a lot. Connor had said that he would do anything he could to help. And I knew I should know better, should have learned by now, that people say an awful lot that they don't necessarily mean, make promises they don't necessarily keep. (In my head I heard my father's voice: 'Of *course*, I'll bring you to the beach next weekend, Tory. Of *course*, I'll be there for your school play.' I shook my head and banished those meaningless words.)

I reminded myself that Connor had probably said it – "I'll do anything I can to help" – just as a conversational convention. But somehow, somehow, I felt that he was different, that I *could* trust what he said. I gave a short laugh, acquiring strange glances for myself as I walked towards the bus stop – maybe I really could trust Connor. Or maybe I was just fooling myself.

Chapter 10

I went home and dashed for the phone. No matter that, since Connor would have phoned the mobile had there been any news, I knew deep down that there would be no message from him. And there wasn't.

And, of course, there was no message from Ray. It didn't look as if he was going to ring me at all, reassure me at all, no matter what the PI Damien Moriarty had said. He was obviously quite happy to leave me wondering about Lucy's fate, for the rest of my life probably.

In fact, I thought, as I listlessly made and ate a sandwich, it was worse than that. It wasn't that Ray knew I would be worried but decided anyway not to allay my fears. No, it was that Ray, with his usual total lack of empathy, wouldn't even have considered matters from my point of view. The idea that I might be worried, that I might need some information wouldn't even strike his consciousness. And that was worse because that meant there was no possibility of him changing his mind. If he knew I was worried and didn't care, the tiny possibility always existed that some morality would hit him and he would repent of that position. But if he didn't hold any particular position in the first place, there was no reason to change it. Ever.

I looked at my watch, it was just gone five o'clock. Too late, probably, to ring any of the management agencies. Still, I looked up the listing in the *Golden Pages*: there were ten or twelve agencies. I tried all the numbers in case people were working late. But if they were, they weren't answering the phone.

The long summer evening stretched, mocking me. And now that my frantic *doing* was finished for the day, there was space and to spare for the overpowering thoughts of my daughter to encircle me. Lucy, where are you? I wondered desperately. Even as I'm sitting on this sofa, uselessly kneading my hands, you are somewhere on this planet. What are you doing right now? Are you sleeping? Or playing? Except that I can't imagine you simply playing. But I hope you are. I hope you're happy and content and peaceful enough to play. I hope, even though it means you would have forgotten me, that you aren't missing me so much that it's hurting you.

How quickly would a two-year-old forget her mother, adjust to her new life, I wondered. I had no idea, didn't intend to find out. But it meant that I had no idea now if Lucy was frantic, upset, missing me and needing me. Or if she would have happily adjusted to her new life, the new people around her.

No! I realised. Even eight-week-old puppies know they've lost their mother. How much more, and for how much longer, would a bright, intelligent, two-year-old human? Yes, she would forget me eventually, adjust to her new life eventually. But not yet, and I didn't for one moment intend to have her away from me for long enough to forget me.

So, wherever she was right now, on this bright evening, and whatever she was doing, she *was* missing me. And even though that thought scratched painfully across my heart, even so, at some deep, shameful level, it eased me too. We were still connected emotionally, we were each still missing the other, each still hurting from lack of the other. And guilt and shame sat vigil with me as I rejoiced in some awful way at my daughter's grief.

With an effort I shook myself out of my paralysis. Sitting here fretting over her wasn't going to find her. All over Dublin, in venues big and small, bands were going to be playing tonight. And surely one of those bands, or of the people in those bands, would know where Ray was. The music industry was fairly incestuous, after all – everyone seemed to know everyone else. If I went into the city centre now and covered as many venues as I could, asked the people playing there if they knew Ray's whereabouts – there was every chance, I told myself, that I could find him. And hence Lucy. It could be all over by this evening. And not a moment too soon.

I ran into the bedroom and threw on some clothes

which were smart enough to go out in, to pass the bouncers' dress code, and I headed into the city centre. I parked in a dark underground carpark, and got out of the car. Where now? I cast around in my mental map of different pubs in which Ray had played, pubs which tended to play Ray's heavy style of music. I knew them all – or most of them anyway – having spent hours and hours of my life sitting in them, either listening to Ray play, or listening – along with a torrent of criticism and derision – to other bands play.

Foley's first, I decided. It was nearest. When I got there, and paid my entrance fee, I saw that the band – all three of them – were just setting up. I walked up to the stage.

"Hi!" I called.

They stopped what they were doing and looked down at me, and then I saw them cast a quick covert glance at each other. A smug glance, a glance which told of the glamour of being in a rock band and the women who wanted to embrace some of that glamour by being with the musicians. A glance which wondered between them which of them would get lucky with me that night.

"Yes, love?" asked one of them.

"I was wondering if you knew where I could find Ray Rafter. He's a rock musician too. He played with bands like *Archery, Whispers and Shouts, The Fundamentals*. Would you know of him? Or any of those bands?"

Another quick glance between them. Maybe they had been a bit premature about counting their rock-chicks before they were snatched.

But, give them credit, they thought about it. And eventually the consensus was that they had heard of Ray Rafter, of course. But they didn't know what he was doing now, hadn't bumped into him for a while. One of them, however, volunteered that as far as he knew *The Fundamentals* were playing in The Top Hat. Did I know where that was?

I did. I thanked them for their help, wished them well, and turned away. Went up to The Top Hat, saw that, yes, *The Fundamentals* were playing there, so I paid my entrance fee and went in.

The band had already started playing, and I studied them as they performed. Yes, I thought I recognised that guy there, what was his name? Jim. I think.

I waited until they took a small break, and I called, "Jim, Jim!"

He looked down – so I *had* got the name right!

"Hi, Jim, Tory here, do you remember – Ray Rafter's girlfriend."

"Oh yes," he said, recognition coming into his eyes, "how are you doing? Haven't seen you in ages."

"I'm great," I said impatiently, "but listen, I urgently need to contact Ray. Have you any idea where he is?"

He thought about it. "Ray? God, now you say it, I haven't seen him in ages. But tell you who might know – Phil Moore. Remember he was with us?"

I nodded, although I didn't.

"Well, he's with a band called *Juice* now. They're playing at Morgan's. You might like to try there."

"Thanks! I will."

I turned to go away and he called after me, "Tory, don't be a stranger now! Come back and hear us play when you've got more time. I'll buy you a drink after."

"Fine, fine," I was saying over my shoulder as I turned away again.

So it was off to Morgan's with me. The band playing there, I saw from the abundant posters displayed around, was indeed called *Juice*. They had also started their session – the evening was getting later now – and the very walls and ceiling seemed to physically vibrate with the decibels they were pumping out. I could do nothing while they were playing, so I stood near the stage, to one side. And despite myself my body began to move with the music. They were good, I decided. Not great, but good. And I *had* loved all this music, the dark pulsating energy of a good band giving it all they had.

But the minute the song had stopped I was calling urgently up to the drummer, "Please, please, can you help me?"

He looked down at me.

"Which one is Phil Moore?"

"That would be me."

If he said so – I would have sworn I had never met him before.

"Hi Phil! I don't know if you remember me. I used to be Ray Rafter's girl. Do you know where Ray is now, by any chance?"

He smiled down at me, a sly smile. "Why, you looking for a grand reunion? I heard he walked after you got yourself a baby off him."

"You'd be amazed to know why I want to speak to him!" I laughed, holding onto the illusion of good temper with an extreme effort. "And I thought of *you*. I thought you of all people would have kept in touch with him." Not true, of course, as I hadn't even remembered him, but I was hoping a bit of flattery would do the trick. And it might even have done so, I'll never know, but just then the lead singer called over with more than a hint of impatience. And sarcasm.

"Phil? Any time you're ready? Wouldn't want to interrupt you, of course, but just in case you decided you might like to actually *play* tonight, we'd be more than happy to accompany you."

"Yeah, yeah," said Phil sulkily. But he picked up his drumsticks.

And I had, perforce, to wait until the next break. And as it turned out, I had wasted my time by doing so. Phil had obviously used the time to do a bit of thinking.

"I don't know where he is, and I wouldn't tell you if I did," he informed me. "If Ray wanted to contact you, he'd have done exactly that. I wouldn't want any ex-girlfriend of mine tracking me down, I can tell you, so I'm not going to help it happen to somebody else."

"Please," I said, "it's really urgent."

He looked narrowly at me, then shrugged unconcerned. "As I already told you, I don't know where he is. I really don't," he said a bit more softly, and I had to believe him.

Disconsolately I turned away and left that pub. Where to now?

Grungy Joe's, I decided. That was a great music venue. So I headed over there, paid my entrance fee and went in. I didn't recognise any of the group, but nonetheless, as soon as there was a break I asked about Ray. And I asked the group called *Acid Rain* at Flanagan's. And I asked the lads in *Lock Up Your Daughters* who were playing in Lord's. And two or three others whose name and venue I can't even remember – they all blurred after a while.

As the night passed it became more and more difficult, as people got drunker and drunker. Being a woman going into late-night pubs on your own was an unnerving experience to say the least. Men seemed to think of me as fair game, as though the only possible reason for going out on my own was to pick up some man. And each of them thought that *he* was the very man I had been looking for even if I hadn't realised it myself. No, he was, really, the *very* man I was looking for, each insisted when I tried to kindly tell them to piss off and leave me alone. We'd make beautiful music together, baby, one of them even told me. The only music I wanted to make with *him* was a Requiem Mass.

And the volume of everything got louder and louder as the night passed, as laughter became more frantic, more exuberant, and drinks were flying – sometimes literally – and occasionally I witnessed fights breaking out, which was scary enough in the bars even though they were very quickly quashed by the bouncers, but even more frightening as I walked alone through crowded revelling brawling streets.

And all this for nothing. Almost everybody I spoke to knew of Ray, had met him, but hadn't heard from him for a while. And not one person knew where he was now. Several of them offered to ask around, to tell Ray I was looking for him if they met him. And even though I knew that word-of-mouth was the best way to find him, it was also the most dangerous seeing as then he would get to hear I was looking for him. (Although, how could he think I wouldn't be?) And so each time I had to laugh lightly and tell them not to bother, that it was only a whim, I had just half-wondered about him, wouldn't have minded bumping into him, but it wasn't important.

And if any of them wondered why I was coming into bars and pubs on my own and coming straight up to ask about something that was only an unimportant whim, they certainly didn't say. And I just had to hope, based on nothing at all, that if they did meet Ray in the next short while, they wouldn't think to say to him, "Hey, funny thing, your ex was in the other day looking for you."

I went home at last, with sore feet and an aching heart.

I got into bed and lay there, and images of the night swirled around in my head, disjointed, as if seen through a kaleidoscope. And eventually I slept fitfully, tossing and turning, dreaming of me and Lucy standing beside a stage somewhere, and the stage was so high I couldn't see over it, but I knew we desperately needed to get onto that stage, or to talk to whoever was on it, and I was holding Lucy even as I was trying to climb the stage but it was so smooth and I kept slipping down again. And I kept shouting up to whoever it was who was up there, to help me up, to talk to me. But there was no answer, just a frenzied laughter.

Chapter 11

Wearily I took a peep at the bedside clock. Oh God, it was half past nine! With a muttered curse I flung back the covers and ran into the sitting-room. I dialled work and asked to speak to my boss Sinead.

"Sinead," I said, "remember I told you I'd be back today? Well, I'm sorry, but Lucy's illness is continuing longer than I thought and I won't be able to come in today. In fact, I don't know when I'll be in again. Can I arrange to take all my annual leave? I should have three weeks left."

Sinead's husband Dr Moran had delivered Lucy and Sinead had always been, I felt, especially fond of her because of that. She gasped, "Oh dear God, Tory, is Lucy okay? No, of course not," she answered herself, "that's stupid – clearly, you would be here if she was. I hope," she paused delicately, "that it's nothing serious?"

"Not too serious," I hastened to assure her. "She just has . . . has . . ." What illness, I wondered frantically, would be long-lasting without being serious? ". . . er . . . Scarlet Fever."

There was a studied silence down the wires. "I see," she said eventually. Sinead is many things, but stupid is not one of them. It was very clear that she knew *something* was irregular about all this.

"Okay," she said slowly.

I had been working there a year, and had proven myself trustworthy and honest in that time, and maybe this was helping me to be given the very large benefit of her huge doubt. "This is most irregular, but I'll talk to Cathy and get her to put you on annual leave for the rest of the time you have available. I'll get her to email your return date back to you."

"Thanks, Sinead, I really appreciate it."

I took a breath then, in, as if I were about to speak. For a long second I was tempted, so tempted to tell her everything. Sinead was so competent, surely she would be able to help me? In the absence of anybody else, it would be wonderful to lay this trauma at her feet, ask her, like a child myself, to please sort it out. But then I shook myself. I couldn't. I couldn't possibly. Sinead would no doubt insist that the gardai be brought in, and might even go over my head if I refused. She's wonderful, Sinead, don't get me wrong. But she's very assertive, and very sure that she's always right. So I realised I couldn't.

"What?" asked Sinead, when it became clear I wasn't going to say anything.

174

"Nothing, nothing. Just to thank you again for your flexibility."

And so, with her good wishes to Lucy ringing in my ears, she hung up.

I hung up the phone in my turn, and looked around me. This was now the fourth day without Lucy. I had been doing all I could, hadn't been wasting time. But time was still passing, and she was still without me. Out there somewhere. Beginning her own new day.

I rushed to the phone and rang the number of the first management agency. A young-sounding woman answered.

"Hi," I said brightly, "my name is Grace Tobin, and I'm a freelance music journalist. *Hot Press* have commissioned me to write a piece about up-and-coming guitarists, and I had a few names in mind, and I need to contact them. I was wondering if they were on your books?"

"A *Hot Press* article?" she breathed. "That would be great. Who are the guys you're looking for?"

"Ray Rafter is one," I said, "and the others are . . . are John Murphy, and John Quinn," better get a bit more imaginative, "and . . . and Aloysius Huntley." Shit, that was probably a bit *too* imaginative.

"Hang on a second." She put me on hold and I heard classical elevator-music. Honestly, would you not have thought that a company which specialised in music could do a bit better? I clutched the telephone hard, my knuckles white. A few moments later she came back to me. "No," she said regretfully, "I'm afraid we don't have any of those guys on our books. But you know, if you get in touch with them, be sure to give them our name – we're always interested in representing good talent."

"I will," I promised meaninglessly. "Thanks for trying anyway. Goodbye."

I tried another, and then another. All without success.

About an hour later my fingers were dialling the number for the last possibility.

"Hi," I said brightly – but the brightness was flagging now, a real struggle to achieve, "my name's Grace Tobin, and I've been commissioned by *Hot Press* to write an article on up-and-coming guitarists."

"Have you now?" asked the woman at the far end of the line, interested. "I know the lads in *Hot Press* pretty well. Who commissioned the article?"

Shit, shit, shit, shit. I tried desperately to think of what to say, but my brain had seized up.

"Are you still there?"

"Yes. Yes, I am." I cleared my throat. "Actually, to be totally honest, I'm not a music journalist at all. The thing is, I'm trying to trace my ex-boyfriend, he's abducted my daughter, and I know he's a musician so –"

"Indeed." The voice was stern, not – it appeared – terribly impressed with my having tried to lie to her.

"Please," I said, and my voice was plaintive. "Could you check your records to see if he's a client of yours. I won't get him into trouble, honest. I just want my daughter back." There was silence as she obviously

176

thought about it. "Please," I said again, "she's only two. She'll be missing me, God knows I'm missing her. Her name is Lucy," I said, as though this detail would sway her. "I really need to find her."

I stopped then. I had stated my case. I didn't see what else I could do.

Her voice, when it finally came, was sharp. "You definitely won't get him into trouble? We don't need bad publicity for our clients. I'd be mad to help you do something like that."

"No, no," I gushed, "honestly. I just want Lucy back, that's all. I *swear* I won't take it further – there would be no publicity." I actually had no idea whether or not I would take it further, I hadn't thought beyond actually getting Lucy back. But I would say anything it took.

"Okay," she said reluctantly, and I could hear in her voice that she wasn't sure if she was making the right decision, "hold on while I check our records. What's the name?"

And so I gave her Ray's name, and then I held on as requested, and a few minutes later she was back. There was relief in her voice as she said, "No, we don't represent him." Relief for her, perhaps, at not having to be responsible for getting one of their clients into trouble, no matter my promises. But no relief for me, with this last chance at finding him through a management agency proving fruitless.

"Thanks," I said listlessly, "thanks for looking."

"No problem," she said, positively ebullient, and totally on my side now that there was no conflict of interest. "I really hope you find him, and your daughter."

"Thanks," I said again, and hung up.

Wearily I went and got dressed. Ate some breakfast. And then the phone rang.

"Hi, Tory?" said Connor's deep voice. "Listen – good news! Murtagh has just phoned. He did, believe it or not, ask around as he said he would, and he managed to find someone who has some information about Ray."

"Where is he?" I asked, my voice shaking.

"He's down in Waterford. Murtagh's informant says he joined a band called *The Drones*, and they've been gigging in Waterford city."

"That's great! Oh, thanks, Connor."

A note of caution came into his voice as he said, "The only thing is, Murtagh's informant didn't know exactly where they were gigging, which venue, I mean."

"It's okay," I said. "Waterford's not that big. And anyway, I might be able to help there. I have a copy of *Hot Press*. I'll just look it up."

"And then what?"

"And then I'm going down to Waterford! Like – now! There's no point ringing the venue, even assuming I do find the name of it now. They wouldn't be open this early, and even if they were, they probably wouldn't give me Ray's contact details over the phone. And you know, Connor, even if they did, what use would it be to me? I don't want to talk to him on the phone. It would be too easy for him to avoid the issue, to move on, even."

"I agree," said Connor.

I continued, "No, I just want to land in front of him, and force the issue. And besides, if Ray's in Waterford, that's where Lucy is, so that's where I'm going to be. So, as I said, I'm going now!"

"I thought as much. I'll be over straight away."

"Right," I said uncertainly. "But you don't need to – I'll keep you informed.."

"I'm coming with you. You don't really think I'd take it this far and let you head off on your own? I want to see this through. It would be like leaving the cinema halfway through the film, otherwise." But although his words were flippant, I got the sense that it was more to him than just wanting to see the story through.

"That's wonderful," I breathed.

"How exactly do I get to your place?" he asked, and after I told him he reminded me, "Pack an overnight bag. We'll book into a B&B there."

I opened my mouth to protest, mostly because of the money issue, but he was continuing.

"After all, by the time we get down there, and find the pub, we'll have to wait until evening till they're on, and wait until they're over before we can follow Ray to his home. So it'll be late. And Lucy will be disorientated – it'll be better to get her settled as soon as possible after we get her back, don't you think?"

It all made sense, so I didn't protest.

Especially as he was finishing, "And don't forget, Tory. Pack some of Lucy's clothes."

And that thought gladdened my heart so much. It made it so real!

"I'll pack her favourite toy, too," I said, and laughed with sheer joy and excitement.

Chapter 12

I packed in record time and while I was waiting, looking out the first-floor sitting-room window every five minutes, I looked up my copy of *Hot Press*. And sure enough *The Drones* were playing in a pub in Waterford. Jolies, it was called, and its address was given too. The address meant nothing to me, but once we got down there, I thought to myself – almost delirious with excitement – we could ask anybody where it was. We would find it easily.

About forty minutes later Connor's low silver car pulled up outside, and I ran down the stairs to the front door and flung it open. I waved at him, then grabbed my case and my coat and ran out to his car.

"Hi," I sang out, wildly excited at the thoughts of getting moving, at the thoughts of actually going and getting Lucy, at having a positive lead. He grinned at me, and opened the boot so I could put my case in.

"Hang on, there's a toy to come too." And I ran back to the house, and fetched her favourite cuddly toy, Nana-Bug, and ran back to the car, closing the front door behind me this time. I put Nana-Bug into the boot too, and Connor closed it.

I hopped into the passenger seat and belted up even as he was doing the same on the driver's side. He turned on the ignition and, checking the road, pulled into the traffic.

"We're mad going this early, of course," he said.

"What do you mean?"

"It's just gone twelve o'clock, we'll be in Waterford by about three o'clock, and then we'll have hours to wait before the gig starts, before we have any chance of even seeing Ray."

"Oh yes . . . I hadn't thought of that. I just had to go now. I couldn't have borne to have waited here in Dublin. I had to be moving towards Lucy."

"I know," he said gently, "that's why I didn't even suggest waiting. But I'm just warning you that there will be some hanging around once we get there."

He turned onto the M50, and began driving south along it.

"Connor," I said earnestly, "I'm so, so grateful that you're coming with me. I really am. It means the world to me."

"No problem," he said easily.

I looked over at him. He was sitting comfortably, relaxed, in the low seat. His right arm was resting on the open window-sill, and the wind was blowing through his short hair, ruffling it slightly. He was steering confidently with his left hand, the long fingers comfortably holding the steering wheel.

"But why?" I asked him.

He glanced briefly at me. "Why what?"

"You know. Why are you helping me? I don't like to look a gift horse in the mouth, as they say, but . . ."

"You're wondering what the catch is?" he suggested gently.

"Yes," I said baldly, now that he had put it into words. "Yes. That's it."

He gave a big sigh then. "Isn't it a hard world we live in, all the same? That kindness should be questioned, should be suspect. But I understand . . . I'm not giving out to you for asking. I'd probably be the same in your shoes. Most people would. And that's the sad thing."

He fell silent then as he completed a tricky bit of overtaking, and maybe as he contemplated the sadness of it all. Once he was cruising on the inside lane again he came back to the subject.

"It's a good question," he said, looking into the rear-view mirror, hitting his indicator and taking the exit off the M50. "I've asked myself the same question. I certainly feel impelled to help, as if it's totally the right thing to do, as if there is no other choice. And I don't mean no other choice in a negative way. I mean that deciding to do this is easy, because it's the only thing to do. In fact, 'deciding' itself is the wrong word, because deciding implies a choice, doesn't it?"

I nodded as he came to a stop in the traffic queue to

get onto the Mad Cow Roundabout and hence, eventually, the road to Waterford.

"So I've been asking myself the same question, as I said. And, you know, we humans are pretty complex beings, I've always thought it. There's never any one straightforward motive, is there? And some of my reasons are downright noble, though I say so myself," he looked over at me with a mischievous grin, which faded as he added, "and some, of course, are not quite so noble."

The traffic moved then, and he moved with it, onto the roundabout where he was stopped by a red traffic-light.

"One of the noble reasons is, I think, genuine niceness. Genuine kindness. There's a fellow human-being in trouble, and I'm in a position to help, so I will. But of course, along with that comes that delicious feeling that comes with helping someone else selflessly – feeling so good about myself, about the kind of person I am. So how selfless is it really?"

"Does it matter," I asked, "if someone else is genuinely benefiting?"

He shrugged. "But that's the question, isn't it? Where does noble stop and selfish begin?"

"But does it matter?" I persisted.

"No . . . no, I suppose not." He paused then and overtook a lorry. When he pulled back into the inside lane he didn't continue.

But I was fascinated to find out his motivations. "What else, Connor?"

"Hmm? Oh, yes. Another reason – I suppose is that that, deep down, it's nice to play the part of the archetypical knight in shining armour. What man doesn't have a fantasy of rescuing a beautiful woman? It's nice to feel heroic once in a while." He glanced over at me and grinned. "But there's more to it than that. My heart turned over when you turned up at my door, bedraggled and woebegone . . . and then when you nearly fainted when you heard Ray wasn't there. I'd have to have been made of stone not to want to help out there."

He stopped then, and I asked, "And what about the less than noble reasons?"

He kept his eyes resolutely facing straight ahead as he said, "Ah, yes. The ignoble reasons. There's only one really, and I'm not that proud of it. But I'd rather be honest and tell you." He gave a big sigh, and I felt a tinge of trepidation. What ignoble reason could he possible have?

"I know I told you that I had written off the money Ray owes me. And I had, at a certain level. But it's one of my things, Tory. I absolutely *hate* being treated injustly. I treat others fairly, and it just gets to me when people rip me off. Like Ray did. It's not about the money he owes me – God knows it would be handy, but it's not the point. No, it's the fact that he ripped me off and, so far, has got away with it. I probably would never have done anything about it if you hadn't turned up. It wasn't important enough on its own. But it certainly helped me decide to help you. I now have the justification to go after him and sort out my own issue with him. I know," he turned briefly and grinned at me. "Doesn't show me in a good light at all, does it? But it's the truth." He changed the subject then, onto something lighter. "Remember Murtagh commented on your name, made a joke about you being called after the British Tory party? I got the impression you'd heard that one before."

"Only about a million times," I said dryly. "Sometimes if I can be bothered I make a joke about my mother being in Labour and changing her mind."

He grimaced theatrically. "That's *dreadful*!" he groaned.

"I know," I admitted, laughing, "it *is* awful, isn't it? But honestly, if someone's stupid enough to think I'm named after the Tory party, do they not deserve that?"

"Fair point," he conceded gracefully. "So, how *did* you get your name?"

"My parents spent their honeymoon on Tory Island – you know, off the coast of Donegal – and I was conceived there at that time."

"That's romantic," he said.

There was silence for a few moments as we drove. And then I said softly, "Not really."

He said, in the most *extremely* neutral tones possible, "Oh."

There was silence for a little while longer, apart from the hum of the car and the murmur of other traffic. And I thought about it. I didn't talk about it much, hadn't really explained it before. I had started to tell Ray after some long time together. But he hadn't really wanted to hear it. He was a great believer in living in the moment, in not dwelling on the past, in not conceding that your childhood had any impact on the way you were as an adult.

I took a deep breath and said, "Thing is, I think my mother called me Tory in order to remind her that her marriage had, once, been happy. If only for a week or so."

His eyes remained resolutely on the road ahead as he said, so quietly I nearly wondered if I was imagining it, "Hmm." Acknowledging what I was saying, and that I had said it. Showing willingness to listen further if I chose, but not probing.

"My father had always been a very devout man, she said. It was one of the things that attracted her to him. She's got great faith herself. And it seemed to indicate steadiness, security. But after they married he began drinking a lot. Or maybe he had always been a heavy drinker, it's just that she hadn't realised until after they were married. Whichever – you know the way drink doesn't make you do anything or be anything that you're not already. But it exaggerates . . . so that you become nearly a caricature of what you were."

"Yes, I know that."

"So," I took a deep breath, "he is an incredible combination: a religious nut and an alcoholic." I laughed a little. "He uses his religion to justify his drinking. 'Sure doesn't the Good Lord condone drink? Didn't he change water into wine?' he says, long and often. 'And didn't he drink wine himself, even at the Last Supper?' And he's very hard to live with. He's very controlling, needs to have his way over every little detail, literally. What time meals will be on the table, the television programmes we'll watch, the suitable topics of conversation, appropriate reading matter allowed into the house.

"And he's totally inconsistent in his moods. It all depends on his drinking. And so the whole house revolves around those moods, his temper, his expectations. Growing up it was always the glance between my mother and me, the secret code indicating his current mood, the better to know what to do or say. Or what not to do or say.

"It made it very lonely," I continued, my thoughts back in that bleak, unpredictable childhood. "Even though I started off being popular at school, I couldn't bring friends home. And therefore I hesitated to go to their houses, when I couldn't return the hospitality, and so those friendships withered. I think they thought I was stuck-up, because, of course, I couldn't tell them why I wasn't inviting them home. I felt like I was living this big secret, this awful lie, so I could never be close to people, in case they'd guess that the laughter and the chat and the details of summer picnics were all fantasies.

"And he had no time for me. I wasn't a boy, and Mam didn't conceive again. I always seemed to do the wrong thing, say the wrong thing. He never hit me," I clarified urgently, "never. But the lash of his tongue was worse than any beating, and apart from that he never seemed to notice me.

"Once, though," I said wonderingly, "just once, and

he was sober at the time, he reached out his hand to me, and he ran his hand the length of my hair, and he told me, 'Tory, you have beautiful hair,' and that was the only nice thing he ever said to me, the only time I ever remember him even touching me."

I stopped and Connor asked quietly, again in a way in which I could ignore it if I chose, "What about your mother?"

"Oh, my mother," I sighed. "She's lovely, my mam. But she's so under his thumb. Slowly, year after year – second after second, perhaps – he's worn her down. She's learned that the only way to a peaceful house is to pander to him always. Do you know," I burst out, "she's never even seen Lucy!"

"What!" he burst out, that fact penetrating even his studied neutrality.

"It's true," I said, and my throat was suddenly hurting. "He hadn't known I was living with Ray – that sort of information was always on a need-to-know basis with him, and it was amazing how little we felt he needed to know. And she never told him I was pregnant. But once he asked why I hadn't been to visit them for ages and she was going to make some excuse, she told me, but she hesitated too long and he knew something was up, and he got it out of her. And when he heard I was pregnant out of wedlock, as he put it, he was quite upset. At least," I sobbed a little laugh, "that's what Mam said. I'd say that was keep-the-peace speak for the fact he went ballistic. She did admit that words like 'whore,' and 'Jezebel' were to be heard.

"Anyway, he said then that no woman of such loose morals – oh yes, that was one of the phrases used too – was setting foot in his house and I wasn't to come there again. Mam told him when Lucy was born, hoping he'd soften when there was an actual baby, but he didn't. Just told her that if she thought I was going to be bringing a . . . a . . . fatherless b-b-bastard," I managed to get the word out, "into his house, she could think again.

"And for ages after that she was going to come up to Dublin for a weekend to meet Lucy. Each week there were plans made, and each week they were cancelled for one reason or another. Until I stopped inviting her because I knew I was putting her in an awful position. She simply couldn't please both of us. And . . . well, she has to live with him. Better that there be peace there."

Connor made a sound then, a sound that's not a word but more of an exhalation of breath, which was expressing disbelief and all-too-much belief and pity and empathy all at once.

"Would she not leave him?" he asked.

"I've asked myself that a million times," I said. "I even said it to her once. Ages ago, before I was pregnant, when I could still visit and put up with him for her sake. And I'll never forget her face. She looked so incredibly sad, so trapped but yet so resigned. And she reminded me that they were of a different generation to me, that she lives in a small rural area. That she mightn't seem to me to have much, but what she did have – a community, a standing, friends of a sort – that she would lose all that if she left.

"And she asked me where she would go, at her time of life, with no skills as such. And when I pointed out that there was a grand farm of land there, and that there were laws which would give her a fair share, she pointed out that my father would gladly ruin himself with never-ending court cases before she saw one sod of clay of one field. That he would consider himself totally justified in doing so because by his lights she would be breaking her sacred marriage vows. Which she would, she told me. She believed in them too. She had to believe in them, she said, because if she didn't, it would make a mockery of the twenty-five years of her life she had lived by those vows.

"But she was happy enough, she told me. She said I wasn't to worry about her. She had, as she said, her place in the community, her volunteer committees. And above all, she had me, and that was worth it all.

"It was probably meant to make me feel better, Connor, saying that last. But oh God, the burden of me, *me*, being compensation enough to have had your whole life wasted. I don't feel she's had a fair deal at all. And I feel constrained, somehow, to have the happiest, most successful life possible, in order to make it somehow more worthwhile for her, you know, that my life *was* worth that much, that it *was* worth her lack of one."

I paused then, and there was silence in the car. But it was a warm silence, an embracing restful silence. The monotony of the drive, the fields and trees and industrial estates flowing backwards past us, our seating positions which meant we had the privacy of not looking into each other's eyes, all conspired to make me feel comfortable sharing all these confidences.

And there was, I suppose, a sense of declaring myself to him. Letting him know a little about me. To see behind the façade. I've done a lot of reading about how adult children of alcoholics turn out, and they all seem to have a big problem with trust issues. And I thought that if Connor was going to be my friend, whatever form that friendship might take, he would have to know all this, and accept it – my past, my background, my baggage – well, I'd rather know now than later. And so I continued:

"I couldn't wait to leave home, and I suppose I did so before I was really ready. I don't know how mature I was, really, having been treated like the littlest of children all my life, not let make any decisions. Well, that's not true. I *do* know how mature I was. And the truth is that, although I didn't realise it then, I wasn't in the slightest bit mature. I didn't have a clue really. And then when I met Ray I thought he was great. The exact opposite of my father! No religion, not dependent on drink or drugs – at least, when I first met him, he wasn't into drugs – and he was so totally laid back he'd never try to control you. Except," and I gave a mirthless laugh, "that in a bizarre way, he *was* so incredibly like my father. Although it took me a good while to figure that out, to realise why I was experiencing a lot of the same emotions all the time. Emotions like fear and stress and anxiety and a desire to please at all costs."

I stopped talking and after some moments Connor asked, "And in what way was he like your father?"

"He also *was* a religious nut, and he also *was* addicted. Although, in his case, his religion and his addiction were the same, and they were his music. And we all had to worship at the shrine of his music, and that included not disturbing him early in the morning, when he'd been up late playing. And you know, when Lucy was a baby, and I was still at home, I joined a Mother-and-Baby group in the local community hall, and it was great. And I started to make friends there. But . . . when it started moving into friendship, into informal visits between mothers, I had to ease off. I couldn't have women and noisy babies and toddlers in my house in the mornings, because God forbid they would waken Ray. And that was exactly like my home situation, when I couldn't bring anybody home, had to back away from proffered friendship."

I laughed, a little bit uncertainly, and pushed a wisp of hair which had escaped from the plait back behind my ear. And I continued, "And by being so laid-back he was totally controlling, in a funny way," I tried to explain: "Because he would never organise anything, he was controlling a situation in which I had to organise everything, from making sure bills were paid, to doctor's appointments, to – oh," I said impatiently, "everything! And because he was too laid-back to worry about housework he was controlling me into a situation in which I either had to live in a mess or do all the housework. And because he was too laid-back to worry about contraception, he was controlling it so that contraception was my responsibility, and, of course, when it didn't work, that was my fault too. I could go on," I finished flatly.

"I get the point," he said gently.

"And now he's controlling me again," I said bitterly. "The very fact that I'm sitting here in this car with you, going to Waterford on a Thursday afternoon – none of this would be happening if he hadn't taken Lucy from me. Oh, God, Lucy!" I burst out anguished.

Connor raised a hand from the steering wheel to place it gently on mine and to give a soft squeeze.

"Did you get to find the name of the pub Ray's band is playing in?" he asked then, clearly intending to bring my attention back to the present, to practical matters, to drag my mind away from the awfulness of my home situation.

"I did! And the address."

"Great. And I've managed to book us into a B&B in the town for tonight. So . . . we'll go to the gig, hang around at the back so Ray doesn't see us. We'll follow him back to wherever he's living, confront him, get Lucy, bring her back to the B&B, stay there tonight and come home tomorrow."

"Sounds like a plan!" I said happily, enjoying hugely the images his words were conjuring in my mind.

After that there didn't seem a whole lot to say, and we drove in silence. But it was still a comfortable silence. And I spent my time thinking, as I had been for the past days, about the Ray and Lucy situation. "If he's gigging," I mused anxiously, "what does he do with Lucy when he's out in the evenings? God, I hope he gets someone to mind her. Someone kind."

"I'm sure he does," soothed Connor.

I gave him a sharp look, knowing fine well that there was no way Connor could know that, but grateful that he had tried.

"I still don't get it, though," I said. "I mean, I've been thinking about this over and over. Why on earth would Ray even *want* Lucy? He had absolutely no interest in her all her life. I don't think he ever even held her when he was living with us – or only once or twice, begrudgingly anyway. Why the sudden change of heart? Could it really have to do with him facing his mortality, like he said? It just doesn't sound right. It really doesn't."

Connor shrugged helplessly. "I don't know either," he said. "He certainly never mentioned her to me, nor spoke of children in general."

And then it hit me, deep in the solar plexus, and I clutched myself in my stomach and bent over as I gasped, "Oh Connor, Connor! What if he's taken her for some adoption ring? What if he's sold her to a childless couple? Somewhere abroad, you can't do that here. Oh, dear God!" And then it got worse, the worst it could possibly be as another, truly awful thought hit me, "Jesus, Connor, pull over. Pull over quick!"

And he picked up on the urgency in my voice and, glancing quickly in the rear-view mirror and indicating, he pulled over onto the hard shoulder and stopped the car. I managed to unclip my seat-belt and open the car door, but I didn't have time to get out, didn't even have time to take the seat-belt off me before I was retching violently, vomiting and vomiting without end, onto the tarmac. Even after my stomach was empty I was retching and retching, hurting but still gagging every time I tried to stop. I felt his hand on the back of my neck, being there for me without intruding.

Eventually my stomach stopped heaving and I sat back up, shaking and shuddering, the horror of what had just occurred to me riding over me like a tidal wave, buffeting me – terrifying me with its enormity.

Connor reached over me to the glove compartment, opened it and took out a box of tissues. "Here," he said, handing me one.

I nodded my thanks at him and wiped my mouth.

And then he handed me a bottle of mineral water. I nodded my thanks even as I was unscrewing the top. I took a mouthful, swilled it around my foetid mouth and then spat it out.

But I still had to face what I had been thinking of. I gave a long shudder and I gasped it out, "Connor, what if it's not an adoption thing? What if he's sold her to a paedophile ring?"

And as I said it my stomach heaved again, and I leaned once more out of the open car door, retching uselessly, and even as I was doing that I could hear his sharp intake of breath, his shocked, whispered, "Oh, God, no!"

When I sat up again I saw that he was sitting with

his head in his hands. He must have sensed, or heard, my movement, because he looked up at me then.

"Tory," he said, and his voice was sombre, "do you really think he would do such a thing?"

"I would have said no," I told him. "I mean, you knew Ray. He was a waste of space, but he was harmless. But it's out of character for him to take her at all, so I obviously don't know him as well as I thought I did. And you know, Connor," I whispered, "you hear about paedophile porn all the time – they must get the children from somewhere. To make the porn, I mean. I've never really thought much about the details of it, about where those poor children come from. And Lucy is so beautiful, she really is. People used to stop me in the street to admire her. She's so pretty. I already told you that."

"Yes, you did," he said, and it shocked me, how shaken he looked. Dear God, if only he had laughed off my suggestion, pooh-poohed it – then I could have thought I was over-reacting. But as he was taking it seriously, it obviously was a real possibility, a valid concern. Dear God, preserve her.

He took a long shuddering breath, and he said, "This changes everything, Tory. This really does. Obviously if he has done this, has . . ." he took another breath and then forced the word out, "has . . . sold her, then we *must* tell the gardai. We certainly don't have the resources to track her once she's out of Ray's hands. And the threat of her coming to harm is not relevant any more, if he did this." He gave a hollow laugh, "If he did this, then she could hardly be in any more danger than she already is. We're just outside Carlow," he told me. "We can find out where the garda station is there, and go and report this."

"But if he hasn't done anything like that with her, then what? Then the original situation applies, that we can't involve the gardai, because he's threatening to hurt her if the gardai get involved."

"Tory," said Connor softly, "you have a huge decision to make. You have to decide whether Ray took Lucy to keep himself and if so we won't contact the gardai. We'll keep going as we have been. Or, if he could have taken her to, oh God, I can't believe I'm saying this, but to sell her on either for adoption or . . . or the other thing. In which case we have to tell the gardai, get their help. You know that."

I nodded.

"So which is it?" he asked inexorably. "If we're going to tell the gardai, the sooner we do it the better – the trail will be cold enough already after this time."

"I know," I said miserably. "Oh God," and I put my own head in my hands, as we sat there in the car on the side of the road outside Carlow. "I have to decide, right now, exactly what Ray has done, because what I – we – do, depends totally on that. Keep searching ourselves, if I conclude that he *has* kept her. Or, as you said, go to the guards if he hasn't. What do you think, Connor? You knew him too."

But he was shaking his head, sadly, kindly, but surely. "No, Tory, I'm sorry, but I can't help you there. I don't know him well enough to comment. And even if I did – God knows, the price of getting this wrong is so high that I couldn't possibly help you make this decision."

I had known it really. It was down to me.

And I thought about Ray, thought hard about him. I'd lived with him for two years, I felt I knew him well. And now everything – everything! – depended on how well I knew him. How accurately I could predict his motives, his actions.

And it kept hitting me like a drum: he was not a bad man, not a cruel man. "He's not evil," I said. "He wouldn't go out of his way to help you, but he would never deliberately hurt anybody. I don't think he would do that, Connor. I don't think he would sell his daughter. It would be so out of character."

"He has threatened to harm her if you get the gardai involved," Connor pointed out, his expression wishing he didn't have to, but that he felt it was important.

"I know. And that's out of character too. As is taking her. I know, I know. But, Connor, as you said, I have to make this decision, and the price for getting it wrong is my daughter's life. And I have to say that I don't believe, I cannot believe, that Ray would sell his daughter like that. And yes, I know I'm betting my daughter's life on that, and yes, I am that sure." I wished I really *was* that sure. How could I be? But I had to make a decision, one way or the other, and deep down, in my gut, the home of instinct, I had a kind of surety that Ray had not sold her on. It was all I had. It had to be enough.

TRACY CULLETON

"Okay," said Connor, "so we carry on as we have been?"

"Yes."

He turned back in his seat and turned the key to switch on the ignition, and pulled onto the road again, and we continued our journey to Waterford. And both of us knew, and neither of us said, that I could be wrong. That I could have made the wrong decision. And that I wouldn't know either way until we found Ray. And that we had to, now, carry that extra burden with us, of not knowing if we had made the right decision. Or rather, if *I* had made the right decision.

"He wouldn't do it," I said again. "He just wouldn't. We'll find Lucy tonight after all, and then it will all be okay." And I know I was trying to convince us both. Connor briefly took his eye off the road and gave me a sympathetic glance.

Another hour and a half brought us onto the approach road to Waterford city, just before you cross the river Suir into the city proper. Connor handed me a piece of paper with, it turned out, directions written on it. "Can you direct me from here?" Between us we soon found the B&B – a big modern two-storey house – and parked the car in its carpark.

"Come on," said Connor, getting out of the car. "We'll take in our bags and Lucy's stuff, and leave them in the rooms."

We went in and registered, and the landlady directed us to two adjacent rooms on the first floor. I went into mine and had a look around. It was fine – immaculately clean, a bit floral for my taste, but really, what did that matter? I was only staying there one night, not hiring their interior designer.

Soon Connor was knocking on my door, and when I answered it, was asking, "Do you want to go and get something to eat?"

"I'd love to." I grabbed my bag and joined him on the landing, and we left the house and walked the short distance into Waterford, passing a park on the way.

"Oh look," I said, pointing at the park, "a playground! Maybe we could bring Lucy there tomorrow!" I had pushed all the dark possibilities aside. Lucy was here in this city and in a few short hours would be in my arms.

"We could," he said, and I could hear the grin in his voice. But I didn't see it. I wasn't looking at him – I was staring hungrily at the playground, imagining Lucy in one of those swings as I gently pushed. Or maybe coming down the slide, slowly, with my arms holding tight onto her.

He took my hand, and squeezed it gently, and I realised that he had noticed what else I was doing – my eyes were searching that playground on the chance, the tiny chance, that Ray and Lucy might be there. Hard though it was to imagine Ray in a children's playground. But if he was indeed interested in being a father, then it was barely possible that he might visit a playground as fathers all over the world do with their children.

And as we walked on, further into the city centre, my eyes were swivelling non-stop, looking at everyone we passed, in case I would find Lucy that way. Could I really be so lucky as to find her that easily – to just spot her in the street? No, was the answer as it turned out. I wasn't to be that lucky.

We found a pub which was serving food, got our meal and sat down. And before I sat my eyes moved over the rest of the clientele. No Lucy. And I sat facing the door so that I could watch who was coming in, just in case – just in case – it was Ray and Lucy.

We began to eat but then he said, "Oh hang on, wait till I show you." And he took out his wallet, opened it and took out a business card which he handed to me.

I took it and read it aloud: "'Shane Murray, Band Manager.' With, I note, an address on Merrion Square, no less! He must be doing well, the same Shane Murray."

"Oh, he is," Connor assured me, "very well, indeed, for a manager with no bands yet."

"And a mobile phone number," I mused, "which, if memory serves, is very similar to yours."

"Very similar," he agreed. "As in, identical."

"Where did you get the business cards? And why?"

"The 'where' is easy. I have business card template software, and proper business-card paper to print them on. The 'why' is . . . I don't know, Tory . . . I have to admit I got a fright when Murtagh Levi was able to identify me, and know my address. So I printed these out the other day, so I'd have something to hand out which didn't identify me."

"Good idea," I told him. But then I realised something. "But Connor, we're not going to need business cards.

We're not going to need to represent ourselves to people. We're going to find Ray tonight, follow him home and get Lucy."

"I know. I know," he said. "But I printed these out before we heard where Ray was, and I put them in my wallet and forgot about them until now."

"But you won't need them?" I persisted. "Seeing as we *are* going to find Lucy tonight?" I was looking for reassurance. "Sorry, sorry," I added then, caressing my forehead with my hand, "you don't know any better than I do."

I changed the subject then, determined to bring back the light mood of a few minutes ago. It had been so nice, so relaxed, and I needed a break from the worry and the grief and the uncertainty and the constant fear gnawing away at the pit of my belly.

So I asked him, in a silly pseudo-Germanic-psychiatrist's voice, "Tell me about your childhood."

"What do you mean?"

"Well, I've told you all my secrets in the car coming down here. What are yours?"

He grinned. "I don't have any secrets. Whiter than white, that's me!"

"Connor!" I said, mock-frustrated. "I mean your life, your past. I don't really know anything about you – and it's time for *me* to get to know *you* better, because you probably know more about me than any sane man would ever want to."

He laughed. "Hardly. I'm sure there's lots more to know about you. Like, do you have tickles. And do you suffer from PMS? And do you like having your feet rubbed? And what your idea of the most romantic date would be. And –"

"Connor!" I warned.

He grinned, pleased, it seemed, that he had been able to so effortlessly wind me up, and he held up his hands in good-humoured surrender.

"Okay, okay. I concede. So, what do you want to know about me?"

I shrugged. "Everything."

"Oh God," he groaned, "not *everything*!"

"Yes," I confirmed, "absolutely everything. Parents. Siblings. Previous jobs. Favourite holiday. Greatest dream. Previous relationships. Tea or coffee? Red wine or white? Manchester United or . . . or whoever it is men follow if they don't follow ManU," I finished weakly. Pity, I'd been on a roll.

But Connor was studying me now. "Tell you what – that's a lot of questions, a lot of information. Way too much information to give you all at once – we don't want you to spontaneously combust. So, here's the offer. I'll give you that information a bit at a time, and if you want it that badly, you'll have to stay friends with me long enough to get it. Do we have a deal?"

I raised my glass of water to him, and said, "Deal."

And truth to tell, it didn't seem to be that arduous a deal. I could cope bravely, I decided.

And he raised his glass in return to touch mine, and smiled, and we clinked glasses.

"A little on account," I suggested.

"Okay," he said dubiously, "try me and we'll see."

"Parents?" I asked.

"Two," he confirmed.

"Connor!"

"Okay," he said laughing, "right. My mother's called Joyce, and my father's Dan. She stayed at home with us, and he's a builder. He has his own company."

"Do you get on with them?"

"I do. Mum particularly. But they're both great. We have a real laugh together."

"Siblings?"

"One sister, Jenna. She's married to Ben, and they have one baby and another on the way. She's great too."

"Sounds idyllic," I said enviously.

"It's not bad, I have to admit. But it's far from idyllic. Dad and I have our moments. And Jenna and I really only get on well now that we're adults, but we used to fight dreadfully when we were growing up together. And even now, we don't have that much in common, seeing as she's married with family responsibilities, and I'm young, free and single. So far."

"What about previous relationships," I asked then, going back to my list.

"Ah yes. That." His face darkened, and he took a deep pull of his pint. "I had one serious relationship for the past seven years, until about six months ago. So serious, in fact, that we were living together, engaged."

"What happened?" I asked, fascinated, horrified.

"I gave up my job," he said bitterly, lifting his glass again and finishing it in one go. I found myself watching, fascinated, the way his neck muscles moved as he did so.

"How could you giving up your job mean the end of a seven-year relationship?" I asked, confused. Maybe I had misheard.

"It meant the end of the good times, financially. Temporarily, I hoped, and in return for – hopefully – even better financial times later. And you know, it wasn't as if we were destitute or anything. It's just that we had to cut back on the luxuries for a while. But it turns out that she liked the lifestyle we were living, and didn't want to give it up for any length of time." His tone was still bitter. "I thought she loved me for me, not for what I could provide. But obviously not. So she went off and found another high earner. A steadier one, obviously, one who wasn't going to start chasing dreams or anything silly like that. Another one of those?" he said abruptly, and indicated my empty glass.

"It's only water, but I'd actually love a glass of Guinness, please."

He went off to get it, stomping his way towards the bar. I'd obviously touched a nerve there. But still, I needed to know. Or at least – I conceded to myself – I wanted to know. And now I did: he wasn't that long out of a previous long-term relationship. I shouldn't have been surprised, though. It would have been a bit strange – not to mention a matter of concern – if a man in his mid-thirties hadn't had at least one serious relationship in his past. He came back with the drinks a few minutes later, and even as I took mine and nodded my thanks, my eyes were frantically searching throughout the pub, just in case Ray and Lucy had come in while I was engrossed in chatting with Connor. No. No, they hadn't.

"So," said Connor, taking a long drink, "what do we do now?"

"Let's find the pub that Ray's playing in tonight. So we know where it is."

"Okay."

"Do you think, Connor, that when we do find the pub, we could ask the barman there if he knows Ray, if he knows where he lives? We might be able to find them this afternoon, find Lucy that much sooner."

He shook his head. "I understand your impatience, Tory – these last few hours must be torture. But if you think about it, it's exactly the wrong thing to do. Anybody who knows Ray is automatically going to take his side against strangers asking for him. And it would be too high a risk to have the barman say that he doesn't know Ray, and then to ring him the minute we've left. Those couple of hours would be all he'd need to get away. And we'd be back to square one then."

I nodded morosely. "Worse than square one, because we would have no leads. Okay, we hang on then."

So we spent the afternoon exploring Waterford, doing touristy stuff. But it felt – to me anyway – as if we were just going through the motions. The light banter and chatting of lunch-time was gone, put away, as if by mutual agreement, to await a more appropriate time. And always, always, every step I took, my eyes were swivelling, trying to take in every side at once, searching always for the littlest glimpse of Lucy's dark head. In vain. There were dark-haired two-year-olds a-plenty. But none was my precious Lucy.

About eight o'clock we had something to eat, and then eventually, at long last, it was time to go to the pub where Ray was playing that night.

There was a growling level of nausea low in my stomach as we walked towards the venue. I didn't know if it was excitement or dread. Both probably. Excitement at the prospects of getting Lucy back. But dread at any unpleasantness I – we – would have to encounter before getting her. Ray had gone to a lot of trouble to get her; he was hardly going to hand her over easily. And also, I had to admit it, dread in case this was another dead end. I kept reminding myself that the information was good – Murtagh's friend had given the name of the band playing at this particular pub, and they *were* playing at this pub. I had to believe, had to decide to believe, that it hadn't been a sick joke.

"Connor?" I said.

"Yes?"

"You don't think this is all a sick joke on the part of Murtagh, do you? You know, I took it as proof that the very band he mentioned was in *Hot Press*, playing here. But, and I don't really want to think it, didn't let myself think it before now, what was to stop Murtagh just reading *Hot Press* himself, picking any band in any city, and just sending us off on a wild-goose chase?"

"I've thought of that too. And, Tory, I don't think

that's the case. What possible advantage would there be to Murtagh in doing this? The pleasure of wasting our time? I don't think he would do that. He's a pragmatist. People in his line of work have to be. Yes, he sent us wrong on Tuesday night, at first, but that was to try to steer us away from him. There was good reason, then. But there's no good reason to send us erroneously to Waterford. And you know, people like Murtagh have plenty of enemies, comes with the job. They don't, I imagine, go around making more enemies for the sake of it. So, I can't be sure – we'll soon know, won't we – but I'd say the information is good."

And I followed his reasoning, and agreed with it, and felt marginally better, longing for the moment when I would have Lucy safely back in my arms.

Chapter 13

Very soon we reached the pub, paid our cover charge and went into the murky gloom. We found a seat at the back, where we couldn't be seen.

Connor whispered, "I'll be back in a second," and I saw him go over to the bar. This was going to be tricky, I realised – the bar was at right angles to the stage, in full view of it. And we couldn't risk Ray seeing either me *or* Connor. After a few minutes Connor returned with two drinks.

"Sorry to be a cheap date," he said, putting them down on the table, "but don't actually finish these. They're just for show – I don't want to go to the bar again this evening. It's too near the stage for comfort."

"I was just thinking the same thing," I agreed.

So we sat and waited and after some time the band came on, and started setting up. I eagerly scanned the stage for Ray. But a moment later I was turning in despair to Connor, to find that he was already looking at me.

"He's not there," I whispered. He couldn't have possibly heard me over the noise of the band doing the one-two-three-testing and the loud chatter of our fellow audience-members, but it was pretty clear what I had said. I felt hollow, kicked. It was one disappointment too many, one barrier on the road to Lucy too many. I felt near tears; tears of fear and grief, yes, but also tears of sheer, bloody, overwhelming *frustration!* Why did it have to be so hard? Why couldn't I have my little girl back?

And I was weary, weary of the fear and the grief and the wondering and the searching and the lack of normal life and missing my darling girl, and part of me – a huge part of me – wanted to be a little girl myself, a little girl who could depend on others to sort stuff out, a little girl who could curl up into a little ball and make it all go away.

Connor leaned forward and, clumsily across the table, folded me into his sturdy arms and held me tight and I leaned my head against his chest and breathed heavily, searching for control. And I realised, what I had always known really, that it didn't matter what I wanted, that curling into a little ball and giving up were just not possible. I would just keep going, keep searching. For as long as it took to find her. As macho military types were wont to say in the testosterone-laden films: failure was not an option.

"We'll stay anyway," I whispered to him. "We'll talk to the band-members. They're our only link."

He nodded his agreement and sat back in his own chair. We sat nursing our drinks, not speaking to each other, just waiting, as the band started playing.

Connor reached out a hand then, and covered mine where it rested on the table. He squeezed it once briefly, in solidarity, before removing it, but I could still feel its residual warmth on the back of my own hand. I smiled my thanks at him, and I don't know if he got it, but my message was, 'Thank you so much for helping me out, thank you for being my friend, thank you for being here with me during all this. It's almost impossible to keep going, but it would be *truly* impossible without you.'

A couple of hours passed as we just sat there, waiting. Eventually the band finished playing, to great applause. Had they been good? I had no idea, no interest.

"Come on," I said to Connor, and without even waiting to see if he was following, I made my way to the stage. "Hi! Hi!" I called, trying to get the attention of any of them. There were lots of groupies around, also trying to get the lads' attention. But none of them had as pressing a need as I did, and that made me audacious. In fact I hopped right up onto the stage.

"Hey," said the lead singer, looking around at me.

"Listen," I said urgently, "where's Ray Rafter? I thought he was playing with you."

"He was, but he's not any more. He left the band."

Okay, I decided, so *now* I'm going to curl up and cry and scream and just let go. But no, a tantrum was a luxury I couldn't afford. I asked, "Where is he now, so? I need to contact him."

Some of my desperation must have communicated itself, and he misinterpreted the reason for it. He looked me up and down with derision. "Knocked you up, has he? Don't you know, you stupid bitch, that it's up to you to mind you. And there's no way I'm telling you where he is. Fine mate I'd be, grassing up a pal."

Infuriated, I put my face close to his, and even as I was recoiling slightly from his pungent breath I was hissing, "I am *not* pregnant! I just need to speak to Ray Rafter!"

"Oh my dear," came Connor's voice, speaking in indulgent, amused, not to mention patronising, tones, "do you not remember what I was telling you about playing it cool?"

I swivelled towards him, ready to go through him for a short-cut. What *was* he on about? But he stared at me steadily, and his eyes seemed to signal something I couldn't read. But I simmered back down, deciding that *he* obviously knew what he was doing even if I didn't, so I'd best let him get on with it.

The lead-singer had also swivelled (we probably looked, from Connor's perspective, like a pair of co-ordinated puppets), and was now also looking down onto the floor, to where Connor was standing.

Connor introduced himself. "Shane Murray," he said and he took out his wallet from which he removed one of the business cards he had shown me earlier. He proffered it to the lead singer who took it and read it. It was comical to see his expression change as he read it: it began being truculent and hostile, from which it segued gracefully to interested before careening swiftly on to become positively ingratiating.

Connor was speaking again: "I've been dealing with various venues, you know, the Point, the RDS," he said airily, and I nearly laughed at the avid expressions on the faces of the band members at the mention of such prestigious venues, "and they've promised me they'll give me a few gigs if I can get a good band together. And I heard about your band, and came down to check it out. And I have to say, lads, you were great."

Well, they were hovering around him now like teenagers around a boy-band, short only of offering to have his babies. Although, give it time.

"What's your name, son," Connor asked the lead singer, avuncularily (if that's a word), and I have to say I thought the 'son' was a bit rich given that Connor was probably only ten or so years older than him. But it did give Connor the right air of gravitas, I suppose. Of avuncularity (again, that's possibly not a word).

"Jimmy Dunne, sir." Not the sharpest knife in the drawer, obviously, not finding it at all suspicious that Connor would have heard of the band but not known the name of its lead singer.

"And I'm John Carr . . ." put in one of the other band members and Jimmy Dunne hastily introduced the others.

"I, and my assistant here," Connor nodded gracefully at me, and I, going along with it, nodded equally gracefully back at them all, "have driven all the way from Dublin to hear you, and as I said, you were great."

But then he looked regretful. "The only thing is, we had heard Ray Rafter was playing with you."

"Ray?" said one of them reflectively, "Well, he was all right but he recently left the band. Er, artistic differences."

"Where did he go?"

They shrugged in unison, not terribly interested. It seemed that they would much prefer to return to the fascinating topic of potential gigs at The Point.

"He didn't say," said one after a few moments. "Thing is, those artistic differences we mentioned? It meant we didn't exactly part on the best of terms. And we didn't ask where he was off to. We were just glad to see the back of him."

"Oh, that's a pity," said Connor, looking very downcast, and I knew he did feel downcast at that news (although not for the reason the lads thought), but still, it was positively euphoric compared to how I now felt. "I really wanted him as part of the package. If we don't have him it could be, well – I'm sorry lads – but that's probably a deal-breaker." He surveyed their woebegone faces then. "But if there's any way you could find out his contact details, let me have them, then we might be able to manage something."

"We know another guitarist, a really good one," put in one desperately. "We've signed him up to replace Ray. He was going to be here tonight only he couldn't make it."

Connor shook his head regretfully. "No can do, I'm afraid. Ray or nothing. Do you think that the, er, artistic differences could be overcome for the sake of a recording contract?"

"Oh yes," they said eagerly, almost falling over themselves in their urgency to reassure us.

"It's such a pity then, that you don't know where he is."

"I guess we could try to find him," said one dubiously.

Connor shrugged. "Well, if you do that would be great. I'd officially audition you all together. But don't worry if you don't. I mean, I liked your sound as I heard it this evening, and I've heard that Rafter's very good . . . but, no offence, you'll understand. There's a lot of good bands out there. So if you don't find Ray, no harm done."

They exchanged glances of increasing dismay. No harm done to him, maybe, but *lots* of harm done to their ambitions.

"I mean," said the dubious one, now no longer dubious, "I'm *sure* we could find him. Find out where he is, I mean. And contact you then."

"Sure, sure," said Connor casually, looking exactly like one who's pretty much lost interest. "Well, look, you've got my card. Ring me if you get any news. We're staying in Waterford tonight and heading back to Dublin tomorrow. But, as you can see my mobile number's on that, so you should be able to reach me."

"We'll ring you," promised one fervently. I looked sharply at him, wondering for one heart-stopping moment if he knew more than they had been letting on. But no, it was clear by his nervous expression that they were just doing their best to bluff, to promise they could contact Ray and then try and do so.

"Yeah, that'd be great," said Connor, and then, to me. "You ready to go?"

I nodded, and with a last "Look forward to hearing from you," to the band we turned and (to the sound of their exuberant whispers to each other) walked out of the pub.

Chapter 14

It was a beautifully clear night, mild, with just the tiniest, refreshing, whisper of breeze coming off the river. A night for lovers to stroll hand-in-hand along the riverside as, indeed, many were doing. Not a night to have your hopes of finding your daughter crushed yet again.

"Shit," said Connor fervently.

"Shit," I said, even more vehemently.

"That's what I meant," he said.

We started walking disconsolately up the quay back in the direction of the B&B.

"Now what," I asked. "Will we head home? Back to Dublin, I mean. There's nothing for us in Waterford."

He gave a short laugh. "Tory, it's nearly two o'clock in the morning. And I don't know about you, but I'm exhausted! Aren't you tired? It's been a long day."

"You're right. Okay, we'll stay the night here."

"And," he went on, "I think those lads have a great incentive to find Ray for us, so I'm hoping we'll get a call tomorrow morning. And you never know, he may well be still in Waterford – after all it's the last place he was seen, apart from Dublin, so it's not totally a bizarre idea."

"Fair point," I said dully as I trod alongside him.

"We'll rest now, regroup in the morning when we're not so tired."

"Okay."

He chuckled a little ruefully to himself. "I do feel a bit bad, though, getting the hopes of those boys up. I hadn't realised I was such a good liar. And I don't really want to think of their faces when they realise they've been had, that I'm no more use to them in their quest for stardom than . . . than," he cast around him for inspiration, and then, obviously taking it from the night-sky, "than the man in the moon."

"Hmm?" I looked at him as if he were speaking a foreign language. "I have to admit, I have absolutely no sense of guilt about what we've done." I gave a short laugh in my own turn. "This is how this has already changed me. Before I *would* have had some sort of conscience about lying to those lads, getting their hopes up. Now, compared with the enormity of getting Lucy back, it seems like absolutely nothing. Maybe the end does justify the means after all. And then," I went on, thinking aloud, "so how can I take the high moral ground against Ray? He probably thinks the same, that the end of having Lucy justifies the means of taking her from Carol's place like he did. What's the difference?"

We had reached the end of the path just then and Connor reached out a hand and grasped my elbow in time to stop me unthinkingly walking onto the road under an oncoming car. Once it had whizzed past, the driver ignorant of the fact that he had nearly had a paste of me under his wheels, we crossed the road.

"Thanks for that. I wasn't watching."

"No," he agreed, "you had other stuff on your mind, really."

"Still do. I thought we'd have Lucy by now, that I'd be carrying her in my arms. Though we'd have got a taxi. I was imagining that, you know, how she's heavy now, too heavy to carry all the way back to the B&B. And it wouldn't have done for you to carry her, no disrespect, but – "

"I know," he said softly, "a stranger to her, when she's been through enough."

"Yes. So I had it all arranged in my mind how we would get a taxi." I gave a bitter laugh. "I didn't tell you, but I looked up the phone book before we went out, and I've a couple of local taxi numbers programmed into my phone. Ha." I laughed without humour, at my own folly.

We walked a pace or two in silence, turning up the side-street towards the B&B, and then he said, "To get back to your question – what's the difference between you and Ray? Everything, I would have thought. You told a little lie, he stole a child. Very different."

"Okay," I conceded. "But still, all this is turning me into somebody I don't recognise, someone I never thought I'd be. Someone I'm not sure I like."

"What do you not like?" he asked neutrally.

"Being able to lie like that, and not even care. That was never me. Wishing the tortures of the world on Ray. I think I'm getting hard from it all."

"Maybe. I don't know you well enough to say. But could you look at it the other way around? Another word for 'hard' might be 'strong', after all."

That resonated with me. I said thoughtfully, "Mmm," and we continued walking, Connor giving me space to think, until I said, "I think you're right, you know. I was always too eager to please people, too scared of upsetting them. I know, I know, you don't have to be a psychologist to know that that came from my childhood. But remember I was telling you how Ray was so like my father?"

"I do."

"Well, I'm only realising it now, but I was contributing to that pattern too. With Ray, I was playing the part of my mother: docile, desperate to please. I let him away with his behaviour, I facilitated it. The only thing I ever stood up to him on was Lucy. He wanted me to have an abortion. And, dear God, I shudder when I think of it, but I seriously considered it. Not because I wanted to, but because *he* wanted me to. And having stood up to him about that, I spent the rest of the pregnancy trying to stop it affecting him. But that's over!" I held my chin a little higher. "I'm going to be strong from now on, stand up for myself, for myself and my daughter. And if people don't like it they can bloody well lump it!"

"Good for you! You're already being strong, the way you're searching for Lucy."

"Yes, I am, amn't I?" I agreed, pleased to think of myself like that. It was so refreshing after years – literally all my life – deferring, trying to please.

And then I thought of strength and how I had it and could ask for what I wanted. And how I didn't really have strength, how I was weary and exhausted from the abortive search for Lucy, but that I could get strength from Connor, soak it up from his seemingly inexhaustible supply. And I thought of the loneliness I felt always, even before Lucy had gone, and the piercing loneliness now that I didn't even have her. And I thought of Connor's strong arms and how they had felt around me, and the sound of his heart against my ear and the masculine scent of him.

At least, looking back now I think that's what I was thinking. At the time the thoughts were swirling around my head but they were unfocussed, unidentifiable, un-nameable. But they caused me to do this: they caused me to place an arresting hand on Connor's arm as we walked. He stopped and turned towards me, an expression of mild questioning on his strong face. And I reached up my hands and clasped them at the back of his head and drew his mouth down to me, and placed my mouth on his and kissed him. He stood alertly rigid for a moment, not responding. I persisted, softly moving my mouth against his. And then he reached his hands behind me – I could feel them upon my waist – and he drew me towards him, against him, until we were standing body-to-body, length-to-length.

And I surrendered myself to the sensations – the feel

of his hard chest against me, his strong thigh muscles pressing against mine, in between mine, the feel of his hands on my waist, the softness of his short spiky-soft hair under my hands and above all, the feel of his face against mine, slightly rough so late at night, but warm and soft and wonderful, and the feel of his tongue as it penetrated me, explored my mouth, and the taste of him as I explored back. I heard his ragged breathing and heard – or felt, I wasn't sure which – the fast beating of his heart, and I rejoiced in it all. And I could feel him hard against me then, and I felt my legs weaken and I had to concentrate to remain standing. I hadn't realised that I had missed this, had refused to think about it. But now that his hands, his mouth, his body were all showing me in their own way how much they desired me, and now that my own hands and mouth and body were answering joyfully, I realised how much I had, indeed, missed it. But it couldn't have been with just anybody, just because. No, it had to be with Connor, and it had to be in this moment and at this precise location, on a street somewhere in the city of Waterford as we kissed exuberantly, not caring who saw us, like teenagers rather than responsible, respectable adults.

And eventually he pulled gently away from me and I felt bereft and empty and abandoned. He was breathing hard, and so was I, and his eyes were hooded.

"Tory," he whispered hoarsely, but I couldn't tell what he meant by that, or what he was thinking, and then he took my hand and we walked in silence the remaining distance to the B&B. And even as my blood still raced around my body as we walked together, even as my body was still humming joyfully, I was wondering what he was thinking, and I was even wondering what I, myself, thought of it all. And then I put thoughts away and just walked with him through the dark night, conscious of the feel of his hand in mine and the sound of his breathing.

We let ourselves into the B&B and crept upstairs, mindful of the late hour and other sleepers. We hovered outside the doors of our respective rooms and I wondered, *now what?* And I didn't even know what *I* wanted to happen, so how could I know what I hoped he would do? I had calmed somewhat after that kiss, although my pulse was still strong and I knew I was still aroused, physically ready to receive him. But was I emotionally ready? I only knew him three days, after all. But such an intensive three days was like three years with anybody else.

But still . . . it didn't seem wise to be beginning a new relationship under the circumstances.

Connor, tall and saturnine, was standing there looking at me, his dark-haired head tilted very slightly, the faintest ghost of a smile on his generous mouth. I got the impression that he was totally aware of my thinking process, and that he was giving me the space to come to whichever conclusion I would.

And I thought, for possibly the hundredth time – which wasn't bad in only three days – what a *good* man he was. No doubt he would have loved to have ended this evening together with me. And equally no doubt, he must have had a fair idea that it wouldn't have taken much on his part to seduce me into his bed – I was already half-seduced already after all. He could, with all honour, have taken that half-step towards me, kissed me again, slow, seductive, until I was asking him, *begging him,* to take me. But no, he was standing there, waiting for me to decide. And as the seconds – long, long, seconds – passed, he must have realised what decision I would come to even if I didn't yet know it myself, because he bent towards me, and he dropped the softest, gentlest kiss on my forehead, and he said, "Goodnight, Tory. Sleep well. We'll talk in the morning." And he gave me the most heart-stopping smile, and turned to his own door, opened it, and went into his room, closing the door behind him even as I was still standing there.

I mentally shrugged, and went into my own room. How gentlemanly of him, I thought again, as I brushed my teeth and undressed. Unless – a thought hit me – unless he just didn't want to, just didn't fancy me.

I got into bed and pulled the covers over me. Maybe that was it, I thought miserably. Maybe kissing me once was enough, maybe he didn't want to repeat the experience. He *had* seemed to enjoy it, though. Mind you, some men enjoy kissing rubber dolls, don't they? It was hardly a major achievement, really, to have turned a man on.

I lay there and tried to sleep, but I was feeling more and more miserable. It didn't take me long to decide that yes, indeed, Connor had decided against seducing me because he didn't want to.

And then, of course, thoughts of Lucy began swirling around in my head. My direct thoughts, I mean. On some level my thoughts (no matter what else I was doing, thinking or speaking), were constantly with her since Monday. But now, as I lay there, I could think of her, didn't have to put those thoughts of her to the back of my mind in order to concentrate on the search for her.

I couldn't *bear* the realisation that, yet again, a lead had proven to be a dead end. Yet again my arms were empty without her, and I was left wondering where she was and what she was doing and how she was being looked after.

And I was so unutterably alone.

Before long I was sobbing into my pillow, and I tried to keep it quiet, I really did. But perhaps my sobs were louder than I realised and/or maybe the walls were thin, but after some time I heard a gentle knocking on my door.

"Tory, are you okay? Tory? Will you let me in? Open the door."

I stumbled out of bed and opened the door, and as soon as he stepped inside I flung myself into his arms. "Oh Connor," I sobbed, and let myself go to that wonderful relief of truly abandoned weeping.

And Connor wrapped his arms around me and held me tight and patted my back, and whispered things like, "Hush now, it's okay. It's all going to work out. You'll see. It's okay."

And eventually my sobs had decreased to the intermittent hiccupping stage and I pulled away a little. "Thanks," I said using my hand to wipe away a – no doubt appealing – mixture of tears and snot from my face. "Sorry about that."

"It's okay," he said gently. "What are friends for? Come here a second, though," and he steered me into the bathroom, turning on the light on the way. I blinked in the sudden brightness, and somehow he had a warm damp facecloth in his hand and gently, like a father with a baby, (or at least, how I have always dreamed a father would be with a baby) he wiped my face clean. And I have to say, I did feel a *lot* better for that.

"Thanks," I said again.

"Come on into the bedroom," he said, and led me there. It was dark, with only the light spilling out from the bathroom to illuminate the room, and the atmosphere was seductive, intimate. But Connor didn't seem to notice. He sat me down on the bed, and then lifted my legs up into the bed. He tenderly pulled the covers over me, and tucked me in, again just like a father with a child.

"Don't go," I said urgently.

"I won't," he promised, "not until you fall asleep."

He sat himself down on the end of the bed, pulling his knees up under his chin and leaning against the old-fashioned end-board. For the first time I really looked at him and I noticed that he was wearing a T-shirt and sweat-pants. His feet were bare. And in the light from the bathroom I could see his arms as they hugged his knees, beautifully curved with defined muscles. And his thighs were taut against the material, and it all looked so appealing. So enticing.

I nodded at his T-shirt and sweat-pants, desperate to lighten the atmosphere a little, and asked, "Designer pyjamas?"

"Oh, of course," he said wryly, "nothing but the best for this body!" He smiled self-deprecatingly then: "Fact is, I don't have a single pair of pyjamas to my name, usually sleep in a T-shirt if it's cold and nothing if it's warm enough. But you know, I wanted to be more modestly dressed than that in case the sight of me made you lose control and you jumped upon my maidenly body!" And even though I had earlier jumped upon his (okay, not terribly maidenly) body, he said it in such a tone, with such an expression, that it was clear he meant it as a joke and not as a dig.

I made myself smile, said lightly, "Thanks! There would have been a huge danger of that, so it's just as well."

He waved an arm airily. "Don't mention it." He shivered then, asked, "Do you mind?" and without waiting for an answer he slipped off the bed, lifted his end of the duvet and got back onto the bed, tucking the duvet around his bare feet. It was a strangely intimate moment, this man under the same duvet as I – albeit how little of him was under it – on the same bed – albeit at the other end of the bed – in the half-light in the middle of the night.

"You were crying," he observed softly. "The whole situation, I suppose?"

"That, of course," I said. And I remembered my earlier vow, that I was now a strong woman, able to ask for what I wanted, and I said, "As well, I suppose my feelings were hurt. That you didn't . . . that you didn't want to . . . you know, come in here with me."

He laughed then. "Tory! Are you suggesting that the reason I went alone to my bed was because I didn't want you? Are you mad! Of course, I wanted you. Didn't my kiss tell you that?"

"I thought kissing me put you off. I know I'm really thin. Ray always used to comment on it. More meat on a spare-rib bone, he used to say. Built for speed rather than comfort, he used to say."

"Ray was an arsehole," said Connor definitively, and I looked at him, surprised a little at the expletive. "No, he was," he continued, "and no doubt he still is. And he is a fool, and you are a bigger fool, Tory, if you take his opinion on *anything* as having any validity."

And his words spread over me and I felt this tension leave my body as I realised the truth of what he said. I might be talking about moving on from my childhood conditioning, but it was going to take some practice.

"But I *am* skinny," I said.

"Elegantly slender," corrected Connor. "And Tory, I do understand how difficult it is to feel good about yourself when you've been given feel-bad messages all your life. But self-esteem is an inside job, I know this. Remember I told you how I was so skinny and nerdy as a child, always being beaten up? And that our family life, although good, wasn't idyllic, that Dad and I had our moments?"

"Yes."

"What I didn't tell you was that my father was a brilliant rugby player in his day. He was capped several times for Ireland, he was that good. And he's a big burly fella, well-used to hard physical labour. I take after Mum's side; they're all fairly willowy. And I have to tell you that he was *not* impressed by this skinny, un-sporty, bookish son. To be fair to him he never said anything, never made it clear. But children know anyway. And I found that difficult growing up. I felt terribly misjudged. I mean, on one level I had lots going for me: I was clever, doing well in school, I was kind, I had a good sense of humour, people liked me. I was very ambitious, always trying to beat my last score, my last achievement. But he wasn't appreciating those things about me, he was instead judging me for not being the things *he* wanted me to be: robust, competitive against others rather than just against my own previous best, sporty. And as I said, I felt terribly misjudged.

"But one thing I learned, Tory, is that people take you on your own evaluation, mostly. They have neither the time nor the interest to figure anybody else out that much, so they're quite happy to take an opinion that's handed to them. And if you go around thinking bad things about yourself, that's what people will pick up on, even subconsciously. I can't remember the exact numbers but the famous 'they' now think that something less than ten per cent of our communication is verbal, the rest is non-verbal. You are saying so much when you don't know it. So, start practising thinking well of yourself. Don't judge yourself any more on your father's evaluation, or Ray's. They are both unhappy men, as far as I can gather, in their own way, and you don't need to take their stuff on board.

"Sorry," he finished, "I'll get off the soapbox now. But nothing annoys me more than someone with everything going for her, going around poor-mouthing all over the place. If you could just see yourself through my eyes, even for just one minute, you'd never need convincing of this again. Sorry, *now* I'll get off the soapbox."

I put his comments away in a corner of my mind to think about later, but I was still concerned about my original issue, and I returned to it: "So that wasn't why you went to your own room?"

"No, Tory," said Connor dryly, "it was not. For the record I wanted nothing more than to whisk you off your feet and into my bed and under the length of my body. It was one of the most difficult things I've ever done, walking away from you."

"Why did you, then?"

"It's not the time, is it? Not when you're so confused and upset about Lucy," he asked gently. "I shouldn't even have kissed you in the street, but I couldn't help myself when you turned to me. It had been on my mind a lot of the day and when you kissed me . . . well, I knew I shouldn't, but . . ." He shook his head.

"And what about now? How do you feel now?"

"Now I think this conversation is heading in a

dangerous direction, so I'm going to ask you to lie down, and I'll stay here while you go to sleep."

Okay, I thought. I lay down as he requested. It was wonderful to lie there, so aware of him at the other end of the bed, hearing his steady breathing, the occasional sound of him moving a little. I felt so safe, so comforted. But still . . . I would feel even *more* safe and comforted if he were lying beside me, holding me.

"Won't you lie beside me?" I asked. "Hold me? Just till I fall asleep."

"Best not," he said, amusement in his voice. "That really *would* be playing with fire."

As I lay there I thought it might be quite fun playing with fire. Hot. Sizzling. Searing. Passionate.

"Goodnight, Tory, we'll resume the chase in the morning. Sleep well."

"Sleep well," I echoed.

There was silence for a moment or two and then he cleared his throat. Nervously, it seemed. "Tory? You still awake?"

"Yes."

"Do you remember earlier today you asked me why I was helping you in the search for Lucy and I told you all my reasons?"

"Yes."

"They were all true, I'm not saying they weren't. But I have to confess that there's one more reason. The minute I met you I was attracted to you, and I . . . well, it certainly wasn't an argument *against* helping you, the fact that I would get to spend time with you. I wasn't going to say anything until you had got Lucy back, I felt you had enough on your mind. But now . . . now that you've kissed me, I'm wondering whether that means you might like me as well. In the same way." He hadn't literally phrased that last as a question, but there was a question in his tone all the same.

"I see," I said, my head spinning. So, it was out in the open now. Our mutual attraction. I had been protesting, both to myself and to Carol, that I wasn't interested in him, and sure, at some level I wasn't. At that level I was concentrating on finding Lucy, and, as he had said, I wasn't in a position to be getting involved.

But at another level, I knew that I *was* interested in him. Hey, what's not to be interested in: tall, attractive, intriguing, kind, takes responsibility seriously, bit of get-up-and-go about him – look at the way he was self-employed.

But what on earth did he see in me?

"What do you see in me?" I asked.

He gave a short laugh into the darkness. "Are you joking? Everything! You're gorgeous-looking. You must know that. And your courage and your determination, which you've been demonstrating so totally these past few days. Even when it's getting hard, you're keeping going. And sure, there's lot of other stuff I'd like to get to know about you, like your sense of humour – which obviously hasn't been much in evidence recently. But there'll be time for all that later. That's what I'm saying." His voice trailed off then, in nervousness perhaps.

"It's hard to think beyond getting Lucy back, Connor. But . . . I am very, very grateful for all your help. And, yes, the tiny little part of me which isn't consumed by fear and longing for my daughter, is able to think that, yes, after all this is over, we might be able to . . ." It was my own turn to let my voice trail off.

"That's good," he said and we both lapsed again into silence. I wondered what he was thinking.

As I lay there I moved my feet a little, and they came into contact with his. His feet were warm now, and I lay there appreciating the touch of them in the silence and the semi-dark. I couldn't help it, I moved my feet a little and rubbed them softly against his, and it was suddenly the most erotic experience I had ever had. Excitement surged through me at the surreptitiousness of it all, touching his feet under the covers while ostensibly we were being chaste. I moved them again, and this time I was rewarded by his sharp intake of breath, and that too sent a current of electricity though every atom of my body.

I listened to his breathing and wondered was he listening to mine.

And I thought about him: a generous man, who had taken a stranger into his house and let her sleep on his couch while he tried to find the required information. A man who had given pretty much the last two days to help that stranger. A kind, sensitive, honourable man who would turn down a sexual encounter rather than take advantage of a woman's confused longings. And, let's not forget, a tall, lean-but-muscular, decidedly handsome man, with sharp angular features under nearly-black cropped hair, deep blue eyes whose eyebrows frequently rose quirkily in amusement and humour, a generous broad mouth (unfair that that looked so good on him and so, well, big, on me) which smiled often and readily, in laughter and compassion.

And ... and ... a man who was making no secret of his interest in me.

I thought about it. After my upbringing, whose prime message was that you can't depend on anybody, it took a huge leap to trust Ray. And, of course, I knew now that trying to depend on Ray was slightly less a good idea than building a house on a sandbank, but at the time ... Anyway, point being, it had all conspired to make me very wary, very distrustful.

But Connor . . . he seemed, if I could trust my judgement on anything, to be a totally genuine person. And I thought, he would never let me down. He wasn't promising marriage or lifelong commitment at this point, but that was okay too. I just knew that if I were to get involved with him, he would be honest and treat me honourably.

And I lay there and thought of that long torso, those long legs, the flat of his stomach and how his muscles had contracted under my touch, the sensation of his neck, his earlobe under my mouth, the feel of his hair brushing my face as I had kissed his neck. And I felt so empty, so unfinished, and thought about being filled, of being completed.

It had been so long since I'd been with a man, and our earlier kiss had just served to waken dormant desires. And more, I was intrigued by him. It certainly wasn't love, or anything like it, so soon. But there was . . . something. It was as if I was standing at the beginning of a journey, and I could see the road going off into the distance, growing narrower and narrower with perspective, going up and down little hillocks, winding its way around lakes and using bridges to cross streams, until it reached an end point. And that end point was Love. So . . . I – and Connor as well? – were on this road which led directly to Love. But it was a long road, and either of us could turn off at any point. But still, *that* was the road we were on, distinct from a million other possible roads.

So there was something which might well be leading to Love, and there was honest sexual desire between us.

But for me, that night in Waterford, there was more, it was more complicated than that. There was loneliness, and fear, and the desire to banish those if only for a little while. Also there was the desire to feel a pair of arms around me, embracing me so that I could take comfort from that. Also it was the desire – the need – to have a connection with another human being, to know that on that dark, silent, scared night, that I did, in fact, exist as more than a sorrowing mother whose life seemed to be dedicated to searching for Lucy.

And overwhelmingly, it was the desire to stop thinking for a while, to stop the crazy thoughts constantly running through my head as I worried about Lucy and feared for her and grieved for her, to stop thinking and for some period of time just feel. Just be sensate.

I'm not proud of what I did next, I truly am not. Connor had been so good to me, and deserved at the least honesty and respect from me. But what he got was a demanding need. Was I using him? I possibly was.

I slipped out from my bed. Connor raised his head and smiled enquiringly at me. I said, "I'm just – " and I nodded towards the bathroom. I did go into the bathroom, and closed the door. After an appropriate time I flushed the unused toilet and came out again, turning off the light, and walked back in the darkness towards the bed. Connor, expecting this, didn't look up, didn't react. But instead of returning to bed I walked behind him where he sat at the end of the bed, and it was only in that last second that he registered what I had done.

"Hm?" he asked. What are you doing? he meant.

I didn't answer in words, I didn't need to. He got the message because by then I had begun nuzzling the side of his neck, just under his ear. It was soft, and warm, and I could feel his ear against my cheek, and his short hair rasping a little against my temple.

"Tory," he said, and his hand came up, and maybe he had been going to still me, ease me away, but his hand found the side of my face and it rested there, holding me softly.

"Tory," he began, but his voice caught in his throat. He began again, "Tory, don't."

"Why not?" I muttered, as I moved my lips, brushing

237

them against his skin, until they found his earlobe, and I nuzzled there, and sucked it and nipped it slightly, gently.

"Tory, don't," he said again, but in my own defence I must say that he didn't exactly sound like he meant it.

And I ignored his statement and he didn't pursue it, and we were like that for a moment or two, as I nuzzled and sucked and licked and kissed his earlobe. His breath was loud in the dark night.

I licked inside his ear then, and he sucked in his breath, breathed my name, whether in entreaty or admonition I couldn't tell, and I put my arms around him. And maybe I had moved too far, too quickly, because he pulled away from me then leaving me bereft, and then I knew by the sound of his movements that he had turned around towards me, was kneeling on the bed. I couldn't see his face, his expression, in the darkness, didn't know what he was thinking.

"Tory," he said softly, "Tory, sweetheart, don't. It's not right."

"It felt right," I whispered, thinking: he called me sweetheart!

A heartfelt sigh: "God, it did," and his voice sounded like velvet in the darkness. "But, you know, you're in a very vulnerable place right now, and I don't want to take advantage of that. Part of trying to be a decent human being, but also, Tory, I want us to have every chance when we do get to begin a relationship. I don't want you to hate me, resent me, because I took advantage of you at this awful time. And, when we come together, I want to know that you really want to, that it's not just a function of confusion and bewilderment and what's going on."

"You're not taking advantage of me. *I* was coming onto *you*. And I do really want to." I noted vaguely that he had correctly identified the confusion and bewilderment component of what I was doing, but I brushed that aside, I wasn't giving that thought house room.

"I had noticed," he said, and his tone was dry and there was a hint of amusement in there too, "and I'm going to ask you to stop now, because, truly, I am *this close*," and although I couldn't see his fingers to see how close that was, I gathered that it wasn't very far at all, "to forgetting all my good intentions, all sense of being honourable, and . . . well, forgetting everything except my desire for you."

"I want you, Connor," I said. "It's okay, it truly is. Please, please come to me. Don't make me beg."

"It's not about making you beg!" he said impatiently. "You must know that. I'm just trying, with a huge amount of difficulty, to try to hang onto a little common sense here."

I got up onto the bed, also kneeling, and I moved towards him, and I leaned forward and I whispered, "Please, Connor," and I picked up his unresisting hand and placed it on my breast. And I heard him saying thickly, "Oh God," as his thumb moved roughly, deliciously, across my nipple, and then, "Tory, are you sure? Really?" But now it sounded as if he were begging me for reassurance, that if I had said, no I'm not sure, let's forget it, he wouldn't have been able for that.

But that wasn't going to happen. I whispered, "I'm sure," and I reached for his mouth with mine. My mouth landed in the darkness on his chin and I plotted my way from there up to his lips, and when I reached there his mouth was open and he kissed me softly.

And then, quicker than I could register it, his hand had whipped up and seized the back of my neck, and he was pulling me down, down, on top of him, twisting his legs so he was lying flat on his back and I was flat against him, feeling the long lean deliciousness of his body, and his mouth was open and covering mine, and his tongue was invading and he was kissing, kissing, and I was kissing back, matching thrust with thrust, bite with bite.

And wildly, mindlessly, clothes were removed somehow, and there was no conversation, no words, no thoughts even. This was pure sensation, our bodies communing in an age-old elemental manner as we kissed and nibbled and bit and sucked and caressed and enfolded and embraced and at the end, came together, bodies joining in a wild, sucking-in-of-breath sensation. And he stopped then, not moving, just enjoying – I supposed, and I surely was – the very fact that he was filling me, completing me. But that didn't last long, couldn't last long, and I grew impatient and I moved against him, whimpering my need. And he groaned low in his throat, spoke for the first time, said into my neck, "Stop moving. I want to savour, oh fuck it –" and he matched me then thrust for thrust and groan for groan and the feeling grew and grew and we moved faster and faster and I truly did not know any more where my body ended and his began, and I never felt so wanton but neither did I ever feel so safe, and even though I had a dim impression that it was hurting, so hard after so long, that sensation was far, far away, and I was still hurling myself against him in my need and desire and passion, and he was meeting me more than halfway, and in the end I reached my orgasm and I clutched the muscles of his back and pulsated around him and he was still then, letting the moment be mine, perhaps enjoying witnessing my release. And when I had finished he moved once, moved twice and then made those little mewing sounds deep in his throat and I felt him pulsate in his turn, and he called on various deities and in the end he collapsed onto me, breathing again into my neck, our bodies slippery with sweat, our hearts thudding in concert, and I moved my hand and caressed the back of his head, his short-but-deceptively-soft hair, and I breathed in the glorious smell of fresh, virile, male sweat.

Eventually he grew heavy on me and I moved a little. Immediately he responded, pulling out of me and lying beside me. But he put his arm around me and gathered me tight to him.

And as we lay there I enjoyed the post-coital glow, the gentle pulsating of my blood in my veins – not quite calmed yet – and the feel of his arms around me. I had this sense of togetherness, of mutual joy, of beginnings and promises and futures together and commitments and partnership. At least, that's the sense *I* was getting. For all I knew he was thinking, "Great shag, how soon can I decently go back to my room?" Or worse, "Mediocre shag, how soon can I leave?"

And even as I was pondering that, he stirred a little beside me, and I heard him say sleepily, "Ah yes, but will you respect me in the morning?"

And I said, replete and satisfied, and reassured, "Connor, after showing this much prowess as a lover, I respect you right now!"

And he laughed a little, and then he dropped a kiss on my forehead and said, "Thank you, my beautiful."

And a few moments later I heard the deep steady breathing of his sleep, and happy in the moment I relaxed my head onto his chest and slept myself.

Chapter 15

I slept straight through until I woke with a start. I glanced at the watch on my wrist: my God, it was gone ten o'clock. What had me sleeping in so late? And then the memories of the previous evening swept over me, and a realisation of a pleasant ache between my legs came to me, and I remembered.

Oh God, Connor and I . . .

And I groaned and I covered my eyes with my hand. Connor and I . . . last night . . . Shame swept over me as I recalled how I had thrown myself at him . . . I whimpered to myself . . . I was so pathetic, having to beg a man to take me.

And then the guilt hit me, and a furious self-loathing filled me, bubbling up inside my stomach. My Lucy, my daughter, was out there, experiencing God-knows-what, and I was indulging myself in sexual flings.

Was there ever *anybody* so low? So despicable?

And worse, Connor – that decent, kind man – I had used him, used him out of my need to forget for a while. And wham! More guilt about Lucy as I challenged myself: what kind of mother are you, needing to forget, no matter how briefly, that your daughter was missing? And I remembered how Connor had tried to talk me out of it all, and felt sick to my stomach with shame at the realisation that he had more awareness of Lucy's predicament than did her own mother.

Where was he anyway?

I had barely time to register his absence and wonder where he was when I heard him knocking on the door.

"Tory!" he called cheerfully. "Tory, it's time to wake up. Tory," he called more loudly, "are you awake?"

I'll ignore him, I decided desperately. I'll ignore him and after a little while he'll give up, realise it's useless and go back to his room. Indeed, go back to Dublin without me. I can get the train back. Sounds like a plan; I need never see him again. Need never have to look him in the eyes again after what I've done.

And I curled up and pulled the duvet over my head while I waited for him to give up on me. And I was aware, try though I might to deny it to myself, of a hollow feeling in my heart at the thought of never seeing him again. I've ruined it, I thought miserably. It could have been so good. If only I had been patient enough.

And sure enough, a few moments later the knocking stopped and I could hear his footsteps, faint upon the hall carpet, walking away.

And that was truly the lowest, lowest moment. No Lucy, no Connor. Just me left alone with a woman I was bitterly ashamed to be.

But then a second later I heard a ringing sound. What was it? Oh yes, my mobile. I picked it up and looked at it and the little screen confirmed that, yes, it was Connor ringing me.

And I stared at it, and I realised that Connor wasn't going to go gently into that good road back to Dublin. He wasn't, despite mutually occurring hope and fear, going to give up that easily. If I didn't answer the phone the next step would be getting the master-key off the landlady. In fact, he might be doing that right now, worried about me not waking. That would be just too, too, embarrassing, having her turning up at the door. I definitely wouldn't survive that.

So I answered the phone.

"Hi," I said dully.

I don't think he registered my tone. "Hi, sleepy-head," he said exuberantly, "something must have worn you out to have you sleeping so late!" He gave a laugh of innocent delight. "But look, Tory, it's gone ten o'clock. It's time to be getting back to Dublin."

"Right."

"So, will you let me in? I need to say a proper good morning to you."

"No, no," I said hastily, "seeing as it's late. I'll just have a quick shower and get dressed and meet you downstairs."

"Okay," he said slowly, sounding puzzled, a little

hurt. "Fine, why don't you do that? Are you hungry? We've only about fifteen minutes until breakfast is officially over but I could tell her that you're on your way, I'm sure she wouldn't mind."

"No, no, I'm not hungry," I assured him, my throat closing over at the thought of food.

"Fine, see you downstairs then." He rang off.

Slowly I pushed the duvet away from me, and the morning air was cool on my naked body. I climbed out of bed, laboriously as I have seen old women do, and padded my way to the bathroom. As I stood under the shower, its warm water washing – to my regret – Connor's touch away, I wondered what difference it was going to make to the search for Lucy. The fact that we had now slept together, I mean.

Was he going to expect this in future, as part of the package for continuing to help in the search? I needed him, I realised, as I lifted my hands to massage shampoo into my scalp. I needed his ongoing help. In truth, I realised, I didn't think I would have got even this far without him. Both in terms of his practical help, I thought as I lathered my hair – look how he had managed to get information in The Derby Rig – I couldn't have done that alone – and in terms of his emotional support during this totally horrible time.

But – the crux of the matter now – would he expect me to sleep with him again? I didn't think so, I decided. If he did expect that he wasn't the man I thought he was. Look how he had been last night, I reminded myself. I practically had to pin him down before he responded. *He* had been trying his best not to complicate the issue. But thanks to me, the issue was now well and truly complicated.

And I had quite possibly just messed it all up, I acknowledged disconsolately as I rinsed my long hair. I couldn't possibly move into a relationship with him, sleeping together as couples do: in joy and commitment and laughter. Not when I was feeling so guilty about even this one night. But it's never the same with a man once you've slept with him.

Well done, Tory, I told myself sarcastically, stepping out of the shower and drying myself abrasively. You've really messed this one up.

It seemed like way too quickly that I was dry and dressed and had to face him. I picked up my overnight bag and, even more sadly, the bag of Lucy's toys, and headed downstairs, and into the dining-room.

His face lit up when he saw me; he got to his feet and came over.

"Hi! Good morning." And he bent to kiss my mouth, but I turned my head so that his kiss landed clumsily on my cheek.

"What's wrong?" he asked anxiously, his bright expression dimming.

I shrugged.

I wasn't prepared for what he did next. He gripped both my shoulders, hard, holding me with a pressure that was a fraction *this* side of hurting. And he demanded, "Look at me," in tones that were brooking no disobedience. Nervously I raised my eyes to his, looked at him, my muddy eyes to his clear blue furious ones.

"As long as we're together," he hissed, "never, *ever*, do that to me. If you've got a problem, tell me. Don't – just don't! – come to me with a face on you like that and then refuse to tell me what's wrong with you."

I looked at him wordlessly, recognising the truth of what he was saying, but not sure how to formulate the words.

"Now, I've paid already, so we can go – this isn't the place to be discussing anything. We'll go somewhere else. Come on."

And without waiting, sure I would follow, he stalked out of the house and to the car. I followed him, and by the time I got there he was sitting in the driver's seat, but he had left the boot open for me. I put my stuff in the boot and closed it. And I realised something wonderful, something liberating. Connor was furious with me, boiling-mad furious. *And I still felt safe!*

How could that be? I wondered as I got into the car and put on my seat-belt even as Connor was pulling away. I used to live in terror of my father's temper, and I had made sure, in Ray, to pick a man who never lost his. There were never many issues to deal with between Ray and me, I made sure of that. But he never lost his temper over those issues which did pop up. Sure, he might have dealt with issues by ignoring them, by removing himself either emotionally or literally, and that was all equally dysfunctional. But he never lost his temper.

And here I was sitting in a car being driven by a set-mouthed, grim-faced man, whose hands, I saw, were holding the steering wheel tight enough to turn his knuckles white. And yet, *I still felt safe.*

I hadn't come up with any understanding of that contradiction in the two minutes before he pulled the car into the side of the road and switched off the ignition. I looked up and realised that we were outside the park. The park we had passed yesterday, the park whose playground I had envisaged bringing Lucy to this morning.

"Come on. We'll walk and you can tell me then," he said, unbuckling his seat-belt.

"Connor, I can't," I pleaded. "I had imagined bringing Lucy here this morning. Don't throw it all in my face. Don't make me walk in there."

"Sorry," he said, chastened at that, without in any way being diminished in his anger and hurt and whatever else he was feeling. "Sorry. I didn't realise. But we need to talk, and the B&B wasn't the place to do it, neither was it here in the car while I was driving. Hang on."

He reached into the little door-pocket on his side and took out a map which he opened and looked at. After a moment he said, "Okay, there's a beach. Here, look," and I looked where he was pointing. "We'll go there."

He did up his belt again, turned on the ignition, glanced over his shoulder before pulling out onto the road and began driving towards the beach. And in his grim silence I was able to continue thinking, wondering, how I could feel so safe with him even though he was furious?

And I realised, as we drove, that the answer was exactly that: I could feel so safe with him simply because I *did* feel so safe with him. No matter how angry he might be, how furious, he wasn't going to hurt me, he wasn't going to shout obscenities and cruelties which ripped my whole psyche apart, or spit out sneering observations about my awful personality/ body/manner/all of the above. He *was* furious and, I acknowledged, with justification, but his fury was going to be directed at what he felt was unacceptable behaviour, and not at *me*.

And how did I know that? Again, it was because I felt safe. My intuition, or whatever, knew it, and was passing the message on to me by its very lack of anxiety.

Not that any of this should indicate that I was looking forward to the forthcoming conversation. I wasn't, not one bit. But, I kept coming back to the fact: I was safe.

And before long we reached the beach and Connor parked. "Come on," he said, his first words to me since outside the park, and I got out too. We stepped onto the beige sand and began walking towards the sea. The tide was far out and so there was a reasonable distance to walk, and the beach was nearly empty apart from a man walking his dog, and a young woman jogging by the water's edge, her long legs and arms flowing rhythmically, gracefully, as she ran. The sky on this June morning was bright and blue and seemed so high, so incredibly far away, unreachable, and the sand was smooth underfoot, with faint pleasant sound of shells crunching as we stepped on them, and a delicate salt-scented breeze caressed our faces. And as we neared the water's edge there was the gentle, therapeutic sound of the wavelets lapping softly against the shore. That might calm Connor down. I hoped.

"Right," he said resolutely, and his body language was unambiguous with his hands stuck firmly in his jeans pocket, and his gaze stuck firmly on the far distance. "Tell me what's going on. Last night we made love together and it was totally wonderful for me. And you know, I thought it was pretty good for you too . . ." He cast a sideways glance at me, and it occurred to me how we women are always aware of our own vulnerabilities, but never think of men's. Maybe all this time he had been panicking, feeling miserable, because my change of attitude was all down to my having had a dreadful experience with him. And he continued as I didn't answer, "I mean, I know men always think they're better lovers than they are, and that a woman can fake most convincingly. But I thought I knew, and I thought it was good for you."

He stopped then, and cast another glance at me, waiting for my answer, my verdict.

And for one teeny-tiny moment, and to my shame, a part of me really, desperately, wanted to agree with what he had suggested, and tell him that my problem was, indeed, with his sexual prowess. It would stop him asking any more questions. I wouldn't have to share my own doubts, my own vulnerabilities. But at the cost of totally undermining his confidence in himself. *And* taking into account the minor detail that that wouldn't be true. And so the better part of me managed to prevail, and instead I said miserably, "It *was* wonderful, Connor, better than wonderful."

He gave an impatient shrug then, "Well then, why the miserable face this morning, the rejection?"

And my sympathy of a moment ago fled, my sympathy at men's carrying the burden of sexual performance was replaced by huge irritation with the whole gender, as I realised how they thought that sexual performance was the be-all and end-all. If I was sexually satisfied, he was asking, then, ergo, what possible reason could I have for being unhappy? Nuances such as shame, or guilt, or fear . . . if they escaped even the notice of a sensitive – by the standards of his gender anyway – man like Connor, what chance was there for the rest?

"Connor," I said acerbically, "it's not all about sex, you know."

"What's wrong with you then?" he asked. Not unreasonably, I had to begrudgingly admit.

"I feel dreadful," I finally admitted.

"Why?"

"I feel so guilty," I admitted, "carrying on like we did last night when Lucy –" I began, only to be interrupted by him furiously slamming one fist into the opposite palm.

"I knew it!" he yelled. "Didn't I say that to you last night? Well, didn't I?" he demanded when I didn't answer. "Didn't I say that last night wasn't the right time, that there was too much else going on? But you insisted, you said it was okay, didn't you? Well, didn't you?"

I nodded miserably.

"And now," he yelled, making me glad that the beach was almost deserted, "now you've decided that you will feel guilty after all! For God's sake, Tory, cop onto yourself. Of *course* we're in an awful situation. *Of course* it's not the right time to be beginning a romance. But we did begin our romance, our relationship, last night. So now what do you want? To pretend it didn't happen? To push me away? Well?" he demanded, and I shrugged helplessly.

He took a deep, shuddering breath, ran his hand through his short hair, and spoke more calmly, "Look, Tory, there isn't some Cosmic Accountant up there, keeping score of how happy or unhappy you are, and awarding you points towards getting Lucy back the more you deny yourself. What we did last night doesn't mean you won't find her. It doesn't work like that. And even for yourself," his voice was positively gentle now, soothing, seducing me into his point of view, "getting close to me, allowing yourself to begin a relationship – none of that means that you love Lucy any less, does it?" I shook my head and he pressed home his advantage, "Being with me doesn't mean you're any less committed to finding her, does it?"

"No, of course not."

He turned towards me then, paused in his walking,

and took both my hands and swung me so that I had to face him. "So, Tory, the two things are not mutually exclusive. You can be with me *and* find your daughter. It's okay. It really is. Do you understand?" He went on when I didn't answer, "Do you?"

I nodded, less than emphatically. Yes, I did understand, rationally, but there was still a lump of guilt, low in my belly. And he must have picked up on some of that from my expression. He sighed and shrugged. "Think about it, Tory. Think about it. That's all I'm asking."

He released one of my hands, but held the other tight, and it felt warm and safe tucked into his, and he resumed walking. I fell into step beside him.

"I *know* this is an awful time," he repeated, "and it's certainly not the beginning to a relationship I had ever dreamed of. I'm really looking forward to when Lucy's back, for lots of reasons. But one of those reasons – a less important one, for sure, but still valid – is that then I'll be able to court you traditionally. You know, meals out, flowers, picking you up from your place and bringing you out on a proper date. But until then . . . well, this is the situation we're in, so this is the situation we have to work with. And I'm so happy that I've met you," and he squeezed my hand a little, for emphasis, "and I do think, over and over, how ironic it is. If Ray hadn't taken Lucy, you and I would never have met."

"Yes. That thought had occurred to me too," I said, and then illumination hit me, and I realised why I felt so bad about being with him. "Don't you see? *That's*

254

why I feel it's wrong to get together with you. Simply because of that. It's like I'm saying it was okay for Ray to take Lucy, because I got you out of it. And it *wasn't* okay for him to take her, and maybe I feel that if I deny what I feel for you, don't be with you, I'm reasserting that he was wrong to take her. It doesn't make sense, does it?" I realised. "But that's how I feel."

"But being with me doesn't make it okay what he did," he protested.

"I realise that in my head," I said urgently, keen that he would understand, "but I have to come to *know* it here in my heart," and I thumped myself lightly on my chest.

He nodded his head slowly. "I see. I understand, or at least I think I do. So," and he gave a little laugh, aiming – but not succeeding – at being relaxed about it all, "where does that leave us?"

"I don't know. Certainly, once Lucy's back, we can get together, do all those things you said – you know, the dates, the dinners."

I paused and he asked, "And until then?"

"I don't know. Let me try to get my head around it. You're right. In one way there's no point in waiting. It would be great to have at least one good thing in my life, give me strength to keep going. But Connor, it still doesn't feel right. It still feels as if there is this – what did you call it? – Cosmic Accountant up there. It still feels as if I can somehow make bargains – you know, if I deny myself now, please give me Lucy back. And if that's the case . . . Connor, what if I don't?"

"Don't want to *be* with me until Lucy's back?"

I nodded, and he shrugged, before bending to pick up a stone. He flung it into the air and watched as it completed its arc and splashed into the sea. "If you don't feel right being with me, then don't do it," he said then. "I'll be sorry, needless to say, but I'll respect it. I don't want you unless it's right for you. I *did* make that point last night," he said with heavy irony, "and even though my common sense was overtaken by . . . events, it still holds true."

If only I had left it there. He understood – or seemed to – my quandary, and his anger at me had dissipated in that understanding. But there was one more thing I felt I had to clarify, and so I persisted, trying to make myself clear, "But what about looking for Lucy? Even if I don't . . . if we don't . . . will you still –"

He interrupted, releasing my hand to take a half-step away from me, the better to look at me, and his voice was rich in disbelief. "You're asking me if I'll still help you look for her even if you won't sleep with me?" I nodded, and he continued, shock and derision rich in the timbre of his voice, "Which means the corollary, that you're asking me whether I'll refuse to help you *unless* you sleep with me."

"No," I said, "I didn't mean that." Even though that *was* what I had been wondering to myself that morning, and so, yes, possibly, it was what I meant. And he knew it.

"Yes, you did. Oh, yes, you did. That's exactly what

you were saying. Jesus, Tory," and there was disgust in his voice now too, and he was shaking his head in hurt and disbelief, and his blue eyes were narrow slits as they looked me up and down as if unable to believe what was standing in front of them, "is that really what you think of me? God, that is the most . . . the most incredibly insulting thing *anybody* has ever said to me."

"I didn't mean that," I repeated, stricken, and he was looking at me as if I was something he had to scrape off the bottom of his shoe. "When you put it like that – that's not what I meant."

He turned suddenly, decisively, and strode away, back towards the car. I ran after him, calling, shouting, "Connor, wait, please listen! Connor! Don't be like that. I didn't mean that the way it sounded." I caught up with him. "Connor," I pleaded, "please listen to me," and I was crying now.

In response he picked up his pace even more, which meant I had to resort to an ungainly trot to keep up with him. "Connor," I panted, "please stop. Please listen to me. Please talk to me." He marched on without acknowledging me, his eyes, his gaze, resolutely facing forward, his sharp profile closed and grim.

"Connor!" I wailed, and reached out and grabbed hold of his arm. Not breaking stride he shook off my arm – not roughly, but emphatically – and carried on.

I gave up and slowed to a walk, and trailed behind him, the physical distance between us hence growing by the moment, symbolising, echoing the emotional distance between us too. I was crying, and berating myself roundly. *Of course*, he was angry, I acknowledged. It was a truly awful thing to have accused him of. No wonder he was cross, any man would be. Any decent man, that is, which he was proving himself to be more and more, even as I was proving myself less and less worthy of him.

It's just as well, I muttered to myself, that he found out now what I'm like. It'll save time in the future. No point getting close to him and then having it all go wrong at some time in the future.

He had reached the car now, I saw, and was sitting in the driver's seat, waiting for me. I was grateful for that. I could hardly have blamed him if he had just driven off. Mind you, it was going to be an extremely uncomfortable drive back to Dublin. Although perhaps not quite as uncomfortable as walking back to Dublin would be. Or even walking back to Waterford to catch the train.

I slowed my walk, not wanting to have to face him again, but still, eventually, inevitably, I reached the car and opened the passenger door, slipped into the seat, put on my belt. Connor was staring straight ahead, his face set hard, and, I noted, a little tic was jumping on his jaw-line. God but he was *furious* with me, and with good reason. But still, strange though it was, I still knew I was safe. No matter how furious, how angry, he wouldn't use that anger to justify flaying me with his words, desecrating my whole personality, my whole character. He might, however, I acknowledged, have a few choice home-truths for me. *If* he were ever to speak to me again.

He checked in his mirror to make sure the road was clear and then pulled into it, and began driving home.

Chapter 16

Once we were through Waterford city and on the road back to Dublin I took a deep breath prior to speaking to him. But as I did so, glancing nervously at him, I saw his face tighten up even more, which I wouldn't have thought possible, and his hands grow even whiter against the steering wheel which, again, I wouldn't have thought possible. So I released the breath without saying anything.

It was a long silent drive back to Dublin, and as uncomfortable as I had predicted.

We pulled up outside my house and he spoke for the first time. "Here we are," he said, which – to judge by his expression – roughly translated as: 'Here we are at last, thank God. So would you mind getting out of my car as quickly as you can and if I never see you again it will be too soon.'

I had to speak now, if I was going to speak at all.

And I stayed resolutely in the seat. If he wanted me out he was either going to have to manhandle me out, I thought mutinously, or listen to me first.

"Connor," I said tremulously, and my hands were kneading together in my lap, "Connor, I am *so* sorry I can't tell you. I never meant it like that. I really didn't."

His jaw moved and then he spoke in a monotone, "Well then, Tory, maybe you would care to enlighten me as to what exactly you *did* mean, since you've been trying to tell me what you didn't mean."

I thought about it, thought about what I had said, and try as I might there was no other interpretation to put on it. I couldn't think of any nice explanation with which to pacify him.

"I'm sorry," I said at last, knowing how weak it sounded. "It's just that, Connor, I'm not used to dealing with men as decent as you. My dad, my first boyfriend, then Ray – they were all pretty awful to me, and I suppose I'm used to looking for the worst, expecting the worst – "

"Which, of course, ensures that either you'll find it, or will convince yourself that you've found it," he put in bitterly.

"– and I was thinking of what you were doing based on what I'm used to. It's not a reflection on you at all, do you see that?" I pleaded. "It's just, well, like I said, I'm not used to being treated well."

Silence descended then, and I waited for his verdict, his opinion on what I had said.

Eventually it came: "Tory, I take your point. You

weren't judging me by *me* but by them. But Tory, never mind the fact that that's unfair to me, it's also really stupid of you. Yes, you had an unfortunate time with your father, with Ray. But to go through life carrying that experience with you means that you are doomed to repeat it. Don't you see that? Our situation is a classic example: you've met me, and I venture to suggest that I'm a fairly decent man – I'd treat you right. And you're doing your best to mess it up. And I think you very well may have succeeded."

An iciness surrounded me at that last, encasing my heart, and I literally shivered.

"And if you keep that up, you'll consistently push away the nice men, and keep the ones who treat you badly. And prove to yourself, over and over, your belief that men are bastards. Well, good luck to you. I'm not getting caught up in your drama – you take that road alone, lady. Because your father may have treated you dreadfully, and Ray treated you dreadfully, but," and he banged the steering wheel for emphasis, and shouted, *"I am not going to pay the price, take the punishment for what they've done!"* He took a deep breath and added more calmly (although, 'more calmly' is a relative term), "I won't do that." There was silence for a moment and then he added, "You told me how you now realise how you were contributing to the dysfunctional relationship you had with Ray, by playing the docile, facilitating role your mother played with your father. Can you not also see that you're contributing to this as well, in a bigger way? You're implying motives to me that I just don't have, and building whole scenarios based on that, and at the end of this process out pops a conclusion – but it's a conclusion based on your own assumptions and hence on flawed information. And so, it's a flawed conclusion. In computers we have an acronym: GIGO. It stands for Garbage In Garbage Out. If you feed erroneous information into a computer, you'll inevitably get erroneous results. And it's exactly the same with you – you're feeding wrong assumptions into your brain and coming out with wrong conclusions."

I thought about what he had said, and I had to admit it made sense. I *was* making assumptions about his behaviour and motivations based on my prior experience. And yes, that was all I had known to date, so it was understandable that I would do that. But if I wanted to break away from the dysfunctional patterns I had been experiencing so far I was going to have to change my own behaviour, and my own beliefs. I was going to have to experience him as himself, not as a carbon copy of other men.

"You're right," I said humbly then. "That's exactly what I was doing. I hadn't realised it myself. But now that we know that, surely you can understand why I said what I did on the beach. It *wasn't* about you. It wasn't being insulting to *you*. So, please, can you forgive me?"

He shrugged. "Look," he said wearily, "I'll forgive you, if that's what you want. No problem. But for now I think you'd better get out – we both need some space from each other. And I'm tired. It's been a tough few days – for you more than for me, I know that -" he added softly, "and I'm feeling like an emotional football right now, my feelings having been kicked all around the place. I was high as a kite after we got together. It was like a dream come true. And then to be told you regretted it, and *then* to learn what you really thought about me and my motivations." He sighed deeply and shook his head despairingly. "I need to think things through. About you and me, I mean. So you go on in now," he said, surprisingly gently, "and we'll talk tomorrow."

"Okay," I said numbly, and I got out of the car. Connor pressed some magic button and the boot opened, and I retrieved my stuff. I returned to the open passenger door and stuck my head in. "Goodbye," I said, "thanks again for all your help. And my apologies again for accusing you of . . . of that."

He nodded. "And I haven't forgotten about Lucy. No matter what, I'll see that through, I promise. I have to admit I'm all out of ideas right now, about what to do next, but hopefully some rest and space and my head will be buzzing with new ideas. Okay?" And he smiled at me. A forced smile, true, a real making-an-effort smile, true. But at least he *was* making the effort.

"Okay," I said. "Goodbye." And I stepped back, closed the car door, waved at him – I don't know if he saw it – and turned and walked up my path.

Once inside I sadly put Lucy's stuff away, and my own dirty clothes in the wash. Now what? It was only about three o'clock – the rest of that day stretched empty before me, mocking me with Lucy's absence.

Chapter 17

I lifted the phone and rang Carol.

"Hi, how did it go?" she asked urgently. "Did you find them?"

"No. No, we didn't," I said disconsolately. "He *was* in that band, but left about a week ago."

"Oh no! You must be feeling awful."

"I am. And Carol, if you're not doing anything, I would really love some company right now."

"I'll be right over," she promised. "In fact I had been trying to get hold of you. I left a message on the answering machine," and as she said it I noticed the blinking red light.

"Oh, right," I said, "what were you looking for me about?"

"I'll tell you when I see you," she promised.

She was there in no time at all.

I met her at the front door and we moved into each

other's arms and hugged hard, and I felt a little of my pain ease somewhat. When I pulled back a little I realised that there were tears running down my face. "Thanks, Carol, thanks for coming."

"It's okay," she soothed, rubbing my back, whispering to me. "It's all okay. It's all going to be okay."

"Come on into the kitchen," I said, making an effort to regain control of myself.

She sat at the kitchen table while I made a pot of tea, and when I had joined her and poured us a mug each she said gently, "So tell me."

And I did, all about turning up to find out that the band was now Ray-less, and that they didn't know where he was. "They're going to try and find him. At least they said they would," I told her. "Connor managed to convince them that he could get them a big gig."

"Connor?" she enquired. "Would that be the luscious landlord?"

"It would," I said dourly, and she raised a questioning eyebrow at me.

"We had a row," I told her. " I don't think we're still on speaking terms. Still," I said bravely, "it was very good of him to give me the help he has done."

"Pity," said Carol. "You deserved a nice relationship."

I shrugged, and took a sip of my tea, and I could feel the path its warmth traced down through my body, and it was comforting.

"So what now?" she asked diplomatically. "About finding Lucy, I mean?"

I shook my head despairingly. "I don't know. I really

don't know. The leads have just totally dried up. So far, each one has led to the last. But unless those lads we met last night manage to come up with something . . ." my voice trailed off.

"God, it's an awful situation," Carol whispered, half to herself it seemed. But then she said, "Tory," in serious tones.

I looked up at her. "What?" .

She took a deep breath. "Tory, I've been thinking, and I can't believe I'm even going to say this, but – now, Tory, you know I love Lucy every bit as much as you do, right?"

Well, she couldn't possibly love her as much as I did, but I knew she loved her lots – so I nodded in agreement.

Carol went on, "And I'm missing her just as much as you. I'm really hurting here too."

"Oh, God," I said, stricken, ashamed at my own selfishness. I reached out a hand and placed it on her arm. "Carol, I'm so sorry. I never thought."

"No, no," she said, "I'm not saying this to look for sympathy, I honestly am not. I know you must be suffering much more than me – you *are* Lucy's mother, after all. I'm just the childminder. But I *do* love her, and I *am* missing her, and I'm saying all this, not to look for sympathy, really, but more in the hope that you will feel that in some small way I have earned the right to have an opinion about what the best thing to do now might be."

She finished her little speech and looked anxiously at me, waiting for my opinion.

"Of course, you have the right to an opinion!" I said. "Of course, you do. And since I'm totally out of ideas about what to do next, I'd really appreciate yours."

"You mightn't like this," she warned. "I don't like it myself, to be honest. But I've really been thinking about it, and I was trying to put myself in your shoes, as much as I can. And what I was wondering was this," and she took a deep breath.

"What?" I asked nervously.

"I was wondering – what exactly are your rights over Lucy?"

"What do you mean?" I asked, confused. "I'm her mother. I'm her legal guardian. At least," I corrected myself, "I think I am. It turns out I should have organised legal custody, but I didn't. But at the very least I have equal rights with Ray, surely,"

But Carol was shaking her head. "I don't mean legally," she said, "although that's going to be important too. No, I mean morally."

"Morally?" I repeated. "Well, *that* one's easy. I'm her mother, I have every moral right to her. She's my daughter, after all."

"But what does that *mean*?" Carol persisted. "What I'm trying, very clumsily I know, to get at, is to ask what happens when your rights as her mother are in conflict with her own rights."

"I don't understand." My breath was coming faster now, I began to feel besieged. I was beginning to realise that, wherever this conversation was going, I wasn't going to like it. But I persisted: "My rights as a mother aren't in conflict with her rights. I want what's best for her, after all, and that's to be with me."

"Ah, but is it?" asked Carol sadly. "That's my whole point. Given that Ray has threatened her life if you try to get her back, I was asking myself – and oh Tory, but I hated to ask this question, I hate even to be saying it to you – if you have the right to risk her life."

"But Ray only threatened to harm her if the police got involved," I said. "He didn't say anything about hurting her if *I* found them."

"True," Carol said, "and I've been clinging to that myself as I've been thinking about this. But I was wondering – and God knows I hope I'm wrong – if, even so, he would react badly if you found them. Badly enough to . . . to . . ." words clearly failed her then, and she fell into silence, but her anxious despairing expression said it all.

My eyes were darting back and forth now, from her face to other points around the kitchen, like an animal at bay looking for an escape.

"He wouldn't!" I said, and I was distressed to observe a note of pleading in my voice. "He wouldn't hurt her just because I found them. I've done what he said, kept away from the police. He wouldn't . . . he couldn't."

"I don't know Ray, obviously. But in the dark nights when I'm lying awake wondering where Lucy is, how she's doing, I kept asking myself how he would react. And it seems that if he wants her this badly, did all this to get her, he wouldn't just hand her over if – when – you found them."

"No." I had briefly wondered this myself, wondered

how it would go when I did catch up with him, and had put the thought to the back of my head to be dealt with if-and-when it happened. Find him first, that was the important thing. "No, he mightn't just hand her over. I'd have to persuade him, convince him that I would share custody. But there's a world of difference in refusing to hand her over – and I couldn't physically make him –" (but Connor could, I thought, Connor could) "– and hurting her when I found them."

"True. And I hope to God you're right. But it just struck me as a possibility. And, given the gravity of the situation, a possibility you should consider. *Would* he, *could* he do as Charlotte Riordan's father did? Hurt her in order to stop you getting her back? And remember what we already spoke of, how Charlotte's mother wished she *hadn't* risked Charlotte's life. How she wished Charlotte was alive, even with her father, than dead. I can't imagine the guilt and remorse that poor woman must be feeling," she said sombrely, "and, Tory, I couldn't bear for you to go through that."

I shuddered at the thought of poor Charlotte's mother, and the burden under which she must be spending her days.

"It wouldn't apply," I said, and I wished my voice sounded more certain. "Ray wouldn't hurt a fly," I said as I had been saying for days now, it seemed. But then I had to admit to her, as I had done to Connor, "But I don't know. Taking her is so out of character, and the way he manhandled you, that I'm finding it impossible to predict his behaviour at all."

"Exactly," she said, but her expression showed exactly how much this was hurting her too, and I thought of what a miserable morning she must have had, debating with herself what the best thing might be – to share this thought with me or not. And she said urgently, "Do you see what I mean, Tory? He *might* hurt her if you find them. And – oh God! – can you take that risk?"

I shook my head, not so much in answering her question, but in confusion and doubt.

"Think about your options," she suggested softly, kindly, empathetically. "What would happen if you decided not to risk her wellbeing by finding her – no matter how hard that would be . . ." She was visibly distressed at the prospect. "You'd be guaranteeing her safety. What greater gift can a mother give to her child? She's young; she would settle quickly into life with Ray; she would be happy. So it's not for *her* sake that you're trying to get her back, it's for yours. Because *you* want her back, *you* want her with you. But do you have the right to do that, to put her life at risk for your own benefit?"

I tried to argue back, floundering, "But *would* she be happy with Ray? He's never even managed to successfully look after houseplants before. I don't *know* that she's doing well with him."

"No, there is that," she acquiesced, looking very relieved at my finding the flaw in her argument. "I suppose I was thinking that he would definitely be looking after her properly, seeing as he went to so much trouble to get her, but you're right, it doesn't necessarily follow."

"And there's more," I said, pressing my advantage. "It can't *possibly* be in Lucy's interests to leave her with someone who thinks so little of her that he would threaten her life to keep her."

I should have quit while I was ahead. As I said that last statement Carol was looking at me intently, compassionately, and so, so, sadly. And I realised, and I said, "You think I'm the same? You think there's no difference between Ray, who'll *threaten* her life to have her, and me who'll *risk* her life to have her."

Her compassionate silence was answer enough.

"Oh God," I whispered, "what does that make me?"

"A mother who loves her daughter very, very much," she whispered back. "Don't be beating yourself up. But what I'm asking, and what only you can answer, is this: what is the most loving action to take now? Where does love end, and ownership for its own sake begin?"

"It's like the story of Solomon in the Bible," I said, anguished. "It was the true mother who would give up her child for the sake of its safety, the false mother who was happy to risk his life to validate her ownership."

"No, no," insisted Carol, "it's not like that at all," and then, anguished in her turn, "Well, yes, I suppose it is." She finished her tea in a large gulp. "I'm so sorry, Tory. I really, really, did not want to say this to you. You had enough stuff going on. But I felt that I was being guilty of *my* part in risking Lucy's life if I continued to let *you* risk her life without saying anything to you. Do you understand?"

I could only nod, tears streaming unchecked down

my bowed face, dripping unheeded onto my chest. Carol laid a soft hand on my wrist, and we sat like that for some unknown time.

"What do you think I should do?" I asked. "Just forget about her? Let Ray have her?"

"I can't answer that," she said softly. "That is absolutely not my place. How you answer it is entirely up to you. But I know what I hope you do . . ."

"What's that?"

"I hope you don't listen to a word I've said, and go and find her. Because I'm missing her as much as you are, and I want her back too," and she made that unique sound of someone swallowing, pushing back, a sob. "But even as I say that I know that that is *me* being selfish, that is me putting my need to have her over my love for her. And I'm not proud of it, but that's how I feel."

"No," I said listlessly.

"I'm sorry, Tory. I'm so sorry. But it had to be said. It really did. I would have felt so guilty, as though I had her blood on my own hands, if I hadn't said it to you and something did happen to her. Which pray God it won't," she finished fervently.

"I know it had to be said, and thank you for saying it. But Carol, would you mind going now? I think I need to be alone."

"Sure, of course, yes, okay," and in a flurry of hugs and promises and apologies she was gone.

And I was left in the empty house. I went to bed, no matter that it was only just after five o'clock, and I lay there and wept. Not only did I not have Lucy, but I no longer – now that I acknowledged the truth of Carol's words – had the justification to find her. *And* I'd messed up everything with Connor. And as I lay there on that bright summer's evening, with the sound of children's laughter and friends' chatter coming in through the open window, I wondered what was even the point of being alive.

And I'm ashamed to say it but I seriously considered ending it all, right there and then. I wallowed in sadness and depression and self-pity – all with good reason, perhaps – and I was thinking in absolutes. I'll never be happy again. I'll never see Lucy again. I'll never see Connor again. There's no better future for me. This is it, this loneliness and despair for the rest of my life. I'm no use to anybody. Nobody will miss me.

Around and around in my head, like some malevolent mantra these thoughts swirled, as I lay on my back on my bed, with the back of my arm pressed to my eyes.

But slowly, from somewhere, from the depths of my subconscious – there came a tiny germ of a voice which managed to ease itself into the minuscule gaps between my negative thoughts, which whispered softly: *nonsense.*

And I idly, curiously, almost, asked that little voice, what do you mean, nonsense?

And then it spoke a little bit more acerbically, sounding incredibly like Mary Poppins saying 'spit-spot', and it told me that I mustn't give up, either on my life or on Lucy. And it told me that Lucy did need me, that she was missing me, and that there's such a bond between mother and child that it's not a case of passing her on like an unwanted puppy. And it reminded me that even if I *had* totally messed thing up with Connor for now, who was to say how it would end? And even if he never did want to speak to me again, there was a whole future out there waiting for me to go and claim it. And it told me sadly that it hadn't realised I was such a coward and such a wimp. *And basically*, it said, *cop onto yourself. Stop lying there feeling so sorry for yourself – get up and find your daughter.*

Okay, okay, I muttered crossly (but relieved too), and I got up out of my bed. But once I was standing beside the bed I asked it, asked my wise subconscious: what if Carol's right and Ray will hurt – kill, I acknowledged, let's not mess around with euphemisms – will kill Lucy if I found them? Look what Charlotte Riordan's mother said, I reminded it, about wishing she had left Charlotte with her father.

Good point, it acknowledged. *That's a tough one all right.* If one's subconscious can give a sigh, that's exactly what mine did. *But look, we don't know that Charlotte's mother was quoted accurately. And even if she was, she was speaking in the immediate aftermath of Charlotte's death, from the depths of her grief and shock. Who's to say what she's thinking now? She might know now that she did the right thing. And this situation is different – you're not Charlotte's mother, Lucy isn't Charlotte. And Ray is a different man to Charlotte's father. Don't think of them and their situation – think of you – us – and your – our – situation.*

And so I thought about it. I thought hard about it.

What would Lucy want if she could make a choice? She would want to be safe, above all. She would want to be with me, I knew that. But what if those wants were mutually exclusive? Would she choose to risk life to come back to me?

Would she? Would she?

What would life with Ray be like for her? Assuming, of course, that I did concede defeat, let Ray keep her. Was I just being selfish to risk her life to get her back? Was it all about me, and my needs? Was I putting those needs above Lucy's wellbeing?

The core question was: never mind my own feelings, what was the best thing to do for Lucy?

Eventually I answered some of those questions. But to this day I don't know how much of it was justification, finding reasons to justify what I wanted to do anyway, and how much of it was genuinely for Lucy's sake. I don't examine this very much, scared to look deep within, scared to find out that I was only pleasing myself no matter the cost to Lucy.

But the answers I came up with were these: Lucy would want to be with me, above all. Ray was no sort of a father. She would have no quality of life with him. Lucy deserved the best, and I honestly believed this – I told myself – that it was best for her to be with me. I could continue to look for her with a clear conscience. And I would!

I moved then, went and washed my face and had a drink of water. And I was ready – if not enthusiastic – to face the world again.

I rang Carol. "Hi, Carol, it's me. I've got good news for you! No matter what Ray has threatened, I'm going to get Lucy back! Don't know how yet," I admitted, "but I am! And I'll do it without risking her life. Again, I don't know how yet, but I will!"

"That's great!" she said warmly, but there was a little fear in her voice too. "I . . .I can't wait to see her again, Tory. That's great news!"

"I'll keep you up to date," I promised.

I went and made myself a sandwich to eat, and while I was washing up afterwards the phone rang.

"Hi, Tory, it's me. Connor," he added unnecessarily, as if I wouldn't recognise the deep timbre of his voice. His tone was neutral – carefully so, it seemed to me.

"Hi, Connor," I said, a little breathlessly.

"It has just occurred to me, Tory, that I have been very stupid."

"Oh yes?"

"Yes. Do you remember when I asked you had you done a search for the bands Ray had been involved with? And you said you had."

"That's right. I did."

"Where did you search?"

I explained about getting the two magazines and looking for the bands to be listed, and about ringing past venues.

"Is that it?" he asked when I was finished.

"Yes." I was puzzled now. What else could I have done?

He sighed, and gave an ironic chuckle. "That's what I was afraid of. You see, when I asked if you had 'done a search' I meant something very specific – I meant a search on the Internet."

"Oh no!" I gasped. "I didn't do that. I never thought of it."

"There was I, thinking I was being very jargon-free to say it like that – I mean, to say 'do a search,' instead of saying 'google it' like computer-heads do!"

I could hear the smile in his voice and it felt very good to be even that close, via the phone-line, to his smile.

"I assumed you'd know what I meant. But that was a stupid assumption. And it only occurred to me just now that you had said you were fairly computer-illiterate."

"Oh," I said. "And do you think it's worth doing a search now?"

"I surely do," he said emphatically, "and I could end up being very angry with myself over the wasted days if we find something. But still, I hope we do find some information. Can you tell me the names of the bands he was in?"

I went through the names with him and he wrote them down.

"Okay," he said, "I'm going to hang up now because I'll need the phone-line to go online with. I'll check these out and I'll ring you back. Okay?"

"More than okay," I said. "Thank you!"

I hung up and hovered by the phone waiting for him to ring back. About fifteen minutes later he rang back again.

"Partial success," he said. "I did a search on Ray's name first, seemed the obvious thing to do. But I didn't get anything on that, apart from a couple of reviews on gigs he did a long time ago. So I did a search on the band-names. I didn't get anything on three of them, but the other two have a web-site each. *Archery*, and *Whispers and Shouts*. And there's a contact number for each of them. Gotta pen?"

"Yes, yes, I do," I said, my heart in my mouth.

"There's a Derek Flynn in *Archery*. Here's his mobile number." He called out the number as I carefully wrote it down, thinking, *Derek Flynn – oh joy!* "And here's a number for an Anthony Doran," and again, he gave me the number.

"Thank you, thanks so much," I said fervently, "thanks, Connor, that's great. I'll try those now. I'll ring you back, let you know how I've got on."

"Well, actually," he said, sounding most unusually hesitant, "thing is, Tory, I was wondering. Could I come over? To talk, I mean. There's something I want to say to you."

I felt a shaft of fear, low in my belly, but I said, "Sure, come on over."

When I had hung up from him I put the thoughts of what he could possibly want to say to me to the back of my head, and dialled each of the mobile numbers. To my disappointment both of them went straight onto answering service. To my disappointment, but not to my surprise, really. After all it was – I glanced at my watch – ten o'clock on a Friday evening. Both men were probably playing on stage somewhere, and would have their mobile phones switched off. I'd have to wait until the morning to try them again. But still, I consoled myself, at least it was another lead, another step to take.

Before too long I heard a ring on the doorbell and sure enough, it was Connor.

"Come in," I invited him.

"Actually," he said, "do you fancy going for a drink? I could murder a pint right now."

"Sure," I said, "just let me get my jacket." As I ran up the stairs I reflected that whatever he had to say to me couldn't be that bad, if he was willing to say it to me in front of lots of other people. Either that, I acknowledged to myself, or it was so bad that he needed the safety of other people around while he said it. Oh well, I thought as I pulled my long hair out from under my jacket, I'll know soon enough.

"There's two pubs within walking distance," I told him when I rejoined him. "One is very trendy and likely to be very busy, but it is *the* right place to be seen. The other is quieter, tends to get an older crowd, and it would ruin your image in no time at all if it were discovered you had been there."

"I'll risk my image. Maybe we can go to the trendy pub another night, when it's just for fun, but for now, like I said, I want to talk to you."

So we headed off in that direction.

"Oh, did you get hold of either of those guys?" asked Connor. "Sorry I didn't ask you immediately."

"That's okay," I said, "and no I didn't. Not at this hour on a Friday night."

"Of course, I didn't think of that. Tomorrow, then."

"Yes, tomorrow."

After that, by tacit consent, we spoke of inconsequentialities until we got there and were sitting down with a drink each in front of us.

"You had something you wanted to say to me," I prompted, unable to bear waiting even another moment.

"Yes, I did." He shifted uncomfortably in his seat, shucked off his jacket, took a sip of his pint. "Thing is, Tory, I owe you an apology about earlier today."

I felt my whole body relax as he said that. If he was giving me apologies then, maybe, possibly, he was no longer angry with me. Maybe, possibly, there was still a chance for us.

He was continuing, "It was all very well me pointing out your stuff to you. And to be fair, I still stand over what I said. But I did some serious thinking since this afternoon, and I've realised that as well as this being about *your* patterns, and your reactions, it's also about my own patterns, and it's not terribly nice to admit it, even to myself. Remember I told you how my father misjudged me when I was a child because I wasn't macho enough to please him?"

I nodded.

"Well, it's something I've acknowledged to myself, that I sometimes set it up that I'm misjudged in relationships. Like you – like most people, I'm realising – the very thing I fear most I create. And I *hate* being misjudged! It pushes every button I have – like what happened on the beach." He paused and then continued reflectively, "It happened with Karen, my ex-girlfriend that I told you about. I told you she left because I was no longer able to provide her with the luxuries she had become accustomed to –"

I nodded again in acknowledgement.

Connor grimaced then. "I suppose I don't like to admit it even to myself, and it's hard to say to you, but although that's all true – I didn't lie to you – there's more to it than that. I didn't tell her I was going to give up my job. I thought she would misjudge me, think I was crazy to give up a good job, threaten to leave me if I did that. And, of course, I really feared being misjudged. So, I didn't tell her I was planning it. In fact, I didn't tell her until after I had done it. I presented it to her as the classic *fait accompli*.

"And *that's* a large part of why she was so angry. We were living together, as I told you, engaged, planning to get married. And, she felt, justifiably I now realise, that it wasn't right for me to make such a huge decision without at least running it by her. And she judged me really harshly for having done this, and I got upset because I was being judged – misjudged, I felt, of course." He paused then, and took another drink from his pint glass before continuing, "And yes, it was an issue for her, that we were going to be on a budget for a while. She did say something, for example, about us not being able to go skiing that year. And so we muddled on for a while in mutual distrust and animosity, and I was neither surprised nor that disappointed when she told me she had met somebody else. The steady secure guy I told you about.

"I was very angry for a long time. But now I understand my contribution to the situation – it wasn't totally her fault. And maybe she was playing out *her* patterns. I don't know. She never talked about her past much. But maybe being lied to, information being hidden from her, was what really pushed *her* buttons. And maybe there was a fear of poverty somewhere deep in her psyche." He shrugged. "Who knows? And so, there on the beach when you said that thing. I could have been calm, could have realised that you weren't being insulting to me as such, that it was a result of your past, your experiences that you said this. But no, you pushed my buttons and I immediately reacted. Overreacted, you might say."

I was listening, fascinated. But quite despondent too, at what he was saying. "Are you saying that we are all constantly doomed to be at the mercy of our programming, our patterns?"

"Yes and no," he answered. "You understand, this is just my opinion. But it seems to me that, yes, we are destined to repeat these patterns, and react mindlessly to them – until and unless we notice them! Until we acknowledge them, accept them. Then we have the choice about whether to respond to them or whether to choose a new way of behaving. But it's hard to take that instant of noticing, that instant of decision-making – usually we're a mile off down the road of our learned response before we stop – if we stop – to realise that it's our programming influencing our behaviour, not our decisions. After all," he said wryly, "it took me *hours* today to calm down enough to realise what was going on, why I had reacted the way I did."

"It *was* an awful thing to say," I acknowledged.

"It was," he shrugged, "but I'm over it now. And to answer your question, no, I am not going to make helping you find Lucy conditional upon you sleeping with me. Of course I'm not. Having said that, are *you* going to make sleeping with me conditional upon finding Lucy?"

In other words, I realised, he was asking whether I was going to try to give this relationship a go, even now. Or was I going to cling to my guilt, my fears of the Cosmic Accountant whose existence wasn't even real, and trade joy and happiness with Connor for a better chance of finding Lucy?

To be honest, if someone really would offer me that trade – yes, in a heartbeat. (Such agreement to be binding only until I had her back.) But given that he was right, that there was no Celestial Weighing Scales, apportioning luck and success in one endeavour in inverse proportion to success in another, then no, I wasn't.

"No, I'm not," I told him then, and he looked at me then, really looked at me. And he smiled and the corners of his eyes creased up and he reached over and squeezed my hand.

"I'm sorry," we both said together, and then

laughed, and my heart felt as much lightness and joy as it possibly could in the absence of Lucy, and I relished the feeling.

"Imagine," I said then, "our first row!"

"Indeed," he said, grinning at me. But then his voice grew serious. "There's something else, Tory, that we need to talk about. We didn't use contraception last night. Is there any chance you might have conceived?"

Oh, dear God, yes. We hadn't, had we? I never even thought of it. I remembered Lady Bracknell's famous line in *The Importance of Being Earnest*. The other famous line, not the one about the handbag. Well, I remembered the gist of it. Something about losing one parent being misfortune, losing two being sheer carelessness. And I thought of conceiving Lucy by accident, and thinking that that was misfortunate (although of course, it wasn't really), but that conceiving another little baby like this could well be considered sheer carelessness. Whoops.

And I desperately tried to calculate dates, but I'm afraid I had never been that good at actually keeping track. I remember at school we were told to have a little calendar, a year-on-a-page type of thing, and to put a circle on the first day of our period, and a little line crossing through the dates after it to indicate how long it lasted. Every time we went to the doctor, we were assured, they would require this information (no matter, it seemed, if we were at the doctor's for anything from an ingrown toenail to a throat-infection), and if we didn't have this information the doctors would be cross with us.

And I had decided crossly that they didn't ask boys to do anything similar, no 'tell me the date of your last wet-dream' for them, oh no, and therefore, I, in a heady and (in retrospect) terrifying mixture of neo-feminism and bog-standard teenage bolshiness had decided that I was *not* going to do this. A blow for freedom, or something.

And do you know what, when I went to the doctor pregnant with Lucy, and I couldn't tell her the date of my last period, it turns out *they were right in school*, because she *was* cross with me! Very cross, I remember, as she sighed and wrote a letter requesting a scan so we could find out the due date.

And, I confess, I hadn't learned anything from that experience so that now I still didn't know when my last period was. And hence, wasn't too sure if I were likely to have conceived last night or not.

"Well?" he asked, as my silence progressed.

"I don't think so," I said then. "I think we're safe."

I don't think I sounded definite enough, though, as he threw a sharp glance across the table at me. "You *think* we're safe?"

"Well, more than *think*," I assured him, quickly putting my left hand down beside my left leg where he wouldn't see it, and crossing my fingers. "I mean I'm almost certain that we're safe. In fact," I laughed, "it would be a miracle if I were to have conceived. Yes, yes, it would."

"Well, let's hope so," he said sombrely. "Now wouldn't be the right time for us to conceive a baby. But," he added, and looked over at me again, "if you have, it's okay. We'll sort it out, I promise. It'll be okay. We'll manage."

"Good," I said, heartfelt, then, "But it doesn't matter, because I'm actually not pregnant. I'm sure I'm not."

"Good," he said, and smiled at me, and I got the sense that he wasn't the slightest bit taken in by it all. But also that, yes, whatever happened we would sort it out. Together. He wasn't going to do a Ray and reject all responsibility.

"And here's to ringing those guys tomorrow, and getting a solid lead to Ray," he said, raising his glass.

I raised mine too, and we clinked together. "To finding Lucy!" I said and he echoed that: "To finding Lucy!"

That night, as he was undressing me, he whispered, "Will you unloose your hair for me?"

And I reached behind and pulled off the elastic bobbin at the base of my plait, and gently he pulled the braid apart. When my hair was loose he ran his fingers through it, luxuriating in it as if it were the finest silk, and he rubbed his face against it, and he whispered, "I have so dreamed of feeling your hair brushing against my body. Will you do that for me?"

And I did, and his sighs and groans and closed-eyes and whispered encouragement were my reward.

Chapter 18

And it was a gift to waken the next morning and find him sleeping beside me, and I turned and moulded myself against him, and in his half-sleep he reached for me, and made an "mmm" of satisfaction deep in his throat, and I lay there just relishing the feel of him against me and the sound of his breathing and the beat of his heart against my back.

But even as I was doing this I was very aware of the time on my beside clock. It was only just gone eight o'clock, and so it was too early to ring the two lads, and that was the only reason I felt justified in lying there against my lover.

But an hour later found me sitting on the edge of the bed reaching for the phone. I reckoned that nine o'clock was still too early to be ringing such night-owls as musicians, but tough, basically.

I dialled Derek first, simply because it was the first

number. And because I wanted to get it over with, talking to him. I had remembered him once Connor had given me his name, and he was a creep of the first order. Thinning blond hair, a pale body running to fat even though he was only in his early twenties, skin which looked like the surface of the moon, added to all the personal grace of . . . of . . . actually, I couldn't think of anything which had as few personal graces as he did. A dyspeptic rhino, maybe, but that comparison was being unfair to dyspeptic rhinos, to be frank. He made quite a serious pass at me once, when I was about seven months pregnant, and you have to ask where exactly serious passes stop and attempted rape begins. Ugh.

After a long number of rings the phone was sleepily answered. "'lo?"

"Hello, is this Derek Flynn?"

"Who's looking for him?" The voice was suspicious, not-quite-hostile.

"Hi, Derek," I carolled as cheerfully as if he had admitted being himself. "This is Tory O'Neill. Now, you probably won't remember me but –"

"Ray Rafter's girl," he said.

"So you do remember me!" I gushed, at some level hating myself for being so artificial, and at another level not caring at all. The ends justify the means.

"Sure I do," he said, sounding a little bit more awake now, and a little bit intrigued. "Fine thing like you, of course, I remember. I always thought Ray was mad to let you go. Told him that too, many a time. Anyway, what can I do for you, my dear?" His voice seemed to suggest that whatever he could do for me, he hoped that it involved exchanging bodily fluids, and inwardly I shuddered.

But, keeping my voice as light and casual as I could I said, "I was just thinking about old times, you know how it is. And I was remembering the craic, the fun, we all used to have. And I was wondering, if you're in touch with any of the gang, maybe we could all meet up again sometime soon."

"That's a good idea – but here's a better one," he crooned. "Why don't just you and I meet up – forget about the others?"

Ugh! And, you know – there was something about the changed tempo of his breathing, but I was getting the distinct impression that on the other end of the phone-line he was busy playing with himself as he spoke to me. Double-ugh!

"In fact," he continued, "what are you doing today? We could maybe get together later. Or you could come over here now, if you wanted." He put a leer in his voice, probably thought it was seductive. "I'm still in bed, Tory, and I'm keeping it warm for you."

Keeping the bed warm? I wondered half-hysterically, or something else? Didn't want to ask, didn't want to know. I will *kill* you, Ray Rafter, I thought to myself, I will *kill* you for putting me through this.

"Not possible today, I'm afraid," I said, trying to put some regret – but not too much – into my voice. "We *could* do that another time, though. But what I was thinking of was more along the lines of a reunion. Are you in touch with any of the old gang?" I was anxious to get the information and get off the phone, but equally anxious that he wouldn't realise how desperately I wanted the information.

"I'm in touch with a few of them," he said reluctantly.

"Oh right," I said breathlessly. I may even have lisped slightly, but I'm certainly not confirming that. "Would you like to give me their numbers, and I'll ring them and arrange something? But you must tell me first, of course, when *you'll* be available, so I can make sure you're there, above anybody." (Barf!)

"Ah, don't worry about that, I'll arrange it," he said.

"I don't mind doing it," I said, striving to sound casual, although I'm not sure how well I succeeded.

"No, no, I'll do it," he said, and there was amusement in his voice and I got the distinct impression that he was playing with me, that he knew I was after something other than a grand reunion, and that he was enjoying teasing me with possibly getting what I really wanted, or possibly not.

"That would be great," I said, sounding as grateful as I could. "What about tonight?"

"Tonight's good," he said. "Doherty's at about nine?"

"Sure thing! And, er, Derek, before you go, who are you still in touch with? Who's likely to be there?"

"Oh, I've no idea, not until I see who's free, obviously."

"Yes," I said, trying desperately to un-grit my teeth, "but who will you be ringing?"

"Oh, I'll let that be a surprise for you," he said. Yes, he was definitely playing with me.

I gave up at this point. "Okay! I'll see you at Doherty's later."

And I put the phone down and gave way to my frustrated rage, *'argggghing'* all over the place, making faces and claws of my hands.

"What was all that about?" asked Connor, amused, propping himself up on one elbow.

"Oh, you might well think it's funny, but that little *creep* was doing my head in. Ugh," I shivered in disgust, "he wanted me to go over there now and join him in bed." I screwed up my face involuntarily at the merest prospect of that. "And now I have to turn up at some pub tonight, and he *says* he's going to try to get some of the old gang back together. And I have no idea if that includes Ray, or not. Or if he is even going to try to get anybody else, or if it's a plot to get me to meet just him."

"He'll get a shock if he does that, and you walk in with me, won't he?"

"But you can't come! What if Ray *is* there, and he sees you?"

"Well, what if Ray's there and he sees *you*," asked Connor reasonably. "How is meeting Ray in a pub going to get you Lucy back? And when he sees you he'll know straight away why you've arranged this – not for the pleasure of his company, needless to say."

"I know!" I wailed. "I didn't want to arrange this meeting! I wanted Derek to give me the phone numbers but he wouldn't! And I was going to get you, or Carol maybe, if you thought he'd recognise your voice, to ring Ray pretending to be a journalist writing for *Hot*

Press, arrange to meet him at his place for an interview. I had it all worked out!"

"Hang on, calm down. Look, let's not worry about all this unless we have to. Why don't you try the other guy? If he has Ray's contact details we're laughing. If not, then, yes, we'll have to work something out about this meeting tonight."

"Okay, good idea." So I dialled the other number. It was soon answered.

"Hi, is that Anto? Anthony Doran?" I asked.

"Yep," said a cheerful voice, "what can I do for you?"

"You mightn't remember me, but my name's Tory O'Neill, and I used to go out with Ray Rafter."

"Ah, the famous Ray Rafter!" he said, in distinctly less cheerful tones. My heart sank a little. It didn't sound like Anto was going to be the founding member of Ray's fan club, never mind keeping in touch with him.

"I – well, I was wondering – if you were still in touch with him," I said even though I felt it was probably a futile exercise.

"No, I am not. I saw sense. Way too late, but I saw sense." It wouldn't have taken a psychic to figure out that Anto felt hard-done by something Ray had done. Still, that might work to my advantage.

"I saw sense too," I said, "but unfortunately he's come back into my life in a bad way, and he's taken my daughter."

"What!"

I quickly explained, to a background of empathetic

curses on the other end of the phone-line. And I finished, "So, I understand that you're not in touch with him, but I really need to contact him, so if you knew anybody who knew where he was?"

"I'll ask around," Anto promised, and his voice was grim. "There's no way he should get away with that!"

So on mutual good wishes Anto took my number and promised to do what he could.

I hung up and turned around to explain to Connor, but I saw by his face that he had got the gist of it. "So, you've got a hot date with Derek tonight?" he asked wryly.

"Looks like it," I said, equally wryly.

Connor flung back the covers with a burst of energy and began pacing around the room. And I sat there and enjoyed the view; long legs, lean but muscular chest and back, nicely muscled arms and legs. Flat stomach. And that intriguing, untidy mix of wobbling bumps and lengths at his groin, so *there*, so different from our own neatly-tidied-away groin. I looked at him: the rest of his body all smooth flowing muscular curves, every part of him gliding gracefully to meet every other part of him, and then this protuberance, and I thought – not for the first time – of how men's bodies always look as if God made the rest of them first, and He took great care about it, a Designer who loves His work. But then at the end, He realised there was something missing, something fairly necessary. But maybe He was bored at this stage, or late for a meeting or something, because men's bodies always looked as if God had stood at the far side of the room and thrown those missing pieces at the man, letting them land and grow where they would, no matter that they ended up looking like a clumsily laid afterthought. But fascinating, though, endlessly intriguing and fascinating.

"Come on. Let's get up and dressed," he said, prosaic when I was being philosophical. "I'll bring you out for brunch, and we can plan our strategy for this evening."

So an hour or so later found us sitting in a pleasant café, eating brunch.

"So, about tonight? Are you going to go?"

"I think so," I said. "It's the only lead we have at the moment. But how to play it? To be honest, I wouldn't feel safe being on my own with Derek. He's a bit of a thug. He made quite a robust pass at me once, a bit *too* robust, if you know what I mean."

Connor shook his head. "You're not meeting him on your own. Don't worry about that."

"Okay," I said, "let's think of the possible scenarios. When I turn up there tonight, either there's going to be Derek on his own, or Derek with some other people but not Ray, or Derek with some other people including Ray."

"If it's Derek on his own, you just turn on your heel and leave."

"I can't do that, Connor, not immediately anyway. What if somebody we want to meet turns up late? I'd need to be there for that."

"True," he said. He rubbed his chin reflectively – his

295

deliciously unshaven chin, I might add. "Okay, let's think of it from the opposite angle. What if Ray *is* there? Do you want him seeing you? Seeing me? Or seeing us both?"

I thought about it. "I would rather have confronted Ray somewhere else than a crowded pub. But right now I'll take him wherever I can find him. If I can meet him I can at least talk to him about it all, persuade him that I'd be happy to share custody, talk him into letting Lucy come back to me."

"Hmm," Connor said sceptically.

"And anyway, I think that's the least likely scenario, to be honest. Ray and Derek parted on not-great terms, I think. What I'm hoping for is that Derek *will* bring along some of the others and they'll know where Ray is. It's a long shot, I know, but . . ." I sighed and took a sip of my tea.

"But if he *is* there," Connor insisted, "what are we going to do? Honestly, Tory, we're going to need a plan for each scenario."

I thought about it. "Okay," I said, "what about this? I go into the pub on my own, but you're waiting in a car somewhere outside. If Ray is there I'll try and talk him into letting me have Lucy back. Even if he won't he'll have to leave the pub at some stage anyway, and I'll quickly ring you and alert you, and you can follow him home. In fact, I'll have your number as the last number dialled on my phone so I can ring you really quickly. And once we know where he lives, it'll be easy to get Lucy," I finished triumphantly, "and in fact, you waiting outside will work with the other scenarios as well. If Derek's there on his own I'll join him for a while, ask him if he's expecting anybody else. If he says no, I'll just leave. If he says yes, no matter that he might be lying, I'll join him for a while. In either case, if he tries to stop me leaving, or starts groping me while I'm there, I can just press the ring button to dial through to you. If the phone rings and you answer it and I'm not talking, then that's the signal that you're to come into the pub to help me. Okay?"

"It's all sounding very melodramatic," Connor grumbled.

"Well, can *you* think of a better idea?" I challenged. And it transpired that, no, he couldn't. And so we agreed on that for a plan.

The rest of the day passed quite pleasantly. Although the forthcoming evening, and the crazy hunger to find Lucy never left my mind, I accepted that I was doing all I could for now. We went into the city centre and went for a walk along the canal, and had a late lunch in the National Gallery restaurant.

Then we went back to my place and went to bed for an afternoon nap, seeing as it was going to be a late night, we told ourselves.

And then we showered and dressed, and it was time to go. I dressed up in smart black trousers and an emerald-green shirt: the bare minimum to pass a dress code. I didn't bother with make-up seeing as I was hardly going out on the pull. And Connor was still wearing that day's clothes, so we swung by his place for him to put on a more respectable outfit, in case he did have to make his way past bouncers and dress-code enforcers to get into Doherty's. We both hoped, needless to say, that that wasn't going to be necessary, but we both agreed that it would be *awful* if I needed him and he wasn't allowed in.

And so, eventually it was time, and we headed into town, deliberately late enough to miss the shopping crowd, but early enough to get a parking space near Doherty's. And so we sat there for a couple of hours.

"It'll seem strange when this search is over," I said. "It's been the focus of all attention for six days now, but in one way it seems like I've been doing this forever. Any memory of another life seems like a vague dream."

"I know what you mean," agreed Connor. "It will seem strange, but not for long. Soon all *this* will seem like a bad dream, to be forgotten, as we get on with our lives."

"God, I hope so," I breathed. "Sometimes I feel as if I'll never find Lucy, that I'm destined, like the Flying Dutchman, to eternally follow this path without it ever coming to an end."

"Hush now," said Connor, "don't be thinking like that. Tell me about Lucy."

"Lucy," I said, and I could hear the smile in my voice even as I said her name. "She's beautiful, as I told you. And she gives the most wonderful cuddles, and the jammiest kisses! She has the prettiest smile and the most infectious laugh. She hates the colour yellow – I think I told you that – but she loves pink. Oh, she's a real little girl that way. The Barbie-er the pink, the better. And it drives me mad! Being this neo-feminist as I told you, pandering to this pink-for-girls is something I *swore* I would never do. But, you know what, I do it, and I'd do it a hundred times more. Because it makes her happy, and after that, so what? She loves her bath-time, it's always a row to get her out, no matter how cold the water has got! She's quite advanced in her speech – not quite genius level," I told him, anxious to prove how fair-minded I was about her, how objectively I could see her, "– but still . . . she has lots of words and short sentences."

And as we sat there I spoke at length about the delight that was my daughter. I spoke of her birth and the totally unexpected overpowering love I had felt, and I spoke of her first tooth, and her first word, and her first step.

And throughout all this – and plenty more – Connor listened, interested. And if I hadn't fallen in love with him already, that was the moment I did. When he listened raptly to me as I went on and on about Lucy's brilliance. Either he *was* genuinely interested, or he cared enough to make sure he gave the impression of being genuinely interested – in either case, it was a powerful way for him to be for me. And as we sat in my little car, and we waited until it was time to go into Doherty's, and I spoke at length about my daughter on this clear June evening, with the sound of revellers-to-be passing by the window, I fell totally in love with him.

And it seemed so simple, and so right, and I was able to tell him: "I love you," I said then.

And he smiled at me and said, "That's good. Because I love you too."

And despite the circumstances – or maybe because of them – it was the sweetest moment, as we held each other's gaze, muddy eyes to blue ones, and acknowledged and shared our growing love.

"So now," he said when it was time, "after all this, after acknowledging we love each other, I now have to let you go in and meet a repugnant lecher. It really goes against the grain, Tory."

"I know. I'm sorry. But it really is the best way. I'll be back as soon as I can, I promise."

I kissed his cheek, and he held his hand to the back of my head, and then I got out of the car and walked into the crowded maw that was Doherty's pub on a Saturday night.

Chapter 19

Derek was there, sitting just inside the door. Alone.

"Hi!" he said, his face lighting up when he saw me. He stood and gave me a kiss on the cheek. Ugh! He was even fatter than I remembered, and his face even more cratered. And while I was on the subject, he'd even lost hair since then too.

"Sit down. Sit down," he said expansively, his gaze on my non-existent cleavage. "What'll it be?"

"I'll get my own," I said, still standing, "and please, allow me. What are you drinking there?"

"A pint of Heineken," he said quickly. Chivalry was all very well, but a drink bought for you is a drink bought for you, after all.

I went to the bar and got his Heineken, and a mineral water for myself. I winced at the price, but paid it nonetheless.

When I was seated at Derek's table – but carefully

opposite him – I asked casually, "So . . . who else is coming?"

He grinned at me, and his gaze was avaricious, and his pointy yellowing teeth were feral. But he surprised me. I was expecting him to mutter something about nobody being available etc etc. But no.

"Johnno's coming, with his bird Claire. And Mickey – do you remember Mickey? Johnno and Mickey used to be in the band with Ray and me. I think Mickey's bringing some girl as well."

I said a silent prayer of gratitude.

"So, how have you been, Tory? Thanks for this by the way – cheers," and he lifted his glass and took a drink of it.

"I've been great, Derek. And you? Still playing?"

And we made stilted painful small-talk for about twenty minutes. And I was beginning to wonder if any of the others were coming at all. But then Derek looked over my shoulder. "Hi, Johnno, how's it going?" and I turned to see Johnno – at least, I assumed it was Johnno, I could have sworn I had never met him before, but I must have done if he had been playing with Ray. And he certainly seemed to remember me as he was holding out his hand.

"Hiya, Tory, how's she cuttin'? D'ya remember Claire?"

And Claire and I said hello, but that was the last word she spoke that evening.

And it seemed that no sooner were they sitting down with a drink than Mickey arrived on his own.

They all seemed pleased to see me, and it was quite touching, actually. I wouldn't have recognised any of them (with the exception of Derek, of course), but they seemed to remember me okay.

"How's the babby?" asked Johnno.

I forced myself to swallow and I said brightly, "Oh, she's fine."

And as the evening wore on, and the drinks were consumed, I deliberately steered the conversation into a nostalgic direction, which was quite a feat as I couldn't remember which incidents these guys might have been involved in, and which involved other bands, other people.

"Do you remember that gig in Goatstown?" I asked, holding my breath, and releasing it when Mickey chimed in, "Oh yes, that was gas! The way it was a strip-club and we didn't know, but we didn't mind anyway!"

That hadn't actually been the incident I had been thinking of – maybe my memory *was* of another band. But still, it was working.

"And Ray was great craic, wasn't he?" I asked disingenuously.

"Oh, he was, the best," they agreed, the alcohol having cast an affectionate glaze over any bitter memories they might have been holding.

"How's he doing now?" asked Mickey, articulating with care. "Have you heard how he's getting on in London?"

London?

"London?" I asked, very, very casually.

He looked surprised. "Oh, did you not know? He rang me about a week ago, really excited. He'd got taken on by this great band in London, the next U2 he said. He was moving over there straight away. God," he said enviously, "it really sounded like a great break."

Yeah, until it isn't, I thought cynically, but didn't say.

"What's the name of the band?" I said.

"Em, what was it again?" He thought about it while I waited in an *agony* of hope, while all the time trying to keep an expression of light unconcerned interest on my face. "I think it was called *The Deadmen*. Something like that anyway. Might have been *The Headmen*."

"Interesting," I said politely. "And do you know where they're playing? Or where they're based? It would be great to send him a card."

"A card? Oh, right, a card." He thought about it again, staring at the roof for inspiration, and I picked up my glass of water with trembling fingers.

"It was in Earl's Court," he said at last. "Can't remember the name of the pub, exactly. But I know it was an Irish pub, with an Irish name. And there's not too many of them around there, they're mostly Australian bars there, he told me."

"And you're sure about this?" I asked urgently.

He looked at me, surprised. My intensity must have seeped out, I was no longer merely showing mild interest.

"Yes, I am," he insisted. "Irish bar in Earl's Court, band called *The Headmen*, or something very similar to that. I got a text from him only yesterday saying how well it was going."

"A text!" I said, delighted. "You have his mobile number? Oh, Mickey, you wouldn't give me his mobile number, would you?" I wheedled. "I'll text him my good wishes, much better than sending a card!" Out of my peripheral vision I could see Derek looking at me suspiciously. Luckily the ambient noise was too loud – I hoped – for him to hear our conversation.

"Sure thing," said Mickey amiably, and he took his own mobile phone out and went through his address-book until he found Ray's number. (Which was different from the one I had – he must have changed phones.) Trying to hide my delight and excitement I quickly programmed it into my own phone.

"One more thing," I whispered to Mickey, "don't tell Ray, will you, if you're in touch with him. I want to surprise him."

"Sure, no problem." Mickey shrugged, and lifted his pint glass, looking disappointedly at its empty bottom.

"Let me get you another one of those," I offered grandiosely, and to the others, "Same again?"

As I was waiting to be served at the bar I debated whether I should try to impress upon Mickey the necessity that Ray not know I was asking about him. It would be good to be sure that Ray wouldn't hear, but then, on the other hand, I didn't want Mickey to realise the importance of this – better that he should just think it was casual conversation.

I wouldn't, I decided as I shouted the order over to the barman, fighting with the laughter and loud chatter all around me. I'd say nothing more to Mickey, hope he would forget. And I'd have to hope that Derek's interest wasn't strong enough for him to pump Mickey.

In fact, I realised as I took the drinks and handed over enough money to keep a small country going for about three months, we would have to move quickly before Ray got to hear of my interest. Not that I was exactly going to hang around: 'Oh yes, my daughter's in London, I'll pop over and get her back in a day or two.'

But one thing I did have to hang around for, and that was the duration of that drink. It would have been way too obvious to have suddenly departed immediately after getting Ray's details from Mickey. So I made small talk and laughed and tried to move my leg away from whoever (I wonder) was playing footsie under the table, and *willed* each of them to hurry up and finish their drinks. But this late in the evening the rate of consumption had slowed down.

But at last, at last, Mickey knocked back the last of his pint and stood to buy the next round. I quickly finished my water and stood too. "Sorry, lads," I said in regretful tones, "but I have to go now. It's getting too late for the baby-sitter, you know how it is."

They looked at me blankly – no, they did not know how it is, it seemed.

"It was great meeting you all!" I gushed. "We must do it again soon, bye."

And I turned to go, but Derek's voice stopped me. "Tory, wait," he called.

I turned and looked back at him. He was getting to

his feet, lifting his jacket. "I'll go with you. Make sure you get home safely." He didn't wink lecherously at the others, I'm pretty sure of that, but they got the point anyway. And Johnno and Mickey looked at him enviously. At least Johnno looked enviously until Claire glared at him, whereupon he went back to admiring his nearly empty pint glass.

"Oh, that's okay, Derek," I said. "I'll be sure to get home safely. You see, my boyfriend's waiting outside."

That stopped him dead in his tracks. "What? Your boyfriend's been outside all this time?"

"Yes, yes. You see," I said, improvising wildly, "he's very jealous, very jealous indeed. Pathologically jealous, in fact. And I only just managed to persuade him to let me meet old friends at all, but only on condition that he could wait outside for me. And if he saw me leaving the bar with you, well . . ." I raised the palms of my hands up in a who's-to-say shrug and shook my head sadly, "I don't know what he would do."

"Oh," said Derek looking nonplussed. "Oh, right. Well, that's okay then." He laughed and sat down, "I don't have to stir myself then. That's good. Yes. You'll be getting home safely anyway. Great. Great. Yes, Mickey, I'll have the same again, so."

I nearly – not quite, but nearly – felt sorry for him.

I said goodbye again, with an insincere hope that I'd see them again soon, and left the bar. It was like a cool shower on a hot day: getting out from the hot, airless, cacophonous atmosphere into the (relatively) fresh air and (relatively) silent night outside. I ran up the road the short distance to where Connor was sitting slumped in his car.

"Hi!" I sang out, pulling open the door, which made him jump.

"Hi," he said, sitting upright and looking appraisingly at me in the orange light of the street-light aided by the smaller interior light of the car. "Good news? You look as if it's good news."

"The best!" I said as I got into the car, and put on my seat-belt. "Connor, I know where he is! I've got his mobile phone number!"

He put on his own seat-belt and carefully pulled onto the road, even as he was saying, "That's brilliant! Oh, that's great! Where is he? Will we go there now? Get Lucy back this evening?"

"Ah. Yes. It's not quite that easy. He's in London."

"London!"

"Yes. He's playing in an Irish pub in Earl's Court. Johnno – the guy who told me – didn't know the name of it, but he said he thinks there's only one Irish bar there. It's not a very Irish area of London, seemingly. And the band is either called *The Headmen* or *The Deadmen*."

"So . . . ?" said Connor in the tones of a man who knows the answer he's going to get.

"So we go to London! Tomorrow! First thing!"

But Connor was sounding dubious. "How reliable is this information, Tory? It's one thing having a wasted drive down to Waterford. But the time and money involved in a wasted trip to London . . . well," his voice trailed off, his point made.

I grimaced although he probably couldn't see me in the flickering orange light of passing streetlamps as we drove out of the city. "I know, Connor. But I have to, I just have to. And the information *sounded* solid. He – Johnno – spoke to him only last week, he said. I mean, I'll understand if you don't come . . ."

"Of course I'll come," he said impatiently. "I just hope that it's not a wasted trip, that's all."

So we drove to my house where I packed a bag with clothes for a few days, and a change of clothes for Lucy. I smiled sadly as I folded the tiny trousers and top, and I held them to my nose and breathed in. But there was – of course – no residual scent of her, just the smell of washing detergent. Soon, though, soon I would be holding the real thing in my arms, and I could bury my face in her neck, her stomach, and breathe in the wonderful scent of her as much as I wanted. Just before we left my house I turned back and on sudden inspiration found an old snap of Ray. I placed it carefully in my wallet.

We then drove to Connor's place, and he packed for himself. And then, magic! He went online and booked us our flight tickets, just like that, and printed them out. I was so impressed! And *then* he found, and booked us into, a cheap hotel.

"I am so impressed," I said, "that you can do all this from your desk!"

"Wait, there's more!" he said with a flourish, and he tapped some more keys and lo, on the screen in front of us, was a list of pubs in Earl's Court. There was just one

Irish pub, a place called O'Neill's! And along with its name and address, a *map* to it was given too!

"This is going to be so easy!" I said, literally jumping up and down and clapping my hands.

"Hang on," warned Connor. "I know it looks good, but listen. There is so much information on the Internet, it's incredible. But Tory, there's no control over the quality of it. Look, this site was set up by beer-lovers, to share their favourite pubs. But there could be other pubs that these guys don't like enough to include, or maybe even haven't heard of. But yes," he conceded with a grin, "it's a very good place to start."

"I'll have to figure all this computer stuff out," I said.

"I'll teach you," he promised, and we smiled at each other with a sense of a delicious future just waiting for us. And there was a lightness about us, a sense of anticipation, a belief that somehow this was it! Somehow we had managed to find Ray – it certainly was the most solid lead yet – and for the first time I could believe, deep down and in my soul, that I would soon have Lucy back in my arms.

Chapter 20

I awoke with a shock as the alarm went off. But it soon came flooding back to me – we were flying to London this morning! To find Lucy! I jumped out of bed calling as I did so, "Connor, Connor, wake up!"

And his sleepy voice answered, protesting, "I'm awake, honest I am. But a cup of coffee would complete the process."

And I laughed and rushed downstairs to the kitchen and made us both coffee. When I walked back into the room with the full cups, their aroma filling my nostrils, I stopped dead in the doorway. Connor was sitting upright, his head and back against the headboard, the covers bundled carelessly around his waist. And he just looked so *edible*. His angular face, so beautiful, sexily unshaven so early in the morning, his eyes closed. I remembered how I had said to Carol that he wasn't actually that good-looking, only attractive, but I realised now as I looked at him that I was completely and utterly wrong – he was *gorgeous!* I gazed at his firm, elegant shoulders, his bare chest with just the right amount of dark hair, the promise of untold delights hidden under the covers, just waiting to be snuggled into.

He opened one eye then. "What are you doing standing in the doorway like that? Trying to torture me with the tantalising smell of coffee, but no actual coffee to drink?"

"Actually, I was admiring the view," I said, and was rewarded with a huge smile crossing his face.

"Glad you like it," he said. "Would you like a close-up view? *After* my coffee, though."

"Love to, but not enough time," I said regretfully.

"No," he sighed, but amiably, "probably not. Have to set the alarm for earlier next time."

"You mean next time we are looking for my daughter?" I asked sharply. "Next time, there isn't *going* to be a next time!"

"Next time we have to leave early for anything, I meant. Here, woman, will you give me that coffee? Now!" he half-pleaded-half-commanded.

Laughing I crossed the room at last, handed him his coffee and sat on the edge of the bed drinking my own.

And after our coffee we washed and dressed, and were soon on our way to the airport. We parked in the long-stay carpark and got the shuttle-bus to the terminal. Checked in for our flight, and wandered down to the gate. Sat there and waited for the flight to be called.

"It's amazing," I remarked, "no matter how quick flying itself is, it's all the bits around it that take so long." I looked at my watch. "It's going to be two hours from the time we got to the carpark until we actually take off! And the flight itself is under an hour!"

"I know," he said idly. "Next time we'll bring the private jet, okay?"

I opened my mouth and he said hastily, "I know, I know! Next time there isn't going to be a next time! I meant next time we fly anywhere."

And as we waited I suddenly thought of Carol. I had to ring her, share this great news. So I took out my mobile phone and was soon talking to her.

"Carol, guess where I am!" I said exuberantly, and without waiting for an answer I told her. "I'm at the airport! We know where Ray is! He's in London, and we're going to find him there and get Lucy back. Isn't it wonderful!"

"That's great! Oh Tory, I'm so delighted for you. Oh, fingers crossed here, and everything else I can find to cross! Ring me when you have her, won't you?"

"I will," I promised, laughing, "and we'll bring her to see you the minute we get back!"

"I can't wait! Oh, Tory, this is great!" and she laughed with delight. I understood – I felt like laughing manically myself at the sheer joy of tracing Ray at last.

But when I rung off from her Connor was looking serious. "Tory," he said, putting a hand on my arm, "Tory, it's a good lead, I know. But please, don't . . ."

"I know. I'm not to get my hopes up. It could be a

false lead. But it's not! I feel it in my gut that it's not!"

And he looked at me, and I could see him debating which was the lesser of two evils: to prick my balloon now (perhaps needlessly), or to let me enjoy at least this period of time, and be let down (if I was going to be let down) when it happened. And after a moment he sighed and changed the subject, obviously deciding to let me enjoy my relief and excitement for as long as I could.

And eventually our flight was called and we queued like everybody else to get on board in the quintessential aircraft-shuffle.

And then the aircraft was being pushed back, and then the engines were revving prior to hurtling us down the long runway and throwing us into the air.

"Is this a good time to tell you," I said, swallowing hard and grabbing his hand and clinging to it, "that I'm a nervous flyer?"

"As good as any, I suppose. Don't worry. It's going to be okay. Just hang onto me."

And I closed my eyes and did just that. And some time later he said, "You can open them now," and I realised that we were right up there above the few wispy June clouds, and when I looked out the window I could see the Irish sea below, and once even, and I was squealing like a child with the excitement of it, a ship below us.

"Look, Connor, look at that boat down there. Is it one of the ferries, do you think?"

And then we were flying over Wales and on this

clear day I could see its outline as clear as any map, and I felt like God with this superior viewpoint.

And then it wasn't so good as we began our descent, and my stomach didn't like that at all, and I was hanging onto Connor's hand again. But still I was fascinated as we flew in over London – my God, the sheer size of it! – and look, there's the Thames!

And we dropped lower and lower until eventually we landed with a mild bump, and the modulated tones of the cabin crew told us that we were now in London Heathrow (whew, got on the right plane, then!), and thanked us for flying with them, and looked forward to seeing us again soon, and tried to push their hotel for us to stay in.

We disembarked and headed for the London Underground station, and as we queued for tickets I was nearly overpowered with the amount of people, their sheer energy, their focussed movements as they all hurried towards their goal. And my God, but there was such a variety of colours of skin and styles of ethnic dress, and as people passed me I heard snippets of such a babel of languages, most of which I didn't even recognise never mind understand. And even when the passers-by were talking English, it was being spoken in every accent you could think of. At first I thought it was because we were at the airport but as time passed and the phenomenon remained the same I realised that it wasn't to do with being at the airport, but rather was a feature of modern London.

We got a Tube map with our tickets and I was

delighted to see that Earl's Court was on the same line as Heathrow Airport, and not too far away either.

We took the train as far as Earl's Court and quickly found our hotel, and checked in.

The receptionist keyed in our details: "How long are you staying?"

"Tonight for sure, we'll know more tomorrow about our plans."

And as he tapped away he made conversation. "You're Irish, yeah? You sound Irish."

We confirmed that we were indeed, Irish.

"Just flew in this morning, yeah?"

"That's right."

"Here you go," he said, handing us our card-key. "I hope you enjoy your time in London."

We gave him our thanks and went and found our room, and dumped our bags.

"Now what?"

"Now we go and find that Irish pub!"

But as we passed through the lobby I stopped. "Hang on," I said, "let's ask the receptionist . . ." and I walked up to him.

"Hi! I was wondering . . . we're looking for Irish pubs in Earl's Court, and we know about O'Neill's on Earl's Court Road. But, do you know about any other Irish pubs around here?"

He looked at me incredulously, and asked in tones of let-me-make-sure-I've-got-this-straight: "You've flown all the way from Ireland, where, I understand, there are *thousands* of Irish pubs, to try and find more Irish pubs in Earl's Court?"

He shook his head disbelievingly, and I could just see him storing this up to tell his friends. You'll never believe what happened to me today, he'd be saying, talk about stupid Irish people!

But, credit where it was due, he did think about it. "There's a pub called The Leprechaun," he said as we winced, "and it's here, look," and he took a map and pointed it out.

We thanked him and left the hotel. O'Neill's first, we decided, seeing as it was nearer. We found it easily and went in. It was just about lunch-time and the place was busy with diners. We ordered some lunch ourselves, and a drink, and sat and ate. And all the time I was looking everywhere. "Imagine," I said to Connor, "this is possibly the very place where Ray is playing tonight!" And he smiled and squeezed my hand briefly.

After an hour or two the pub all but emptied, most people – it seemed – preferring the bright June outdoors to its gloomy interior. I couldn't blame them – if I hadn't been on a mission I think I'd have been the first person out the door.

We casually made our way up to the bar and placed our empty glasses on the bar-top.

"Thanks, mate," said the barman in a rich Aussie accent, as he took the empties. "Same again?"

"Sure thing," said Connor, "and whatever you're having yourself."

"Oh, thanks, mate!"

When he brought us our drinks I asked him, my heart racing at being so close to finally closing on Ray, "Tell me, do you have a band playing here called something like *The Deadmen* or possibly, *The Headmen*?"

But he was shaking his head, "No, love, we don't. Nothing like that at all."

"Are you sure?" I asked desperately, and he cast me a sympathetic glance even as he was insisting that he was sure.

"We do have bands playing here," he said, "but they're called nothing like that." And he rattled off four or five band-names: *The Quigleys, The Fields of Athenry, Black Velvet, Skibbereen*, and sure enough, none of them were remotely like the names we were looking for.

"As well," I said disconsolately to Connor, "they all sound like they do very traditional music, and Ray wouldn't be caught dead doing all the diddley-I-dee stuff. A proper rock singer, he always insisted he was. Denim and leather, not Aran jumpers, you know."

But just on the off-chance, having come so far, I showed the barman the picture of Ray. He shook his head. "Sorry, love, don't recognise him. But to be fair, that doesn't actually mean anything. I'm so busy that I sometimes barely register that the band has started, never mind who's playing in it."

Connor sighed heavily. "We'll try The Leprechaun, so."

And we gave our thanks to the friendly Australian barman and made our way onto the street, blinking at the unexpected light and warmth. And we found our way to The Leprechaun. Where it was the same story. No *The Deadmen*, no *The Headmen*. A few traditional bands, okay, but that was it. Specialising in rebel songs, he told us proudly, reliving the centuries of occupation and re-fighting the War of Independence every night. And no, he didn't recognise Ray's picture either, but he had the same proviso as our friendly Australian barman, that he was so busy he wouldn't recognise Ray even if Ray *had* played there.

Well, I thought I'd throw myself under the nearest bus. Connor had been right after all. It was another false lead. To have come so far, spent so much money – and far, far, worse, to have spent so much time – and have it all be for nothing. We were still no nearer finding my Lucy, and it was going to be a week tomorrow since she had disappeared. And yes, maybe, the boys from Waterford might still get back to us with some information, no matter how unlikely that might be. And yes, maybe Anto might manage to track him down, but the odds of that weren't great either.

And as we trailed towards the door Connor said softly, "When we get back we're going to have to contact the gardai."

And I said, "I know," even though my heart sank at that thought. Charlotte Riordan had been missing for over a year with her father before the gardai managed to track them down. How could I possibly do without Lucy, worry about her, live without her, for possibly a year, not knowing how she was, what conditions she was being kept in? And all that time hoping that the gardai *would* find her, but with it hanging over my head that the nearer they got to finding her the more danger she was in.

But just inside the door I stopped suddenly, so suddenly that Connor banged into me from behind.

"Look!" I hissed, and I pointed to a poster on the back of the door. *The Wren Boys* it said proudly, and underneath was a picture of four lads in jeans and Aran jumpers, grinning proudly at us. And there, to the very left, holding his guitar, was Ray!

I whirled around and clung to Connor's arm. "It *is* him, isn't it? Tell me I'm not imagining it," I begged.

And he clutched me back and he was grinning so widely I thought it must hurt his face. "You're not imagining it," he said, over and over again. "You're not imagining it. It *is* him!"

And eventually we calmed enough to read the handwritten information at the bottom of the poster. And Ray was due to be playing in this very pub, that very night!

And we marched back to the bar and confirmed that yes, that information was correct, *The Wren Boys* would be playing there later that evening. Officially at about nine o'clock, he said, but for sure some time before ten. But then he looked anxiously at us.

"You're looking for one of the lads in that band? Is he going to get into trouble? I don't want to be responsible for you finding him through me."

"We found him through the poster," Connor pointed out reasonably, and I was nearly talking over him, desperate to get my point across, terrified that even at this late stage we could lose Ray, and I was saying: "But listen, please listen. He's got my daughter. My little girl. She's only two! Don't warn him off, please. We're not going to do anything to him, just get her back. We're not even going to involve the police," I said – although I still had no idea whether or not we would, but I would have said anything . . . *anything*, to have got him to agree not to tell Ray we were looking for him – "We just want my daughter back safe and sound, that's all. Are you a family man?" When he nodded I said urgently, "Think how *you* would feel if you lost a child – that's the situation I've been in for a week now. Please don't tell Ray. Please don't!"

And he looked at me appraisingly and slowly he nodded and said, "Okay, I won't."

"Oh, thank you, thank you," I said, and I would have flung my arms around him but for the intervening bar counter. And then I thought, and I asked, "I don't suppose you know where he lives, do you? No, silly me, sure you weren't even sure he was playing here. But someone here must have contact with someone in the band," I insisted. "Maybe we could find out now where he lives and go and get Lucy now."

And I saw by his eyes, by his body language – crossed arms, a step taken back – that this was a step too far, and I think Connor had seen it too because he said quickly, "Ah, no, Tory. He's done all he can to help us. Leave him. We'll sort it out ourselves."

And I slipped off the bar-stool and Connor and I left the pub. And once on the street outside, I turned to him, and my sight was blurred with unshed tears of joy and I flung myself into his arms, and he held me tight and swung me around and then I was crying onto his neck, and he was saying mindlessly, *'Oh, thank you, God! Oh this is great, brilliant'*. And although most of my thoughts and my emotions were involved in the sheer joy and exuberance of having found Ray, even so, a little part of me was able to recognise and acknowledge and appreciate the fact of Connor's joy and excitement. It was a gift he was giving to me, and to Lucy, a little girl he had never even met – that he was as concerned to get her back and as joyful at having found Ray as I was. And I loved him for it.

"Will we go and buy her a huge toy?" he asked then.

And I said, "No, let's not. Not until we definitely have her back," and he understood that I didn't want to tempt fate.

And it was felt strange then, to be so excited, but having nothing to do. We just had to wait for time to pass until that evening, until we could meet Ray. And we couldn't settle to doing anything else. We were in one of the most exciting cities in the world, and we couldn't concentrate on any other activity. It seemed far too prosaic to simply go off and pretend to be tourists, and there was nothing that could attract our attention – or certainly, mine – that could compare with the thoughts going around and around in my head: *We have finally found Ray. We'll have Lucy tonight!*

And so we just went back to our hotel, and we went to our room.

"It's so frustrating to just wait, knowing that Lucy's somewhere near here," I said. "I want to go and get her *now*. It's been far too long already."

"I know," Connor soothed, "but honestly, just a few more hours, that's all."

We sat on the bed ostensibly watching television, but I for one couldn't concentrate, and I don't think Connor could either. We channel-flicked, neither of us registering what we were watching, and made desultory conversation, and waited for time to pass.

"Here's what I think we should do," said Connor at one stage. "We'll go to hear them play tonight, and we'll follow Ray wherever he goes after. Which hopefully will be straight to his home. He does have a baby to look after, after all," he said sardonically. "But even if he goes clubbing or whatever, we'll follow him. He'll have to go home *sometime*."

"How will we make sure Ray doesn't see us?"

"We'll just have to keep out of his sight. Hopefully there'll be a big enough crowd that we can hide at the back. We'll go to the gig late, when the pub is full."

And so about eight o'clock we went out and got something to eat, and after that – and my heart was thudding painfully on the inside of my chest-wall, and I was clutching Connor's hand – we went back to The Leprechaun. As we made our way there, I started laughing.

"What's so funny?" asked Connor.

"I'm just thinking about Ray. In a traditional Irish

band. Doing rebel songs, no less. In an Aran jumper! He always *hated* that kind of stuff. And now he's doing exactly that! And I know, Connor, it doesn't reflect very well on me, but I'm *delighted!* There *is* a God after all. There is Divine Justice after all! Because this really is the third circle of Hell for Ray! And I was thinking of what he told Johnno – that guy in Doherty's," I explained, "about the band he was in here in London. The next U2, he said. I think he was covering up, and there's no band with a nice rock-sounding name like *The Deadmen.* Or any variation thereof," I said, skipping a little. "No wonder he came to London – if he's doing stuff like this, he would just *die* if people he knew got to know it!"

Connor laughed in his turn. "Depending on how vicious we feel, we can tell all his friends in Dublin the truth. Mind you, he won't be playing in any band, not once he gets done for abduction."

"No. Or maybe 'Jailhouse Rock'," and I laughed long and loud even though it wasn't that funny. But this laughter was nothing more than the physical manifestation of some of the second-by-second stress I had been under for the past week. And as I listened to myself I realised that it could easily get out of control, could easily end up as hysterics. So I took several deep breaths and calmed myself. I then thought of something else. Maybe Connor would have the answer.

"What if he drives away from the pub, after? We can't assume that he lives locally. And they might have a van or something, you know, for the musical instruments."

Connor said, "Then we jump into a taxi and say, 'Follow that car'! I've always wanted to do that."

And laughing together, totally delighted with the prospect of seeing Ray in his downfall and of getting Lucy back, we reached the pub – fashionably late.

We paid our cover charge and went into the back-room which was obviously used for gigs, and immediately my eyes were anxiously – indeed, frantically – scanning the raised corner of the room which passed for a stage. And sure enough, the band were already on the raised corner of the room which passed for a stage. And equally sure enough – there was Ray among them! I let out a breath I hadn't realised I had been holding, hadn't realised that a part of me had been terrified that something would go wrong even at this late juncture. I just stared at him, nearly unable to believe it, that after searching for him for all this time I had finally found him!

And Connor was pulling me, urging me, to what proved to be a table at the right at the back of the room, and I gave thanks that he, at least, was being sensible. The room was dark, and the band probably couldn't see much, but still . . . it was much more sensible to be sitting down than standing right inside the door.

I sat down and thanked God, over and over, that we had found Ray at last. All the false starts, all the wrong information, all the worry . . . but we had found him. And, having found him, we would soon find Lucy. I called out to her in my mind: *I'm only a couple of hours away from you now! Hang on, my love, I'll be there soon!*

And we sat while the band went through its repertoire, and certainly the rest of the audience seemed to enjoy it, shouting and whooping and joining in and begging for encores. No encores, I begged silently. Let's just get this over with.

And at last, encores notwithstanding, the band bowed their last bow and began packing their stuff away. Connor and I watched them intently. The rest of the audience were still there, chatting now and laughing together, and drinking their last drinks, so we were still hidden. And eventually the musical equipment was packed away, and the band-members walked the length of the room towards the door – Connor and I ducked our heads, but I don't think Ray was looking in our direction anyway.

As they passed one of the lads said, "Who's for heading on to Doran's?" and one or two of the others said they would. I held my breath and listened intently, but was rewarded to hear Ray say, as he passed through the door, "No thanks, Jack. I think I'll pass."

As soon as the door closed behind them Connor and I were on our feet, grabbing our jackets and heading after them. Connor cranked open the door a fraction, and looked out. A couple of seconds later he said, "Come on," and we walked into the main pub in time to see the doors to the street closing gently. We hurried across the pub, and out the door. We then stopped and stood in the lee of the doorway and sneaked a look out. A grubby white van was parked outside, looking urine-yellow in the glow from the streetlight, and the band-members were busy putting the drums and other equipment into it.

When they were finished one of them said, "Ray? Do you want a lift?"

Again I held my breath. It was all very well Connor joking that we would get a taxi, but this wasn't Hollywood. There was no script promising us that a taxi would arrive just as we needed it, and no director ensuring that that would happen. And looking around the deserted streets I realised that we would never get a taxi in time. As I waited for Ray's answer I started reciting the van's registration to myself, over and over.

All this in a heartbeat, but in the next heartbeat Ray was saying, "No, thanks. Not if you're going to Doran's. It would be out of your way. And it's a grand night for a walk." And as my breath rushed out in relief I could hear Connor beside me give an equally heartfelt sigh.

The rest of the band-members piled into the van, and they pulled off with a beep goodbye on the horn, and a wave from Ray. He hefted his guitar-case more comfortably onto his back, and began walking. And stealthily, we began following him.

And God knows we were such amateurs at this surveillance lark, but luckily he was an amateur at being followed. And if it even looked as if he were going to stop and check behind him, Connor and I would turn towards each other and place our mouths together as if we were a couple kissing, appearing nothing more than an ubiquitous romantic-after-a-night-out-and-a-few-drinks-and-can't-wait-to-get-home couple, and even as we were doing this we were nearly getting eye-strain, trying to keep Ray in our peripheral vision. And twenty minutes later he turned into a small driveway, and walked up it, unlocked the door and went into the house, closing the door behind him.

And we looked at each other in delight, and I whispered, "Lucy's in *that* house! Come on, let's go and get her!"

And no matter that it was heading for midnight, and no time to be disturbing a child – I didn't care. She was in that house and I was going to get her and that was it.

I marched up the small driveway and knocked on the door, and stood back and waited for it to be answered.

And as I stood there the doubts began to hit me. Surely, *surely,* she had to be there. I couldn't have made the wrong decision about Ray selling her on. No, I told myself firmly. I couldn't be wrong. Well, I told myself resolutely, we would soon know. In a few moments we would know. And I felt sick to my stomach as I waited to find out if I had gambled incorrectly with her safety, her life.

At last I could hear the sound of approaching footsteps from behind the door, and a moment later it opened, and there stood Ray.

Chapter 21

Everything happened very quickly then, far more quickly than it takes to relate it. He saw us and his expression seemed to indicate that all his nightmares had come together.

"Tory!" he gasped. "Connor! What are you doing here? Together? How did you find me?"

But that was as far as he got before Connor had moved and taken him by surprise and had his arm twisted behind him.

"Look," he blustered, "Connor! You know, I'm sorry about the rent, I really am. But I had no choice, I really didn't. I was stuck financially," he said, and he was bleating now, "and I was going to send it to you as soon as I could, and I *will*. Jesus," he said, his expression, his voice, changing now to being aggrieved. Ray was being hard-done-by here, it seemed clear as he continued, whining, "You didn't have to follow me all the way here, you know. Over two poxy months' rent, I mean, Connor, how desperate can you get?" he finished, scrambling – it appeared – for the moral high ground.

But I was sweeping into the house now, and Connor was wheeling Ray back from the doorway to make room for me, and I closed the door.

And I was not in the slightest bit interested in answering Ray's whiney self-justifications, nor in his famous two-step to spin the situation so that he was firmly in the right. I put my face right up against his and I hissed: *"Where is she?"*

And I had to give him credit for the confusion he managed to put on his face as he blubbered, "Where's who? Tory, what's going on? What are *you* doing here? And with *him*."

And I wasn't even going to be drawn into playing his games, into answering his proof-of-innocence questions. After writing his note admitting he had taken her, was he now about to pretend he hadn't? Asking what we were doing here! And his look of surprise – did he really think we would be taken in by that?

"Where is she?" I demanded again.

"Who?" he asked, still looking confused and puzzled. If I hadn't known better I'd have sworn it was genuine. But I had been taken in way too often before by Ray's 'genuine' expressions.

"Lucy," I snapped, "where is Lucy? Come on, Ray. You already admitted you have her – don't insult my intelligence."

"Lucy?" he echoed, his confused expression deepening. "She's not here. Why would she be?"

"Oh, for Jesus' sake!" I shouted. "Will you stop with the innocent act! Where is she, Ray? Tell me now, or I swear I won't be answerable for what I do to you!"

"Or me," said Connor, yanking his arm a little. "I'll help her, no problem. Where is Lucy?"

"Honestly," he moaned, "I swear – ouch! – I swear she's not here. Honestly, Tory – you're welcome to look all over the house. You won't find her – because she's not here!" he finished on a roar.

"I will!" I said, and I looked at Connor and he nodded to say that it was okay, that he would keep hold of Ray. And I frantically opened the nearest door, which was into the sitting-room but Lucy wasn't there, and then the door at the end of the hallway, which led into the kitchen, but she wasn't there either. And then I desperately ran upstairs, opened all the doors – the bathroom, no she wasn't there. A bedroom – in which a couple were making love – I couldn't see her there – I even ignored their squeals and "What the –" and looked under their bed, in their wardrobe. Without even having acknowledged them I opened the next door – the last door, which opened into another bedroom – Ray's, I supposed. But there was no little black-and-curly-haired girl there either. And worse, there was not one single sign that she had ever been there. There were no children's toys, no plastic cups or plates, no child's clothes in the wardrobe or drawers. Oh yes, I searched, and I searched well. And found nothing.

And then I heard a howl coming from somewhere, echoing around the walls of the house, and it was only as I was flying back down the stairs like an avenging Fury that I realised that it was I who was doing the howling.

And I rushed up to Ray where Connor still held him, and – out of control now – I slapped his face, and all my fury and fear and longing and stress and anger were in that slap, and it hurt my hand but I barely registered that. "Where is she?" I screamed. "What have you done with her?"

And I howled again and I was sinking to my knees in the hallway and I was crying, sobbing.

"You've sold her!" I shrieked at Ray through my tears, and the taste of bile was bitter in my throat. "I thought you wouldn't do that. I thought that there were some depths you wouldn't sink to. But I was wrong about you, and I am going to be cursed for the rest of my life for not having known how low you are, what an excuse for a human being you are! But it is nothing to the way you'll be cursed for what you've done."

And Connor was saying, "Tory, Tory, calm down," even as he was saying to Ray, "Come on, Rafter. Tell us. We haven't come this far to let you deny it all."

And then with a supreme effort I stood again, regained some control, knowing that I was going to be no use to Lucy if I collapsed in hysterics. She still needed me, more than ever now that I knew the worst.

Ray was still staring at me. "I don't have her," he shouted, and he twisted as best he could in Connor's grip. "Connor, I don't have her. I never did. Tory's gone mad. She was always unstable. I've no idea why she thinks I have Lucy."

"You stole her!" I howled at him, and I took a step forward, towards him, not sure whether I was going to kill him or physically force some answers out of him. And he tried to take a step backwards, moving further into Connor's none-too-gentle embrace, it obviously being the less awful option. "You came looking for shared custody and when I wouldn't give it to you, when you knew you wouldn't get it legally, you stole her! Tell me what you've done with her!"

"I *didn't* steal her!" he protested. "Look, Tory, calm down –"

"Calm *down?*" I yelled.

But he shouted over me: "I did ask you for custody, okay, but it was only a whim. Tory, listen to me! I was drinking and smoking and I got to feeling like I told you – worried about my mortality, and it seemed like a good idea at the time. But the next day I saw sense. What would I do with a child?"

I had asked myself that very question a hundred times.

"Honestly, Tory, listen to me. There's something wrong here."

"There surely is, and I'm looking at it," I spat out.

"No, listen," he implored, his voice rising both in tone and pitch, "I didn't take Lucy. I don't know what you're talking about. Honestly, Tory. Have I ever lied to you?" He swallowed that last and hurried on, "I'm telling you the truth, honest. I didn't take her."

I heard voices from upstairs, I looked around. It was the male half of the couple I had interrupted. "Ray," he was shouting, "are you okay? Will we call the police?" He didn't sound too keen on that option, though.

And Ray, it transpired, wasn't too keen on that option either. In fact, he was certain that he didn't want that to happen "No!" he yelled back. "No, shit, don't involve them," even as I was shouting at them, "Yes, phone the police. He's sold my daughter. I'll need their help to get her back!"

And Romeo hovered irresolute, perhaps wondering how badly they needed flat-mates – maybe they could manage the rent on their own if they gave up eating or something.

"Don't listen to her!" Ray hysterically shouted up at them. "Don't phone the police whatever you do. Just go back to bed. I'll be fine."

Giving one last anxious look, but perhaps glad to get off the hook, Romeo moved away.

Ray turned his attention back to me. "I don't have your daughter," he yelled, trying to get through to me.

And then Connor spoke for the first time since we had entered. And he released Ray, but his look told him that he would be able to overpower him at will, and Ray, rubbing his sore arm, nodded a little to acknowledge this. And Connor said, "Listen to him, Tory."

"I don't have Lucy," said Ray again. And there was some kind of truth in his voice, and that stopped me a little, and we stood, staring at each other. He was backed up against a door at the end of the hallway now, and we were both breathing heavily.

"Where is she, Ray? What did you do with her? Please, please, I beg you, tell me!"

"I didn't take her!" he shouted then, frustrated. "I swear, I haven't seen her since that night in the flat when I watched her sleeping."

"Ray," I said shortly, despairing now of ever getting him to admit the truth, "you wrote me a note saying you had taken her. Threatening to harm her if I went to the police. Well, I'm going to the police now, I can tell you. She can't be in any more danger than she is already. But how can you say now you didn't take her when you've already written a note saying you did!"

"A note? No, I didn't! Honestly." He clearly gave up on me then, and appealed to Connor. "Will *you* listen to sense even if she won't? I wrote no note. I took no child. I made no threats. And please don't call the police. Nothing to do with Lucy," he stressed urgently, "something else."

Drugs, we all realised.

I looked at him, confused now – he sounded so genuine. But then, I reminded myself, he always did. It was part of his charm, part of his way.

"But I saw the note," I protested, but there was something niggling at the back of my mind.

"You saw a note?" asked Ray. "Written by me? Saying that I had taken Lucy?"

I nodded, but there was that funny feeling . . .

"You couldn't have," he protested desperately. "I didn't write one. How could you have seen it?"

"Tory," interjected Connor in his deep baritone, "have you still got that note?"

"Yes, yes, I have. But it's back in Dublin."

"And you're sure it was from Ray?"

No, no, I wasn't, there was *something*, something I should have thought of.

"Yes, how did you know it was written by me? Was it in my handwriting?"

That was it.

I whispered, "It was typed. Even your name was typed. Oh dear God – it never occurred to me, I just read it. I was so shocked by what it said that I didn't even really register that it was typed."

And the knowledge, the realisation was rushing at me like a train, like a tidal wave. And I was standing on the tracks, standing on the beach, watching the train, the wave, hurtling towards me, knowing that its arrival was inevitable and that the impact was going to knock me over, pulverise me, sweep me away.

The knowledge arrived with a huge roar in my ears and a thump like a fist between my breasts.

I swivelled around and faced Connor. And I could see by his face that he had realised too, but I said it anyway. Whispered it anyway. "Carol . . ." I breathed, and he nodded, his face sombre.

"That's why she was so keen to keep up-to-date on

what was happening," I said breathlessly, "why she kept in touch, kept checking how it was going. I thought it was concern, God help me, I was grateful for it," I gave a short bitter laugh. "but it wasn't a bit. It was to keep track of where the hunt was, to know how safe she was from us – me – discovering her deception. And, dear God, I told her we had found him! She'll know – she must know – that as soon as we find Ray we'll know the truth."

And my breaths were coming quickly now, so quickly that I could hardly keep up, and my heart was thudding furiously, and the miserable hallway seemed to be spinning around me, and Connor's worried face was whirling past me dizzyingly, and even Ray looked mildly concerned as his head rushed by me, and somewhere I thought I could hear Lucy calling for me, and over her cries Carol was saying, "But you want her to be safe. You don't want to risk her life. What sort of mother are you?"

And even as Connor was saying anxiously, commandingly as his blurred face passed me for the twentieth time, "Tory? Tory . . ." I realised that I was well into the early stages of a panic attack. And I nodded briefly to him, and reached out my hand to his arm to anchor myself – at once the room slowed in its dizzy spin. And I concentrated on taking deep breaths, slowly, in and out, in and out, deep, slow, until I was calm again and the room was once more stationary.

"I *will* give in to the abandonment of hysterics once this is over," I told Connor grimly, "but I can't afford that luxury now." And he was shaking his head, no, you can't, even as I was continuing, "Not when Lucy still needs me to get her back, to stay calm, keep strong for her."

And somewhere deep down there was the beginning of a sense of the deepest, bitterest betrayal. But I didn't have time to concentrate on that either, to acknowledge it, or any other of the emotions which were swirling around inside me. I had to concentrate, had to keep my cool, to plan my next move.

"I told her we had found Ray," I said again. "She must realise that we'll know the truth as soon as we see him. And," and my voice was trembling as I said it, "she must have some Plan B in mind, for when we did find him."

"You mean, as soon as you saw me and then finally accepted the truth," put in Ray belligerently, rubbing his sore cheek where I had hit him. I threw him such a look, though, that he decided the better of it and subsided, contented himself with giving me hard-done-by looks.

"She doesn't know we found Ray," corrected Connor. "You rang her from the airport to say we knew where he was, but for all she knows it could have turned out to be false information like when we went to Waterford."

"Yes, you're right," I said, some small level of relief easing into me. "She doesn't *know* we're on to her. But, on the other hand, she must know it's a possibility. I'll have to ring her, tell her we didn't find him, hope she'll think she's safe, stay where she is."

"But you can't ring her tonight, Tory."

"No," I realised, "no, I can't. Not at, what? Two o'clock in the morning. It would never look natural. First thing in the morning, then?"

"Yes, first thing in the morning."

Ray had abandoned his poor-injured-me pose, obviously realising that it had been getting him nowhere. And something must have eventually penetrated the carapace of his self-absorption as he looked from Connor to me as we spoke in turn, like a spectator at a tennis match.

"What's going on?" he asked then, bewilderment on his weak face. "What *is* the story with Lucy?"

"Don't worry about it, Ray," I said wearily. "Why break the habit of a lifetime? Come on, Connor."

But Connor said, "Hang on a sec, Tory." And then to Ray, "While we're here, there's the little matter of two months' rent."

"What! Ah, Connor, come on!" he said indignantly. "Something's going on with Lucy, she's obviously missing somewhere, and *you're* worried about money! It's my daughter we should be all thinking of now, not rent," he finished piously, as if *he* were the concerned father and Connor merely an unscrupulous mercenary money-grabber.

I saw Connor begin to smile, I think he was amused, but *I* saw red.

"You bastard, you complete and utter waste of space, you . . . you worm!" I yelled. "Your daughter could have starved to death this past year-and-a-half for all you cared. Connor has never even met her, but he's been more a father to her than you ever were or will be. He's been helping me look for her, which has been costing him money and time, and *you're* accusing *him* of being more concerned about money?"

"It's okay, Tory," said Connor, and he spoke softly to Ray. But it was the kind of softness that had you looking around for the big stick being carried. "Ray, I'm glad you're so worried about Lucy. And so, maybe you're right, maybe we won't worry about the rent. But as Tory mentioned, I'm out of pocket over this search, so maybe, as such a loving, concerned father, you might like to reimburse me my expenses so far, and pay for the time I've spent looking for *your* daughter. And that comes to," and he mimed a brief calculation, "now, isn't that such a coincidence? It comes to exactly the same as the rent."

And Ray knew when he was beaten, and he had the sense to concede at last. "Okay," he said churlishly, "I'll get it."

And he disappeared upstairs and came back with some notes which he handed to Connor, who counted them.

"What's this?" said Connor, as if puzzled. "This isn't enough."

"It is! When you convert euros to sterling – "

"No, no," said Connor, still softly, "I don't think we'll bother converting at all. I think, given that I've come all the way to collect this, we'll say a one-for-one exchange rate."

And Ray glared at him, knowing well that this was

going to cost him half as much again, and Connor just smiled benignly at him, and stared him down. And so with a muttered curse Ray went upstairs again and returned with some more notes which he flung ungraciously at Connor.

"Pleasure doing business with you," said Connor, and turned away and without either of us looking at Ray again, we left the house and walked down the street, back towards the hotel.

Connor perused the notes in his hand before stuffing them into his pocket. "Drug money," he said conversationally. "I never thought I'd see the day I'd be handling drug money. Mind you, if it's good enough for the Criminal Assets Bureau, I guess it's good enough for me."

I knew that at another time I would appreciate Ray having got his come-uppance about the money. But for now . . . now I was thinking furiously, trying to compute the different information, the way the game had changed. Carol had her, not Ray . . . What was the best – the safest thing for Lucy – to do now? I thought about it as we walked through the mild night, our footsteps echoing slightly on the pavement. God, it was so tempting to go into the nearest police station, to hand the responsibility over to them, get them to contact their Irish colleagues. If we did that, the gardai could be at Carol's house within half an hour, and a brief few minutes after that Lucy could be safe. Or dead.

And then Connor cleared his throat. "What do you think about contacting the gardai now?"

"I've just been thinking about it," I acknowledged, "and it's very tempting. Especially as we now know where Lucy is – in Carol's house, so the gardai could just go straight there. And in some ways I feel a lot better knowing that Carol has her. Carol loved – loves," I hastily corrected myself, "*loves* Lucy, and she wouldn't hurt her. In fact, Connor, that's the only reason I can think of why she's done all this, why she's taken her – because she loves her so much she wants more than just childminding hours with her. That means that she'll be well looked-after. And at least Lucy knows Carol. It's not like she's with a stranger. And Carol *does* know how to look after children. I was terrified," I admitted, "that Ray would neglect her, simply because he didn't know what to do." I knew I was getting off the point here, not wanting to deal with his basic question. But he persisted.

"So, we'll go to the police?" he asked again.

"I don't know," I admitted. "Thing is, Connor, Carol's obviously unbalanced to take someone else's child, and that's scary. And her love for Lucy is obviously obsessive, which is equally scary. It means that Lucy will be well-minded only as long as Carol's control over her isn't threatened. That obsessive love might make her hurt Lucy to avoid having to give her back, exactly as Charlotte Riordan's father did. It's no coincidence, I'm sure, that that's the example Carol used in the note – it's obviously on her mind. It's what she has threatened."

"You've just contradicted yourself," Connor very reasonably pointed out. "First of all you said Carol wouldn't hurt Lucy, and now you're saying she might."

"I know," I admitted glumly. "Okay, let's do this. I'm reasonably certain that Lucy will be safe as long as nobody tries to get her back, and will be in danger if Carol feels anybody has found her. Right now she doesn't know what's going on. She knows that we had a good lead to Ray, but doesn't know if it panned out or not. And she's expecting me to ring as soon as I have any news, so she probably figures that she's safe at least until she hears from me. "So what I think we should do," I concluded, "is to just go and get some sleep. Or try to. And ring her in the morning and try and convince her we haven't found Ray. And play it by ear from there. It will be easier once I've spoken to her, I can try and judge what she's thinking."

"There's nothing we can do tonight, for sure," agreed Connor, "if we're not going to go to the police. So, yes, let's just try and get some sleep, and get the first flight back to Dublin in the morning."

So we went back to our hotel room, and Connor looked at the schedule in his wallet. "First flight is at eight o'clock. That means we have to be at the airport by six, which means leaving here around five. And it's now nearly three o'clock." He sighed. "Look, Tory, you lie down and have a couple of hours' sleep, and I'll pack and check us out, and wake you again at five. Okay?"

"Are you sure?" I asked, but not protesting much. I was *exhausted*.

And when he said that, yes, he was sure, I pulled back the covers and slipped under, still dressed, pausing only to take off my shoes. As I lay there I could hear him moving quietly around the room, softly opening and closing drawers.

Chapter 22

It seemed like no time at all that he was gently shaking me awake. I sat up, my eyes gritty, my mouth dry. I brushed my teeth and washed my face, and we were ready to go.

We went downstairs in the dark silent hotel, and I felt – despite Connor's assuring me that he *had* checked out and paid – like a thief sneaking out. As we reached the lobby he told me, "Turns out the Tube doesn't start running until six, so I've ordered a cab. Think of it as Ray's farewell gift to us."

So we sat in the black cab as it drove through the silent streets towards Heathrow. Neither of us spoke. I was half-dozing on his shoulder and I'd say he was trying to doze as well.

We got out of the cab when it reached the airport, paid the driver and thanked him, and checked in for the flight – luckily there were two seats left.

We sat in the departure lounge waiting for the flight to be called. Dawn was coming as the earth was turning on its axis and it was again our turn to face the sun. But it was still bloody early, and everyone waiting was quiet, half-asleep. To judge by the clothes, they were mostly business-people heading over for meetings, and there was no excitement, no novelty, no sense of an upcoming holiday to compensate for the early start.

I tried to doze, but thoughts were surging through my mind. Thoughts of betrayal beyond imagining, and manipulation, and lies and duplicity.

"Connor," I whispered into the church-like quiet.

"Hm?" he whispered back, dragging himself with obvious difficulty back from half-sleep.

"Connor," I said, and my anguish was sharp in my voice, and my anguish was like a knife in my heart it hurt so much, "Connor, she has played me for a fool."

He became fully awake then, knowing that this was important to me, knowing I needed to speak it out.

"She knew I trusted her, and she took that trust and used it to her advantage. She knew I wouldn't question what she told me, wouldn't look for holes in it because of the trust I had for her. And she was *so* clever," I whispered miserably, bitterly. "She must have got the idea to do this after I told her, in all innocence, about Ray asking me to share custody. That made it all so plausible. I totally believed her," I wailed, shaking my head helplessly, and Connor reached out and grasped my hand. "And you know, I was surprised that Lucy would go without distress to a stranger like Ray, but

346

Carol told me that she, Lucy I mean, was quite happy with strangers . . . and I took that. I thought that Carol knew her better than I did." The tears were rolling unchecked down my cheeks at this stage.

And the insights – the jagged, excruciating insights – were flooding me now, and like a religious penitent with a metal-tipped whip, I was hitting myself endlessly with them, bringing each deceit out into the air, and flailing myself with my stupidity for having believed them.

"And do you know," I whispered aghast – stunned equally at her audacity and at my own gullibility, "I'm thinking back, and Connor, the way she was looking anxiously at me as I phoned Ray's mobile – I thought she was anxious because Lucy was missing and anxiously hoping that I would contact him, but, of course, if I *had* got through to him, it might have been over then, so she was actually anxious that it *wouldn't* happen . . . And the way she wouldn't let me come to her house any more – there was always an excuse. She always came to my place. That's obviously because Lucy was at her house, but I never thought anything of it . . ." I was still shaking my head, in disbelief and exasperation. "God, what an fool I was! And Connor, do you know what's the worst?" I breathed.

He shook his head, held my hand tight, and his blue eyes gazed into my indeterminate ones as he told me without words that I could share this with him, that he would take it all onto his broad shoulders, his strong psyche, that he would hold it and carry it for me, with me, that I didn't have to do this alone.

"And the worst thing is," I whispered hoarsely through unshed tears, "she had the *cheek*, the total cheek, to come to my house and suggest that maybe I was being a bad mother by trying to get Lucy back, you know, that I was risking her life. She said that maybe I should just let Ray keep Lucy! – for Lucy's sake, she said. She steered me towards the biblical story of Solomon – but she was so clever that it was actually I who used that example."

"What?" Connor burst out, aghast. "Are you serious?"

I nodded tearfully, "Yes. And she was suggesting, very subtly, mind you, I never saw through it, that I would be like the false mother in the Bible if I kept looking for Lucy!"

Connor was shaking his head in disbelief.

"I know it sounds stupid, Connor, but she was *so* clever that I never suspected. She was speaking as if she was really reluctant to say all this, and that she hoped I would still try and get Lucy back, because she, Carol, was missing her. And of course, it's obvious now, she was hoping I would give up the search, so that she could sail off into the sunset with Lucy." I gave a bitter, unamused laugh.

"But you didn't give up," Connor reminded me. "So she didn't win, despite her best efforts. Your love for Lucy kept you searching regardless."

"But she still has Lucy," I reminded him in my turn.

"There is that. But not for long."

"No." I brightened a little. "Not for long."

Eventually the flight was called and we drooped our way onto the aircraft. The flight home was so different from the flight over. Then, I had been buoyed up at the thoughts of finding Lucy, I had thought I'd be doing this return trip with her on my knee. Now I was sunk in misery and exhaustion, and I just dozed as much as I could, propped against Connor's shoulder. He was sitting in the middle seat, with nowhere to rest his head, so I don't know how much sleep he managed to get.

We arrived in Dublin airport and disembarked. As we walked from the gate to the arrivals hall (a day's exercise in itself) I looked at my watch. "Twenty past nine," I said. "It's probably too early to ring her. I don't want to alert her by ringing her too early."

We went from the arrivals hall to the long-term-carpark shuttle bus. One came along pretty soon, and a couple of minutes later it deposited us at the carpark.

We sat into the car and I looked at my watch again. It was a quarter to ten now.

"It's time," I said, and even as he was nodding I was opening my mobile phone and with shaking fingers I began to dial Carol's number. And then, halfway through dialling it, I stopped. And I thought.

I was a poor liar at the best of times, I knew, but now my daughter's safety – possibly her life – was going to rest on how well I managed to convince Carol that her secret was still safe, that we still thought it was Ray who had Lucy.

As I had said to Connor, it was a fair bet that she had a contingency plan – a Plan B – to be put into action if, or when, I discovered it was she who had Lucy. And I was pretty sure I wouldn't like what that involved. So,

I debated, I had to hope that she had not yet acted on her Plan B . . . and I had to convince her that there was no need to do so.

Much better to have Carol and Lucy still at Carol's house. We would still have the problem of how to get her back, of course, but at least we would know where she was. We would be that much ahead of the game.

And worst of all, I was going to have to speak nicely to a woman I now hated, the very thought of whom made me want to vomit, a woman whose name would stick in my throat as I tried to say it. But say it I would have to, *and* without making obvious any of the revulsion I was feeling.

So I took a deep breath and redialled the number. As I sat there in the car in the long-stay carpark of Dublin's airport, with cars pulling in and others leaving, and excited people decanting themselves and their cases from their cars prior to flying off, and tired travellers returning to their cars after their trip, and everybody intent on their own lives, I listened to the phone ringing. Please let her still be there, I begged a deity in whom I wasn't sure I believed. Please let her not already have gone off with Lucy.

The ringing continued and I began to fear the worst, as I stood there clutching the phone to my ear, aware of it hurting me as I pressed it against my head.

"No answer?" asked an intently watching Connor.

"No answer. I'll try her mobile."

I rang her mobile number and listened to it ring. After three or four rings it was answered.

"Hello?" said Carol, her voice wary.

I took a deep (and I hoped, silent) breath. This was it. "Carol," I said, anguish and despair in my voice, and *that* wasn't acted, "Carol," and I allowed a sob to creep into my voice, and again, that wasn't hard, "he's not here!" I wailed, "I can't believe it, yet *another* dead end!"

"Hush," she said soothingly, "calm down. Now, how do you know he isn't there? Are you sure?"

"The pub management have never heard of him," I said, thinking, you bitch, you total bitch!

"Oh no," she said, sympathy dripping from her, and was it my imagination or was she deliberately overplaying it now? Or was it just that, now that I knew it was all false, I could hear the insincerity I had never before looked for, had never before noticed. "If the management has never heard of him, that means you have no leads to follow."

"No," I said, but then, realising that it would be better if she thought I was still following the false trail I revised what I was saying, "except that I've just rung Johnno back, and now he says he thinks he just said the wrong area by mistake. You know, the wrong part of London. He told us it was Earl's Court, but he thinks now it was Kilburn. So I'm on my way there now. It'll be a much harder search, of course – looking for an Irish pub in Kilburn is like looking for straw in a haystack – so finding the right one will be a long job. But I'm going to do it," I told her, determination in my voice, "I'm going to keep looking over here until I find him."

"Good for you," said Carol approvingly, and I

marvelled despite myself at her coolness, the way she could lie so barefacedly.

"So I'm on my way now," I said, "and I'll ring you as soon as I have any news, and let you know how I'm getting on." As I was speaking a large aircraft took off literally over my head.

"Sorry, I couldn't hear that," said Carol, "what on *earth* was that noise?"

"A truck," I lied, "a huge truck just rattling past. Honestly you'd think they wouldn't let them into the city centre but they do. Anyway, I said I'm going to Kilburn this morning, and I'll let you know how I get on."

"Do that," said Carol, and her voice was warm and concerned as she said, "Oh Tory, poor you. You've been through so much already. It's been so difficult for you."

"Yes, well," I said, managing, with *huge* restraint not to shout at her, not to yell at her that she could put her false warmth and concern right where the sun don't shine, and while she was at it she could bloody well give me my daughter back, "it *has* been tough, but you know, what else can I do?"

"Nothing else," she said, and then: "Well, Tory, do ring me as soon as you've any news. God knows I'm as desperate as you are for you to find Lucy again – I'm dying to see her too."

You lying *bitch!* I managed not to say. "Okay, Carol, I'd better go. The sooner I start the sooner I'll find him."

"And is that luscious landlord still helping you?" she enquired sweetly.

"No, no, he's not. Remember, I told you we had a

row. Nope, it's just little old me," and I gave an ostensibly brave laugh. "Anyway, Carol, I'll talk to you soon, bye," and I rung off to the sound of her calling, "Good luck!"

"Well?" asked Connor anxiously, "how did it go? Do you think she bought it?"

"I don't know. I think so, but I can't be sure. I think so, though," I said again. "She didn't sound suspicious at all. Commiserated with me about the dead end, was sympathetic for all I was going through," I literally gagged as I related this, and Connor put out a hand and placed it on my shoulder, "wants to hear how I get on."

"I bet she does," he said sardonically.

"Do you know, that was the most incredibly *surreal* conversation ever. Neither of us spoke one word of truth . . . I was lying to her, and she was lying to me, and I knew *she* was lying to *me*, and she may well have known *I* was lying to *her*, and if so she knew that I knew she was lying to me. But both of us carried on regardless, sticking to our part of the script. It was bizarre."

"It sounds it."

"I told her you were no longer in the picture, I thought it might give us some advantage, although I can't yet imagine what. But I'm trying to think, and I can't remember, when I rang her to say I was going to London to find Ray, did I say *we* then, or *I*? And if I said *we*, did she pick up on it?"

And he tried to think back, but he shook his head, "I can't remember either. There's nothing you can do about it now, though. She knows what she knows, or suspects what she suspects."

But I was worrying about it. "But if she remembers me saying *we*, she'll know I was lying when I said you weren't helping me any more. And if she knows I was lying, she'll know I'm onto her – why else would I lie to her?"

"Tory, Tory," he said, "what's done is done. Stop trying to second-guess her like this – you'll crack up if you go too far down that road. So what now?"

"We go to her house."

"Right," he said, switching on the ignition. "Will you direct me?" As he drove off he asked, "How do you think we should play it?"

"She's either there or she's not," I said, thinking it through. "If she's still there it's because she did believe me, and she thinks I'm still in London. And she doesn't know what you look like, even if she didn't believe me that you're no longer part of this. So, if she's still at the house, I think you should just knock on the door, say you're an insurance salesman or something, and overpower her with that fancy karate stuff you used on What's-his-face – Murtagh's stooge – and on Ray. And if she didn't believe that I'm still in London, if she has put this famous Plan B into action, either she's not there, in which case there's no problem you knocking on the door. No advantage either," I acknowledged, "but no problem. Or she *is* there and Lucy is . . . is . . ." I couldn't say it, "in which case you overpower her anyway. Sound like a plan?"

He nodded, wearily rubbing his hand against his forehead. "Okay. In that case, I think I might go home first. You know, have a shower and a shave, and change into a suit so that I look something like an insurance salesman."

"Good idea."

So we drove to Connor's house and he spruced himself up. I couldn't help staring at the finished result. I had never seen him in a suit, never seen him so formal. He looked even more handsome, but somehow he looked sterner, less approachable. And he looked almost de-sexed as the suit hid his strong arms, the well-muscled chest, the bulge at his groin. I shook myself. "You look perfect," I said. "She won't know what's hit her."

"Perhaps literally," he said self-mockingly as he led the way back to the car. "Tory, I know this is the best way, and I know I can overpower her without hurting her, and I know what she is, but still . . . I really don't feel comfortable about using force on any woman." He caught my sharp look. "Don't worry, I will, I know it's the best thing to do, but I'm just sharing with you that I don't like the idea."

And I thought mutinously that he didn't have to like it, he just had to do it. I hadn't yet dared let myself really think about how Carol had betrayed me, or let myself feel too much about it, because I knew such thoughts, such feelings, would overwhelm me at a time when I needed all the self-control I could get. But equally I knew that those thoughts and feelings wouldn't leave any room for sympathy for her.

So we arrived at Carol's road, and drove past her house. Her car was gone from the driveway. "She wasn't at home when I rang," I said. "I got her on the mobile, remember?"

"I'll try the door anyway," he said, driving on and parking around the corner. He got out of the car. "Stay here. Keep your head down. I'll be back."

And off he went and I was left sitting there, every atom of my body a quivering little ball of anxiety, wondering how he was getting on, what was happening. I knew he was right – there was no way we could risk her seeing me, but still it galled me to be left sitting there just waiting.

But as it turned out I didn't have to wait long. It was only about five minutes later that he was knocking on the passenger window. "Come on," he said bluntly, his face grim.

I clambered out of the car, asking as I did so, "What happened?"

We walked together back to the house, and he tersely filled me in. "She's not there, as you said. There's no answer. And her next-door neighbour saw me knocking on the door, and going around the back, and like a good citizen or a nosy old lady – take your pick – came out to see what I was doing. And she told me that Carol has gone away for a few days. To Wales, on the ferry. But she, the neighbour, has a key to the house. She won't give it to me, though, not surprising, I suppose. So can you see if you can talk her into it?"

Carol's house, when we reached it a few moment later, looked dark and deserted, and it somehow had an abandoned air of a house which knew its occupant had gone for more than just a few days. Or maybe I was being fanciful.

And I was still wondering why Connor looked so grim. This wasn't great news, sure, but something in his demeanour made me think that he hadn't told me everything. And he hadn't.

He paused, cleared his throat awkwardly and took a deep breath before saying, "Thing is, Tory, she said that Carol went off on her own," and his face showed how much he had not wanted to say that to me.

My hands went to my face. "Oh no. Connor, no!"

"That's what she said. It mightn't be as bad as . . . well, really bad. Come on." He strode up the driveway of the next-door house. "Her name's Mrs Dooley," he told me. "I need you to get the key off her, and I'll – I'll go into the house while you wait outside." And as he was ringing the doorbell I realised with a dreadful clarity exactly what he was thinking, exactly why he didn't want me to go into the house with him, and I blanched.

But I didn't have time for more than that. Mrs Dooley must have been hovering the other side of the door as it began to open immediately after Connor's ringing the doorbell. It opened only about four inches, and we realised that she had left the door chain in place. We got a narrow view of a small old lady with a hooked nose and rheumy pale-blue eyes – or at least, the eye we could see was pale-blue and rheumy and I assumed the other one was also. She was staring balefully at Connor, obviously not at all sure whether to trust him or not.

"Hello, Mrs Dooley, it's me again!" said Connor, and his voice was bright and his expression cheerful, but I could see by a narrowness in his eyes, a tightness to his posture, exactly how much this cheery tone was costing him. "As I told you, here's the young lady, Tory, who's Carol's friend."

And Mrs Dooley turned her gaze to me, and her face lit up. "Of course, I know you!" she said. "Oh you naughty boy," she said to Connor, "telling me that was Carol's friend – why, isn't it her niece! Hold on a second." And the door closed, and opened again, fully this time, the chain having obviously been released. "That's right, you're Carol's niece, aren't you? Haven't I often seen you at Carol's house with the little girl! Oh," she sighed, "Carol is forever telling me how fond she is of you, and of course, of the little girl. Her grandniece, Carol always reminds me, and how lucky she is to be able to mind her for you." She laughed coquettishly. "You'd swear nobody ever had a grandniece in the world before now, the way Carol goes on about her."

Connor and I exchanged the merest of puzzled glances as I said, "That's right, Mrs Dooley. I'm her niece. And I thought that Aunt . . . Aunt Carol," I managed to get my mouth around the words, "would be here, but you're saying she's gone away?"

"That's right. She went, let me see now," she paused to think about it, to search her memory, "it would have been yesterday morning, I think."

Connor and I exchanged sharp glances at that information: she must have left just after I had phoned as we were on our way to London, and told her we had found Ray's whereabouts.

"And she's going to Wales, you say?"

"That's what she said, dear. At least, she said she was getting the ferry to Wales, but that she was going to explore some of England too. Oh, she was looking forward to the trip! She was so excited, talking nineteen-to-the-dozen. My poor old ears could barely keep up with her, I don't mind telling you."

Another glance between Connor and me. Excited? Or manic?

And now we were coming to the crux of the matter. I said, forcing myself to keep my tone gentle, relaxed, "And you told Connor she was travelling alone?"

"Why, yes, dear. I don't know, in my day no lady would have dreamed of travelling alone like that, with no man or companion to help her. And I asked her, are you going to be able to manage like that, all on your own, with nobody to help you with the child? But you know, she said she would be fine, and she – "

But with the sound of a rush of blood pounding like the wind through my ears I didn't hear what else she said. Not after she had said that most beautiful word, *child*. But I felt my whole body relax, and I could see that Connor, too, had let a breath out, let his tightly held shoulders ease slightly.

Okay, Lucy was still missing, and we had no idea where she was, and she was on the way to Britain – and you could easily get lost in Britain, if you had a mind to. But . . . but she was still alive!

"Mrs Dooley, you mentioned Carol gave you a key?" I said.

"Oh yes, dear, that's right. She said I could give it to you. 'Give it to my niece, Mrs Dooley,' she told me. 'Give it to nobody else.' Let me see, what did I do with it?" And she turned and tottered back into the gloom of the house, leaving Connor and me still standing at her doorway.

And after a few minutes she returned, and handed me a door-key. "There you are, dear. I knew I had it somewhere!"

"Thank you, Mrs Dooley, I appreciate that," I said even as I was backing away, down her drive.

Back up Carol's drive, and I inserted the key into the door and turned it. It opened and I went again into that familiar house, Connor following behind.

"Tory, we should phone the police now," he was saying. "We'll never find her in Britain. We'll certainly need their help for that."

"True," I said, looking around me, "but it can wait a few minutes. If she left yesterday morning she's long gone now. A little longer won't make any difference." I walked into the sitting-room, saying to him over my shoulder, "Because, you know, Connor, I think there's something a bit suspicious about this."

"The woman's taken your daughter and disappeared and you think there's something suspicious? No shit, Sherlock," he muttered sarcastically.

I glanced over at him, and saw to my remorse that

he was looking haggard with exhaustion. He hadn't got *any* sleep last night, I remembered, apart from whatever doze he had managed to snatch on the aircraft, and if he cared at all – which he certainly seemed to – the stress of it all must be getting to him too. As I looked at him, tired and depleted, I got a sudden picture, a ghost-like image from the future, of him as an old man. And so I didn't respond as I had originally been tempted to, by hitting back with some smart comment.

"Apart from that," I merely said, as I poked around, looking to see what I might find, "do you not think it's all a bit handy, her telling Mrs Dooley her travel plans? And her leaving the key for us?"

"Good point," conceded Connor. "Sorry for snapping."

"Don't worry," I said, and I went over to him and put my arms around him, and he put his arms around me, "You're tired; we're both tired," and we clung together for a moment or two, drawing strength from each other.

Reluctantly I pulled away then, and continued my search. And I came to the little wicker bin beside the fireplace. As long as I knew Carol it had contained each day's paper waiting to be read before being discarded, and sure enough, I saw, Friday's paper was in there. But something else too. I covered my hand by pulling a fold of my jumper over it, and pulled it out.

"Look," I said, showing it to Connor, "a ferry brochure. With," I added as I looked inside, still careful to leave no fingerprints, "the details for the Dublin-Holyhead service carefully ringed. She was subtle enough to put it in the bin, but still . . . I think it's all a massive red herring. She's trying to put us off the scent."

"I agree with you. Which means," he said, his voice full of relief, "that we can be sure the one place she isn't, is Britain. And of course she can't get any further than that without a passport for Lucy. So at least she's still in Ireland."

"Unless it's a massive double-bluff," I agreed, "which I don't think it is. She's clever, but not that clever. I hope."

I went into the kitchen then, Connor following me.

"Ha," I laughed shortly, "look." And there on the notice-board beside the sink was a press-cutting, where there had never been a press-cutting before. CHARLOTTE FOUND DEAD! read the headline. It was one newspaper's version of the tragic story of Charlotte Riordan, killed by her father. "It's a warning," I said bitterly, "a reminder to me. Clever enough, though – although it's a bizarre thing for her to have, it admits nothing. It would mean nothing to anybody but me." I looked around, but there was nothing further of interest in the kitchen. "You can see now why she wanted us to have the key," I said. "She's been leaving all these messages for me. Just in case we broke in, rather than talking to Mrs Dooley – she couldn't bank on us doing that. And even if we did talk to Mrs Dooley, well, there's no harm a message being repeated, is there?"

We went upstairs, and there was one final message for me there. A little red sock, lying forlornly under a bed. It was unclear whether Carol had realised it was there, but no matter, it was a clear signal as to where Lucy had spent the past week.

We went downstairs again, into the little sitting-room.

"Now what?" I asked, weariness and fear overcoming me, hoping Connor could magically make it all better, fetch his noble steed and go and rescue the fair – albeit very young – maiden. But Connor's only human, and Connor was tired and weary too, and he shook his head despairingly.

"The gardai?" he asked. "Really, Tory, do we have any choice now? We have no idea where she's gone, none at all. Nowhere to start searching."

"Not the gardai. You saw that message she has left us. I can't risk Lucy's life, Connor. But you know, something you've just said, about where she might have gone. There's a thought simmering just below my consciousness, some information . . ." I said slowly.

"Where? It would have to be somewhere she would feel safe, somewhere she would have resources," he said.

As he spoke the memory came nearer and nearer but it was still tantalisingly out of touch, but then: "Hang on, I think I have it . . . no, it's gone, damn!" I looked at him. "There's something, Connor, though. Something she said once – oh, if only I could remember it!"

I looked around the room, hoping for inspiration, and my gaze landed on the two photographs on the television. "Her sons," I said, pointing them out to Connor. "They might know where she would be."

He tiredly wiped his eyes. "And do you happen to have their phone numbers?" he asked, unsuccessfully trying to ask without sarcasm.

"No. No, I don't. But look, I know it's a long shot, but why don't we take the photos out of the frames, there might be some identifying details on the back."

"Okay." Connor shrugged. "When you've no sensible ideas you might as well act on any and all ideas." So he went over and picked up one of the frames and began to unclip it at the back. He removed the cardboard back, and then said, "Oh . . ." and we could both see it – a portion of a magazine article. Recipes, if memory serves. I lifted it up, and turned it over. And at the bottom of the photograph we could now read the caption, which had been previously hidden by the frame. *"Dermot Murnane,"* it read, *"graduating from UCG after his parents had been told he wouldn't live to his fourth birthday."*

"Good for him," I muttered. And, truly, it was. But it didn't help us. "She cut that picture out of a magazine!" I said, incredulous, shaking my head at her audacity, and luckily Connor managed to rein in his sarcasm and didn't comment on my stating-the-bleeding-obvious. "He's not her son at all! And the other one's probably the same."

Connor wondered aloud, "Was she planning this all along?"

"Maybe. Or maybe it was window-dressing for her childminding business," I said. "You know, to make people more confident in her. Seeing as she was the mother of two sons she obviously had experience in looking after children. And the fact that they're both graduating . . . it sends its own subliminal message, after all. Not only did she raise two sons, but she raised them well enough that they went off and got degrees. She probably hadn't planned to abduct Lucy from the very start . . . I hope not anyway!" I said slightly hysterically. "It probably just came to her as she grew to love Lucy. In her own twisted way."

"Okay," said Connor, trying to regain control of the situation. "Well, we knew that the photos were a long shot, even if they had been genuine. Look, are we finished here? This place is giving me the creeps. Let's go somewhere else, you might find it easier to remember there, where Carol might have gone."

"Good point."

So we left the house, shutting the door behind us, and returned to the car.

"My place?" he asked, and I nodded distractedly, still desperately trying to think of what it was that Carol might have said that would give a clue to where she had been.

"Stop thinking about it," he said. "It'll never come if you push it. Just think about something else and when you least expect it, you'll remember."

"Good advice," I said ruefully, "but hard to follow. Hard to make myself stop thinking when I'm so desperate."

When we reached his house I realised just how grubby I felt, having been wearing the same clothes since yesterday morning. I was also exhausted, and a wash might revitalise me. So I asked him, "Can I have a shower?" and he waved a be-my-guest gesture. And I stood under the shower and let the accumulated grime of the past day and a half wash away from me. And as I did so I remembered! Or at least, I half-remembered. If there was ever a time to shout 'Eureka,' this was it.

"Connor!" I shouted instead, jumping out of the shower, half-washed though I was, "Connor," I yelled, throwing a towel around me and heading for the door. And he had heard me and was just outside the door as I opened it.

"A holiday home!" I said. "It was a holiday home her family had – still has. It was when we were talking about my name, and she said it was just as well she wasn't called after the place her parents honeymooned, because it would have sounded so strange as a name!"

"That's great! Where was it?"

"Ah," I said, "that's the bit I can't remember. It was only idle conversation a long time ago. But I do remember that it was in County Cork. And I think I must know it, and have known it's on the coast, because I remember when she was talking about it an image flashed into my head of her at the beach."

"Would you know it if you heard it?"

"Yes," I nodded, "yes, I'm sure I would."

"That's great!" he said again. "Look, you get dried and dressed, and I'll get out my road-atlas, and we'll go through it until we find it."

I frantically half-dried myself, and pulled clean clothes out of the weekend-bag I had brought to

London, and was sitting on Connor's sofa in little more time than it took him to get the atlas out.

And slowly, carefully, we began going around the coastline of County Cork, saying each name we came to. "What'll we do if we don't find it?" I worried. "Maybe it's not big enough to be on this map."

"It would want to be *very* small not to be on this," Connor assured me, "and if that's the case, we'll just go straight out and buy a really detailed Ordnance Survey map. We'll find it."

But it didn't come to that, because quite soon after we found it.

"Cilltubber," I said triumphantly, pointing to its name which sat on the west Cork coastline. "That's it!"

"Are you sure that's what she said?"

"Positive!"

"Tory," he said cautiously, "I don't want to always be the pessimist, but is there any chance she could have just picked that place to tell you about. I mean, if she's devious enough to fake photographs of sons . . ."

I thought about it. "No, I don't think so. We were talking about my name, and she said it in the context of what she would have been called if she had been called after her parents' honeymoon destination. And she mentioned that the family had, and still has, a holiday cottage there. No," I said, thinking again, "even liars can't lie all the time, Connor. It's too exhausting. And the way the subject came up, I'm sure . . . I'm almost certain . . . that it was genuine."

"Right then," he closed the book decisively, and

stood up. "Come on then," and he reached out his hand and pulled me up too. "We're off to Cilltubber, County Cork."

Buoyed up by finding this information, I stood up, and we hugged, and he whispered in my ear, "It'll soon be over," and although I knew he couldn't know that – that there were a million things that could go wrong before we found Lucy – it was good to hear.

Chapter 23

So we hefted our still-unpacked weekend bags and left his house for yet another journey in the search for Lucy. We were soon heading out of Dublin, on the N7 which would bring us, four or five hours later, to Cork city. And then, another hour or so to Cilltubber. A long journey. But hopefully – this time – a profitable one.

I yawned hugely then – the night's wakefulness was catching up with me.

"Why don't you try to sleep?" Connor suggested. "And then if you don't mind, I'll wake you in a couple of hours and you could take over driving for a while, so I can have a doze."

"Sure," I said, "good idea."

So I slept as best as I could, and it must have been better than I realised, because the next thing I knew he was saying my name in my ear, and I woke and realised that we had stopped.

"I thought we'd stop for lunch," he said. "It's just gone two, and neither of us has eaten all day."

"Good point," I said, stretching, and then getting out of the car and stretching some more. He had parked outside a pub which stood on its own in the middle of nowhere. But it offered food, and to judge by the huge variety of counties indicated on the registration plates of the cars around us, not to mention a few British cars, it got lots of passing trade.

So we went in and ordered sandwiches and soup. As we were eating it he said, "While you were asleep I've been trying to think how we should play this. How we find her when we get to Cilltubber, I mean. And I have to admit that I haven't come up with any solutions. What I have done, however, is to identify lots of problems," he said proudly but with a wry expression mocking his pride in this dubious accomplishment. "Right, all this is assuming that she *hasn't* double-bluffed us about going to Britain, and that she didn't lie to you about her family holiday home in Cilltubber, and furthermore assuming that that's where she's gone." He sighed, and then began listing the problems, enumerating them on his fingers: "First of all, we don't know exactly where in Cilltubber she lives, so we'll have to find her. You said that her parents had the holiday home there?" and when I nodded he continued, "That means that she's probably well-known in the area, if the family have had the house that long. Which is good because it probably means lots of people know where she is. But the bad news is that the local people are probably going to have their loyalty firmly on her side, unless we can show good reason why that should not be so. So we'll have to be really careful about who we ask for directions to her house.

"Secondly, there's the fact that she mustn't see you. I'll be able to go as I please, but the problem is that I've never seen her. That's not insurmountable, you'll be able to describe her well, but we still have to remember that. Have you still got that photo of Lucy in your purse?"

"I have," I said, and I got it and handed it to him.

"I mean, I'm sure I'd recognise Lucy from the last time I saw the photo, but just to refresh my memory . . . Mind you, we'll be very lucky if I get to see her – Carol is probably keeping her well hidden. The other problem is that even if we find her house, we'll need to take her by surprise, get to her before she can harm Lucy. And you know," he added wryly, "I've clean forgotten all that training the SAS gave me, in – you know – skills such as covert reconnaissance, hostage negotiation, and rescue operations. And she's probably going to be on her guard. She might have forgotten telling you about Cilltubber, especially if it was said as casually as you said. Or she might be assuming that you haven't thought of it, haven't remembered it. But she will still be alert, she can't not be, not when she's got someone else's baby. Oh, Tory, I still think we should go to the guards, you know."

"We will," I said, realising that he was right, that we couldn't keep going like this. "If this doesn't work, we will, okay. But, please, let's try this first."

"Okay," he conceded, taking another bite of his

sandwich, "but now that I've applied my massive intellect to identifying the problems, I'll leave you the easy job," he waved an airy hand, "of finding the solutions."

"There's another problem," I admitted. "People locally might not know her by the same surname as I do. She told me she's widowed. Now, that dead husband could be as much a fiction as the two graduate sons, but if not, she wouldn't have her maiden name any more. Women of her generation rarely kept their own names."

"Hmm," he said, raising his eyebrows and shaking his head in disbelief at the task we were setting ourselves.

I hurried on, "But it's not as bleak as that. We *do* have some advantages. For a start, like you said, she probably doesn't expect us to be able to find Cilltubber, and she doesn't know you. Also, we still have her mobile phone number – I don't know yet how that will be of use to us," I admitted, "but it might. And we know what car she drives."

"So, we'll drive around looking for her car?"

I shrugged. "Unless you can think of something else?"

He shook his head. "Remember, *I* identified the problems, it's *your* job to come up with the solutions." But he smiled deprecatingly at me. He threw back the last of his pint, and finished his sandwich. "Come on so."

When we got to his car he asked me, "Do you mind driving for a bit? I'm totally exhausted."

"Of course not!"

We got into the car and he showed me the route – it was actually very easy, follow the road we were on until we reached the outskirts of Cork city, and then take the by-pass under the Jack Lynch tunnel, and onto the N71, and keep going until we hit Cilltubber.

"I can do that," I said.

He looked at his watch. "It's three o'clock, give or take. We should be there before six. I never thought of getting accommodation there, but we should be able to find something."

"Right."

We drove off, and I was a little nervous at first with having this much engine-power at my disposal. I was more used to my own car, which did zero to sixty in about five minutes. As long as there was a tail-wind and you spoke to it nicely. Before long I heard a gentle snoring and Connor, bless him, was fast asleep, and I relaxed into the union with the car, and the gentle throbbing of its engine and the incredible responsiveness of its pedals. And the miles flew past until I was coming into Cork city. Unfortunately it was now rush-hour, and while getting onto the ring-road was easy, getting along it wasn't so handy. But still, I shrugged philosophically, what else could I do? And I inched my way along with all the other drivers caught in the traffic, and not one of us admitting that we weren't just caught in traffic, we *were* the traffic.

And eventually, about an hour and a half after we left Cork city, we reached Cilltubber. I pulled up just past the metal name-plate which had informed me that this was, indeed, our destination, and which had welcomed me, and I shook Connor gently awake.

"Okay, here we are."

I eased back onto the road and drove slowly further into the town. We only got about a hundred yards before I spotted possible accommodation for us.

"There's a hotel," I said, indicating the low, white, elderly building bearing the sign, *Cilltubber House Hotel,* on the right side of the road. "Will I go and see if they have rooms?"

"Sure."

So I parked and got out, and made my way into the rather dreary lobby and managed to book a double room. Connor and I brought our bags up to the room and looked around. It was clean, you could definitely say that. But the décor looked like it came from *The Land That Time Forgot.* Heavy dark wood-laminate, swirly carpets with the static shining off them.

"Have you any idea whether the house was in the town, or outside it?" asked Connor, and I shook my head.

"No, 'fraid not."

"Well, look, it's going to be bright for a few hours yet – why don't you get some rest while I take a walk through the town, or as much of it as is doable, depending on its size, do it logically, and see if I can find her car."

"Sounds like a plan," I said, and I gave him the details of the car. "It's a red Nissan Micra, and the first bit of the reg is 03D, and I can't remember the number exactly but it's got the digits 275 in it, which I always remember because – believe it or not – that's Lucy's birthday – the 27th of May."

"Okay," he said, "you stay here, so, and I'll head off.

This is mad," he said, shaking his head. "This is no sort of a plan at all. It's very possible that I *will* pass her house, but if she's out in her car, I wouldn't even realise that. But we might consider that part of the town searched. Or, otherwise, do we keep checking the same parts of the town over and over? Without even knowing for sure that she's here?"

"I don't know," I had to admit. "Just give it a day or two, Connor. Let's do our best. And if it doesn't work, we'll go to the police like we agreed."

He gave his graceful shrug, "Okay," and came over to me, kissed me full on the lips and held me tight. "I love you," he said. "I'll see you later."

And I held him tight back, relishing the feel of him within my arms, the solidness and warmth of him.

After he had gone I was restless and on edge. There was a television in the room, okay, but I couldn't really settle to watching television under the circumstances. I know, I decided after about forty minutes of aimlessly wandering around the room like a caged panther, I'll go down to the bar for a drink. I'll try to strike up conversation with someone. You never know who might know something.

So I did that very thing, and settled myself at the bar, but with my body angled so that I could see the door and also the window onto the street. I didn't think she would come into the bar, nor walk past – surely I couldn't be that lucky – but worse again would be if she did do either of those things, and I missed her.

"What'll it be?" asked the young handsome barman in that unique, melodious Cork accent.

"A red wine, please."

He got me a mini-bottle of red wine, courteously unscrewing the top and pouring a little into my glass.

"Cheers," I told him, as I took a sip.

And so he began to talk to me, with a mixture of professional courtesy and, I suppose, interest in a woman sitting alone in a bar, no matter that I was probably ten years his senior. "You down here on holiday?" he asked, polishing some glasses.

"Just for a few days. Just arrived today, and I must say, you've got a gorgeous town!" Not that I had seen any of it bar the hundred metres between the boundary-sign and this hotel, but it seemed a fair bet, and also a fairly ingratiating thing to say.

He smiled then. "Ah, it's not too bad. We like it."

"And does it get on your nerves, being taken over by tourists like me in the summer?" I said coquettishly.

"Ach, no, of course not!" he said diplomatically. "We love to see the tourists coming, brings a bit of life into the town, you know like." *And a lot of money* – the thought floated unspoken above both our heads. "Mind you, it's nice off-season too. It's quieter when it's just ourselves. So we get the best of both worlds," he added hurriedly. "Oh, excuse me," and he went to the far end of the bar to serve someone else.

But he was back as soon as he had done that – the glasses at my end of the bar obviously needing a lot of polishing.

"I was wondering, though," I said, taking a sip of my wine and licking my lips sensuously after it, (or what I hoped was sensuously, I didn't have much practice in this – for all I know I looked like a post-dinner Rottweiler), "how do the locals feel about people buying holiday homes here? I mean, obviously if people are staying somewhere like the hotel here, they're contributing to the local economy. But if they have their own home, they're using the amenities when they feel like it, without necessarily contributing a whole lot."

His eyes darted left and right, looking for rescue. God love him, he was about twenty, and beginning to realise he was out of his depth a little. Henry Kissinger he wasn't, and his powers of diplomacy were being seriously stretched. I decided to help him out a little.

"I think that if *I* lived here I'd resent it. In fact, now that I think of it, a friend of my mother's has a holiday home around here. But she says her case is different, that they've had the holiday cottage here since she was a child, so that she's practically a local herself."

"Really," he said, moving away a little, and I got the sense that whatever meagre attractions my company might hold for him were finely balanced against my demanding conversation, and that the balance was about to tip in favour of abandoning me for more relaxed company. So I hurried on without, perhaps, the casual unconcerned air I had hoped to maintain, "In fact, would you know her? Name of Carol Moore? She's about fifty, fifty-five maybe? And she's been coming here since she was a child. I'm pretty sure it was Cilltubber, anyway. Wouldn't that be hilarious," I said urgently, leaning forward towards him a little, and I was going to – I swear I was – grab his wrist if he edged just *one* more step away, "if she lived near here? I could pop in and visit her while I was here."

"No," he said shaking his head, "no, I don't know her. Maybe the manager would, though. I'll go and ask," and off he scuttled.

And I sat back on the barstool and took another sip of my wine. Well, I had really blown that, hadn't I? Be discreet, we had agreed. Above all don't let news get back to her that you're looking for her, we had said. And now this young barman would be regaling his family and friends with the story of this mad one from Dublin, and the manager would be next to hear the tale and might consider it worth chatting about. Connor would go through me for a *shortcut*.

A fifty-ish man approached me then. "Excuse me? I'm Paudie Connor, the manager here. I understand from young Michael that you were looking for somebody?"

"Carol Moore," I said, looking him in the eye. "She's a friend of my mother's and I just remembered that she has a holiday home somewhere in West Cork. I *thought* it was Cilltubber, and I just asked – Michael, was it? – on the off-chance. Would you know her?"

And sometimes, just sometimes, it *is* as easy as that. Sometimes the gods do smile on poor eejits like me. Once they'd finished rolling around their celestial floor, in their all-consuming mirth at the frantic search I had been undertaking for the past week, they took pity – bored no doubt of putting obstacles in my way.

Because the manager's eyes lit up and he said, "Carol Moore! Indeed, isn't it true what they say, it's a small world! Of course, I know her. I used to play with her and her brothers when they'd be here in the summers. She hasn't been here for a while, though, too busy minding other people's children, she told me. So I don't think you'll find her here – I'd say you'll find her house empty."

Don't bet on it, I thought, but aloud I just said, "Well, is it far from here? It might be worth while just popping up on the off-chance, if it isn't too far."

"Oh, it's not too far at all. Indeed it's not. No, you just go out of the hotel, and take the road back towards Cork. But just after the National Speed Limit sign, there's a left turn. In fact it's the first left turn after here. Take that, and Carol's house is about a hundred, hundred and fifty yards up there on the right. It's easy to miss, though, it's down a little rutted laneway, so you have to watch for it carefully. But that's the only laneway on the right side of that road until you come to a crossroads about a mile further on."

"That's great!" I said, and then, more casually, "Yes, we must drop up to her, if we have time. Thank you for your help. I really appreciate it. I must say, you have a lovely hotel here. We're staying here tonight, and so far we've been really well looked after . . ."

And for a minute or two I wittered on about the brilliance of his hotel, possibly overstating the case, and his broad smile grew more and more fixed, as he busily disclaimed my compliments, "Oh, you're too good. Well, we try of course. It's wonderful to hear, but we're only a small hotel, obviously . . ."

When I finally drew breath and he was able to make a graceful exit, it would be hard to tell which of us was the more relieved.

Casually I slipped from the bar stool, and I sauntered upstairs to our room – I was even humming nonchalantly to myself. Once inside though, I was frantically pulling my mobile phone out and dialling Connor's number.

"Connor," I hissed exuberantly, "I've found her! I really have! Come back now and I'll tell you about it."

"What? Are you serious? Where? Okay, look, I'm only a minute down the road, I'll be there straight away."

And sure enough a minute or so later I heard his knock, and he rushed into the room as soon as I opened the door.

"Tell me," he said, and I did.

"Oh, dear God," he said, and he put his head back in gratitude, and pleading, praying, I realised, "Please, please, let this be it. Please let it not be a different Carol Moore, or some other disappointment for us." He turned back to me then. "Okay. Let's go now and see if we can find the laneway. We won't be able to approach her yet – if it's up a laneway it will be hard to sneak up. But let's check where it is exactly."

We left the room, and he said, "We'll take the car, it will be much less conspicuous than walking up that road."

So we drove the short distance back out of town, and turned at the next left turn. We drove at a sedate speed – without being suspiciously slow – up that road, and sure enough, well-hidden by summer growth, but there if you were looking for it, was a little laneway. I got a glimpse of a rutted path with grass growing on the middle as we passed. Connor continued driving and about half a mile further on he pulled into the verge and parked. And we congratulated ourselves, and laughed, and kissed and hugged and high-fived.

"I don't want to drive past her house again," he said then. "Let's see if we can get back to Cilltubber another way."

"There should be a crossroads a bit further on, the hotel manager told me there was." And there was, and Connor took a left turn there and kept taking lefts until we came back to Cilltubber, approaching it from the other side. And you know, it *was* quite a pretty town, but I barely registered it.

He parked again in the hotel carpark and we went back to our room. And once in the room we hugged and kissed and held each other full-length. And I was wondering to myself if I was mad to get this excited again, after my hopes being dashed so much. But . . . it just seemed so real, so possible. We knew that Carol had Lucy, and now we knew where her holiday house was. And there was every chance that that's where she was – she certainly wasn't in her own Dublin house, and she would need *somewhere* to hole up. So I could be – *was*, I told myself firmly – only about a mile or so, less as the crow flies, from my sweetheart. In no time at all, hours at most, I would have her back!

Reality intruded then. "How are we going to do it?" I asked, looking up at Connor. He smiled down at me and kissed my forehead. He drew me then onto the bed, and we sat together, close.

"I can't knock on her door pretending to be selling something. It's not going to work in such a secluded house. I imagine insurance salesmen and the like wouldn't be selling in such an out-of-the-way place. In fact, I can't see how I can just knock on the door at all – it would make her suspicious. So what I'm thinking now is that we'll walk up to the house tonight, when it's dark or nearly dark, and we'll slip down that lane. And, well, basically, we'll break into the house."

"But how are we going to do that?"

"Break a window if we have to," he said. "It'll probably have to be something like that."

"But she might hear a window breaking," I persisted, "and it might give her enough time to harm Lucy. That's the problem. She has to have *no* time to hurt Lucy. Because she might be like Charlotte Riordan's father, who didn't care about getting convicted for it – he knew he wasn't going to get away with it, but it didn't matter, once she was dead."

"Yes, I know," he said wearily. "What about going back to Plan A, then? Will I knock on the door pretending to be a Jehovah's Witness or something. You see, I only need her to open the door – I'll have her then, like I did Ray and that guy, Murtagh Levi's sidekick. But would she even open the door to a strange man in the circumstances?"

"Perhaps not," I admitted. "Not with her secret to hide."

"The other option is to recce the place, make sure she's there, and just hang around outside until she comes out – which she must do *some* time. It wouldn't be that easy, though, remaining unhidden for possibly days, while still being near enough to see her come out. You see – "

"Yes, I know, you've forgotten that bit of SAS training as well," I said impatiently. But much though this frivolity was annoying me, I could understand it too. It was his way of coping with the tiredness, the stress, the responsibility of getting this right, and the fear of getting it wrong.

"Look," he said at last, "let's go and get something to eat now, keep our strength up. And let's go out after dark tonight and see what we can find out. Let's make sure she's living there, for one thing. And maybe she will do something silly like leaving a door unlocked. I know, I know," he said as I began to protest, "unlikely, but it's worth a try."

So we did that: ate in the hotel, and then went back to the room to wait for darkness, which, given that this was June, was a long time coming.

And as we sat there on the bed, holding hands, waiting, he said, "You know, Tory, it's been an adventure."

"It certainly has. Not one I'd have chosen, obviously. But it's certainly been an experience."

"Think what a story we'll have to tell, once it's all over. You know, when we get back to real living, and mix with other people again, and they ask how we met. And think of how we'll be able to bore our grandchildren in years to come – and I include Lucy's children in that, obviously – by telling the tale over and over. Although," he added reflectively, "maybe Lucy's children mightn't be bored, they might like to hear it. 'Tell us again how you saved our mother from that nasty evil woman, Grandad,' they'll say."

"I can't think of you being a granddad," I said lightly, wondering why I had experienced an immediate lump of dread in my stomach at his words, wondering why I was experiencing such discomfort. Possibly – indeed, probably – it was at the thoughts of us being old enough to be grandparents.

"No," he added morosely, "neither can I. I haven't even been a father, yet, after all!"

"I've learned a lot from this," I said, changing the subject. "I feel much stronger. I used to let people walk over me, but no more. I used to be very reactive, now I feel I'm much more proactive. I'm stronger," I said again, "much stronger. Nobody's going to walk over me, ever again. It's been a hard lesson to learn. It's been the worst week of my life, and God knows I wouldn't have chosen this. But given that it did happen – there have been gifts out of it, that's all I'm saying. As long as . . . as long as we do get Lucy back safe and sound."

He squeezed my hand in response.

At one stage in that eternal evening he took out his

mobile phone. "I'm dialling Directory Enquiries," he told me, and when he got through, "Yes, would you have the phone number for Cilltubber Garda Station, please? Thank you."

I looked enquiringly at him, at which he said, "Obviously we'll ring the guards *after* Lucy is safe. Won't we?"

"Yes, of course, sorry, I didn't think of that. I haven't really been able to think of anything after I get her back."

"That's understandable."

And eventually it became dark enough for us to go on our mission. We both wore black jeans, and as dark a top as we had with us. And we left the hotel, and picked up a torch from the car, and then began walking towards Carol's house.

"Great, a romantic full moon," grumbled Connor. "Typical."

"Do you want to delay the rescue for two weeks?" I asked him sharply. "We'll do with what we have."

"Yeah, I know."

We reached the left turn, and walked up it until we reached her laneway. And in silence we began to walk down it. Immediately it grew darker, the overhanging trees cutting out the moonlight. It was eerie, it truly was. Here I was, a city woman, used to smooth (well, smoothish) footpaths, constant street-lights and noise, sneaking my way down a rutted laneway in the pitch dark and total silence. On a mission straight out of a thriller. On we went, slowly, feeling our way, for, I don't know – fifty or sixty metres maybe, until we came to a little clearing.

And there, lit by the moonlight which once again had access, standing low and squat in front of us was an old single-storey stone cottage, with a corrugated iron roof. We were looking at its gable wall – luckily windowless – so its front door and the windows at its front were facing to our right. Which was good, nobody in that house could see us. Not yet. And there was even better news: we could see the spillage of light from one of the windows. Somebody *was* staying there!

Connor squatted then, and by the moonlight I could see what he was doing – he scooped up soil and smeared it over his face and hands. Immediately he became less obvious. He obviously *had* remembered something from his SAS days after all, I thought dryly, either that or from watching Arnie Schwarzenegger and Sylvester Stallone films. He indicated that I should do the same, and I did.

And then slowly, silently, we moved towards the house. He led the way first around to the corner between the gable and the back of the building, and indicated that I should wait there. There were two little windows at the back, with a door in between them. He went up to the first one, peeping in at an angle. He then crawled under the line of the windows – I was very impressed – past the back door to the next window. He looked in there in the same furtive manner, and then turned and waved for me to join him. Copying his movements, I did so. He pointed to the window, and I looked in.

And there, lying on a small bed the far side of the small room, fast asleep, was my Lucy! I put my hand to my mouth with an inward gasp. She was *there!* We had found her at last! Tears prickled my eyes as I gazed on her. Her curls spilled over the pillow, her long lashes lay on her cheeks – still chubby, I noticed in delight, she didn't seem to have lost weight – her hands curled into little fists.

With an effort I composed myself. She was there, but we were here, and we didn't have her safe yet. The phrase, *so near and yet so far,* came to mind. The window, I noted, was an old sash one. I took hold of the bottom half and tried to slide it up. But that would have been too much to hope for. The fact that the hotel manager knew Carol had obviously used up my total allocation of good luck already

Silently Connor moved past me, and tried to open the back door, with a similar lack of success.

Shrugging, he indicated that we should return to the lee of the laneway, and quietly, silently, we did so.

He put his mouth close to my ear then. "I think the best thing we can do is wait until Carol goes asleep. It's nearly midnight, and that first window we passed looks like being her bedroom. So we should be able to tell from the lights going off and on when she's going to bed. We'll give her an hour or so after that, and then break in. We'll try the front door on the off chance that it's unlocked, but failing that we should be able to break the glass in Lucy's room without any of it hitting her. Okay?"

"Okay," I agreed, and so we moved a little bit into the vibrant plant life beside the path, and sat on the ground in front of a large tree, leaning our backs against it, all the time watching the spill-over of light pouring out of the window at the front of the house. It didn't take long for my bottom to get numb, but I sat and endured. This was the last hurdle now towards getting Lucy back, and if a numb bum was the price, I would pay it gladly.

"Breaking the window might terrify Lucy," I said.

"I know, but it can't be helped, assuming the front door isn't unlocked."

And not too long after that the light at the front of the house was extinguished, and a few minutes after that we saw light pouring out of the window nearest us at the back of the house, as Connor had predicted. It tapered to a narrow beam of light then – possibly curtains were being closed. And five or ten minutes after that, the light went off, and there was darkness.

I shifted uncomfortably. I was getting cold now too, as well as uncomfortable. "I think I'll stand for a while," I whispered, and did so, wrapping my arms around myself. He stood too, and held me length to length, and we took comfort and warmth from each other as we stood there, swaying slightly together.

"I'm impatient," I whispered in his ear. "It's torture being this near to her, but, she's not safe yet. And I know we're increasing the odds by waiting until Carol's asleep, but it's hard."

"Not long now," he whispered back. "Look, I've

been thinking about it, and this is what I think we should do, based on my vast SAS experience –"

"Stop with the SAS jokes," I snapped, then, "Sorry, I'm just scared and nervous."

"Sorry too," his voice was warm in my ear. "I'm scared and nervous too, that's why I'm doing it. But I'll stop, okay. But do you want to hear my plan? Failing opening the front door, we'll smash Lucy's window with a rock – as I said, the bed is far enough from the window that none of the glass can hit her. And I'll wrap the rock in my sweatshirt to minimise the noise. But Tory, I'd say that window is too small for me to get through, and I'd better not waste time trying – so you're going to have to get in. I don't know exactly how it will work, how much glass will fall away with the first blow – most of it, we'll have to hope. Obviously waiting until Carol's asleep gives us a little more time, but it's too much to hope that she'll sleep through the sound of the glass breaking even if we muffle the noise as much as possible. So it's going to be essential that we can clear as much of that window as we can, as quickly as possible.

"So, we're going to have to be careful. I think I'm probably going to lift you in, so that you don't have to try putting hands or feet near any remaining shards in the window. And once you're in, as quickly as you can, push Lucy's bed over in front of the door to block it. That'll buy us some time. And then grab Lucy and hand her out the window to me. I'll place her on the ground. and I'll lift you out again."

"Sounds good," I said, shivering with fear and cold.

Well, terror actually. It was surreal, standing under this tree in this country laneway, discussing breaking into a house to mount a rescue operation for my daughter. Things like this didn't happen to people like me, surely? I kept waiting to wake up, convinced on some level that this must be a dream, to be in such a strange situation. But no . . . it was no dream.

"And before all that," ended Connor, "we'll phone the police. That way we should have time to do all that before they arrive, but it will be good to know they're on their way, in case it all goes wrong."

I saw the sense of that. It had gone far enough – we were going to be in enough trouble with them for going this far on our own – I wasn't sure if we had broken any laws yet by not involving them – but breaking and entering was a crime, last I heard. And once we had Lucy back, it needed to be out of our hands, and into the care of the appropriate authorities.

So about half an hour later, Connor took his mobile phone out, and handed it to me. "You ring. It will be better if they hear a woman's voice. Say you're calling from Carol's house and that you're about to break in to rescue your baby which she had abducted –"

I interrupted him. "That sounds too improbable. They'll never believe that – I hardly believe it myself. I'll pretend to be Carol, say I've heard a prowler outside. They should come up quickly enough for that, but not quickly enough to get in our way – they'll probably just come anyway to humour me, thinking it's some woman getting frightened of a fox or something."

"Okay," he agreed, "that's better. It's the last number dialled, so just ring it now. And while you're doing that, I'll find a rock."

And the phone rang for some time and eventually came a relaxed voice, "Cilltubber Garda Station, Sergeant Farrell speaking, can I help you?"

"Oh, Sergeant, this is Carol Moore – I'm calling from the house and I wonder could you come up. I've just heard a prowler outside, and seen the beam of a torch. I'm here on my own and I'm very nervous. Please come quickly. I'm really scared!"

"Will do, Mrs Moore," he said, and even as he took a breath to speak, I said "Thanks!" and in my nerves rang off, cutting off whatever he had been about to say.

"He's coming," I told Connor. "Unfortunately I rang off before he could finish whatever he had to say, but they're on their way and that's the important thing. So let's do this now."

"Okay," he said, quickly taking off his jacket and sweatshirt, before replacing the jacket over his T-shirt and wrapping the rock in the sweatshirt. And then we ran as quietly as we could towards the house.

Connor lifted the wrapped rock and smashed it against the window. The glass shattered with a noise which reverberated around the whole world, as far as I could tell, so loud was it in contrast to the country night-time silence which it broke. But the window had smashed well – there were only a few stray shards sticking out of the frame. And Connor dropped the rock, wrapped his hand in his sweatshirt, and quickly pushed them through also.

He then turned to me, "Come on," and he lifted me and eased me feet first through the narrow window. I landed on the floor, the sound of glass crunching under my feet. And then I did as we had said – I rushed across the room and pushed the bed against the door. Only then did I dare breathe. I lifted Lucy up – dimly registering my surprise that she hadn't stirred through any of this – and a small part of me was able to relish the solidness of her, the touch of her. But most of me had to concentrate on getting us all away safely. So I quickly carried her back to the window and handed her out into Connor's arms. He bent quickly out of my view, to lay her on the ground, and then he turned again to me and helped me out through the window.

Once I was on my feet he turned again and picked up Lucy – who was *still* sleeping – and jerked his head towards the laneway. Now all we had to do was to wait for the garda at the end of the laneway, or meet in the laneway if he was quicker than we thought. It was all so nearly over!

Quickly we moved the length of the back of the house. The house remained silent, no light had gone on in Carol's room. There were no shouts. Maybe we *had* been lucky enough that she slept through it all.

But as we reached the corner where the back of the house and the gable met, we learned otherwise. She stepped out of the shadows towards us, and the moonlight gleamed on a rifle which was pointing directly at us.

"Hello, Tory," she said conversationally. "Very rude to go so soon!" as if it had all been about afternoon tea. "Let's go back into the house and talk about this," and she jerked the rifle in the direction of the front of the house. I glanced at Connor and he gave the briefest nod: we should do what she said. Yes, I thought – after all, the cavalry, in the form of Sergeant what's-his-name, would be here soon. All we had to do was to stay alive until then.

So we walked around the house, me first, Connor carrying the still sleeping Lucy behind me, and Carol and her rifle last.

"In the front door," she called, "and into the room on the left of the hall."

I let myself in the open front door, and through the doorway into what proved to be a darkened sitting-room, lit only by silvery moonlight. Connor followed me and then Carol came too, still holding the rifle. She switched on the light and I blinked at the brightness of it.

"Isn't this nice?" she asked, smiling. "I do love visitors. And you must be the luscious landlord," she said to Connor, "masquerading as the knight in shining armour!"

"Carol, we've phoned the police. They're on their way. They should be here any moment," I said.

But she grinned at me, a 'nice-try-but-you-don't-think-I'm-falling-for-that-one-do-you?' smile.

She looked then at Lucy who was still sleeping in Connor's arms. "She's beautiful, isn't she? I knew you wouldn't be able to resist coming after her once you realised it was me who had taken her. Despite my warning you what would happen if you did. You did understand my warning, didn't you? Even though you foolishly chose to ignore it."

And I looked at Lucy, lying so still, not having stirred in the slightest, even with all the noise and movement, and it hit me then: "She's dead," I gasped. "She's dead!" And the room swayed around me and everything blurred, and Connor had to shout at me, "Tory, she's not. She's not!" and eventually his words penetrated through to me.

"She's not?"

"No, she's not. She's breathing, and I can see her pulse in her neck."

"Oh thank God!" I breathed, but my relief was short-lived.

"No, she's not dead," agreed Carol, "not yet."

I spun around to face her. "What do you mean, not yet? What have you done to her? Call an ambulance. Please, please call an ambulance!"

Carol shrugged carelessly. "You were warned, and warned again. It's all on your head. How does it feel, to be guilty of your daughter's death?"

I could only look at her in horror.

"What have you given her?" asked Connor.

"Sleeping tablets. Lots. More even than the adult dose."

"Oh God, no. Please no." I took a deep breath. I knew I had to get through to her, appeal to her with everything I had. "Carol, you've got to call an ambulance. It mightn't be too late. Don't let her die, Carol. You love her too. You've said so a million times."

"Yes, I love her, but I see now that I can't have her. I thought I could," she said sadly. "I thought you wouldn't find Ray. You mentioned enough times how you had lost touch with him. I admit, I underestimated your determination. And even when I tried to persuade you of the right thing to do – you wouldn't believe it, would you? No, you were too stubborn. *You* knew best," she said sarcastically. "You certainly have proven yourself the false mother after all, by coming here, haven't you? Despite me reminding you of the differences between true love and false love. Really," she tch-ed, "I'm very disappointed in you. To put your own want of her over her very safety . . ."

Sergeant-what's-his-face would be here soon, I thought. We'll be able to phone an ambulance then. Just keep her talking in the meantime.

"Why did you come down here?"

"Once you said you had found Ray's whereabouts, I knew I had to disappear. Even if it turned out to be another dead-end, you had proven your tenacity. You would find him sometime, and then it would be all over for me. And if it was all over for me, then of course it had to be all over for Lucy. You know, I understood Charlotte Riordan's father, why he did what he did. Everyone else – you, the media, all the commentary –

thought he was mad. But he wasn't. He just loved her so much, even though everything conspired against him."

"Please," I begged, tears cascading down my cheeks, "please call an ambulance. If you love her, let her live."

She didn't answer me directly, just looked over at Lucy as she lay comatose in Connor's arms. "She looks so peaceful, doesn't she? Nothing's ever going to hurt her now. Not ever."

"Tory, if she's . . . well, under the circumstances, you had better hold her," said Connor, moving to hand her to me.

But: "Oh no," laughed Carol, "no, I'd much prefer you kept your hands, shall we say, tied-up, with her. I'd feel much safer that way."

And by the way Connor's eyes narrowed I knew that Carol had read him right, that he *had* wanted his hands free.

"Why did you do it?" I asked desperately. Anything to keep her talking until the garda arrived – what on earth was taking him so long? And besides, I really wanted to know why she had done it, why she had put Lucy and me through this horror.

"Why did I do it?" she repeated back to me, eyes wide open as though the answer were patently obvious to anybody with any sense. "Tory, my dear, have you *any* idea what it is like to look after a child day after day? To have her grow in your care, to love her, to mind her, to be like a mother to her. But to have to hand her back every evening. To never have weekends or holidays with her. To have her accept your love and your care and soak it all up and take it all, and then throw it back in your face by going to her mother's arms without a backward glance at you? Have you any idea what all that's like? Do you?" she spat out – obviously this question was not as rhetorical as I had assumed.

"No. No, I don't."

"Well, it's awful. Think how you have felt this past week, and multiply it by a thousand, and that's how I was feeling all the time."

Hardly, I thought, but decided not to debate the point.

"You know," she laughed bitterly, "you women make me sick, you really do. Wanting it all, having it all. Career and children too. As long as someone else rears the child for you. Someone who will love that child, give that child the love you're not there to give. But not too much love, oh no. Not so much love that your own role as mother is usurped. So what you want from us is that we give the child exactly the right amount of love, and that we're happy to be like a mistress, taking the crumbs of time which are doled out. And all for a paltry hundred and thirty euros a week and a box of chocolates at Christmas.

"Why did I do it?" she repeated "Because I love Lucy so much I wanted her all for myself." She said this as if it were the most reasonable thing in the world. "Because I didn't want to share her any more. I didn't want the crumbs any more. Because I would be better for her than you are. She would have forgotten you in time," and it was clear this was something she had already said many, many times . . . to herself, since there was nobody else to whom to say it. "She would have stopped asking for you eventually."

"*Was* she asking for me?" I whispered through numb lips, both delighted at this but despairing too at this manifestation of Lucy's unhappiness while we had been apart.

Carol shrugged, not interested in that aspect of it all. "She would have stopped," she said again.

"I trusted you," I said, the betrayal sharp in my voice, "and you did this to me. I thought we were friends."

"Ha! Trust! Friends!" she spat. "There's no such thing as friendship; there's only mutual advantage," and as she said this, despite myself I felt the tiniest atom of pity for her, that whatever had happened in her life had brought her to that belief. But even that sympathy dissolved as she went on, "And you, Tory, were so desperate for friendship you were easy to fool that we were friends. You were *pathetic,* looking for someone to like you, someone to be there for you. And as for trust, ha, you must be the most gullible fool ever. You'd believe *anybody!* Gullible, gullible, *gullible*! You'd believe *anybody* in your desperation to think the world is the way you'd want it to be. And look at him," and she jerked her head in Connor's direction. "I suppose you trust him too," and her face twisted as all her venom spewed out of her, "you three-times fool! Why would any man want to give up so much time, so much effort, to help *you*, a stranger, find your daughter. Ask yourself, ask yourself, what is he after?"

"Shut up!" I screamed, putting my hands over my ears. "He's not like that. Not everyone's like you, you twisted witch! There *are* decent people out there. There really are!"

"Oh, I'm sure there are," and even through my hands I could hear her, "but how will *you* know which ones they are. *You* with the discernment of a . . . a puppy-dog!"

"Don't listen to her, Tory," said Connor, shifting uncomfortably with Lucy's weight. "This is the last throes of a dying rat, trying to take you down with her."

"'Dying throes'? Who is the one with the rifle here?" she demanded of him. "And you," she turned back to me, "no wonder you don't want to hear it. The truth hurts. You don't want your fantasy of this knight in shining armour to be destroyed. Oh, but it will be, it will. When – assuming you two survive this – he begins to extract his price for his help. Then you'll think back to me and you'll realise I was right, and you'll be sorry you didn't listen to me sooner and save yourself a lot of pain."

"You're mad!" I said. "Stone crazy mad."

She shrugged, uninterested in my opinion. She paused, seemed to be thinking about something, and then seemed to come to a decision. "Now, here's what we'll do. I want you to put Lucy down on that sofa there, and then stand over beside Tory."

"No."

"No? Tory, which would you prefer? Will I shoot

you both while Lucy's safe over there? Or while he's holding her? Best case, I'll miss her and she'll just fall as he falls, and we'll hope she doesn't bang her head or anything serious. Worst case . . ." she shrugged.

"She's dying anyway. Let her die in my arms, or Connor's if you insist."

"Oh, she's not dying," she said impatiently.

"What?" A tiny flicker of hope ignited. Was it true? Or was she playing with me?

"No, I just said that," she laughed, "just to prove to you how gullible you are! You'd believe anything, you would. No, she's not dying. It's just a sleeping pill, an appropriate dose. She'll waken in a few hours, right as rain." She shrugged. "As I said, I knew you'd come, and I needed her quiet and relaxed while I dealt with you. So I'm glad you found me sooner rather than later – it wouldn't have been very good for her to have been taking this for too many nights. Great stuff though, kept her asleep and safe while I was over visiting you, reassuring you, finding out what was happening!

"In fact, Tory," and she smiled evilly, "Tory, Tory," she sang, "guess where Lucy was that day I told you Ray had taken her. Guess!"

Again, I could only look at her in shock, in horror. It had never occurred to me, but, of course, she had to have been –

And Carol read the realisation in my eyes and laughed, delighted with herself, "Yes, yes indeed. She was in my house all along! Upstairs, sleeping peacefully after her first dose of the sleeping tablet! Even as you were sitting crying at my table, she was sleeping upstairs! Even as you were on the phone trying to find Ray's grandmother, she was sleeping upstairs! Oh, Tory," and she was laughing so much at this – to her – hilarious information that she had to wipe her eyes, clumsily because she was still making sure to train the rifle on us, "how I laughed when you had gone rushing off to find her – and all the time she was asleep in my house!" She was barely able to contain her mirth. "Oh, if only you had realised the delicious irony of it! So near to you, but so, so far away. If you had searched the house you would have easily found her. But you didn't, did you? Because you trusted me. That's my whole point, you fool. You trust too easily, and wrongly. Ahhhh," she sighed the last of her laughter and wiped her eyes again.

And suddenly she was serious again.

"Okay, your decision. Will I shoot you while he's holding Lucy, or not?"

"She'd be better off dead than being raised by you," I said.

She pursed her lips a little, seemed to be thinking about it. "Do you think so? Now, there's an interesting question. I think that that one would tax even Solomon. I, of course, think she would be better off alive. I'd take very good care of her, you know that. Assuming she survives me shooting him. You know what," she brightened as an idea struck her, "I think I'll shoot you first, so you die not knowing if Lucy dies too, or lives to be raised as my child."

Would that garda *ever* arrive? Keep her talking. Keep her talking. She was loving sharing her cleverness.

"What did I ever do to you, that you should be so cruel to me?"

She shrugged. "What did the rabbit ever do to the fox, that the fox should eat it? It's simply that it's some people's fate to be the prey, some to be the predator."

"And if Lucy lives, will you live here with her? How will you explain having her? How will you manage with schools and things, with no documentation. And what about us? People will be looking for us. You won't get away with our deaths."

Keep her talking, just keep her talking. Would this garda ever get here?

And just then, he did. There was a knock on the open front door and he called, "Hello, hello, Mrs Moore, are you okay?"

And Carol glared at us, and looked at the rifle in her hands, and I could see the realisation hit her that it was all over. She couldn't – she surely wouldn't – shoot us all?

The garda – along with a junior colleague, we saw – came further into the house, and followed the light into the room, speaking all the time: "I'm sorry it took us so long to get here. You rang off before I could get directions. Are you okay, Mrs Moore. Did you hear any more from those prowlers you reported?"

And in that instant Carol smiled at us, a beatific smile of power regained, and she said, "Oh, Garda, there were indeed prowlers! I have them here."

And he came fully into the room, and took in the scene in an instant: Carol holding the rifle towards me and Connor, who were standing against the far wall, Lucy still in his arms.

"Oh Garda," she twittered, "thank God you got here! Here, take this!" and she handed him the rifle. "It was my father's old hunting rifle. I don't even know if it works! But luckily they believed it did."

And he took the gun, and looked bewildered at us. He had probably seen very few burglars who brought sleeping children on their heists.

Connor handed Lucy to me, and I hefted her up so that her lolling head was in the crook of my neck, and I held her tight, breathing in the warm milky smell of her. And Connor said, "Garda – Sergeant, it was actually us who phoned you. My name is Connor Brophy, and this is Tory O'Neill. Yes, we said there were prowlers, just to get you here. And yes, we *were* the prowlers, but there's a lot more to it than that. May I explain?"

"Go ahead," said the sergeant sceptically.

"Mrs Moore was employed by Tory to be her childminder, for Lucy here," and he nodded towards Lucy, "but last week she abducted her. She threatened that the child would be killed if we contacted the gardai, which is why we tried to find her ourselves. And tonight we found her, and yes, we broke into the house – you'll see the broken window at the back – but it was to get the child back."

"That is preposterous!" exclaimed Carol indignantly. "I have never heard such rubbish in my life. Sergeant, you are hardly going to believe that, are you? Oh dear," and her eyes widened and she clutched his arm winsomely, "you don't think they're on drugs, do you?"

The Sergeant shifted nervously. "You wouldn't know, ma'am." He looked totally out of his depth. I'd say the height of crime he normally had to deal with was after-hours drinking and illegal parking.

"We can prove that what we're saying is true," I said.

"Indeed, can you? Okay, let's be hearing it then." And his tone and his expression seemed to say he was looking forward to hearing whatever I might come up with, but that he wasn't going to believe a word of it.

And then I thought, and I realised. There was actually very little proof of what had happened. Very few people knew Lucy had even been missing. Damien Moriarty, the private detective, did know she had been abducted. But *he* had been told that it was Ray who had taken her, and even then, he only knew what I had told him. It was all hearsay. Ray himself knew the truth, but again, only in as much as Connor and I had said it to him. Besides, Ray was hardly the most reliable witness.

There was the note ostensibly from Ray. It had her fingerprints on it. But she had handed it to me. There was no reason why it wouldn't have her fingerprints. It *didn't* have Ray's fingerprints obviously, but they could argue he would have worn gloves. Although, why would he have worn gloves to write a note to which he put his name? Yes, that was a little bit inconsistent, but hardly proof positive.

There was the newspaper cutting in her kitchen, but it was hardly a crime – a bit odd, perhaps, but hardly a crime – to have newspaper cuttings.

Ah yes, there was the next-door neighbour!

"Sergeant, Carol – Mrs Moore – was seen leaving her house in Dublin last Saturday with Lucy. She told her neighbour that Lucy was her grandniece, and that I was her niece, which isn't true."

"Oh, Sergeant, that Mrs Dooley. She's so old she forgets her own name sometimes. I *never* said I was related to Tory or Lucy. And yes, I had Lucy with me. I *am* her child-minder, that much is true. And I had agreed, out of the kindness of my heart, to mind her here for a few days while Tory went off with her new boyfriend. But they must have hatched a plot to accuse me of this. In fact," she was warming to her theme now, a hand to her breast with the emotion of it all, "that's what they were saying to me just before you came in. They were going to blackmail me for an abduction I hadn't done! How dreadful, to turn my kindness on me like that."

"You told Mrs Dooley that you were going to Wales," I said. "And don't say she got that confused. There was a brochure in your house with details of the ferry to Wales."

"Sergeant," she turned wide eyes to him, "is it a crime now in Ireland to change one's mind?"

"But you just said that you agreed to mind Lucy *here*," I cried, "and now you're saying you had originally intended to go to Wales but decided to come here instead?"

"Oh really," she said, more in sorrow than anger, "do you mind not turning my words against me, like you've turned my kindness against me? It is true that I had been planning a trip to Wales, but when you asked me to mind Lucy I decided to come here instead, not to subject her to the rigours of a boat trip," she finished virtuously.

"But you told Mrs Dooley – the morning you were leaving! – that you were going to Holyhead."

She shook her head sadly at my stubbornness, "I'm sure Mrs Dooley heard me mention Wales, but certainly not the morning of my departure to come here."

She was good, I'd have to give her that. Every objection I came up with she managed to sidestep. There were a few flaws in her act, like the fact that she had only admitted to having Lucy at all after she had been faced with the fact that Mrs Dooley had seen her. But they were subtle, and it didn't look like Sergeant Farrell had picked up on them.

"Look at the child, Sergeant," I said, turning her to face him, and she flopped like a rag-doll. "She's been drugged, and you'll find the same drug here, whatever it is. She told us it was a sleeping pill, before you arrived."

Carol looked abashed at this, and she fluttered her eyelashes at him, "I admit it," she said. "I gave her a little bit of a sleeping tablet. She was fretting tonight and wouldn't settle, and I couldn't bear to see her distraught. But I'm a nurse, Sergeant; I know how much to safely give. And surely if Tory trusted me to mind her daughter, she must trust how I deal with the day-to-day care of her?"

It looked as if Sergeant Farrell had had enough. "Okay, you two," he said, "I am going to arrest you on the charge of breaking and entering into Mrs Moore's house. The attempted blackmail we'll have to look into later, but you've admitted the B&E, so we'll go with that."

"There is one more thing, Sergeant," said Connor authoritatively, so much so that the garda stopped.

"The reason it has taken us so long to find Carol and Lucy is that Carol misdirected us at first. She produced a printed note purporting to come from Tory's ex-boyfriend, the child's father, stating that *he* had taken her, and we wasted a week looking for him. But the point is, since Carol printed that note, you'll find it on her computer."

"You'll find no note on my computer!"

And Connor smiled at her pleasantly. "Did you delete it then? I would have, in your shoes. But you know – well, obviously you don't know – but anything deleted from a computer isn't actually deleted. It's still somewhere on the hard-disk. The average layperson couldn't find it again, but I could. And you might be interested to know – and Sergeant, I'm sure you'll be able to confirm this for her – that the gardai have their own computer experts who would be able to access it, no problem, as easily as you or I walking through a door."

Carol stared at him, horrified, as he went on, "And it wouldn't surprise me if the only fingerprints on your keyboard are yours, Carol. You certainly won't find mine or Tory's on it. And while I admit that that is not conclusive proof that you abducted Lucy, it would certainly have to raise some interesting questions, wouldn't it, Sergeant?"

"Is this true?" Sergeant Farrell started to ask her, but one look at her horrified, frozen face told him the answer. She could have bluffed it, perhaps, if she had been quick enough. But she wasn't, thank God.

I held my breath as he stared at her.

Then he said, "I am arresting you for the abduction of this child," and he laid a hand on her arm, and read her rights to her.

And to us, "And you two will have to make a statement. But first of all you'll need to bring the child – Lucy, is it? – into hospital, get her checked out. I could call an ambulance – *should* call an ambulance, in fact, but by the time it gets here, you'll be in Cork. Where are you parked? I didn't see a car."

"At the hotel."

"Joe," he said to his colleague who had been standing patiently all the time, "you drive these people here to the hotel, and then come back for me and Mrs Moore."

And to us he said, "You go on into Cork with the baby. By the time you get there I'll have contacted them to expect you."

And, clutching my daughter, who was still sleeping scarily deeply, I moved towards the door. But then I thought of something and I turned back to Carol. "What did you give her? The doctors will need to know."

She glared at me and said nothing.

I said, "You've admitted you gave her something. You might as well tell us what it is, and where the rest is. We'll find it anyway," I looked around the small cottage. "It can't be far."

And she accepted the futility of resisting on that one, and said, "It's called Zaleplon. It's in the second drawer in the kitchen."

And Garda Joe went into the kitchen and came back with the box in a clear plastic bag. He said, "It's evidence, we'll hang onto it, but when we ring ahead the hospital we'll give them all the details of it. So, come on, let's go."

And he drove us back to the hotel carpark, and we got in. I didn't have a car-seat for Lucy – it was still in my car, and I hadn't thought of it. So I sat in the back with the seat-belt around us both. She still slept deeply.

And we drove through the dark night back to Cork, and I cradled my daughter, and held her, and I couldn't believe that the nightmare was really, finally over, that I finally had her safe back with me. Just once she was okay, would recover from the drugs she had been given. And I held her tight and wept over her, and her head was sodden with my tears, and I kept trying to dry it with my sleeve.

And Connor, driving, left me to the intimacy of that moment, and didn't speak.

Chapter 24

Eventually we found the hospital and Connor dropped me off while he went to park. I went inside and up to reception. "Hi," I said, "The guards in Cilltubber were to have rung ahead, we – "

But even before I could explain further the receptionist said, "Oh yes, we're expecting you," and she lifted the phone and a few minutes later a white-coated woman came towards us.

"Ms O'Neill? I'm Dr Feehan." And she held out her hands for Lucy.

I said, "No, no, I'll carry her," and she nodded sympathetically.

"Come on," she said. "We'll take her and examine her."

And just then Connor joined us and fell into step beside us.

The doctor looked at him, "Are you the child's father?"

And before he could speak I said, "Yes," and she nodded and accepted his presence.

I was very aware of the angry and resentful glares of other people in the waiting-room as we passed them. But you know what? For that evening, I just didn't care.

The doctor took us to an examination room and I reluctantly handed Lucy over to her. She looked at me regretfully: "We're going to have to pump her stomach, in case she hasn't ingested all the drug, to get rid of it. It's not pleasant to witness. I really think you should wait outside. I'll call you the minute we're finished, I promise."

"Okay," I said, knowing that I wouldn't be able to watch that happen.

Connor and I went out into the corridor and waited silently. And sure enough, a few minutes later the doctor opened the door and gestured that we could come back in. Lucy was lying still flat on the trolley, a nurse making sure she didn't fall with a gentle hand on her chest.

"It wasn't too bad," Dr Feehan said. "Because she's unconscious she didn't suffer from it at all. Unfortunately we didn't get very much. Her stomach was empty. So whatever she was given is well into her bloodstream. I've taken bloods and the lab are analysing them as a matter of urgency. Now –" And gently but efficiently she stripped Lucy bare as I stood watching. Connor was standing behind me, his hands lightly on my shoulders. My poor girl, she looked so little and vulnerable lying naked and unconscious on the white-sheeted trolley.

But . . . but she looked plump, and there were no injuries, except a couple of slight bruises to her knees.

The doctor pointed to those, "They're the only injury I can see. And to be honest, I'd nearly be more worried if I didn't see bruised knees on a child of two. It would indicate perhaps a child which had been restrained." And she lifted Lucy's limbs and moved them this way and that, and they moved easily. She took Lucy's temperature, and wound a cuff around her tiny upper arm and wrote down her blood pressure. She listened to Lucy's heart with her stethoscope, and my heart gladdened at the way Lucy squirmed a little bit, and whimpered a tiny complaint at its cold touch. And she pressed a finger down on Lucy's arm and the depression bounced back easily when she removed her finger. She spoke over her shoulder to us: "She's not dehydrated. That's good."

She straightened and looked at us.

"The guards found three-quarters of a tablet still in the packet, which seems to indicate Lucy was given only a quarter, which should be okay."

And she smiled at me as my shoulders slumped in relief.

"We'll keep her in overnight for observation," she said. "We'll certainly want to see her conscious again before we release her. And walking and talking and back to herself. But she should be right as rain in the morning." And she smiled wearily at us and excused herself, and went off to the next in a long line of people needing her attention.

And the nurse produced a clean nappy and a sleepsuit, and I dressed Lucy in them. And then she showed us to the children's ward. There was a cot for Lucy, and two chairs beside it. "We do have a sleep room for parents," she said, "if you need a rest."

"No," I said, "I'll stay here. But if you want to?" I asked Connor.

He shook his head. "I'll stay here too."

I placed Lucy in the cot and sat down. But as soon as the nurse was gone I lifted her out again and sat down on the chair with her in my arms.

"Do you want the cot blanket?" asked Connor, and when I nodded he took it out of the cot and placed it around the two of us, tucking it in carefully, lovingly, as best he could.

And all the rest of that night Lucy slept, and I stayed awake and gazed at her, and brushed her cheek with my finger, and ran my fingers through her wild curly hair, and cupped her padded bottom, and held her tiny feet, and tried to weep my tears away from her so I wouldn't wet her again. And all the rest of that night I was aware of Connor's presence, and he didn't speak, but every time I looked at him he was looking at me, or sometimes Lucy, and there was a smile on his face. A tired smile, for sure, but a happy, contented, compassionate, relieved smile.

And dawn came early through the windows, along with the rattling and crashing sounds of another hospital day. And the light and the noise penetrated to wherever Lucy was and she stirred and woke.

And she opened her eyes, and her expression when she saw me would have been comical if it hadn't been so poignant. Her eyes opened wide in surprise and delight and she said disbelievingly, "Mammy?" and she reached up her hand and touched my face. And the reality of touching me convinced her, and she said again, joyously this time, "Mammy! Mammy!" And I gazed into her eyes and I laughed, "Yes, Lucy, it's me! It's your mammy. Did you think I wasn't coming for you? Oh but I was. I was. Every minute of each day was a journey back towards you." And I held her to me, and I kissed her and hugged her, and I was crying, and she was laughing, and her plump hands were touching my hair, my face, in awe and disbelief.

And Connor was smiling at us, and his eyes were suspiciously bright.

"Lucy, Lucy, look," I said, and I turned her around to face him. "Look, this is Connor. He helped me find you. Will you say a big hello to him?"

And Connor held out a hand and said, "Hello, Lucy. It's lovely to meet you. I've heard a lot about you."

But Lucy lowered her chin, and stuck out her bottom lip, and glared at him before turning to me and burying her face in my neck.

"Give her time," I said, embarrassed. "I suppose it's natural. She doesn't know you and she's just had a bizarre week."

"Sure," he said, smiling easily.

And the breakfast trolley came around and Lucy tucked into a big bowl of cereal while I watched her, her every mundane movement seeming more beautiful to me than the most expressive ballet.

And then Dr Feehan came back, and looked at Lucy. Lucy gazed suspiciously back at her. "She seems quite recovered," she said, reading her notes. "I'm happy to discharge her. But if there's any problems with her, any at all, bring her straight back, or into a local hospital if you're going home."

"Yes, I will, thank you."

"And I've asked the hospital psychiatrist to come and have a chat with you, about Lucy's emotional wellbeing, now that we're happy that she's physically fine. Will you be able to wait a little to see her?"

"Okay."

"That's good – oh, here she is now." I looked around to see a beautiful black woman coming up to me. "Ms O'Neill? Tanya Umbuka," and we shook hands. "I'm the staff psychiatrist here. Have you got about half an hour?"

I looked at Connor and he said, "I'll go and get some breakfast. I'll bring you back a sandwich, if you like."

So Tanya Umbuka, Lucy and I went into a little room, and she said, "I've read the notes, but they don't tell me much except the bare facts. Would you like to tell me what happened?"

So I told her about the past week, and she was nodding slightly as I spoke, inviting me to tell it all.

And at the end she said, "Okay. Now, we don't have much time – if you like I would suggest you contact a counsellor back in Dublin. But let me tell you what I think for now, and excuse me if I sound abrupt. It's just trying to give you the most information in a short period of time.

"It's very possible that Lucy will have no problems after this. She was with her child-minder, after all, whom she knew well, and it seems as if she was treated well. But we don't know how upset she was being without you for such a long time. Also being given those sleeping tablets might have made her disorientated. And coming to Cork, to a different environment won't have helped. So if she does react, it could be in either or both of two ways. The first is that she might become totally clingy. Not let you out of her sight, I mean, in case you disappear again, since – to her mind – you've disappeared once already. And our advice would be that the best thing to do is to honour that, until she slowly learns that you aren't going to go away on her like that again. The other thing that might happen – and it could happen as well as the clinginess – is that she becomes very angry with you. As far as she's concerned, you abandoned her, and once she's over the excitement of getting you back, the anger and resentment of that might show through. And again, just go with it. You won't be spoiling her; she just has to work through her feelings about this past week. Okay?"

"Okay."

"And now, what about you? How are you feeling now?"

"Tired, but totally ecstatic. I can't believe I have her back!"

She nodded, "Understandable. But don't be surprised

416

if your own euphoria passes in a day or two, and you feel really down. You've been through a tough time, and I suspect that you have suppressed a lot of emotions to just keep going."

"Oh, I have," I said. "There were times when I could feel myself having to stop feeling emotion, to think of the next thing I had to do."

"Those emotions are all still within you, and after the excitement wears off, they'll probably start expressing themselves. Perhaps you might consider going to see a counsellor in Dublin for yourself, to help you through them. Or at the very least, don't be surprised by them, accept them, and just wait for time to heal them."

"Okay," I said, "thanks for that."

And she smiled warmly at me, in a way they're probably taught in psychiatrist college, and we shook hands goodbye. I thanked her and went in search of Connor, glancing at my watch as I did so. I had been over half an hour with the empathetic Ms. Umbuka. I hoped Connor wouldn't be too fed up waiting.

I found him in the cafeteria, sitting with his back to me. And with Lucy still on my hip I went up behind him, and put my free arm around him from behind and kissed his neck.

"Hi," he said. "Would you like some revolting coffee?"

"No thanks, not if it's as bad as that."

"It's worse!" He proved it by taking a last gulp of his, with a grimace and a wiped mouth. "Will we go, so?"

"Yes, let's."

He picked up a wrapped sandwich which had been lying on the table and handed it to me. "That's for you – do you mind eating it in the car?"

We got into the car and drove back towards Cilltubber. "I don't know what you want to do," he said, "but my suggestion is that we go and make our statement to the gardai, then I wouldn't mind a sleep of a couple of hours before driving back to Dublin."

"Sounds good. I'd love to get home, I must admit."

In Cilltubber we went into the garda station and made an official statement to Sergeant Farrell, told him everything that had happened from the beginning, my voice shaking and breaking as I relived it, and I held a wriggling Lucy tight. But wriggle as she did against my constraining arms, she made no effort to leave the safety of my knee. He tch-tch'd a lot, made clear their displeasure that they hadn't been called when Lucy was first abducted. I could live with their disapproval, I decided. After all I had been through, an upset policeman didn't figure terribly high on my list of things to worry about.

Carol was now in her local garda station in Dublin, he told me, having been collected from Cilltubber while we were in the hospital – the Dublin gardai were responsible for the case since the crime, the actual abduction, had happened in their jurisdiction. They would be in touch with me in due course, he said.

And then we were free to go.

We went back to the hotel. Connor crashed out immediately, falling fully-dressed onto the bed. I looked at him somewhat enviously – but there was going to be no sleep for me. No, Lucy was full of beans. Lucy wanted to play, and chat in her own inimitable two-year-old way.

So we played pat-a-cake, and tickles, and pouring water from glass to glass in the bathroom, and we went downstairs for some lunch. I expected my own lunch to be eaten in its usual way – stolen bites in between following Lucy around as she explored. But she sat beside me on the sofa, and didn't stir. She didn't seem distressed – ate her meal well, and chattered away. But she didn't move from my side. And I thought of the bright lively child I had had, and how often I had resented never being able to sit for more than a minute without her heading off, and I hoped that that fearless little girl had not disappeared forever.

After lunch we went for a little walk along a small beach in the town, and had a play in the little town playground. And as I was pushing her on the swing my mobile phone went.

"Hi, Tory, it's me. Where are you?"

"I'm at the playground here in the town. Did you sleep well?"

"I did. Could have done with another four hours, but still, I'm fit to drive back to Dublin now without killing us all. Come back when you're ready – I'll pack and check out in the meantime."

"I'll come back now," and I took an indignant, squealing Lucy off the swings – some things hadn't changed – and walked the short distance back to the hotel. Connor was waiting for us in the lobby.

"Hi!" he said, and "Hi, Lucy," he sang. But she stuck her thumb in her mouth and glared at him again.

"Give it time," I said again. "Just ignore her mostly. Let her set the pace of getting to know you."

"Okay, fair enough," he said equably.

So we said goodbye to the receptionist, and got into his car for the drive back to Dublin. And soon the movement of the car lulled Lucy asleep, and I put back my head and slept too.

I woke when the car stopped. I opened my eyes and looked around – we were just outside my house.

"We're here," said Connor, unbuckling his belt.

We got out and went into the house, and Lucy woke from being moved. She looked around the sitting-room in wonder, as if she had never seen it before, or had thought never to see it again. She wriggled out of my arms and with a squeal of joy began investigating her long-lost toy box. Soon toys were flying everywhere, and I could only smile indulgently.

"Would you like a coffee?" I asked Connor

"I'd love one."

I turned and walked into the kitchen, but was stopped by the most almighty roar of fear and then the most heartbreaking sobbing, and Lucy came running out of the sitting-room as fast as her two-year-old legs could carry her, holding her arms up towards me, piteously weeping.

I picked her up and she clung to me, trying to burrow into me, it looked like.

"That was one of the things the psychiatrist told me, that she might be clingy," I told Connor, with an apologetic look, as I patted Lucy's back and soothed her. "But I didn't realise that it meant she wouldn't even let me go into another room without her."

He smiled tiredly. "I'll make the coffee. How about that? You sit down."

I sat down with Lucy on my knee, and she was still clinging to me like a baby monkey to its mother, and I got the distinct impression that I could stand without even holding her and she would be holding tight enough to me that she wouldn't fall. Then little by little, as the kettle was boiled and coffee made and served, she relaxed, until she calmed enough so that she was only hiccupping every so often to herself.

My stomach growled then, and I realised I was hungry. I glanced at my watch – it was gone six o'clock. Connor grinned at me at that. "Will I order a take-away? I don't know about you, but I don't feel like cooking. And I'm way too tired to go out to a restaurant, even assuming Lucy would be up for it."

"That would be great! The brochures are in that drawer there."

So he rang and ordered pizzas, and soon enough they were there, and we all tucked in, Lucy still sitting on my knee.

Once we had finished he looked at his watch. "I think I'll head on now," he said. "We're both exhausted, and it would be good for you to have time alone with Lucy."

I smiled at him gratefully. "Thanks, Connor, thanks again for all your help. I couldn't have done it without you."

"My pleasure. I'm just so happy that we got her back safely."

At the door he kissed my forehead – practically the only part of me that wasn't covered by a hanging-on Lucy. "I'll ring you tomorrow," he promised.

I looked at him, and thought of how lucky I was to have met him, and how good he was to me. But I couldn't understand the unease which seemed to have settled in my belly.

"Do you remember what we said?" he asked me, "How once we found Lucy we would be able to begin our relationship properly? I think we'll all need a few days to get back to normal, but after that, I'm really looking forward to spending time with you both, just having fun and getting to know each other better."

"Me too," I said, and wondered why the words sounded hollow.

"I'll ring you tomorrow," he said again, and he left.

I gave Lucy a bath, and that was fun, and we laughed and giggled our way through it, and I ended up as wet as she did, and as I soaped her I thought how glad I was to be washing away the stain of Carol's touch on her plump pink body.

We sat in our nightclothes under a duvet on the sofa, and as she fell asleep on my chest I channel-flicked and wondered how I could feel so down and sad when I had Lucy lying against me, her soft breath against my neck, my hand cupping her bottom.

About ten o'clock I switched off the television and unearthed us both from under the duvet. And even in her sleep Lucy protested and adjusted herself so that she was still touching me. I laid her down in my bed and covered her with the duvet, and turned to go and use the bathroom and brush my teeth. But I had barely gone two steps before she woke, crying, flailing, reaching out for me. I picked her up and carried her with me, and brushed my teeth with her on my hip, and placed her on the bathroom floor as I used the toilet.

We went to bed then, and I curled around her, and kissed the top of her head, and I knew by the little snuffling sounds she was making that she was sleeping. But, exhausted though I was, I found it difficult to sleep. As the psychiatrist had said, all the emotions I had repressed all week were flooding through me. Poor Ray – and there's something I don't find myself saying very often – I was even experiencing now the rage and fury I had been feeling for him, even though I now knew that it was unjustified. And the fear for Lucy – I could feel that washing over me like an arctic wave and I lay under the warm duvet and literally shivered with that fear, even as I had my hand on her back and knew she was safe. And the disappointment of each dead-end, the building-up each time when I had been sure we would find her, and the total let-down when it didn't happen.

And then, as the night wandered its way through

the hours, I let myself think of Carol. I experienced like a sharp knife to my gut – it literally physically hurt – the total betrayal she had visited upon me. I thought of all the chats, the shared cups of tea, all the confidences I had shared with her. And each time she was laughing, laughing, at me, amused at my gullibility, enjoying how much she was taking me in. The taste of that betrayal was bitterness.

I thought then of what she had said of my gullibility. God, but I had been so stupid. So incredibly, totally stupid. Naïve beyond belief. I flailed myself with this, called myself names she hadn't even thought of, at how I had believed her, taken her on face value, trusted her totally, never questioned her.

And at some stage, even as I was still berating myself, I fell asleep.

Chapter 25

I woke early the next morning, and immediately the memories of the previous day flooded over me. First of all came the relief. She's back, I thought gratefully, as I caressed Lucy's soft head. She's safe, she's here. I don't have to worry about her any more, worry whether she's getting enough food, whether she's safe. I don't have to worry that she's in the hands of God-knows-who. And I lay there and cherished that feeling, it felt so good.

But despite all that, my mood was as low as the psychiatrist had predicted. What do you do with no solid core of certainty upon which to stand while you judge the rest of the world? When your very perceptions are proven to be invalid? When you can no longer trust the evidence of your own experiences? How, then, with nothing concrete to compare things with, can you know the truth about *anything*?

After some time Lucy woke and her eyes lit up

when she saw me. Perhaps she had, in her little brain, thought she had dreamed seeing me yesterday. I thought, hugely relieved: at least I can know the certainty of *this*, of my little girl, and our shared love and our connection to each other.

She kneeled up and announced, "Lucy hungry."

"Me too, baby girl. Come on and we'll get some food."

I quickly changed her nappy, decided that she could stay in her pyjamas for now. But once again, I had to bring her to the bathroom with me.

We went downstairs and I popped her into her high-chair and got our breakfast, and she was my sunny little girl.

After the meal I lifted her out of her high-chair, gave her face a quick wash, and started washing our dishes. But then she came and pulled me by the hand. I let her take me and she pulled me into the sitting-room. She picked up Nana-Bug, her favourite cuddly toy, and then guided me back into the kitchen. And then she was happy to let me wash up, as she sat on the floor playing contentedly with Nana-Bug. And I thought, horrified: she won't even go from the kitchen to the sitting-room without me.

After breakfast I brought her upstairs, and she played away on the bathroom floor while I had a shower. We went into my bedroom and I got dressed, and then it was time to dress her. But it soon became very clear that Lucy did *not* want to be dressed. She yelled, "No, no, no, no" over and over. She arched her back and braced herself rather than let me fold her into her clothes. She sobbed piteously, tears tracking their way down her face and plopping onto her chest. I began to get more and more frustrated with her – all I was trying to do was to dress her, for God's sake, what on *earth* was her problem with that? And then I remembered the psychiatrist's words, about her being angry with me for abandoning her. And my heart melted. When you're two years old you have so few opportunities to demonstrate your hurt and anguish and fury. And she must be feeling so mixed up right now – needing me but livid with me too. Wanting me there for her, but wanting me to know that I had *always* to be there for her, and needing to punish me for not having been there this past week.

So I let her stay in her pyjamas. I knew I had to go out and get some groceries. But it was June for heaven's sake, she wasn't going to get cold. So what if she looked peculiar?

Connor rang about eleven o'clock. My instant reaction upon hearing his voice was joy, but immediately that joy was subsumed by something else, something I couldn't name, but which was dark and brooding and awful.

"Good morning, how are you?" he asked. "Did you sleep well? How's Lucy?"

"Great. Well, not so great actually. She won't let me out of her sight, literally. And she had her first tantrum this morning, and it was a good one. And I'm tired still – well, more weary after the emotion of the past ten days, I suppose."

"Yeah. Me too."

There was silence for a moment, and I thought in a panic, have we nothing to say to each other without the search for Lucy to provide conversational fodder?

He said then, "I was thinking – I've a lot to do today, I'm a bit behind for obvious reasons. But would you like to come over this evening? I'll cook."

And before I knew it I was saying, "No, don't worry about it. Thanks anyway, but Lucy probably shouldn't be out of familiar places."

"Okay," he said cheerfully, "fair point. I should have thought of it myself. Would you like me to come over to your place then? As you know I'm a dab hand at wielding the telephone to order take-aways!"

And something about the thought of him coming over that evening set that unease in my belly going again.

"Connor, do you mind if you don't? I think Lucy and I need some time together, just to get her equilibrium back, and mine too, come to that. Just for a couple of days."

I could sense more than hear that there was something in my voice, something that knew it was more serious than just a matter of Lucy and me getting our equilibrium back. And I think he picked up on it too, as he said slowly, with a hint of confusion in his voice, "Okay, sure." He asked then, carefully casually, "So, what do you want to say? Will we get together, say Friday or Saturday?"

No, no, I thought. I still didn't know why, but I knew

I just couldn't see him, not now, not even as soon as Friday or Saturday.

"I don't know," I said. "Look, why don't we play it by ear. I'll ring you in a few days when I know better how we're getting on."

It sounded dismissive even to my own ears, and sure enough, Connor had picked up on it too.

He said, and I could hear the hurt and bewilderment in his voice, "Okay, you do that. I look forward to talking to you then."

"Talk to you then," I echoed sadly, and we both hung up.

Oh God, I thought, staring at the phone, what have I done? That was *awful*. He had been so incredibly good to me since we met, giving up a whole week of his life. And it was true, I couldn't have done it without him. And I'm treating him like a double-glazing salesman. But there was something going on, something that knew I didn't want to be with him. No, it wasn't that. I *did* want to be with him. But I felt really wrong about being with him. This unease I had been experiencing . . . what was it?

And like venom Carol's words seeped into my consciousness and I could hear them echoing through my brain:

'Tory, you're so desperate for friendship . . . you were pathetic. . . you must be the most gullible food ever . . . gullible . . . gullible . . . gullible . . . three-times fool . . . why would any man give up so much time and effort to help you, a stranger . . . ask yourself what he is after . . .'

And as I had done before I laid my hands over my

ears. "Stop it," I moaned. "Stop it. Get out of my head."
But the words kept coming, inexorable, inescapable:

*'You have the discernment of a puppy-dog . . . I don't know
what his ulterior motive is, but I know it's there somewhere . . .
truth hurts . . . fantasy of this knight in shining armour . . . he'll
extract his price for his help . . .'*

And Connor's voice, Connor telling me not to listen
to her.

A voice spoke in my head then, and I recognised it
as being the voice of fearfulness. It said, *'That's it. That's
what's bothering you'.* It continued: *'You don't have a great
track record, do you? You trusted Ray and he let you down.
But worse, far, far worse was Carol: think about Carol.'*

Ah yes. Carol who had taken my genuinely given
friendship and my total trust and betrayed them cruelly.
Carol in whom I had had complete faith, whom I had
unconditionally believed . . . Carol who had thrown all
that back in my face, laughing all the while at my
stupidity and naivety. Carol, who by doing all this, had
proven comprehensively that, of the many things in
which I could no longer trust, my own judgement was
first and foremost on that list.

So . . . how could I possibly be sure that I could trust
Connor?

And the fearful voice told me: *'You can't. That's the
whole point. You know nothing about him.'*

It was true, I acknowledged miserably. I couldn't be
sure that I could trust him. Ten days ago I didn't even
know he existed. Everything I knew about him – or
believed that I knew about him – I had learned from him.

A quiet voice spoke then in my head, tentatively putting a counter-argument: *'He could be telling the truth.'*

True, I realised. Most people did, after all. Even Carol had acknowledged that.

The fearful voice rushed in, asking me: *'But how do you know whether he's telling the truth? How could you, with the discernment of a puppy-dog, possibly know?'*

I realised, of course I did, without even any quiet tentative voice to tell me, that Carol had said all this to hurt me – that it was, as Connor had said, her last attempt at wounding me. But that didn't mean that she was wrong.

The fearful voice continued: *'Connor told you not to listen to her. Yes, yes,'* it acknowledged pre-emptively, *'there could be a perfectly innocent explanation for that: nobody wants to be wrongly accused. But also . . . if he did have an ulterior motive, that would be another, equally valid, reason why he didn't want you to listen to her.'*

The fearful voice was right, I thought to myself. The chances were huge that Connor was genuine. Most people are, as I had already acknowledged. But how could I know?

And how could I risk again? That was the real question.

How could I risk opening myself up again, leaving myself vulnerable to the abuse of my trust?

I didn't . . . I really, really didn't think that I could.

'But yet . . . but yet . . .' the quiet voice tried to speak over the tumult, *'you can't accuse, try, find guilty and*

punish somebody because they might do something some time in the future.' This quiet voice reminded me how Connor had asked to be judged for himself and his behaviour, and not to be pre-judged based on how others had treated me. He had been speaking about my father and Ray, not Carol. But the principle was identical, the quiet voice pointed out.

The loud, hurt, fearful voice burst in, overriding that argument. *'He would say that, wouldn't he?'* it forcefully pointed out. *'He would ask not to be pre-judged, whether or not he is trustworthy. You can't take that into account. It proves nothing.'*

It didn't really, did it? I agreed.

The quiet voice – which literally was, I now realised, the voice of reason – tried again. *'Yes,'* it said to me, *'okay. I'll concede that one. But consider this: he has acted with absolute honour ever since you met him. Indeed, he has acted beyond honour, doing far more to help you, a stranger, than you had any right to expect. How much more could he prove himself? What more could he possibly have done to show himself an honourable person?'*

'Yes, yes, yes,' said the fearful voice impatiently, *'he has acted well.'* The fearful voice sounded almost irritated at having to concede even this much. *'But,'* it insisted, *'that still proves nothing. Carol had always acted well, before, hadn't she?'*

'Yes,' admitted the quiet voice of reason, reluctantly.

'And anyway,' the fearful voice pressed home its advantage, *'he had ulterior motives for all his help, after all. He admitted that he had done all this to get closer to you, to*

432

spend time with you. How honourable is that?' it asked triumphantly, sarcastically, delighted at having made such a strong point.

'That doesn't make him dishonourable or untrustworthy,' protested the quiet voice of reason. 'He didn't make any moves on you at all. He didn't tell you about his interest until you had shown your interest in him. And,' it insisted, 'remember this: he didn't put any price on his help.'

'Anyway,' said the fearful voice, quickly abandoning a losing argument, 'that's beside the point. The point is that you trusted Carol when she was totally untrustworthy. The point is that you were totally taken in by her, that you never even suspected what she was thinking, what she was capable of. So therefore, how can you possibly trust anybody ever again because – remember? – you have the discernment of a puppy dog? And, given that you are hurting so much from Carol's betrayal, can you possibly risk going through this again? And, given that you can't be sure of anybody, and that you can't possibly experience this again, then ergo, QED, de facto and all that, you simply cannot risk moving towards a relationship with Connor.'

That was the nub of it, all right. There was no point in me and my quiet voice of reason debating Connor's motivations, Connor's decency. It wasn't actually about Connor, after all. It was about me. About me and my perceptions and the quality of my judgments and my puppy-dog discernment.

I sighed and rubbed my forehead wearily as I finally accepted what this was all about. It wasn't about whether I could trust Connor, it was about me *knowing* that I could not trust myself to make good decisions about people.

"Mammy, I want drink," a still be-pyjama'd Lucy demanded, coming up to me where I stood in the hallway and pulling at my hand.

I smiled at her fondly, thinking ironically to myself that once you're a parent you don't even get the time to have a personal crisis any more. But any irritation I might have felt a week ago was well gone, to be replaced by a joy that at least she was here to interrupt me. How many times over the time she was missing had I begged for the chance to do these things again, the simple mundane tasks of raising her? Now that I had that chance I was cherishing it.

I would be a long time getting over this, I acknowledged, and perhaps one thing I had lost forever was a sense of safety, a taken-for-granted sense that Lucy was inviolable. I already had a glimmering that I would have to struggle against being an over-clingy mother, scared to let her out of my sight.

But one gift I had received from this, a gift I knew would remain with me, and that was the gift of never, ever, being annoyed or irritated by the demands which caring for her made upon me. I had the gift of knowing, in every fibre of my being, that her being here to need me was a gift beyond price, and that honouring those demands and servicing those needs was a privilege, not an inconvenience.

And so I said cheerfully, "You want a drink? Well, then, you shall have one! Come on," and I took her hand and we walked together to the kitchen.

I later managed to get her to agree to getting dressed and to being good in the supermarket by bribing her – negotiating, I told myself firmly, not bribing – with a trip to the beach. And so I spent the afternoon of my first full day back together with Lucy digging sandcastles and paddling on Dollymount Strand. We played and laughed and hugged and hopped and danced and giggled and had a truly wonderful time. On this bright June day the beach was fairly well-attended and I vaguely registered in my peripheral vision different people smiling at us affectionately as they witnessed our huge fun and our total absorption in each other, and I smiled even more broadly at her and relished her safe and happy return to me.

We returned home towards tea-time, both of us tired, dirty, hungry and laughed-out. I fed us first, dirty as we still were, and then we shared a bath and once we were clean and dry we snuggled together under the duvet. Lucy was asleep in minutes, and I just lay on my side and watched her for ages, drinking in the beauty of her, and every so often I would reach out my hand and caress her soft cheek, relishing the sensation of its velvet under my hand.

And as I fell asleep myself I allowed myself a tiny moment to acknowledge that I had been avoiding, all that day, thinking about Connor, or about how I felt about losing him, or about how I would have to tell him this. He's not expecting to hear from me for a couple of days, I told myself even as I knew that that was making excuses. I'll ring him tomorrow, I promised myself.

But I didn't.

I was going to, I really was. But just as I was thinking of it the doorbell rang and I answered it to find a young woman in garda uniform.

"Ms O'Neill? Garda Imelda Ryan. May I come in?"

Soon we were sitting opposite each other in the sitting-room. I leaned forward, keen to hear what she had to say. Lucy was clinging nervously to my leg and I placed my hand reassuringly on the soft hair of her head.

Garda Ryan noted Lucy's apprehension and whisked off her cap, looking immediately younger and more approachable, and beside me I could half-see-half-feel Lucy relaxing slightly.

"Ms O'Neill – Tory – I'm here to catch you up on what's happening. It seems that Ms Moore is indicating that she might plead guilty to abducting young Lucy."

I let out a deep sigh of released tension and she smiled compassionately, "Yes, that's good news. It means you won't have to go through the ordeal of a trial. But it's not all good news. Her solicitor is talking about her pleading guilty but with diminished responsibility."

"What? You're joking! She knew exactly what she was doing."

She made an I-know-I-know gesture before continuing, "It turns out that Ms Moore got pregnant when she was sixteen and was sent to one of those awful homes for unmarried mothers. She spent her pregnancy there, working in the laundry, and when the baby was born – this would have been in 1961 – it was taken away

436

from her and given up for adoption. Without her say-so or her permission," Garda Ryan said heavily, "which was standard for the time. You know that."

I nodded sombrely. Over the past ten years or so I, along with everyone else in Ireland, had been shocked and horrified at the revelations of the abuse which had been done to various innocents in such institutions.

"She never once saw the baby, never knew what happened to it. And she lived on in that place doing what was, to all intents and purposes, slave labour, until it was closed in 1968. Since then . . . she never married, she never had any other children. She seems to have had a very sad, lonely life."

"It doesn't excuse stealing my little girl," I said, my voice harsh as I furiously suppressed a piercing pity for Carol having experienced the permanent theft of her own baby, the theft of those years of her life.

"No, it doesn't," agreed Garda Ryan. "But her solicitor is arguing that while it doesn't excuse it, it explains it. She's arguing that Ms Moore acted as she did as a direct result of the trauma which was inflicted upon her by the agents of the State and the Church – hence the argument of diminished responsibility."

"Oh. And are you – the gardai – accepting that argument?"

"It's not up to us. It's up to the Director of Public Prosecutions. He might. A guilty plea is always preferred – it saves everyone time, money and trauma. And, to be pragmatic, there usually is a bit of a trade-off for that guilty plea."

"That's not fair," I protested.

There was silence for a second or so while Garda Ryan possibly agreed tacitly with me. But she had to keep to the party-line – after a moment or two she said, "It makes sense, though. If a guilty plea had you as badly off as going through a trial and being found guilty, nobody would do it, ever – they'd prefer to take their chances, no matter how small, on acquittal. The DPP doesn't offer deals arbitrarily, though," she assured me, "only if he thinks the defence solicitors have a good argument. Like in this case," she finished quietly.

"What will happen if the DPP doesn't accept the offer of the guilty plea?"

She shrugged a little. "There's a number of possible outcomes. Ms Moore might possibly decide to plead guilty anyway, to save herself the stress of a trial. And, it has to be said," said Garda Ryan in carefully neutral tones, "perhaps to save *you* the stress of a trial. Her solicitor tells us she is very remorseful for what she has done to you and Lucy. But having said that," she sighed, "in our line of work we often experience people who are very remorseful after they're caught – it's hard not to be cynical sometimes."

"Hang on," I said as a thought struck me. "If she's said she's sorry, isn't that an admission? Couldn't you – the gardai – use that as a confession without ever needing her to plead guilty?"

Garda Ryan shook her head. "If it were only that

easy . . . confessions can only be accepted under very strict circumstances, and Ms Moore's solicitor expressing her remorse to us isn't one of them . . . even if she wasn't doing so using a legal phrase called 'without prejudice', which means that although she's saying it, it can't ever be used as evidence against her."

"Oh," I said, drooping a little. "Okay, so what happens if the DPP *does* accept the offer?"

"Well, first, there's another possibility if the DPP doesn't accept the offer and it goes to trial. She might be acquitted."

"*What?*" I yelled, causing Lucy to jump a little and turn towards me. I hoisted her onto my knee and held her tight.

"It's unlikely," Garda Ryan hastened to assure me, "but it is possible. The defence would surely bring up Ms Moore's unhappy circumstances and argue to the jury that she wasn't responsible for what she did. And they might just buy it. You never know with juries; they're completely an unknown quantity."

"But . . . but . . ." I spluttered incoherently.

"And to answer your question," she went on quickly, "if the DPP accepts the offer it will still go before a judge for sentencing. She will definitely get a sentence of some kind," Garda Ryan promised me, "but it might be in a psychiatric institution rather than in prison. And while there would probably be a reasonably long sentence imposed, the judge might well suspend a lot of it."

"It's not fair," I said, "after what she's done."

Garda Ryan grimaced. "It's a mistake a lot of people make, thinking that the justice system is about fairness," she muttered. "Look, between you and me I think I can tell you that the word is that the DPP *will* accept the deal. So Ms Quinn will serve time for this. Possibly not as much as you or I would like, but that's the reality of it, I'm afraid. This is real life, not some fairytale in which the ends are tied up neatly and the good win everything they want and the baddies lose everything."

We were silent for a little while, and I thought about Carol as I knew her now, a woman old before her time who had done me the most grievous injury. God, the hatred, the pain, the betrayal, the desire for the bloodiest and bitterest revenge! But, too, I couldn't help but think of her as a young woman – a girl really – terrified and isolated, brutalised in a large gloomy institution, working until exhausted even as she grew bigger and more tired with her pregnancy, and at the end enduring labour with no help or kindness, just brusque reminders that it was her own sin which had led to this. And no reward for her labour, no infant to hug, no soft head to kiss. Instead . . . nothing. A tinny, resonating nothing. A nothing which was echoingly despairingly silent except perhaps for the reverberation of her baby's cries, the sound of which grew weaker and weaker as the minutes-old infant was ruthlessly carried out of the room and out of her life.

"I'm not going to feel sorry for her," I insisted fiercely to Garda Ryan as if she had been privy to my internal images.

"You don't have to feel sorry for her," she assured me. "She did a dreadful, terrible thing to you and Lucy."

"A terrible thing was done to her," I said despite myself.

"It was. And she's still paying the price in terms of a lonely life, a life so desperate for love that she was driven to think stealing Lucy would make her feel better. And now *you* have paid part of the price for what was done to her. The echoes of that awful time in our country's history are still being felt, aren't they?" she asked me rhetorically.

And I clasped Lucy to me and tried to imagine how it would have been to have had her seized at the moment of her birth and taken from me forever, with every hand of all-powerful Church and all-powerful State raised to take her and prevent me holding onto her, and no hand to help me, no ears to hear my pleas. Tried to imagine the horror of this, and failed utterly – my mind refused to alight on the image, my imagination skitted away before the image could come into focus.

After Garda Ryan was gone I sat and thought about it all, tried to reconcile the burning hatred I felt for Carol on the one hand and the begrudging pity on the other. Eventually I realised that both emotions were valid, that I could accept them both. I didn't have to choose between them. I could hate her and pity her too, all at once.

But I ended up emotionally exhausted and wasn't up to phoning Connor that day.

The next day I woke, sure that I would ring him that day. But firstly there was something else I had to do, and that was to ring my boss Sinead.

"Sinead," I said, "do you remember I told you that Lucy was sick? Well, it wasn't exactly the truth."

"I gathered that," she interjected dryly.

"In a way, though, it was worse than her being ill," I rushed on. "Sinead, she was actually missing."

"What?" came the astounded yelp down the wires.

I quickly brought her up-to-date on the past week, to the accompaniment of her horrified in-breaths and shocked exclamations.

"Oh, my God," she said when I was finished, "that's *terrible*, Tory. Well, look, we'll do anything we can to help here. As well as your leave we'll give you an extra two weeks' paid compassionate leave, how about that? And then, well, as much time as you need, within reason, unpaid, until you feel able to come back to us."

"Thanks, Sinead," I said gratefully, "that's very kind of you. I really appreciate that."

I did too. Time . . . time was now my enemy. Well, really, Poverty was my enemy but Time was its attack force. The rest of my annual leave plus another two weeks' paid leave would give me some leeway. But after that . . . I was faced with the hugest of dilemmas. How could I possibly go back to work now? How could I possibly leave Lucy again? How could I trust anybody with her? Even people in a proper, certified crèche? I couldn't. That was the answer: I couldn't.

But yet, but yet . . . how could I manage without a job? I'd be straight back to where I was six months ago, falling into debt a little more each month. I knew I'd have to make a decision soon but I was paralysed now, and each day I promised myself that surely, definitely, *absolutely*, I would decide the next. Even though, deep down, I knew that I probably wouldn't do it then either.

It was an impossible dilemma, and I could feel my head begin to hurt and my heart begin to ache every time I contemplated it. So I applied the ostrich method of problem-solving by trying not to think of it at all. I knew that wasn't doing any good, but I simply couldn't think of anything else to do. So another two weeks' money coming in was another two weeks during which the solution might magically present itself.

And so that day passed worrying about the future, and what with that and the inevitable day-to-day stuff of looking after Lucy, the day just ran away with me and I headed for my bed that night without having called Connor.

I didn't ring him the next day either. Nor the day after that. Nor the one even after that. Each day I promised myself that I would phone him the next, but I didn't. There was always some reason. Some excuse, rather. And it's amazing how many excuses we can find for not doing something we don't want to do.

And as the days passed it became embarrassing to ring him. Too much time had passed for me to be able to just casually lift up the phone with a cheery hello. He'll get the message, I told myself. It's better this way, I said. We don't have to have any painful or awkward conversations. We can just glide gracefully out of each other's lives.

I refused to let myself think of him, and how angry and hurt he would be. To have given all that help and then to be dropped like this . . . to have been told I loved him and shared his love in turn and then to have all contact just cut off . . . to have been so close together and now, abruptly, so distant . . . actually, I dimly realised and refused to face the knowledge straight on, hurt and anger were pale shades of the emotions he was probably experiencing.

Just as I refused to dwell on what he was probably experiencing, I refused to let myself feel the loss of him. Rationally I knew that once I opened that particular box the pain would overwhelm me. Even with my emotions firmly clamped down I still keenly felt the loss of him. I coped by refusing to miss being able to look at his angular face, his long lean body, his short spiky hair, his large capable hands. I wouldn't let myself miss the sound of his voice and his laughter and the feel of his touch. I stopped myself from imagining the presence of him, the clean masculine scent of him.

After about ten days I got my period. So I hadn't got pregnant by him on that night in Waterford. That was great. It really was, I insisted. I couldn't afford to keep one child, how could I possibly manage with two? And God, the complications of being pregnant by him didn't bear thinking about. I would have had to let him know, or else perpetrate an even greater injustice upon him. So it was super news that I hadn't conceived. Wonderful news. The best possible outcome. It really was.

Chapter 26

The light of the new day woke me. With a groan I rolled over, turning away from the window and its too-thin curtains and tried to sleep again. Beside me Lucy stirred a little, muttered something in her sleep, and then settled again. Sleep, however, eluded me. I sighed and sat up. Another day.

It had been three weeks since I had got Lucy back.

At least Lucy seemed to be getting over her trauma. Each day was easier in that respect at least. She could now bear for me to be elsewhere in our home. I had not yet had the occasion to be separated from her – it remained to be seen how she would cope with that. Or indeed, how I would cope with it. I clung to her as she did to me. I breathed in the scent of her, her curls tickling my nostrils, as much as she would allow me. When I held her our hearts seemed to beat in unison. She was occasionally having tantrums still, however.

Probably a factor of her age (the terrible twos, after all) as much as anything else, I told myself. And I managed to stay calm and loving but strict when she did throw a tantrum. I was still in the running for the Mammy Of The Year award.

We were living quietly all this time. We shopped, we played at the park, on the beach. We relaxed and recovered as best we could. The need to make a decision about my work situation hung over me always, no matter how much I put it off.

And Carol's betrayal – it went around and around in my head like a stuck record. I abused myself over and over for my stupidity, my gullibility.

Not to mention the effort I was putting into not missing Connor.

He'd know by now, I decided miserably as I brushed my teeth that morning. Three weeks on . . . he'd definitely have got the message by now. He'd want to be very stupid not to have got the hint and Connor was far from stupid.

And for one piercing moment I experienced the full pain of his loss and the void which would be my life from now on without him. But a *safe* void, I insisted, brushing my teeth even more vigorously and dragging my thoughts back to my meagre plans for the day.

But later that morning I learned that while Connor may have got the message, may have received the hint, he wasn't going to meekly accept either.

I learned this when he phoned later that morning. He was *furious*. This fury made his previous fury that day on the beach seem like mild annoyance in comparison. Even as my stomach was sinking at the ferocity in his tone, my heart was leaping with some emotion – could it be joy? – at the sound of his voice.

He hissed, and his voice was shaking, "I was actually in the car on the way over to you, but then I thought of Lucy. I don't want her to witness what I have to say to you. So, either you promise to ring me as soon as she has a nap, so I can come over then, or I come over now. And if you promise and then don't ring me, I'll come late tonight anyway. But, Tory, if I were you I would get this over with. My anger isn't going to cool with time. And if you keep avoiding me I'll take any chance, no matter if Lucy's there."

"I – I'll ring you. She normally naps around two o'clock, although I don't know if – "

"Fine, I'll expect to hear from you around then." The bang of his hanging up reverberated in my ear.

With a shaking hand I replaced the phone. I couldn't blame him for being angry. I knew that he had every justification. But that didn't mean I wanted to deal with it either. However . . . I had no choice. I wouldn't put it past Connor to make good his threats, to come over at any time, and he was right, I didn't want Lucy to witness what looked like being a major row.

And my stomach churned with nerves at the prospect. But still . . . I wasn't scared. Nervous, yes. Not looking forward to it – that was putting it mildly. But scared, no.

And I had to acknowledge this: even in the midst of

an awesome fury, he still thought of Lucy and what was right for her.

But... that could all be a ploy. How did I... *discernment of a puppy-dog* ... know?

Lucy did go down for a nap just after two o'clock, sleeping on my chest as we sat on the sofa, and with shaking fingers I lifted the phone on the table beside me and dialled Connor's number.

"Yes?" he barked into the phone.

"It's me. Lucy's asleep."

"I'll be there in twenty minutes." And he hung up.

I eased myself carefully out from under Lucy. She stirred but – thank God – didn't waken. With luck she would sleep for about two hours. Plenty of time for Connor to share his opinion of me.

I watched out the window and it wasn't long before his car pulled up outside the house with a screech of brakes. I had the door open before he could ring the doorbell, and as he marched up the driveway I – despite everything – could only admire his long lean-but-developed body, his handsome dark looks – marred now by the most awful scowl – his very *himness*.

This will be the last time I see him, I thought in despair.

"Come into the kitchen," was all I said to him. Once there I turned to him. "Would you like a coffee?"

"No. This is not a social call, Tory. I would not like coffee. What I would like – the least I deserve – is an explanation." He stood, arms crossed, feet braced apart, waiting, and I had never, ever seen any sight quite so magnificent. Perhaps if I had ever been to Kenya and seen lions imperiously stalking their land, I might have seen something to equal this, but apart from that . . .

I wondered if I said to him, 'You're beautiful when you're angry', whether that would defuse the situation, make him laugh. Perhaps not.

"What is going on?" he demanded. "I'm good enough to help you find Lucy, but not good enough to keep around once you have her, is that it?" And even as I was shaking my head – I don't know if he saw it – he was continuing, sadness in his voice and a kind of defeat, "I have been patient. More than patient. I waited for you to ring me. But you didn't. Three weeks without a word from you, and I gave you space. I knew you would need time for yourself and Lucy. I was patient," he said again, shaking his head a little, "but you didn't ring me in all that time. Were you ever going to ring me? Were you just using me all the time?"

I protested, "No!"

But he carried on, on a roll now, "When you clung to me as I moved inside you, and when you kissed me and put your arms around me and when you sat in that car outside Doherty's and told me you loved me – was all that a ploy to keep me on your side?"

"No."

"When you promised me we'd try for a future together once we got Lucy back, was that a lie? Something to keep me happy so I'd keep on searching with you?"

"No, Connor, no," and I was shaking my head.

"Well then," and his voice changed to glacier-cold, "would you mind telling me why, the minute you got her back, you changed, you dropped me rather emphatically? Would you mind telling me why you haven't contacted me in three whole weeks? I think I deserve an explanation, don't you?"

"It's hard to explain," I said miserably.

"But you'll try." And it wasn't a question.

"Connor, I don't know you."

"Of course, you don't," he spat out, furious again. "*That's* why," he went on in exaggerated terms, as if he were explaining something to a sheep, "we were going to spend time together. To *get* to know each other."

"I mean, I don't know anything about you, apart from what you've told me about yourself."

He looked at me, confused. "Yeah?" He didn't get the point.

I took a deep breath, I knew this wasn't going to go down too well with him, he would probably explode, "Well, how do I know you're telling the truth?"

He looked at me, confusion, irritation and fury-in-waiting equally mixed in his expression. "What do you mean, how do you know if I'm telling the truth?"

"Just that," I said. "I don't know anything about you beyond what you've told me – how do I know if it's the truth?"

"Ah, for – " he swallowed an expletive. "Tory, is this what all this is about? Are you serious?"

"I trusted Carol," I sobbed, "and look how that turned out."

His face paled with his reaction to that. "You are blaming *me*, punishing *me*, because of what Carol did? For God's sake, Tory! First of all you blame me for what your father and Ray did, and now you're putting the burden of Carol's behaviour onto me?" He shook his head, incredulous at my stupidity. "You know what, lady? I'm better off without you and your neuroses, I really am." He sighed and shook his head in frustration. "I thought we'd make a go of it. I thought we could see if we could be good together. But I'm not spending any more time being somebody else's – " he gave a short bitter unamused laugh, "in fact, *everybody* else's whipping boy. Jesus," he whispered to himself, "bad enough being blamed for your own behaviour, but to be judged and convicted for what others have done!" He shook his head again, gave me one last look, and it wasn't an affectionate look. More glaring and contemptuous, in fact. And then he turned on his heel and strode away, out of the kitchen, down the stairs and out the front door, banging it behind him heedless of Lucy.

And I was left standing there in the kitchen, drooping there. He had summed up what my quiet voice of reason had pointed out: that I was judging and convicting him for Carol's crimes. Which was the truth after all. And I recalled how he hated, more than anything, being misjudged, and now I had misjudged him totally. He would hate me forever, I thought miserably. Not that it should matter – if I wasn't seeing him ever again how could it make it worse that he hated me? But it did. Somehow it did.

I went into the sitting-room and looked out the window in order to see his car pull away, to witness and remember my last sight of him.

But the car wasn't moving. It just sat there. From my angle I couldn't see Connor at all, just the low silver car. I stood and watched, expecting that any moment it would pull away.

What happened next, however, was that the door opened and out stepped Connor. He had his head bowed – I couldn't see his face, his expression. He slowly walked towards my door and out of my sight. A moment later I heard the doorbell rang.

My heart pounding, a thousand questions rushing through my mind, I went downstairs to answer the door.

"Hi," he said quietly. "Can I come in again?"

"Sure . . . sure," I said, stepping back. "Come on up."

I walked upstairs so, so aware of him behind me, and led the way back into the kitchen.

"I was thinking," he said awkwardly. "About what you said, I mean." He stopped, sighed, and then took a deep breath. "Again, it's not about me, is it?"

I shook my head, hardly daring to believe that he might be reconciled to what I had said.

"No," I said, "it's about me. I want to trust you, Connor, I really do. But Carol was right, I do have the discernment of a . . . of a puppy." I was crying now, tears coursing down my cheeks, "How can I trust my own feelings about someone? It was bad enough after Ray . . . but I trusted Carol and that was the worst mistake I ever made. And I would have *sworn* she was my friend. How can I trust you? Or rather – because I do trust you, Connor, I do – how can I know that the trust I feel for you is at all valid?"

He suddenly looked very young then, vulnerable, hurt, and my heart went out to him. (But was he putting it on?) "You *have* to trust me," he said urgently. "We could be so good together. All you have to do is trust me. I won't let you down," he pleaded. "I'll be a good father to Lucy, a good man to you."

But I was shaking my head, tears still tracking along my face.

"Don't let Carol win," he pleaded. "Don't let her ruin your life. She only said what she did to try to hurt you. Don't let her succeed."

"I know, I know. But no matter her motivation, she was right. I *am* gullible, I *do* believe people too quickly."

"No, she wasn't right! No, you're not gullible!" He raised his hand in a fist and went to bring it down against a cupboard, but stopped himself, and lowered his hand again. But I noticed that he kept it fisted. And his jaw was held tightly except for a little tic as a muscle jumped. "Look," he went on more gently, "I know she let you down in the worst way. But that's all about *her* – not about you. Tory, part of what's so wonderful about you is your openness and willingness to *be* for others. Don't let her steal that away from you. Don't let her steal your very personality. You were unlucky, that's all. Not stupid, not puppy-like – no matter what she said – unlucky. Think of all the people all over the world who are trusting others every day. And most of them are right, and some are wrong. That's just the way it works.

"And to be alive, to live in this world, you have to take that chance. Not be stupid, I don't mean that. But go on the evidence you see, go on what your heart tells you. And take the chance. If you never trust again, Tory, you'll never be hurt again. But, apart from your relationship to your child – and that will be full of fear – you'll never love again, or know true laughter again, or . . . or I don't know," and he shook his head in frustration at not being able to explain himself as well as he wanted.

"You're saying to go on the evidence I see," I wept, "but the evidence for Carol being trustworthy was there, and my heart said I could trust her, and it was wrong. I can't trust my heart. It's let me down so dreadfully. I would need *proof*."

"Some things don't have proof, Tory. Some things take trust. And faith."

He stood there, tall and remote, but his hands were shaking and his voice was shaking as he said, "We could have been so good together. It could have been great. It really could."

And when he turned and walked away again, across the hall and down the stairs to the front door his shoulders were shaking too, and I thought perhaps that this man, this virile, totally masculine man was actually possibly crying. But maybe I was wrong.

I crossed back into the sitting-room and I looked out the window again, and this time the long low car pulled away from the kerb and out of my sight.

I returned then to the kitchen and sank onto one of the chairs, and I rested my arms on the table and laid my head on top of them, and I cried until I thought there were no tears left, and then I cried some more. I might be there yet, weeping as my tears lapped gently around me, but Lucy woke crying, and I had to wipe my wet snotty face – using a sleeve, I'm ashamed to admit – and go to try to calm her.

And all through the rest of that long day I thought constantly about Connor, and I thought about what he had said. About how it *wasn't* any fatal flaw in me. About letting Carol win or not. About how good we could have been together. I smiled through my tears as I remembered him speaking of our grandchildren.

And I thought of a lifetime with him, how it would be . . . children, grandchildren, laughter, tears for sure, hopes and fears, triumphs and failures. And then I reminded myself that that was only how a lifetime with him *could* be . . . if he were the man he said he was, if he were the man I thought he was.

But how did I know?

And I thought of a lifetime without him. Never to see again that long, lean body, that saturnine face, that broad smile, those blue eyes. Never to again hear that melodious voice, even as it spoke in love, or laughter, or anger. Never to see what I had, for only an instant, fantasised about – him swinging a laughing Lucy above his head. Never to see him as that old man whose face I had briefly glimpsed in his tiredness.

But never, too, to know the pain of losing him. Of coming home one day and finding the locks changed. Or answering the door one day to find officers from the Fraud Office there. Or opening the door to see his real wife and their four children camped out on the front garden.

But none of that last would happen, if Connor were the man he said he was, the man I thought he was.

And I wondered – did I have the courage? And part of me knew that it wasn't any risk at all, that Connor *was* decent, *was* genuine. But a tiny but vociferous part kept reminding me, yes, but you 'knew' that about Carol.

And when I finally went to bed that night, to toss and turn and wonder and imagine and fear and fantasise and dream and worry . . . I still didn't know if Connor was the man he said he was, the man I thought he was.

I think that even as I slept my subconscious was debating the issue, or maybe it was listening to my fearful voice and my quiet voice of reason and was judging the issue. By morning it must have come to a conclusion. Because when I awoke next morning, there was a sureness within me. A conviction deep in my gut where the unease had lain before.

So Carol betrayed me. Yes, it hurt, hurt unbearably. Yes, I felt unbearably foolish. And thunderously, ferociously angry at her. I realised, however, that what Connor had said was true: if I let her betrayal sour me for life, she would truly have won. If, on the other hand,

I took my courage and engaged in life, no matter what, then – and only then – would I have beaten her. Who was it who said, the best revenge is living well? And live well I would, for my own sake, sure, but also to spite her. In fact, I was going to have the most *wonderful* life ever! That would show her!

Better yet, no matter how Carol had betrayed me I would survive the pain of that betrayal. *That* was sweet victory too.

And as for Connor: it wasn't so much a certainty that he was the man he said he was, the man I thought he was. *That* certainty was as it had always been: a 99.9999999% belief in him. No, this certainty was more a certainty in my own intuition. He *was* the man he said he was, the man I *knew* he was.

But this certainty was more, much more. It was a certainty which said, even if I'm wrong, even if that 0.0000001% chance that he's a liar, turns out to be the case – I'm strong enough to cope! I'm strong enough to deal with it. And I am *not* going to live my life in a shadow, terrified to live in order to avoid tiny chances of hurt – hurt which I can overcome anyway.

I wasn't giving my power away any more. I would live and be happy and damn the begrudgers. And I would choose to live and be happy with Connor.

Reality intruded. I would live and be happy with Connor – if he still wanted me.

Well, only one way to find out. I was out of bed in a flash, and I had Lucy and myself washed, dressed (no tantrums this time, I think she took one look at me and sense prevailed), and fed in a length of time which must have been a new world record. And then we were out the door and on the road to Connor's house. I would surprise him, I thought, and so I hadn't phoned ahead.

But in fact it was I who got the surprise, because there was no answer to his door, and in fact, now that I looked, his car was gone. No matter, I thought, full of the courage of my convictions, the determination of my decision. I would just wait for him.

Have you ever tried to entertain a two-year-old in a car for two and a half hours? It's not easy. We waved at passers-by until my arm was going to fall off. We played with the steering wheel and made vroom-vroom noises until my ears hurt. I steered her away from the horn for – at the last count – three hundred and forty-two times. We talked to Nana-Bug and told tales using her as a puppet until her stuffing started falling out.

And by then we were both hungry and fractious, and one of us needed our nappy changed. So we went and got some lunch in a café.

After that I returned to his house. It was still empty. I decided I would give up on my determination to see him face to face, so I rang his mobile. But he had it switched off.

And so I waited there all afternoon. It might sound mad, but I wanted to prove to him that I meant my change of heart, that I was willing to take risks, (and okay, the risk inherent in sitting in a car all afternoon might not be comparable with risking your heart and your happiness, but it was symbolic), that I was in there for the long haul. And even if he didn't come home before I had to leave, I would be able to *tell* him that I had done it. The neighbours would back me up, I was sure. There were two girls, ten years old or so, quite obviously twins, who were walking up and down past the car for the sheer fun of getting waves and giggles from Lucy and Nana-Bug each time – they would surely vouch for me.

But eventually afternoon turned to early evening, and Lucy was hungry and smelly and needed to go home. She really had been very good, considering the day I had put her through.

I would try Connor again tomorrow. I just hoped he hadn't gone off and joined the French Foreign Legion after losing me. Did they even *take* computer nerds in the French Foreign Legion?

But just as I was thinking that, I saw his car coming up the road and pull in front of his house. I watched as he gracefully swung himself out, his denim-clad legs seeming to go on forever. He walked around the car onto the pavement and then I saw his expression change as he registered my car sitting there. As he registered me.

His immediate reaction reassured me somewhat as his face lit up in a broad beam of a smile. But then a slight wariness came over him, his smile dimmed slightly, a questioning expression came into his eyes. He came to a stop outside the car.

I opened the car door and walked around the car to meet him on the pavement.

"Hi," I said shyly.

"Hi," he said neutrally.

"Can I come in and talk to you?" I asked.

"Sure."

I opened the passenger door and lifted Lucy out and we three walked into Connor's house.

Once we were in the hallway I began to speak, too anxious to get my speech over with to wait until we were seated anywhere.

"Connor," I said on a rush, my head down to avoid seeing his expression as I spoke, "I've been thinking about what you said. And I'd like to try again with you. If you'll still have me, that is. You're right. If I close myself down rather than be hurt, she has won and I'm not going to give her that victory. And Connor," I gulped, "I've been so unhappy without you, I've missed you so much." I had lots more to say but I came to a sudden halt, having run out of breath, and my heart was pounding with the fear and stress of admitting this and making myself so vulnerable.

I felt his fingertips on my chin as they gently raised my head, until we were looking at each other, blue eyes to hazel ones. His expression was sombre. I had no idea what he was thinking. Until he spoke.

"I've missed you too," he said, and my heart released the lump of tension which it had been carrying.

He glanced downwards and I could see him making a decision based on Lucy's presence, where she clung to my leg.

"I'd like to kiss you now, properly," he said, "but

461

given a certain young lady's company . . . well, this'll have to do." And he bent and kissed me softly, chastely, on the lips. I fought the urge to fling myself at him, to open my mouth to him. He was right; it wasn't appropriate. So I merely returned his chaste kiss.

"Come on," he said, and led the way to the kitchen, where we were soon ensconced with juice for Lucy and a glass of rich red wine for each of us.

And as evening moved on we spoke. Even as he was moving around the kitchen cooking some pasta for our dinner, we spoke. And as we ate together, the three of us, Connor and I spoke.

We spoke of hurt and forgiving it and moving on from it. We spoke of expectations and promises of explanations. We spoke of a hoped-for future. We spoke of Lucy and how Connor was already half in love with her, he said, and was looking forward to the opportunity to complete the process, and the hopes and fears of us both about her accepting him and coming to love him in her turn. We spoke of fear and moving on despite it. We spoke of love and sharing love and aiming to commit to it. We spoke of the incredible intensive terrifying experience we had shared and we spoke of the incredible intensive joyful experiences we were hoping to share.

And we spoke of practical issues. Connor spoke of his need, now that his software project was nearing completion, to market it and sell it. He spoke of his requirement for a marketing person to do this. Someone qualified, with a degree in business studies and marketing, he said. But at the same time, someone cheap, he clarified, someone who wouldn't mind working for only a little money and a share of the eventual profits in lieu of proper wages. And maybe, eventually, after a suitable probation period, food and board could be thrown in, he told me. And although he granted that so far it didn't sound like a great job, there was one big advantage – a great deal of flexibility. The right person could work their own hours, he said, and could possibly bring a young child to work with them, if that person should turn out by any coincidence to have a young child.

I released a huge breath, and with it released a ton-weight of fear and worry I had been carrying. I said casually, "If I should think of anybody, I'll be sure to let you know," but I grinned at him, and he grinned broadly back.

And late that evening, once Lucy had fallen asleep and had been placed in his double guest-bed, we spoke some more. But this time we were speaking in an ancient language, the very first language of them all, we were speaking in whispers and uncompleted sentences and sighs, all accompanied by the loud rhythm of fast-beating hearts.

I slept that night in the guest-bed with Lucy in case she should waken in this strange place and get a fright. I lay waiting to sleep, with the sensation of Connor's arms, his mouth, his body, still imprinted on my skin. And as I lay, a half-smile on my face, I thought of the future. Of how happy I would be from now on, now that I knew my own strength, knew that I could cope with whatever life would throw at me, now that Connor and I were free to embrace the joy of loving each other, and the joy of loving Lucy.

THE END

Poolbeg 'Write a Bestseller' winner

Looking Good

Tracy Culleton

"I never forget that happiness is a choice and that sometimes you have to make that choice every day."

But it's easy to be happy when you have no problems. Grainne and Patrick are madly in love, with successful careers, plenty of money, holidays and romance. The only thing missing from their lives is a baby, and for Grainne this is fast becoming an obsession.

But on a cold November night on cold hard tiles, Grainne's old life is suddenly and irrevocably ended and a new uncertain one begins.

Now she has to question all she believes and trusts. Now she has to begin again, to find resources she doesn't know she has. Is her new life worth the cost of everything they shared? Is it worth losing Patrick for? Maybe it is.

Of one thing she is certain: the decisions she will have to face will take all the courage she can grasp.

ISBN 1-84223-155-3